the Enigma Dragon

A CATS Tale

Breakfield and Burkey

BOOK 9: Award Winning Techno-Thriller Series

The Enigma Dragon
Charles Breakfield and Roxanne Burkey
© Copyright 2023 ICABOD Press
ALL RIGHTS RESERVED

This book is a work of fiction. All names, characters, places, and incidents are the products of the authors' imaginations or are used fictitiously. Any resemblance to actual events, locales, or people living or dead is coincidental.

Published by

ICABOD Press

ISBN: 978-1-946858-35-1 (paperback)
ISBN: 978-1-946858-71-9 (ebook)
ISBN: 978-1-946858-26-9 (audiobook)

Library of Congress Control Number: 2017914111
Cover, interior and eBook design: F + P Graphic Design, FPGD.com

Second Edition
Printed in the United States

TECHNO-THRILLER | SUSPENSE

Acknowledgments

We are grateful for the support we have received from our family and friends. We look forward to seeing the reviews from our fans. Thank you in advance for your time.

Specialized Terms are available beginning on page 387 if needed for readers' reference.

Control over one's destiny means having the right to fail. Failure is essential to the learning process. Sometimes success is best understood in terms of a failure. But beware of those who tout success from others' suffering. Success has a satisfying feel and taste to it, but it should not be gathered from the defeat or misery of others. Harvesting success from potential victims is why governments try to limit failures. Be not the victim of someone's success.

...The Enigma Chronicles

Old definition: drag·on 'dragən/ *noun/*
A mythical monster like a giant reptile. In European tradition the dragon is typically fire-breathing and tends to symbolize chaos or evil, whereas in East Asia it is usually a beneficent symbol of fertility, associated with water and the heavens.

New definition: drag·on 'dragən/Specialized Term/Digitally Randomized Analog Graphics for Off Net Sequencing

Locations and Primary Cast Members

CATS Team - Luxemburg

Julie "JAC" (Rancowski) Rodríguez and Juan Rodríguez –
Owners of the CATS Team

Eilla Zan "EZ" (Marshall) Waters (CATS operation/communication
headquarters in Luxemburg)

Supported by R-Group staff Quip, ICABOD, Petra, Jacob, Wolfgang,
and Otto

Panama – (Data Center built into the mountain side)
Brayson Morris, member of the CATS team
Mercedes Field, member of the CATS team

Operations in Zürich - (R-Group Headquarters)
Eilla Zan "EZ" (Marshall) Waters, member of the CATS Team
Quip Waters, member of the R-Group
ICABOD

Singapore, Hong Kong, Istanbul
George Jones, member of the CATS team
Summit Hayes, member of the CATS team

New York, Washington D.C. - (Smart City)
Ernesto Gleen, member of the CATS team
Tyler Hebert, member of the CATS team
Jim Hughes, member of a US three letter agency
AIMs Penny and Jenny
Jamie Griffin, newest member of the CATS team

London, New York – (ePETRO)
Marge Barger, ePETRO executive
Mike Patrick, ePETRO executive
Steven Christopher

Iraq Interests
Kashan Nasr
Dabir Nasr
Achmet
Najih

North Korea Interests
Chung-He
Chung-Ho

Tracking Digital Betrayal

Beaten as he was, he could barely stand. Trembling fear was the only reason he didn't collapse in front of them. It was supposed to be a simple drop off, routine like the others, only this wasn't like the others. It was a trap, and he had walked into it only thinking about where to get his adult male entertainment that evening. It was evening now, but entertainment wasn't at the top of his list at this point, only surviving.

His captor snarled, "You were supposed to bring the package straight here, unopened! Did you think we would not notice, western dog?" The brooding man stalked around the prisoner once, then hollered, "Beat him again! I want to see him on his hands and knees whimpering, begging! His betrayal will earn everything we can deliver!"

Several heavy, flexible rubber hoses rained down on his shoulders, back, and arms which did indeed force him to his knees. The blows were designed to cause heavy bruising, swelling, and bleeding just under the skin, but not break any bones. The prisoner felt his strength dissolving under the pummeling.

Finally, through his sobs he cried, "I was phoned to pick up this package and deliver it here. Once delivered I would get a deposit into my account just like the other times. Someone must have gotten there ahead of me and tried to help themselves. I swear that is the truth!"

The captor demanded, "You think we believe you? How could that be possible when no money was missing?"

The prisoner was bewildered and sobbed as he asked, "What do you mean? If no money is missing, then why…?"

A new, confident male voice of authority, outside the circle of punishment, answered, "Because of the tracking device inside the package."

"You are all under arrest. Put down your guns and raise your hands over your heads. We are the…"

The man never finished his sentence as a short burst of an automatic weapon cut across his path. The bullets caught him just below his waist line, filling the area around his body with a blood rain. Gunfire then erupted from both sides. Men dropped to the ground and took cover behind the makeshift shield of those already dead. The body armor of the U.S. security troopers kept most of them from being killed outright, while the cruel captors weren't so lucky.

The gunfire ceased, almost as quickly as it had begun. One of the U.S. security troopers, after checking on fallen team members, went to see what the captive's status was. As he turned the captive over, it was obvious he'd been caught by a stray bullet in the fire fight and would never be able to answer any questions.

The trooper, in a fit of disgust, bitterly remarked, "Hell! After all that monitoring and tracking of this Muslim weasel, he had to go get himself killed before we could find out who hired him. Bastard! Running guns into my country to outfit a bunch of Muslim extremists! The only good news is that we won't have to feed and clothe him while he waits for trial."

A team member hollered, "Rogers, we are missing two insurgents! Looks like they slipped away during the firefight!"

Rogers quickly shouted, "Alright, men, let's pursue and trap them between the secondary line and us. Watch where you fire, since we have our people on the other side. Move out!"

Rogers continued, "Carl, you and Lee maintain a perimeter here in case they double back. Come on, people! With even two of these guys loose, they get a foothold to rebuild."

Carl finished dressing the wounds of a downed team member and stood up to check on the fallen suspects. Lee and Carl checked each body for some type of identity papers.

After checking the last body, Carl looked at Lee and spit before he said, "Here they are! Afghan troops who were brought to the U.S. for intensive counter-insurgence training by our Army Special Forces. They came in, earned some trust, then simply vanished. They had planned this all along. Suck up to the U.S. military in Afghanistan, plead for better training to protect themselves from the Muslim extremists and insurgents in their country, and all the while it was a ruse to get their military on our soil. Might have worked too, if we hadn't intercepted their cell phone calls. They were clumsy, and we got a lucky break digitally tracking them."

Lee shook his head and asked, "What I don't know is how they got all those weapons after leaving the Army compound. There were no weapons missing from the base, so someone must have smuggled them in anticipating this kind of scenario. It always seems like the bad guys have way more friends than we do."

Carl nodded his head but offered no response.

Lee and Carl both turned their heads in the direction of distant gunfire. They both hoped it meant the end or capture of the missing insurgents, but they couldn't be sure.

CHAPTER ONE

A Sneeze in Time
Will Make You Mine!

It had begun quietly enough with the group *Sequentially Nihilistic Efforts to Eradicate Zealots and Extremists*, or SNEEZE. Their charter was to destabilize a government, move a competing organization into the vacuum that was left, and then rule the country through the new proxy government. The process had been occurring little by little, one small country at a time.

An encrypted conference call opened with all high-profile participants present.

Without much of a greeting, the menacing Asian-accented voice demanded, "What happened to our operative? You assured this cabinet that his profile was ideal for the role, and our organization funded the operation. Now entire property contents are being viewed, it seems, by several competing governments. Tell us how we can look at this other than as a total failure on your part."

The calm female voice on the other end of the call soothed, "My dear comrade, there are two kinds of failure in our world. The first, as I expect is the way you are looking at the situation, is like a sports game where the clock has run out and your adversary has won.

"The second, as you should be considering, is for someone to think we have failed and that the acquisition of the data center is simply the spoils of war. We used our SEP routine and wiped the machines. That's what the *Scorched Earth Program* should do, except we left our signature code buried in the special purpose device driver chip, built into the motherboard. In other words, we expected this compromise to occur so that our competitors would bring our technology into their data universe, or as you would call it, their network."

The Asian man smirked softly and remarked, "I am educated and familiar enough with your western culture to observe that your actions frequently mirror Odysseus and the Trojan horse ruse he used to get the Greeks into the city of Troy.

"Instead of arguing semantics on the concept of failure, perhaps you should enlighten the cabinet on the real issue, the next stage of the plan. These plans within plans are becoming tedious as well as expensive. Our approach of subjugating entire populations in our other country conquests proved quite success-ful. We are beginning to question your methodology of exporting this to other countries. Frankly, the cabinet is weary of all this extra finesse you insist on engaging in."

Losing some confidence in her position, the woman looked anxiously at her male companion for a brief moment before she carefully delivered, "I would observe that we are trying to engi-neer events in these other countries for activities and processes you did not need to overcome in your earlier conquests. We are trying to move some more advanced countries and governments into a model like yours, but they still have more freewill that must be subdued in order to introduce our next step of transition. Without controlled chaos being precisely introduced, at the correct time, all we will do is instigate civil war.

"You claimed that you wanted the social infrastructure to remain intact. You indicated that food production was a high value item in these targeted countries and is a necessity to supplement your current shortfall. If all you want is mass carnage and civilization to return to the Stone Age, then simply continue to fund the Muslim extremists who are happy to destroy everything."

It was now the turn of the silent man next to her to shoot an alarmed stare at his counterpart because of her bold statement. The panicked look on his face was almost making her nervous.

It took a few seconds for the Asian on the other side of the call to respond, but finally he interjected, "We can see that you still retain that useless Western female tendency of throwing a temper tantrum when she doesn't have her views totally embraced by the other party."

She swallowed hard and in a thoroughly chastened voice replied, "I meant no disrespect to you, Chung-Ho, or to your cabinet. My organization is prepared to continue with our charter and will continue to cooperate with your team to reach our

mutual goals. However, I would point out that we have a marked preference for our approach in this matter."

Chung-Ho smiled slightly as he firmly stated, "Ah, now that's more like it. Almost an apology, how classically Western of you. Your culture seems driven to point out deficiencies in others and then promptly offer to help the poor backward Asians. It is curious how your *help* always generates profits that flow in your direction.

"You should understand that we are not displeased with what you have brought us so far. This means we can be somewhat tolerant of your insubordination, but we assert that you leave that adversarial attitude somewhere else before joining a call with us. For now, you are permitted to disconnect from the call."

The large woman sat and drummed her chubby fingers, the office light bouncing off her jeweled rings, as she fumed post call. Her girth pressed against her shirt and jacket with sweat beginning to seep through the lower back area as she shifted in her chair to ease her tenseness. Her grey hair, though professionally cut to a medium, low maintenance length, lacked the shine associated with a healthy lifestyle. Her lips were outlined with a brown line and filled in with a deep red lipstick which drew the eye to her full cheeks and sagging jowls. Though sitting, she had a tall upper body with a total height that reached just over 1.8 meters to hold her close to 118 kilograms.

Her somewhat younger male companion struggled to suppress a smirk at her annoyance and finally stated, "Well done, Marge, at containing your feelings and maintaining a near perfect center during the discussions with his high-end ass."

She shot her minion a venomous look and assessed the poor specimen who faced her. Marge reflected on the man she had hired, who topped 1.9 meters, but now sported a pear shape which spoke of indulging eating habits. Mike Patrick's once thick dark hair showed highlights of grey and was shapeless even when combed. His rich baritone voice, once his major asset, seemed less commanding, especially when looking at his reddish nose and puffy complexion, a side effect of his continuous drinking.

In an agitated voice she stated, "Chung-Ho is so fricking smug after inheriting power over his country from his 'Daddy' and the nuclear technology we helped him get! We've built all his cyber assassin technology and trained his team of criminals on the subtleties of digitally pounding his enemies and even brought up that Muslim extremist scum into his Monday morning call for global destabilization. Now, we get treated like second class servants!"

Mike chuckled slightly as he suggested, "Well, I, for one, am glad you stood up to him and gave him a good strong listening to when he told you to remember a female's place. Of course, this might be best interpreted as no back-sassing."

Marge studied him a moment while grinding her teeth and in a strained tone offered, "At least he spoke with me, mister persona non grata! Did you hear ANY warmth in his voice for you, my dull friend?"

He rocked back in his chair, clucked his tongue, and in an annoyed tone flatly stated, "Well, it looks like the little ol' fat boy was right about western females throwing a temper tantrum when they don't get their way. But that's okay, I'm used to it. So, how about we plan our next move?"

CHAPTER TWO

Reality, the Alternate Viewpoint

The younger man practically shouted, "No, you're wrong! Their so-called greatest strength of ethnic diversity and religious tolerance is clearly their greatest weakness! They are a mongrel race of people with no unified voice! They grow their workforce by pretending to be a home for the oppressed outcasts while they are really skimming our intellectual and professional talent for chump change! That country is stealing our future by pirating our next generation of leaders!

"I say we leverage their weakness and pump in our freedom fighters to bring the fight onto their soil! I promise you they will embrace our refugees. Then, with them fully camouflaged among their civilians, we can launch an attack without fear of their stealth weapons dropping on us because they won't risk collateral damage to their own population! Maybe we can't win on our soil, but I am confident we can win on theirs!"

The older, scruffy bearded man took the insolent comments calmly with his facial features not revealing any reaction. This younger man was identical to how he had looked and reacted when he was twenty-five, way before the beard and wrinkles had punctuated his life experiences. He noted his young protégé's intensity was accentuated by his lithe frame at 64 kilograms of sinewy muscles, intense facial features, and closely cropped shiny black hair.

After the elder man mused a moment, he asked, "You think you have enough patience to plan something like this out? What you are proposing takes time and funding, using dedicated freedom fighters who risk being corrupted in their target surroundings before you are ready to strike. You have always advocated strike now, and strike fast. Now I hear you describing a lengthy planning exercise that depends upon our enemy accepting our freedom fighters with no hesitation.

"I would not expect our freedom fighters to be accepted and embraced in their target population with their weapons over their shoulders. Thus, arming them at some point in the future will be another effort which depends upon either regular communications or having them fully briefed on the overall project before they depart. The problem with both of those is that regular communications are easily traced and long-range planning is always subject to change. The fundamental flaw with your approach is that our enemy is always changing moods, politics, and directions, so an erratic foe cannot be counted on to cooperate with our plan."

The eager young man sensed a modest shift of some sort in the older man toward his plea. He wanted to see if this was due to some consideration for his opinion or only because he also knew him on a more personal level.

The young freedom fighter gently offered, "Sir, I sense some acceptance to my recommended approach to taking the battle to the enemy. I find it gratifying that you like my ideas on this matter. Am I allowed to continue my planning approach?"

Kashan responded, "I believe this council should explore all well-crafted plans, but understand, ideas are judged by their merit as either good or bad only after extensive planning and a flawless execution. When you show us that level of planning and forethought, we will then render an opinion of good or bad."

The comment irked the young freedom fighter but, keeping his anger in check, Najih stated, "We have transparent funding from a likeminded comrade. We have given you several proofs of concept that clearly demonstrate the viability of the approach, but you still deny their worth. I need to know why."

The older man smiled, not quite indulgent as he almost teased, "As the phrase is stated by our highland farmers who tend their animals, Najih, *even an old blind camel may find an olive now and then.* This council does not want to gamble on a few olives, they want the whole harvest in the grove. Return to us with the methodology of obtaining the whole harvest."

The smirks from the other attendees only added to his infuriated mood, but the young freedom fighter, Najih, only ground his teeth as he nodded upon taking leave of the council.

CHAPTER THREE

Advice for Guests, Don't Stay Too Long

EZ said, "You know this is really unnecessary, Julie. You and Juan have been overprotective of Quip and me since we started our honeymoon in Jamaica. Plus, it's still continuing, with no end in sight. At some point, you need to stop mothering us so we can live our lives. Yours too. We aren't your children. Speaking of which, aren't you anxious to get back to Luxemburg, to Juan Jr. and Gracie, let alone your home and business? We'll be fine here in our flat."

Quip, growing a little annoyed, asked, "Uh, where is Juan? He isn't doing an electronic sweep on our flat, is he? I have had ICABOD sanitizing this quadrant of the galaxy on our behalf, so can you lighten up a bit? Besides, I don't want him finding our um…adult play room. It's been grand and loads of fun, but you guys need to disengage so we can settle into the newlywed thing here. Got it?"

Juan strolled absentmindedly into the living room, turning a piece of leather gear over and over in his hands, and asked, "Quip, I'm not sure what this device or garment does, or for that matter, who it's for. I mean, it's nicely adorned with metal studs and short chains, but can you give me some contextual clues about how…"

Quip snatched it from his hands and quite crossly demanded, "Gimme that! See, this is what I mean."

Juan gave some exaggerated winks and nods to Quip to assure him that he was actually in the know about what said item was used for, but could rely on Juan's discretion. This only served to further inflame Quip.

EZ sensed that Juan and Quip were on a collision course and promptly interjected, "Hey, guys, let's take this unwanted protection issue up again in the morning, hmmm? We're kind of tired after the trip, and I don't want us to come off sounding negative to your generous support. That will give you time to check in at home and time for us to digest what is needed and, of course, what is practical. Would that be alright?"

Julie smiled a knowing smile, nodded her head, and offered, "Yes, of course, darlings. Your point is well taken. Perhaps we have been a little too overprotective, and frankly, I would like to do our family thing too. Let's take off for the night. I don't want any risk of friction in our relationship."

Juan added, "Hey, it's just that we care about you. Plus, it has been our experience that just about the time you let your guard down, thinking everything is okay, that's when a secondary strike occurs. I'd like to propose that I stay engaged here for a while longer, just to be safe. Julie can head home and begin putting the pieces of our family back together. We all need to feel safe, and we are family."

Quip, a little chastened, nodded and said, "Alright, point taken. There is some logic in scouring for any missed clues before we stick a fork in this episode and call it done."

Julie queried, "EZ, are you alright with this?"

With a tired smile EZ nodded and added, "I'm sure this will all sound better in the morning. Now you scoot. We promise to keep a watchful eye open at all times."

Quip was trying to hurry Juan and Julie out the door, but EZ put her arm into the crook of Juan's and slightly held him back while Julie and Quip moved ahead of them to the door. In a low, mischievous and sultry voice, EZ asked, "Juan, do you really not know how the leather garment is used?"

Usually, Juan was the teaser in these situations, but the sensual undertones of EZ's question caught him off guard. With something of a stammer, he offered, "Uh, well ah, you see…that is to say…it is an unusual…article…that could be multi-purpose… well, I didn't want to seem like a novice in the uh…you see."

Suppressing her grin at catching Juan flat-footed, she politely offered, "Juan, it is used for a comprehensive workout." Juan swallowed hard and, trying to maintain some dignity as the conversation seemed to be sliding into an awkward area of discussion, lamely asked, "Oh, so is the…uh, garment for him or you?"

EZ, grinning like a Cheshire cat, mischievously offered, "Yes, it is. Both parties slide into it with the chains used to…"

Julie, grinning from ear to ear, stepped in to Juan's rescue. "Honey! Stop dawdling! We said we would go and leave them to their own devices. Besides, whatever you and EZ are discussing I want to hear about later because you are blushing profusely! Now come on."

Juan stammered a little more for effect and lamely protested, "But EZ wasn't finished with her side of the conversation!"

EZ grinned at both of them and innocently offered, "Juan, perhaps another time?"

After Juan and Julie had gone, EZ turned to Quip and asked, "What exactly is this used for?"

Quip broke out laughing and then finally said, "That, my dear, is the best gag gift I have ever seen. It is a harness for holding the back legs of a sheep while the shearer shores off the wool of the animal. The additional chains are to hold the shearer up but take the load off his back while shearing the sheep. I think it will be sometime before Juan goes poking around another newlywed's apartment, don't you?"

They both howled with laughter at their gag and antics with Juan.

After waking to a wonderful early morning lovemaking session, Juan and Julie lounged in bed and continued the previous night's discussion.

Juan reassured, "Sweetheart, just give me a few more days here with EZ and Quip to make sure they are not going to be targeted again. Then, I promise to be on a plane home to you and the kids faster than you can say, my wayward Uncle Jesus is safely at the beach now. Everything will be fine with me, but I don't want you to let your guard down."

Julie responded, "I know, but I feel a little guilty leaving you here going over the last details when I should be here helping."

Juan gently reminded, "Now don't forget that the team is all assembled and looking for direction, so it doesn't make sense for both of us to be here with no one driving the business. And you know how Juan Jr. and Gracie are if one of us is not there to monitor them. I mean, think of poor Maude trying to deal with those two growing terrors! We need you home now, and I'll finish up this business as quickly as I can. I promise."

Julie frowned at Juan and scolded, "The last time you promised me something similar, we had to hunt for your whereabouts and break you out of jail!"

Juan somewhat indignantly responded, "Hey, it isn't always my fault! But in the meantime, I need you to also promise not to get into any trouble. It could happen. Right?"

Julie smirked and retorted, "Moi? In trouble? Oh push-tush! I'll be fine. I don't go courting trouble like you, mister accident prone!"

Juan reflected for a moment, then gently offered, "Honey, thanks for saving my backside so many times. If the tables ever get turned, I will be there hunting for you. I just hope it won't be like the time you drug me out of that dungeon in China. It would devastate me to see you that worked over. I will come for you whenever you are in trouble, even though I know it will never happen, okay?"

Julie mushed into Juan and, after a passionate kiss, quickly pulled away and hopped out of bed. She raced to the shower with Juan hot on her heels. They cleaned up after steaming up the mirrors in the bathroom even further. Julie dressed and finished her packing. Juan carried her suitcase as they walked outside to the waiting car.

One more passionate kiss and Julie entered the car for transport to the airport. As the cab pulled away, a stray tear got away from her eye before she could trap it.

CHAPTER FOUR

Round Two May Be a Tie

Even with the conversation only happening over the state-of-the-art speakerphone, the tension was vilely palatable in the room where the two of them sat.

Mike insisted, "I can inter-trade your oil because of this organization with no retaliation from the world powers. The infrastructure is such that, using the methods and procedures we put in place, you can get a fair and reasonable price for your oil, even while the world believes you are stockpiling these resources."

After a long pause, Kashan replied, "ePETRO is too close to the investigations of the U.S., with many of their number trying to infiltrate the thinly veiled enterprise."

Marge knowingly nodded in silence toward Mike as if her former predictions that he was in way over his head were coming to fruition. Mike ignored her and continued with the conversation exactly as he had planned.

Mike laughed loudly, then said, "There! That's my point exactly. If you think the web, you see is what they're watching, then we're very much hidden from view. Those tankers are simply decoys. Our actual live storage is at specific ports which are accessed only by our silent partners. The details and directions for the operations are conveyed by non-electronic means, period. In other words, we let them hear what we want so our efforts are not under a microscope.

"I'm not going to explain the details of my operations to you, but they are insulated from any outside hacking, prying, or any electronic means. There is simply no way to penetrate to the heart of the operation without the hundreds of feet on the street, which I control. Suffice it to say, we have embraced *Digital Eavesdropping Avoidance Through Analog Crowd Sourcing*, or what we refer to as DEATACS, to confound and confuse our competitors and potential enemies."

Mike remained silent, letting the words be dissected by his potential partner. Though he may have found the partnership distasteful from several aspects, he could not deny the fortune that he was building because of this relationship. Marge thought she knew about all of his holdings, but she was only aware of a fraction of his amassed wealth in the Caribbean banks. He glanced briefly at her and saw her smug *I told you so* look of disdain. She was as vicious as he was, but he was grateful that he at least didn't have the heavy sagging jowls that she sported. She was another person he couldn't care less about, outside of her being a means to his retirement. Marge thought her control over Mike was sealed when he lost his love, but she was so very wrong. He would never let her see how he thought until her last breath, which was something he hoped he could engineer soon.

The minutes ticked by until the silence was broken, and Kashan asked, "So, you are in charge of this operation, rather than that whale you publicly report to? We have no respect or tolerance for stupid females who should be at home servicing their men.

"In her case, it would take a desperate man to want to use that for service." Then he practically spit out the next comment. "Women are too stupid emotionally for serious business transactions. They turn red and then become too angry to even speak full sentences. It would lessen the value of our relationship if the beached whale was silently attending this call. I insist you assure me, Mike, she is not listening."

Mike glanced again at Marge to see the immediate effect that Kashan's words were having. He feared she would explode; she was so visibly angry. He reached over and placed the call on mute.

"Marge, you need to leave this room before you ruin this discussion. You know that it is for show and for our end game. Now leave, or I will be forced to end the call and apologize when I call back. He has to trust ePETRO, or at least me, in this arrangement. This, as you know, will weaken our position and my bargaining avenues. This is why we agreed, I am Kashan and his team's point-of-contact."

Marge struggled to gain her feet, her anger causing her to not lift her heavy body correctly from the chair. She was seething but, without a sound, left the room, surprisingly not slamming the door to the room next to his. Her office had an equally private entrance and exit, and he felt certain she would remain there until he briefed her on the remainder of the call.

Mike cleared the phone from the cradle and suggested, "Kashan, you are correct, of course. Even educated women should remain in their place.

"Now, Kashan, are we aligned with the goals for the next three months on the quantity of oil we can use for trade? If not, I have other contacts I will need to make to fill the orders I have waiting. I only reached out to you as we have the longest and most equitable business relationship."

"Mike, we have done business since you demonstrated we could remain out of sight and off the grid. You have stayed out of my side affairs and I out of yours. I don't trust you anymore than you trust me, but business works well between us. I will agree to the supply numbers discussed, with one condition."

The silence after that statement weighed on Mike, and he broke the silence before he meant to. "What is your condition, Kashan?" Mike realized his error in answering too fast and quickly added with a bit of humor in his tone, "The amount cannot change and still work with the cost models, unless you are petitioning to take less."

Kashan chuckled and replied, "You would wish, but no, that is not the condition. My nephew, Dabir, has completed his university education and now requires some real experience. I would like him to work in your London office for the next three months and learn the numbers side of the business. He would not need the intimate details, but rather operate as a standard office worker. He did well in his studies but wants to be close to his friends in London, and I need him to see how work is done in a Western business."

Mike thought about how much of the operation was centered in London and if he would be able to control the access to his information mules. He decided he could but mentally added that Marge could never be told of the fox in the henhouse.

"Kashan, I think that would be agreeable. When should I expect the young man? I would prefer taking care of the details of his addition to the staff personally, to avoid any confusion."

"Good, I will tell him to be there next Monday and ask for you. I will have him carry the signed contract so that we may proceed. But let me caution you not to discuss our business arrangements with him since he is not yet aware of all that concerns me and my organization, nor is he aware of my history of the lessons of fire I gained in the U.S. Agreed?"

Mike paused a moment for effect and said, "Agreed, Kashan."

They continued discussing some of the finer terms of the agreement before disconnecting. Mike was making notes to make certain he briefed Marge on the details when she barged into his office and stood by his chair until he was forced to rise and meet her eye-to-eye.

Marge seethed, "You little piss ant. You will not forget your place and what you owe me. I am in charge of this operation, and you do *my* bidding. Kashan and the rest of those assholes may think women are tools, but I can crush you in oh-so many ways. Don't you ever tell me to leave a room again! Do you understand me?"

Mike appeared to wilt under the piercing stare and nose-to-nose proximity. "Yes, Marge. I was only doing what we had agreed to. I am sorry if you feel I overstepped. I can quit if you prefer."

She stared hard and replied, "You may quit, when I tell you to. Now, get me the details on the final negotiations within the hour. I am leaving this godforsaken city and going back to headquarters tonight!"

Inside, Mike smiled at his good fortune as he nodded agreement to the request.

CHAPTER FIVE

Use an Assumptive Close, Problem Solved

Christopher was prompt for his usual briefing with Marge. Always crisp in his dress uniform, his military haircut with only a hint of warm brown color, dark steel-blue eyes that missed nothing, and with a commanding manner he stood at attention just shy of two meters from Marge until she invited him to sit. Marge reveled in the unqualified respect he showed her. When he glanced down, she couldn't help but smile slightly at her perceived power.

After pretending to complete a task, as though she were engaged in it before he had arrived, she greeted him, "Good morning, Christopher. Please be seated. Has the room has been swept for electronic eavesdroppers?"

With almost military precision Christopher replied, "Madam, the room has been swept every day since our last meeting. My preference is to keep our environment pristine, rather than wonder if it needs to be revisited."

Marge suppressed a slight icy smile at Christopher's efficiency even though it bordered on jealousy. His military background had made him a perfect lieutenant for the DEATACS organization. She reflected about how lucky they were to have him. It had been a true quirk of fate that he had even considered joining the team. If it hadn't been for that friendly fire mistake he would still be with his military unit.

The so-called investigation on the friendly fire incident had been swept under the rug so the higher ups wouldn't be blamed for their careless mistake. His lost right arm should have been penalty enough, but the army discharged him without consideration. He correctly surmised that keeping a *friendly fire* mistake around would not be a smart long-term move. He had been quietly shoved out the door as soon as he was released from the hospital and fitted with an adequate prosthesis.

Christopher had lost his arm, but his mind was solid, almost digital in his detail and recall capabilities. He had focused on improving his mental capacity, which made him perfect for his new role with the DEATACS. The role demanded nothing digital or electronic and everything verbal, so the ability to memorize and repeat accurately was crucial. This was how the organization controlled the analog information mules or AIMs, the watchers, and the aggregators.

Christopher began his update. "The deployment of the watcher plants is proceeding, although slower than I would like. It is difficult to obtain qualified recruits to listen in on sensitive conversations and not resell their information gems to another bidder, double dipping as it were. We've had to terminate our relationship with some recruits because they felt what they had learned was up for auction."

Marge looked dispassionately at him and flatly verified, "Terminated completely I trust."

Without any hint of emotion Christopher responded, "Most completely, madam, per your instructions. Your existing AIMs and new recruits are easier to train and retain. Plus, the time from hire to onboarding is much shorter, if additional resources are needed."

"I attribute this to the flavor of intrigue these assignments have in transporting memorized data sequences across international borders. I've noticed that we seem to have a higher preponderance of female-over-male AIMs. This is of course not surprising considering that females are quicker studies of memorization and are more accurate at repetition than the males we have on staff. Disappointing, but there it is."

Marge smirked at his side comment but did not respond.

Christopher then recounted, "Madam, our biggest challenge appears to be with staffing the aggregators. I am finding a limited number of qualified people who can take in endless amounts of disparate data along with visual images for unspoken nuances in a given situation and render useful application recommendations to achieve the proper pain points. At this stage, we cannot consume the information flood we are receiving and translate it into useful pressure points."

Marge clucked her tongue, and then as she was rotating her head slightly to the left, challenged, "Knowing you as I do, I would expect that this observation has probably chapped your ass, hasn't it? Do you have a recommendation we need to explore?"

Still retaining all of his military-like composure, Christopher responded, "Madam, I know that you wanted all of this operation to be analog. However, you might consider this a problem. Without finding a healthy quantity of cerebral mutants highly engaged and thoroughly motivated to our cause, I am forced to recommend that we obtain our own data center and use Big Data mining techniques to bring this portion of our plan under control.

"Let me be clear, I am not suggesting we rent space on a hosted Cloud Provider data center, but build our own that is completely off the grid. In other words, every AIM drops off collected data from our watchers to the Digital Aggregator for Synthesizing Pressure Points, or DASPP, from the endless data we are collecting. The advantage is we can process more information faster than having to use humans in that role, which would also eliminate their subliminal prejudices."

Marge was uncharacteristically calm at the recommendation and after a few moments of thought asked, "Building a fresh data center, outfitting it with the necessary software and logic routines would take a considerable amount of time. Time is critical now and this sort of modification would throw us off our schedule."

Christopher now sensed an acceptance to his recommendation but, still maintaining his reserve, said, "It occurred to me that we could commandeer the data center that Takeru built, but was compromised by the local authorities. It is completely isolated from the Internet grid and could possibly be repurposed for this project. This would keep us on our timetables because most of what I will need has already been built and carefully stored in our main facility. The main problem I see with this line of thinking is that the local authorities will likely be reluctant to allow anyone to resume operations in the space. It occurs to me that you might be able to persuade them to allow us a restart of our operations, if certain incentives were proposed."

Marge was flattered by the blunt observations, smiled and asked, "How long would you need to re-enable the data center? Software restores, reversing the Scorched Earth Programs, restoring power to the center, and of course, operational personnel who don't ask too many questions. All of this would have to be orchestrated quickly, efficiently, and quietly to make our timetable. That is, assuming I can persuade the locals."

Christopher hesitated a moment before he responded, "Madam, I already have all the piece parts you referred to in flight. I made the heroic assumption that you would be able to handle the one piece of the proposed project that I could not effect. I believe the local authorities are waiting for your …uh, persuasion to be delivered to these numbered bank accounts I have written out for you."

Marge, uncharacteristically, chuckled and said, "Now that's what I like, an assumptive close to a problem now only being seen in the rear-view mirror. Well done, Christopher."

CHAPTER SIX

Information Deluge, Straining the Levees
...The Enigma Chronicles

Quip grudgingly decided to take Juan to the R-Group operations center. He was not necessarily going to share all the secrets of the organization, but at least he could show him some of the capabilities. He had alerted ICABOD that Juan was coming but not for full disclosure, or the proverbial keys to the kingdom. Admittedly, Juan reminded Quip he was not highly computer savvy, but rather more attuned to people and event deduction skills.

Juan was careful not to over-press his position with Quip. Quip had made it very clear that he would be seeing things that his family and the organization would not want shared everywhere. It was a tool that the CATS group could use via Julie or himself. He also explained that even EZ at this point did not have all the details, which was as much for her protection as for the protection of the organization itself.

When they arrived at the operations center, it appeared to be an unused warehouse in the middle of the forest, long forgotten and ignored. If it weren't for the motion-activated camera over the door, which Juan's keen ears picked up the whirling sound of, he would have thought it totally deserted.

Quip grinned as Juan looked up and scoped out the camera, then commented, "If you had walked up without me, it never would have moved. I am impressed that you heard that pitch. It's mostly masked by the general sounds of nature around the building, which of course, we encourage.

"We are going to go in the door, which would not open were it not for my handprint recognition on the panel to the right that looks like a simple occupancy sign for information purposes. You might see a few of the group, but it is early so we may simply be left alone. We subscribe to a three-factor authentication for security. This equates to something you have, something you are, and something you can do. As we go into the entry room you will need to create a profile with these three factors, which are unique to you and security for us. I have set the program to accept you as a member of this building but to allow you access only into specific areas. This is much the same as the network we established for your operations at CATS. Julie and you can see all files and data, whereas EZ or Mercedes, for example, can only see designated areas."

Juan nodded. He appreciated the way Quip explained things without talking down to him. He watched Quip run through the authentication with unique but memorable elements to fulfill security. First, Quip used his handprint on the screen again. Then he recited a bawdy limerick, followed by singing two lines of a theatre show tune Juan recognized from the flight back from the islands.

Juan commented with a grin, "Ha! Does this mean you can sing at the twins' next birthday party?"

If looks could kill, the glare from Quip in that moment would have done it. Quip snarled, "Okay, funny man, give it what you have. When you see the green light, do it again to confirm."

Juan laughed and went through the *have and are* authentication factors. When it got to the something you can do element, Juan executed a karate kick Quip had never seen.

Quip asked, "Does that move have a name?"

Juan replied, "This is called the Scorpion Kick."

"Wow, man, can you teach me that move?"

"Quip, as much as I respect your technical expertise and, heck, even the flexibility you must have to use that device with EZ that I saw at your flat, I would need years to help you perfect that move. It requires extreme flexibility, which I constantly work at, to bring your leg backwards until you can complete the strike with your foot over your shoulder while retaining your balance. It doesn't do you any good to throw a Scorpion Kick only to be flat on the floor afterwards. To be honest, it looks cooler than it is effective. I can get some power behind it but it has to be placed perfectly to be effective. Happy to help you with it, but you would have to be patient and work at it."

Quip thought for a few moments then asked, "Does Julie know how to do this?"

"No, we have not worked on this. There are other defensive moves we focus our training on. I do it to maintain my flexibility."

Quip grinned, "Then I want to learn it. One upping Julie is a winner, if you promise not to tell her that's why I learned it." Juan laughed. "Your secret is safe with me, but it will take some time. I will write down a few things you can do to help stretch and we can do remote sessions if you want. I try to work out an hour or so a day."

Quip visibly gulped. "Every day?"

"Yep, even when I was in the Mexican jail with my Uncle Jesus I worked out. It doesn't take too much space and that tends to help with one's control."

Quip sucked in and raised his chest a bit then replied, "Yeah, good! That works for me too, man. I'm looking forward to the sessions.

"Now we need to go to our meeting room. I wanted to make certain you have the current information for some of the work your team is taking on. We have the location in Panama we are monitoring, then we also have a review of the business ePETRO, which we are also monitoring. This is the place where Jacob and Petra did some computer forensic investigation."

They retrieved coffee and a couple of cookies available on the side of the room as they entered. They settled into some chairs facing a very large high-definition screen. The color was amazing and the detail extremely precise.

Juan joked, "So this is where you watch movies when you're bored. I didn't see one of these in your condo, but it would likely have been hidden behind a wall, right?"

Quip admitted, "As much fun as this is, I really don't like looking at a screen when I am home, other than the modest television we have. I think we both spend so much time looking at screens with our work that other things are far more interesting to look at, if you get my drift."

Juan knowingly grinned and replied, "Don't I know it. We have some very lovely females, don't we?" They both zoned out for a moment before a high chirp sounded, bringing Quip back to business. He keyed in some words and the screen erupted with various summary information reports. Quip began to analyze the information in real time and summarized it for Juan.

Juan was certainly known for his flying and fighting abilities, but felt a bit overwhelmed by the barrage of information coming at him. He tried to listen to Quip and read the screens at the same time.

"Stop a second, Quip. You're going way too fast for me to pick out the salient pieces. Can you slow it down a little so I can capture the right stuff to focus on?"

Quip looked confused for a moment, then quite sheepishly replied, "Juan, I'm sorry. I sometimes get ahead of myself. Julie has pulled me up short the same way. Let me look at this and then highlight out loud the areas that make sense for further investigation or work using your team. I think that will work better."

Juan nodded and was surprised again at how graciously Quip admitted a need to change. He'd always thought Quip believed he was smarter than everyone and liked to flaunt it. Apparently not. Juan then began transcribing the areas Quip highlighted, adding a few reminder notes in places for his take on a few of the items.

They worked on through the morning, pausing for short breaks and taking advantage of the lunch items, which appeared in place of the morning sweets. No one bothered them and the information seemed to just keep flowing. Juan noticed the information continued to be updated and assembled into increasingly logical order. Then it suddenly seemed to stop. Juan looked around as if afraid that a breach in the building had occurred.

Quip noticed Juan's shift and concerned, he insisted, "Juan, it's alright. The timers I put into the system for breaks just kicked in." Then he turned a bit red and admitted, "I had to put these in to make certain I get home in time for dinner. Before EZ, I would keep on working a project until I went nose down on the keyboard. But now…"

Juan grinned and replied, "I do understand total focus. I surely do. Let's take a break. Perhaps you can look over my notes before dinner, and I can call Julie with an update."

"Deal. Um, will you inform Julie that the day was good, like no arguments. She made me promise." Juan heartily laughed and replied, "Sure, but I am glad you told me. She gets too nosey sometimes."

Quip looked surprised by Juan's response. "Yep, she does at times. EZ too!"

CHAPTER SEVEN

The Rain Always Hides Your Tears

It wasn't raining hard, but it was enough to soak one quickly if you didn't have an umbrella and rain gear. The steady rain also made the trees drip increasingly heavier drops, reminding him that he should be moving indoors soon. Mesmerized, Brayson watched the rain water stream down the headstone into the manicured grass, punctuated with flashes of lightning and the ever-closer rumble of thunder. It increased his melancholy for the graveside visit.

With a heavy sigh, he chided himself for having a knack for picking bad weather days to visit her grave site. It was almost as if he was consistently rehearsing her worldly exit so he could punish himself just one more time for not having stopped her sacrifice. She once scolded him for thinking that she could ever be in his life. Now it seemed he only continued to imagine the two of them together as life partners.

Like so many times before, he absentmindedly chewed on his lip as he stared intently at her headstone. The wind whipped up now and again, sending the rain sideways just enough to get under the umbrella, chilling his skin. Completely saddened, he lifted his arm to reach out to the grave marker and, as was so often the case, almost felt her standing next to him. Even though the daylight receded further, the occasional lightning flashes provided enough light to help maintain the mentally punishing scene he almost welcomed.

Almost like clockwork, the scene dissolved into the alarm blaring its wake-up call, pulling him from sleep. This time it was coupled with the noise of a fist pounding on his apartment door, most insistent about being answered. It always took a few minutes to shrug off the mildly depressed state he found himself in after dreaming about her.

Finally, he hollered, "Alright! I'm up, I'm up!"

The loud, familiar male voice boomed commands from outside of the door, with words that verified it was not his first trip to this door. "Come on, Brayson! This is getting old, dude! If you're tired of the group, then resign. Otherwise, get your rear in gear!" Then as an afterthought, the man added, "And don't be making that vulgar hand gesture that you seem to have incorporated into your outlook on life. Move it, soldier! There's a war on, man!"

Brayson made a sour face, added the gesture for good measure, and hollered, "Yes, Drill Sergeant Ernesto!"

Moments later, Brayson exited his apartment, buttoning his shirt as Ernesto pushed the elevator buttons and handed over the extra coffee in his hand. Neither man said a word or even looked at one another as they intently walked toward their destination.

Even with his unruly dark brown hair, Brayson had an attractive squared face with espresso-colored eyes above the dark circles that emphasized his poor sleep of late. At nearly two meters, his strong, muscular build was kept his daily workouts despite his troubled sleep. With hollowed cheeks, his face reflected a reduction from his normal 86 kilos. His schooling and military history showed in the way he walked and held his shoulders.

Ernesto, always ready with a smile and a joke, realized his teammate was still grieving for the woman who had died by her choice. He walked with the same military background, fit and trim and close to the same height, but the darker skin and curly hair suggested a different heritage. His parents, Polish and Italian, were proud of their son, who had graduated from a prestigious university with honors. They had no clue their son was a weapons and explosives expert with a history of covert missions using his many languages and ability to quickly blend into any place.

The team had gathered in the large meeting room where Julie and Juan gave briefings and held conference calls. Julie, also known as JAC, interfaced to the R-Group, with her limited visibility. At just over 1.6 meters and 54 kilograms, she kept in shape sparring in martial arts with her husband Juan, but her real advantage was her trademark megawatt smile. It lit up her bluish green eyes in her pretty face, framed with light brown wavy hair, which she kept in a shorter style since their twins were born.

Juan, her devoted husband, was still in Zürich working with Quip. She escaped into a quick daydream of him. She pictured him next to her, just over 1.5 meters, his stocky build of solid muscle at just over 77 kilograms. His thick black shiny hair, kept in a groomed though longer style, hinted at his Mexican ancestry. Juan's quick wit and smile was what had initially endeared him to Julie, as well as his ability to overcome almost any situation. Theirs was a rich and loving relationship made even stronger by their twins.

Juan was on the video conference bridge as people drifted in. Still, he greeted the team individually with comments about how he appreciated everyone being there, bright-eyed and bushy-tailed, for this early meeting. He seemed to rest his gaze on

Brayson, as if to acknowledge he was aware of the exception to those comments. It was a modest chiding exercise, which everyone noticed, though no one tried to examine any further.

Julie smiled as she said, "Morning, team! Thanks for joining us so promptly. We have a lot of things teed up for pursuit, and a lot of things that are just…undefined.

"You know, usually Juan and I simply go down the list of pending assignments and, based on team availability or skills needed, hand them out. We'd like to do this a little differently this time. We have some new information that we received from some data tracking programs that suggest additional investigation is required in Panama, London, Singapore and others. I want to go over the open assignments, and then I would like the team to decide between yourselves who would make the most sense in a given activity."

A couple of the team members looked uneasily at each other. A couple rolled their eyes at the statement. As seasoned professionals with backgrounds in covert operations, cyber technology, weapons usage, military combat and so forth, they all expected the other shoe to drop. Their background suggested they took orders and then carried out those orders, as opposed to a *make your own decision on the best way to handle the task* manner.

Then Julie quickly added, "Okay, I get the subliminal *is she kidding or what* sentiment. Understand this, folks, you are the best at what you do, and frankly we are getting more business than the team can handle. This isn't the newest management fad thinking, coming out of the MBA University du jour, but our next step in potentially hiring new CATS members. We want competent field agents that can also manage or train others to grow our business. In other words, I need to see you guys begin operating like leaders. We already know you are highly-skilled field operatives."

The team members immediately did an about face in their attitudes and took on a new sense of pride at Julie's statement. They all brightened, except for Brayson. It troubled Juan to see how the discussion fell flat on him. Juan said nothing, as he wanted to see how things panned out.

Julie outlined the pending assignments, and then she used a well-defined kinetic hand gesture on the video conference monitor to move Juan and the open conference bridge to her phone and left the room. She wanted to speak with Juan privately, so the team could discuss and plan the distribution of work.

Once they were out of ear-shot, Juan suggested, "You know, he just might not make it. Now I'm willing to try with everything we discussed, but he simply may not choose to keep going. He did well with the assignment in Spain, but you know as well as I do, since he returned, he has continued to withdraw. It's really his call. We can't force him, or more specifically, I won't force him. Either he is in of his own free will and a team player, or we cut him loose. Anything else is a risk to the group dynamics and our business as a whole. Actually, the risk to himself might be even worse."

Julie studied Juan's image on the video call for a moment and then firmly stated, "As long as he wants to try, I'll give him that chance. I don't want to give up on him, just because he is having a rough patch. Are we in agreement, my darling?"

Juan moved closer to the video camera, lowered his voice, and flatly responded, "Madam, I'm in violent agreement with you. There is no need to try and insist upon having your way in this matter."

Julie broke into her trademark smile and delivered a quick smooch to Juan's image on the video image before she illuminated, "I'm glad you can be reasoned with. Sometimes reasoning with some males can be troublesome."

Juan feigned a hurt look and meekly offered, "I can be agreeable sometimes. You remember that time, before the kids, when you asked me to hook your bra before we left for work? I can help sometimes!"

Lowering her head and looking at Juan from underneath her eyebrows with a critical look, she sighed as she recalled, "Has it been that long?"

Then they both smiled. Julie lovingly caressed the video image before disconnecting the call.

CHAPTER EIGHT

Tall, Dark, and Desirable

Laurie entered Mike's office while he was on a call. He nodded his head in acknowledgement as she waited for him to hang up. She was dressed in her standard grey and black business attire, which seemed to compliment her well-styled, short, almost black hair. What was not typical was her bouncing up and down on her toes as the heels of her pumps clicked the floor. Laurie had a bit of color in her cheeks that offset her pale skin. Mike realized something was up with his twenty-something assistant, and she was not going to drop work on his desk and leave. Her fidgeting finally annoyed him enough to disconnect the phone call.

As soon as the phone was disconnected, Laurie blushed as she exclaimed, "Oh my goodness, sir, there is the most fabulous looking young man in the reception area. He says you are expecting him for a job. I have nothing in my planner indicating you have a job applicant, or that we even have an opening." She hopefully added, "I didn't realize we were hiring again, but I'm happy to train him, sir, in any capacity you wish."

Mike thought for a moment, then recalled the request of his customer. "The young man is a relative of one of our customers. I need to have him complete an application. I want him to get a basic understanding of the overall operations. He can start with opening mail, sorting it alphabetically, and he can relieve the receptionist during lunch and breaks, as a start. I do not want you hovering over him like a love-sick puppy, do you understand?"

Laurie grinned with delight as she practically danced out the door to retrieve the forms to get things in motion. Just before the door closed, Mike added, "When he has completed the application, I will speak to him."

"Yes, sir!"

A scant half hour later, Laurie knocked and then opened the door. "Sir, Mr. Dabir Nasr has completed the forms." She walked toward his desk and handed him the forms.

Mike reviewed the forms quickly and looked up. "Send him in, Laurie."

Laurie ushered the young man in with a blush rising in her cheeks. One nod from Mike reminded her she was not needed in the conversation. She turned and left, closing the door behind her.

Mike stood and extended his hand as the young man walked in, smiling pleasantly. They shook hands and quickly assessed one another. The young man was eye-to-eye with Mike at a bit under two meters, but considerably thinner. His dark hair was neatly trimmed just above the shirt collar. He wore a light tan shirt with a dark tie, over dark slacks. The quality of the fabric was not particularly good, but the cut and fit were definitely current with today's business casual standards.

"Mr. Patrick, thank you for seeing me. My uncle tells me this opportunity is one I will appreciate at some point in my life. I am not certain what you would have me do, but I am willing to learn, sir." He then handed a sealed envelope to Mike. "My uncle requested I bring this letter to you."

Mike accepted the offered envelope and then looked critically at the young man, having detected no sincerity in his greeting. Then again, after knowing Kashan now for several years, this was normal behavior. "Kashan tells me, Dabir, you recently graduated university and have friends here in London. I suspect a lady friend or two as well.

"He asked if you might learn the business essentially from the bottom up, so I will have you go through all the positions in that manner. I trust you will not consider any of these positions insulting or beneath you. I am complying with the request of an old friend."

"Any job is fine as long as I can learn. I do learn very quickly though.

"I noticed your staff seems young and very busy on their phones and computers. Do they work with all the accounts, or are they assigned customers?"

Mike warmed to the subject and replied, "Each representative has specific customers, though a backup is also assigned to an account to cover any time someone is away from the office. You may, after some period of time, be assigned a few accounts to cover, at least for back up. Initially, I want to have you get your initial basic work assignments from Laurie. She and I spoke of some duties over the next few weeks of mail, filing and reception desk coverage. Laurie handles most of my correspondence and is actually in charge when I am out of the office."

Their conversation continued for thirty more minutes as Mike related his background of work in the oil fields as his introduction to the business. Mike outlined some of the work he had done in the United States and how he had worked his way up to his current position. For his part, Dabir related his studies and some of the trade work he had completed in Iran, Turkey, and Saudi Arabia. He laughed as he discussed some of the earlier endeavors before university. In a short time, they had formed a quasi-employer-to-employee relationship.

As they wound down, Dabir looked at Mike and seriously asked, "Is this Laurie your part time female too?"

Mike shook his head and added, "No, and I don't want you pursuing a relationship with her either. She has too much to get done to have her head in the clouds." Dabir wryly smiled, "Yes, sir, I understand. No worries on that front. My taste runs to taller more shapely females. My youngest brother has more curves than your Laurie."

With that understanding, Mike buzzed Laurie.

Laurie entered with a huge grin and look of anticipation. Mike reintroduced Laurie to Dabir and suggested she show him to his work area and get him started.

Laurie looked into Dabir's very dark eyes with adoration and assured him she would take care of getting him acclimated to the work.

CHAPTER NINE

Always Leverage the Assets

Everyone in the CATS group had great respect for Julie and her management style. As business manager she was driven to excel and was always the person in charge. Juan liked his position in the organization as her trusted business partner. He often deferred to Julie on points of contention.

With her take-charge attitude, Mercedes naturally gravitated to leading the discussion concerning work assignments. Because of their respect for Julie, the males in the group tended to permit Mercedes to drive the discussion, all except Brayson. Ernesto and George were very gregarious males and liked to be in the thick of things. Tyler and Summit tended to be more reserved and analytical in their dealings with people. Brayson had fallen into a brooding mood and seemed unable to engage with others, to the point that he seemed to resent the new group assignment.

While everyone seemed to be engaging in the conversation, Brayson drifted off again to the final scene he had witnessed when he watched Gretchen stretch out her arms in front of the window just as the bullet slammed through her body then almost grazed him. He had cradled her body for all too short a time before his cell phone had gone off, warning him that the police were en route and that he had to go. It had torn at him that he had to abandon her lifeless body as his grief had almost consumed him. The scene wouldn't stop playing over and over in his mind.

Finally, Mercedes intruded into his thoughts. "Hey, Brayson, you want to join us over here on planet earth? This is a planning exercise that requires all of our input, and you seem stuck in a disengaged, neutral state. How about putting your big boy panties on, climbing out of the emotional cesspool you seem stuck in, and re-joining the living teammates who all depend upon you?"

Brayson snapped back to reality and slowly looked into the faces of everybody before settling his gaze on Mercedes. His hurt feelings coupled with his growing anger caused him to confront her. "Oh, you think you're neat 'cause you got tits? You're always pushing and pulling everyone without thinking of the bigger picture! You're the kind of person that loves to stomp on gnats in the corner of the room, while there's elephants stampeding down the hallway! Here I am watching you do it yet again!

"Your tendency is to put people in the same old role that you have created for them mentally, rather than looking to grow them in other areas. Why are we not grouping dissimilar skill sets together and deploying in groups of two? Maybe that way someone won't get beaten up or killed!"

The blustery outburst caught everyone by surprise, and no one spoke. Mercedes was quite livid at the dressing down, but before she could respond, Julie leaned against the doorway and interjected, "Well, class, how are you doing with taking on the new assignments? Has everyone had a chance to examine their skill set and feelings for the new roles we have ahead of us, so they can thoroughly tick off other team members?"

Ernesto brightly replied, "Julie, we were just discussing what we liked about each other from an alignment perspective. The team is suggesting we pair up on this go-round to help keep each other safe, as well as for a learning exercise.

"From what I'm hearing it sounds like Tyler and myself could take the first assignment in New York. Summit and George would be the best fit to work the Asian based assignments. Then Mercedes has volunteered to supervise the emotionally retarded Brayson as they hit the Panama data center. The only one left open is the London assignment to review the data and babysit Laurie, the girl hired at ePETRO right before R-group departed. We are kind of out of personnel at this point. The well is dry, so to speak."

Julie's mood darkened a little bit as she questioned, "Oh, so I'm not considered as deployable for a babysitting assignment? What am I, chopped liver? Heck, I have experience with that, and recently too."

The team members melted a little into their chairs at the view of defeat snatched from the jaws of what seemed like a victory, before a chastened Ernesto meekly offered, "Ah, what I meant was with Juan still on assignment, and… well, with you the only one here to, ah… manage the business and…uh, the offspring …I assumed that you would be disinclined to ah…work the field…so to speak."

Julie then broke into her characteristic megawatt smile and teased, "It's alright, Ernesto, I was just yanking your chain. Is everyone alright with their assignments? Now is the time to rethink your partners and responsibilities, not once you get into the field." Julie's focus was primarily on Brayson and Mercedes.

Before Mercedes could respond, Brayson calmly offered, "I believe working with Mercedes in this data center assignment is a good pairing. There is much I can learn from her, and I welcome the opportunity to be taught."

Somewhat stunned at the conciliatory, almost flattering statement from Brayson, Mercedes numbly responded, "I, uh… of course would welcome the chance to learn from Brayson, as he is a most accomplished data center…uh, whatever."

Julie smirked a little but let the situation stand on its own. However, she was unable to resist the final word. "Excellent. By the way Brayson, we females ALL know we're neat, 'cause we have tits!"

Brayson's beet red face perfectly expressed to everyone his mortal embarrassment at the echo of his disparaging remark. The team members chuckled, even Mercedes.

Julie was contemplating her pending assignment in London when the phone chimed, alerting her that Juan was checking in. She answered with "Hello, honey! How is my favorite man?"

Juan, somewhat distracted, answered, "Uh, I'm okay, babe. Just overwhelmed and feeling a little inadequate here at Quip's data center. Jeez, this guy is a mutant! He is working on three, count them, three PCs at a time and coaching me in between, all while holding a call with EZ. What is it that Jacob says? It ain't bragging if you can do it! I used to think he was bragging, but I don't anymore. Anyway, enough on that, how did the assignment exercise go?"

Julie, being somewhat evasive, responded, "Oh, I think it went alright. There was a bit more friction than I expected. They wanted to double team these assignments for cross-training purposes and, well, for better personal safety. A bit more cautious than I was going to suggest, but I want them to try this. They have some real chances to learn from each other."

Juan did the math in his head and then asked, "Julie, doesn't that leave one AIM lead un-accounted for? With me not there, we have one lead not being pursued, unless you are going to split a team or you hired someone already."

Julie, now trying not to answer, responded, "Honey, you know I'm perfectly capable of handling a simple sleuthing assignment by myself. I mean, after all, who taught this group their trade?"

Juan fumbled with the phone but finally grabbed it firmly and insisted, "No, sweetheart, please? I don't want you to do it alone! I'll be back the day after tomorrow, and I can go do it. I don't want you at risk."

Julie smiled at her husband's pleading concerns and said, "Yes, honey, you know I always do what I'm told. I've never worked on my own before, either. I love you."

Juan, now feeling his insides rolling with uneasiness, bluntly stated, "Julie, I know that tone, so promise me you won't go do this assignment. Then, when you ignore my request, please be careful and cautious on the assignment that I know you are going to do even though you shouldn't."

Julie smiled lovingly as Juan pleaded and promised, "Yes honey, I'll be careful. Besides, it's just the babysitting one. Love you."

She then disconnected the call and began creating her new identity for the assignment, recalling a fun evening of old-time movie watching they'd recently shared with her favorite, *Superman III*.

CHAPTER TEN

Pictures at an Exhibition

Ernesto wrinkled his brow at the incoming caller ID but took it anyway and calmly answered, "Lost souls' hotline. You got sore feet? We need to meet!"

Jamie smirked a little and responded, "Don't tell me you've forgotten who this is, bro? You got me and Frieda out of danger in China a few months back, and now I want to return the favor. You see, my lady and I found this scruffy stray mutt. Well, he reminded us of you, so would you mind if we named him after you?"

Ernesto pictured the image of Jamie with his longish blond hair and dancing blue eyes that flashed when his uncontrollable flair for blarney started. Ernesto had felt a certain young earnestness in this Irish rogue. Jamie's computer talents were offset by his constant chasing of the next adventure to capture that pot of gold at the end of the ever-elusive rainbow.

Ernesto chuckled slightly and asked, "How is Frieda? Did she deliver okay? How is your new offspring? Did you get one with the plumbing on the inside or the outside?"

Jamie's smile faded as he replied, "She and the baby are doing fine, Ernesto. Just fine. But that's not what I'm calling about." Ernesto sensed Frieda and the child were a sore subject, so he quickly moved the conversation along. "Enough of the social chit-chat, what's up?"

Jamie began, "I guess you know me well enough to know that domestic life isn't really for me. After little Timmy was born, the family wanted us closer to home, as in her parents' home. I drifted on and ended up working in the Oregon/Washington area. Not a bad gig, waiting tables, cleaning rooms, helping old folks on and off the riverboat that cruises up and down the Columbia and Snake rivers. And OMG, the opulence of those 50 cent tips! Sometimes my cup runneth over from their generosity!

"Anyway, I got off in Richmond, Washington, to get me some variety and culture by taking in the Hanford Reach Museum."

Ernesto, growing impatient with Jamie's monologue, curtly asked, "Jamie, is there a point to this story? I mean, I'm always glad to hear from you, but then you start talking, which ruins it."

Jamie now wondered if it was a good use of his time too but continued, "You know, I'm fairly sure it's your caring, compassionate nature that keeps people coming back for more sarcasm. If you don't have time to listen, then just say so. I called you because no one else would get it." Somewhat chastened, Ernesto offered, "I'm sorry, Jamie, please continue."

Jamie continued, "Anyway, the Hanford Reach Museum had two separate sections. One for the geological history of the area which was okay. But the one I wanted to see was the chronicles on the first U.S. site to be built with the sole function of refining uranium to enrich it into plutonium to make the first atomic bombs."

Ernesto's eyes got big, and he was completely focused on the conversation. He responded, "Really? How come I've never heard of it?"

Jamie, warming to the topic, explained, "Turns out only 1% of the manufactured city of Hanford knew what was being built. The exhibit talked about the B-Reactor, the world's first industrial-scale nuclear reactor, which was built during World War II as part of the top-secret Manhattan Project to develop the atomic bomb. You know what was interesting about this exhibit? The life size photos and atomic bomb schematics that they have in the exhibit. Including some logistical nuclear fission graphs to help understand the fission process."

Ernesto said nothing during the slight pause, so Jamie continued, "There I was taking in all this advanced physics, when a camera goes off next to me. I saw this scarfed Muslim woman taking several photos of the nuclear bomb schematics, but nothing else.

"Then, when I turned to speak with her, she went white as a ghost, not so easy with her complexion. Being the kind of person I am, I took her camera and offered to take her picture in front of the exhibit, just to see what she would do.

"She bolted and headed for the door like Satan was after her. Then, I was honestly trying to return her camera, but she was almost in hysterics. I started yelling at her to refocus and calm down. The guards at the place thought she was trying to steal something, so they intervened and tried to stop her. She wrenched free, turned, and at a dead run, gets through the front door and into the parking lot. There she gets picked up by a car. She and some guy driving with his face in a shadow sped away. We were all standing there scratching our heads, when the guards ask me what was going on."

Ernesto smirked and offered, "I bet you told them she tried to lift your camera. However, since it wasn't taken, you weren't going to formally report it."

Jamie clucked his tongue and whined, "Oh man, I'm sorry, have I already told you this story?"

Ernesto chuckled slightly. Jamie added, "After everything calmed down, I found a quiet place to go over the photos. The only photos on the camera are of the atomic bomb schematics, the B-Reactor, and anything else on how to enrich uranium and how the first atomic bomb was engineered. All of this in a Muslim female's hands who definitely had a scared, guilty look."

Ernesto smiled a little and somewhat sarcastically suggested, "My, what an exciting life you lead. Did you have a similar experience at the zoo, too? Was there anything else about this accidental tourist and her lost camera I should know about?"

Jamie, now irked at the tone of the comment, bluntly replied, "Actually, yes, I think so. She was found dead the day after the lost camera episode. It was all over the news about how badly beaten her body was before she died. I got to thinking that she might be a part of a Muslim terrorist cell looking for atomic bomb information that didn't want to go through the Internet, thereby calling attention to certain keywords being monitored by Homeland Security.

"These pictures are fairly incriminating, but the interesting thing to me, is that this was being collected, not by a computer search engine, but using an analog method that can't possibly be traced back. Fairly clever actually. Might have worked if I hadn't gummed up her works."

Ernesto sat musing for a moment and then asked, "You still have the camera and its contents? Maybe you can ship them to me, along with the make and model of the camera so I can do some detective work on it. Oh, and when was her untimely demise? Or better still, send me the newspaper, so I can at least see what she could have looked like?"

Jamie offered, "I have something even better. When I got the camera away from her, I took a quick shot of her face, which is still on the camera. I'll send them all to you. Now, wasn't this call interesting enough to listen to all of it?"

Ernesto smiled and responded, "Jamie, I will admit that you seem to have a knack for being a lightning rod for rough circumstances. I hope you are wrong, but I can't help feeling that you have stumbled into yet another mess. You take care of yourself and call me if you get any more leads. I'd hate to think we got you this far only to see you get whacked by some Muslim extremists. If they whacked her for losing the camera you now have, it is highly likely they will want it back."

Jamie mocked indignation as he replied, "Me, get whacked? Oh, do come along, young man! This is Jamie the gambler, with the luck of the Irish, we're talking about!"

Ernesto clucked his tongue and responded, "Precisely."

Jamie phoned back to convey the package tracking information to Ernesto. It was an insured and signed for shipment which even with priority would take a few days. Once the business side of the discussion was completed, they transitioned to the more personal side.

Ernesto asked, "Once I have reviewed the contents of the package, are you up for some part-time work, Jamie? Though I understand if you need to be close to the family. Perhaps some of the effort can be a remote support function."

Ernesto kept probing the conversation with Jamie to get at the real story of what had happened before Jamie went on the road, so he asked, "How about some pictures of the three of you so I can see those happy faces, huh? I need to live family life vicariously through yours."

Jamie hesitatingly replied, "I don't have any photos with me, so…so some other time perhaps." Ernesto playfully insisted, "Oh come on, you're a proud papa with an exquisite redheaded lady! You must have some photos on that smart phone of yours. Don't tell me I need to perform a virtual training session on how to access your images folder. Just a few crumbs for me here!"

Jamie hesitated then seemed to struggle to find the words as he haltingly offered, "Umm…you see, it was a difficult delivery and…well, she smiled at me before she…uh…" Jamie's voice got softer and softer as he wiped the tears away from his cheek as his eyes kept overflowing.

Ernesto now wished he hadn't been so insistent on the story, but Jamie continued, "Little Timmy had some problems…Frieda didn't get to see…it wasn't his fault it was, uh… mine. It's always my fault. Her folks never said that, but I, uh…but whenever I looked them in the face, I could see them…I could feel the blame…"

Jamie was now in free form, blamestorming himself, his voice just barely above a whisper when he finished, "Her parents said they would help raise little Timmy and that I was welcome to stay, but…I knew that I shouldn't…I knew I couldn't. Besides, who would want a killer under the roof with them and Frieda's baby? I could see the look in their eyes and almost hear them thinking *you killed our daughter; we won't let you do that to her baby.*"

Ernesto was shamefully quiet at the story he had provoked, and so he said nothing.

Jamie's choke turned into a false laugh, and as he wiped the tears from his face, he used all his now forced bravado to be as cavalier as possible, saying, "So I am now out dreaming and scheming again to get back on top, bro! I have nothing holding me back, so what kind of gig for me did you have in mind? Remember now, I ain't cheap, but I can be your bought whore!"

It took a lot of forced concentration for Ernesto to finally suggest, "We may have need of some freelance work on a problem we are trying to solve. The Muslim female you ran into at the museum is the point of entry into this situation. I am obliged to point out it is going to be dangerous."

Jamie smiled his old gambler smile and offered, "The more danger the better."

CHAPTER ELEVEN

That Means No...
To Both Questions

Christopher tersely stated, "Madam, repeat all the information back to me, please. I have to know that the account numbers and the sums are exactly as required."

Laurie quickly responded with the request and made no mistakes in the numbering sequence, the target names, or the amounts. After a few seconds of silence, she pointedly asked, "Does that conform to your written information, Mr. C?"

Christopher nodded at her rote memorization effort and then continued, "Well done, madam. Now the exercise is to take multiple flight hops and get to Panama for a completed delivery of the transaction, but to quickly return to your duties at ePETRO, so as not to be missed. Once you get to Panama, pull the battery out of the burner phone and do not replace it until your second flight hop back has been completed. Anything that can communicate wirelessly is also trackable and therefore..."

Laurie dispassionately finished his sentence. "A risk for exposure of our operation. Yes, Mr. C, I remember that as well. As far as my cover goes, I have let it be known that I am taking my infirmed mother to an out-of-town specialist and will be back in a few days. The cover story is in place. However, you need to understand that my watcher duties will have to be suspended until I return."

Christopher unflinchingly responded, "Then be efficient with your time and re-engage as soon as possible. Our organization prides itself on minimal disruption to our information flow."

As she turned to leave, Laurie wondered how much harder his heart had to work to pump all that ice water through his arteries.

Mercedes stood staring into the airline terminal crowd with a puzzled look on her face.

Brayson hadn't noticed at first but then settled his gaze on her. He realized that she had stopped processing so he asked, "Are we channeling onto something else? You seem to have stopped moving."

Mercedes, without taking her eyes off her target, in a hushed tone remarked, "That is the target AIM that Julie was going to work with at ePETRO. What is she doing heading out and with almost no baggage?"

Brayson sported a mildly surprised look and, peering in the same direction, questioned, "Are you sure it's her? I mean, it's not like it couldn't be someone with similar looks. At this distance you could mistakenly…"

Mercedes cut him off. "No mistake. And yes, my eyes and cognitive skills concerning people are what got me into that prestigious U.S. spy agency many moons ago."

Brayson smirked a little but then agreed, "Well, let's just see who she is, shall we?" And without waiting for an answer, Brayson quickly walked up to the female traveler, spun her around, and laid a big sloppy kiss on her as though they were long lost lovers suddenly reunited.

Mercedes was aghast at the scene and irritated that apparently their cover was now blown completely by a man who couldn't keep his hormones in check. However, she maintained a fixation on the drama still unfolding.

As soon as Brayson finished his impromptu greeting kiss, he immediately went into abject embarrassment as he sheepishly announced, "Oh my god! Madam, forgive me! A thousand pardons and endless apologies! I thought you were someone else! I…I… don't know how I can make amends for my unforgiveable transgression, Miss…"

Now that the initial shock had worn off and the handsome but unknown gentleman was desperately trying to back-peddle his way out of the embarrassing situation, Laurie, now somewhat amused, asked, "Whoever she is, make sure you maintain the same level of enthusiasm for a proper greeting! My name is Laurie…ah, that's all you need to know. I'll accept your apology, since I am a little late for my departure gate." She added with a chuckle, "I would recommend that you spend a little more time properly identifying your intended target before you launch your next greeting."

Brayson sheepishly nodded and offered, "Again, madam, please accept my apologies. I must confess, though, that I'm not sorry to have had the pleasure of kissing you. Perhaps you will permit me to call on you again when you return to work to confirm my honorable intentions? You are working where?"

About that time, Mercedes strolled up and put her arms around Brayson's waist, and cooed, "There you are, you naughty, naughty boy! Come before this tolerant lady suspects you of being a stalker. Besides, we have a plane to catch!"

Laurie chuckled as Mercedes hustled Brayson toward their gate and the waiting aircraft. As soon they were out of earshot, Mercedes growled, "Was she neat too?"

Brayson smirked and acquiesced, "You were right. Her name is Laurie, and the quick phone photo that I got of her was confirmed by Julie as the target individual."

Mercedes, now somewhat annoyed, responded, "We could have just taken her picture and verified it with Julie WITHOUT having to taste her lipstick. I did the same thing with Julie except that you beat me to it."

Brayson grinned and said, "Well, here is something you could learn from me on verifying your suspicions. Although I doubt you could have comfortably swooped in and given her a hug and smooch with the same cavalier approach that I did."

Mercedes, still irked, snarled, "You're just lucky she didn't just haul off and clock you a good one. I know I would have." Brayson smiled and agreed, "If she had, I would have fallen back to plan B and run through the same scenario with a hurt, surprised look with my hand covering my cheek where she had slapped me."

Mercedes studied him and then added, "When I say clocked, smarty pants, I don't mean slapped. I mean you having to get up off the ground."

Brayson, tiring of the banter, easily redirected the focus and admitted, "You were right, she is a person of interest. We need to tag along and confirm her destination. Julie indicated she is headed to ePETRO soon. If we do lose track of Laurie, Julie will be able to pick up the thread from there, while we work the data center angle.

"An idle question for you. Are you done being mad at me for the impromptu action just because it isn't your style?"

Mercedes looked at him pointedly and admonished, "Let me answer your question with a question of my own. Are you always going to be irrational, undisciplined, and unpredictably dangerous when working with a partner?"

Brayson clucked his tongue and replied, "I guess the answer is no … to both questions."

CHAPTER TWELVE

Three Perps and a Wildcard

Ernesto and Tyler found a spare room to use for planning the New York assignment. With the flight scheduled for early the next morning, they wanted to use the time to outline their approach. The intel they had received from Julie indicated that there were two, possibly three, people that would be landing in New York La Guardia the next evening from two different overnight connecting flights. One flight originated from San José, Costa Rica, while the other from *São Paulo*, Brazil. They both had layovers in Dallas, Texas, for some unknown reason, before continuing on to New York. That was all they had from the flight manifests they'd received.

Tyler had a drier sense of humor than Ernesto, as well as being on the opposite spectrum end of coloring with his blonde hair and piercing blue eyes. They were of comparable height at nearly two meters and equally fit, even with Tyler being three years younger. With their military background, both men could handle nearly any situation with or without arms, though Ernesto promised he was a better sniper, even though the testing for that boast had not occurred.

Tyler thumbed through the information in the folder and began to use the whiteboard to capture the details: travel itineraries, flights, names used where available, and video feed locations. He added their assignment objectives and added pictures of the targets of their surveillance efforts. Initial instructions were to locate and track the subjects, capturing any and all contacts made while in New York. It was undetermined if the subjects knew each other, hence the teaming by Tyler and Ernesto.

Ernesto uploaded photos of the suspected targets into the facial recognition programs to see if they might have a record or get a name. The reason these two females, currently labeled as Jane 1 and Jane 2, had been identified as surveillance targets was because of their entry into two different cities using multiple passports and names. The flights were paid in cash, so there would be no credit card tracing. Oddly, customs officials hardly questioned the females, though from the photos and film, it was obvious they were both dressed for distraction. How Julie and Juan had received the data was something neither Tyler nor Ernesto wasted time questioning. The third photo was of a male who seemed to be very close to one of the females, either as a stalker or possibly a bodyguard. He also had multiple passports.

The male had hit almost immediately in the Interpol database as a citizen of Spain, Santiago Lopez, currently listed as living and working in Argentina for the past four years. His profession was listed as a freelance foreign news correspondent, who was for rent, though no published pieces had been identified to date. The cover provided him a great deal of travel freedom if he truly had a press pass. It didn't, however, explain the multiple passport entries recorded by the customs and immigration data from Brazil. It would be interesting to learn what name he entered the U.S. with the next day.

Ernesto, bored with watching the program run through Interpol and U.S. Homeland Security databases checking for matches, looked at the information on the white board and asked, "Tyler, you seem to have placed Jane 1 on your side to follow. I'm not sure I agree with your taking her since she looks more my type than yours. She has the pretty, wavy dark hair, what appears to be Spanish eyes and lovely curves to match that hair. Jane 2 is far fairer skinned and lithe from the shots we have. If we need to cozy up to them to get our information, she seems more your type."

Tyler raised an eyebrow at the random narrow-minded assessment and replied, "Heck, Ernesto, I didn't realize you had a preference or took notice of such detail. I'm impressed. I had Jane 1 under my side since she has the male stalker slash body-guard, aka press man, in tow, and I didn't want to overtax you, old man."

Ernesto heartily laughed at the quick comeback. He thoroughly enjoyed working with all the team, but Tyler was a hoot. Nothing phased the man, Ernesto observed, and frankly Tyler was a genius at analytics and rapid situational deduction. Then he added, "Old man, eh!? I'm just more mature and can appreciate an assignment with a beautiful female on more levels than a young pup such as you. The male sidekick can be easily neutralized: he appears to be rather skinny and smarmy."

Laughing at themselves, they settled into planning for the possible outcomes envisioned. They enacted the possible scenarios of locating the three people as they deplaned. As long as everyone maintained their flight plans, they had a chance of at least picking up their targets. Julie had indicated that if some other piece of data signaled a change in the targets' arrivals, it would be sent to their cellphones. Their arrival was a good four hours before the targets, giving them plenty of time to stake out their best positioning. Both men were very familiar with the layout of La Guardia Airport.

Ernesto sat pondering the photos of the two females and, rotating his head to one side, said out loud, "I'm not satisfied with giving them placeholder names of Jane 1 and Jane 2. I believe we should rebrand our rogue targets as Penelope and Jennifer. Penelope being the dark haired one that I should follow."

Tyler looked at Ernesto from underneath his eyebrows and deadpanned, "Penny and Jenny? Is that how we want to designate them?"

Ernesto grinned and responded with "Works for me!"

Ernesto then related the conversation he'd shared with Jamie and how he hoped the package being sent would arrive that afternoon. Tyler thought it sounded intriguing, even though he suggested that Jamie might not be the most reliable resource for information. In the end he agreed to review the contents of the package with Ernesto and see what could be done to bake it into their plans while in the U.S.

It was very late when the package arrived. Ernesto laid out the contents on the conference room table for review. Time was growing short for them to depart for the airport, so they made a copy of the pictures provided by Jamie. The original photos and the camera itself were secured in the office safe. Ernesto wrote a quick note to Julie and Juan about the camera so that they could see if prints or anything else might be found on the device to identify the user.

The pictures were precisely as Jamie had indicated and seemed tightly focused on the nuclear fusion attributes openly displayed at the museum. Of course, there were the last couple of the Muslim female and the license plate of the getaway car. They both agreed it was an insightful move on Jamie's part.

Tyler was puzzled by some photos at the front so he asked, "Can you go back to the beginning?" Ernesto shrugged and said, "Sure. Here you go, but what's up? You typically don't wrinkle your nose like that unless something is out of whack."

Tyler studied the first picture. It was a typical male of Middle Eastern descent, but the second picture was a simplistic image of multiple dragons. After a few quiet moments of review, Tyler remarked, "I know we need to go, but I don't understand the significance of the multiple dragons in this picture. It simply doesn't fit with everything else."

Ernesto nodded slightly and commented, "Yeah, I see what you mean. Let's take the pictures with us to review some more while we wait on the flight, but leave any conclusions until after our current assignment is completed and see if our bosses can extract any fingerprints or other useful residue from the camera, okay?"

Tyler absentmindedly acknowledged this suggestion but continued to contemplate the misfit picture as they headed for their transportation.

CHAPTER THIRTEEN

By Land, By Sea, and By Instinct

George had had almost as much as he could tolerate as they approached the final hour of their nearly seventeen hours of travel to Singapore. Even with one of the five-hour legs of flight in First Class, his 1.8 meters height felt like an accordion which had no desire to be compressed any longer. Switching planes multiple times, as well as delays, had proven even worse than he had imagined when the travel was planned. He had just taken a turn in the back of the aircraft to joke with the flight attendants after combing his well-groomed brown hair and brushing his teeth. The laughter and flirting had improved his mood even when he returned to his seat to find his traveling companion still sound asleep.

Though both men had enough military experience to have learned to sleep anywhere, Summit had taken it to a whole new level of sleeping in the zone. His thick dark hair wasn't mussed, no shadow on his cheeks, mustache perfect, and at 1.73 meters, he appeared to fit into the seat comfortably, totally relaxed. George found it annoying that the man was never ruffled.

During the First-Class leg of the trip, they had enough space and privacy to formulate a plan to locate the tankers and to view the travel logs to determine the ports of call they stopped at during their journey. There were a dozen different tankers they were assigned to locate and find additional information on. A portion of these tankers had been tagged at one point by Juan and some locational information had been gathered from those tags, which was the reason for their trip to Singapore. Other tanker identification numbers and descriptions had been provided on a list to George and Summit, with no further detail outside of an estimated route they were to follow, which included a stop in Hong Kong and an unscheduled stop in Singapore.

Summit had suggested he might infiltrate one or more of the Muslim groups in Singapore. The selling and buying of oil from those under trading embargoes was a big deal. Some of the countries under embargoes had Muslim populations. The world might be large but extended families were everywhere for any given population segment. There was a large Muslim population he cultivated and as a community were usually well informed. As Summit knew, not all communications go via the Internet or cell phone. To get this *under the wire* information flow you had to be *under the wire* as well, which meant face to face communications. His fluency in Arabic languages and Chinese would prove invaluable in being able to fluidly move within those groups and learn what was really going on. These people might be willing to share with anyone presumed to be an insider, far easier than through normal law enforcement or diplomatic channels.

George was more inclined to work an angle of reduced security support for the various leadership groups they might have to win over to gain visibility to the ingoing and outgoing shipping manifests. They were interested in the oil cargo origin and the buyers of the products. It was hoped that a pattern might be revealed which would give them their next step. In the off hours while Summit rested, George had been modifying some very sophisticated data gathering tools Julie had provided, which both of them could access from their phones and tablets, storing the information in the cloud. He had created an analytical model that would take the data and extrapolate routes, volumes, and risks in real time. The insight he was looking for was a technique called *skimming*. If all the oil was in fact correctly recorded before it shipped, George wanted to know if all of it got delivered.

Julie and Juan had asked them to prove the shipments were within the global treaty guidelines for the various buyers and sellers located on the manifest. Tall order to prove, period. During their planning discussions they decided identifying the people involved and doing due diligence background checks would be the most useful part of the project.

Summit shifted with ease and grinned at George's screen. He quietly asked, "Were you finally able to get the model to take all the inputs you wanted?" George nodded without looking over and replied, "Yes, and I was able to load it to our devices. Nice cover picture on your devices. I didn't know you liked bikes."

Summit looked a bit startled, just as George had hoped, when he questioned, "You took my devices while I was sleeping? Those are password protected. You could not have had enough time to break them."

George grinned and replied, "I am a fairly happy-go-lucky kind of guy. Because of that, people assume I do not watch and pick up subtleties like how people move their hands when typing passwords. I actually know the passwords to all our team's devices, save one. But, if you tell anyone on the team, I promise I will tell them what I found in the folder labeled personal."

Now looking a bit more frazzled, Summit demanded, "You not only took my private property, but you had the audacity to look in a folder labeled personal. Have you no honor, George? Pictures of my lady friends taken during service to my country is so none of your business. I can't believe you would be so rude and invasive. I am going to insist on a different partner for this project as soon as we land. Now get out of my way, you asshole."

Summit motioned for George to rise and then stood up in the aisle, making certain George saw that his phone was going into his pocket, and stomped away. George had no idea that Summit could get so rattled. He wondered if he should tell him. He was musing to himself the various outcomes of saying something or not when he felt the blow to his shoulder and looked up to find a very angry Summit staring at him, willing him to move.

After Summit resumed his seat and attached his seatbelt, the captain was on the intercom alerting the passengers to the landing in twenty minutes.

George rubbed his shoulder and looked seriously over at Summit. He calmly said, "First, we are not changing teams for this project. Second, I was totally putting you on to see if I could break through that stoic façade you present to all of us. And, third, now that you told me what was in the folder that I only guessed existed, can I see?"

Summit looked like he'd been sucker punched as he shook his head in disbelief.

"George, it amazes me how convincing you were. We will work well together using brute force or pulling really good dialogue out of thin air. I hate you, man."

"Back at you, Summit. Your shirt isn't even wrinkled.

"Go to our cloud data storage and download the updated programs and the plans with a few modifications I worked on while you rested. Let me know of any changes you think we should make, otherwise I think we have it. Now I'm going to take a snooze."

Summit signed on to the airplane Wi-Fi and downloaded the material. He read through it, very impressed with the changes that were made and the way the plan came together. He then carefully went to settings and modified his password.

George chuckled at the reflection in the passenger window and memorized the modified password as he dozed off. This was going to be a fun assignment.

Julie hesitatingly answered the phone rather than let it roll to voicemail. She wasn't prepared for a long discussion. Distractedly, she answered, "Hi, hon, what's up?"

Juan sensed the lack of focus on her part and quickly said, "I know you are trying to get ready for your ill-advised assignment that I wish you'd stand down from, but Quip and company have come across some rather unusual money transfer issues that I thought we could discuss."

Julie, still not focused on Juan's call, absentmindedly acknowledged, "Yes, dear…"

Juan, now struggling to contain his annoyance, insisted, "Okay, let me net this out for you by saying these AIM individuals we are trying to track appear to be part of a money laundering scheme that is almost flawless.

"The ePETRO people appear to be moving product and collecting funds, but nothing is going through the standard bank clearing houses. Nothing is showing up on the corporate ledgers, according to the esteemed Dr. Quip, and yet commerce is being conducted. We are at something of a loss to understand how this is being done.

"Quip and his computer can only loosely put the AIMs in the same proximity of an activity like oil sales with the transfer of funds almost right after that. At this point all we have is circumstantial evidence and no proof. At least no digital proof."

Julie brightened and, now fully engaged, promptly responded, "No digital proof! Of course, that's it! Thank you, honey, talk soon."

Juan gave the now quiet, disconnected phone an incredulous look and flatly said, "Yes dear…thank you dear…good to hear from you too dear…dammit dear."

CHAPTER FOURTEEN

Time to Go to Work

Julie had packed her bag with the twins doing the typical *helping*, by putting additional items into her bag they deemed critical, like the stuffed monkey and sippy cup. Simultaneously, they removed items they felt could be put to better use, like her raincoat to build a quasi-fort between her bench seat and makeup table. She found it humorous and very creative. Every time she or Juan traveled, the twins always tried to help. The great outcome was at least they interacted during all the silliness. It was well worth the extra time it took to pack. However, when the clock chimed eight, she knew playtime was at an end. Neither she nor Juan ever made a big deal about leaving on a work trip. It was just a normal part of their lives.

"Maude, can you please come and help the children get ready for bed? Perhaps, if they are very good, you could help build a fort in the morning with all the chairs in the dining room?"

"Miss Julie, I think that can be arranged. Mister Juan bought a new tarp with Velcro we haven't tried yet. Gracie is usually better at helping with the fort, but Juan Jr. might be able to work this if he wanted to. Perhaps I will have to do it by myself, but then I would get all the milk and cookies inside the fort."

Maude was a little older than Julie, and her blonde hair was a crazy mess of curls while the mischievous grin and dancing eyes proved that she was goading the twins. She had been the twins' nanny since the beginning and loved them. The twins in turn adored her and loved to play all the games she made up. As toddlers they were into everything, especially their parents.

Juan Jr squealed, "Miss Maude, I can do it. Poppy showed me how."

Gracie, not to be left out, added, "We can make the bestest fort together. Race you to our room, Juan." She headed for the door then stopped and turned back. "Love you, Mama, have a good work. See you soon."

Juan Jr. moved over for an extra hug which Julie supplied. "You and your sister be extra good for Miss Maude, please."

Juan Jr. solemnly replied, "Yes, Mama. I will watch out for Gracie." Then he raced off to compete with his sister on something else. Julie watched him scamper away, and she sighed a heartfelt sigh that spoke volumes of how she felt about those two kids.

It took all her willpower to push the delightful scene of her children to the back of her mind so she could re-focus on her business itinerary. Then she said, "Maude, I will be out of touch for a few days until I get settled in London. I will call as often as I can."

"We'll be fine. You said Mister Juan would be home in a couple of days, and we have forts to build and cookies to make. I will send you pictures often."

Julie smiled and returned to finalizing her packing. She was alerted to an incoming text message. The tone indicated it was ICABOD sending the information she'd requested.

Additional intel at ePETRO. 1st, new person added to the team by Mike P. Checking on background of the new person. Will forward when confirmed. 2nd, two positions you applied for are still available. You are qualified for both, and checking of your background is in process. You can review your new work history on your professional page.

Your flight is on time, and you were upgraded to 1st class.

Julie replied with an acknowledgement, which also proved her new burner phone was working as expected. She sent an updated link of her new identity profile to Juan. Then she finished packing and called for a car to take her to the airport.

Julie had arrived late at London Gatwick. Once she found the reserved rental car, it seemed to take forever to find the one-bedroom flat Petra had rented for their use while in town. The flat was tucked back and away from the busy streets, with a modest walk to the Overground rail services, which also had a connection to the Tube if needed. The Overground had a stop within a long block of ePETRO. Julie's plan was to be as mobile as possible and use the rail services as most locals did. The car was only for extenuating circumstances, not routine commuting.

Using the secured wireless already established in the flat, she connected to the ePETRO career website. Her application and cover letter had already been submitted two days ago, and the modifications were also included from a post yesterday. The site held an interesting employment aspect of showing the applicant where they stood with meeting the job requirements. At this point, it appeared five people had applied, but only two had met all of the outlined requirements, herself and one other.

With some special help from ICABOD, she looked at her special view of the comparison with the other applicant, a man named Rob Richie. She had an advantage of speaking fluently in four languages, while he only had two. She sent a special prayer of thanks to her parents for her education. She then logged into the personal email account of her JAC persona and found three emails. One was total junk. One was from the talent acquisition leader for the two positions she had applied for, informing her that her qualifications were under review. The latest email was actually a request for an interview for the next afternoon. She quickly replied with a professional thank you and acceptance.

She danced around the flat putting things away, grateful for her interview. Closing had always been her specialty. She called Juan from her own smart phone which would be placed into the wall safe after the call. Sadly, it rang and rang until voicemail was reached.

"Honey, sorry I missed you. I hope you are continuing the male bonding with Quip during the day, but pushing him out the door in the evening to be the attentive new husband. Things are going well and I have secured the interview for tomorrow afternoon. I feel comfortable I will get the position and be in deep cover. Easy as can be in a nice office building.

"The kids are great and building forts with the tarp you secured. Great for kids to use. You are a good Poppy. I transferred one of their pictures to the special burner phone. ICABOD is monitoring it, but like always it will not be used for any personal conversation. The texts from home were cleared along with all the history, just in case anyone gets nosey.

"I miss you, love you, and will try to find time in a week or so to call again. Please stay out of trouble, Honey!"

CHAPTER FIFTEEN

You're Still Dancing with the Devil

Mike smirked as he responded, "So their Juche, or self-reliance policy, is teeing them up for another horrific famine, probably bigger than the one they had in the mid 1990's. You're saying all they want to discuss is their next nuclear material purchases? Gee, Marge, do you think we can get them to just *buy what's on the truck*? We broker and sell oil, not enriched uranium ore so that the Korean fat boy can send launch vehicles into low earth orbit over everyone's heads! The biological weapons they are building are bad enough, but asking us to include enriched uranium so he can take some nuclear weapons into space to then drop them anywhere? Count me out!"

Now contemptuous as well as irked, Marge declared, "Sober up, bright boy! Use your head! He wants the threat of nuclear weapons so he can trade them to the west as a show of good faith to gain the needed food aid! They have mismanaged so much of their economy that their people are starving. The only way to accept food for a starving public, and save face in the transaction, is to offer to disarm their nuclear weapons stock."

Mike fixed a pathetic look at Marge and mocked, "How humanitarian of him! See how this sounds. I won't nuke your country, and to show you how magnanimous I can be, I will let you feed my starving population. Aren't I sweet?"

Marge clucked her tongue and visibly strained to keep her temper in check. When she felt in control she bluntly stated, "They will still buy our oil stocks, but we still need to figure out how to convert their lousy Won currency into something that will spend. Where are you on that?"

Mike modestly reined in his sarcasm and replied, "Not very far without a convincing scenario. However, you are going off the deep end on this one.

"Let me try and wrap my head around your current scenario. The North Koreans managed to thoroughly piss off the Russians by defaulting on 90% of their loans, so now they will only deal in rubles for oil purchases. Since the collapse of the Soviet Union, the Russians have stopped handing out subsidies just for towing the communist line.

"Then you have the Chinese trying to distance themselves from your partners. That is in part because the Chinese recognize they kind of like the high lifestyle that free market economies can deliver, so they don't want to subsidize their neighbors anymore when their eyes are on the profits. The only thing that your partners can produce in quantity is a bloated communist bureaucratic workforce and low-grade high sulfur content coal. Oh, and neither of these are marketable by today's standards.

"On the other side, we've got some fresh lunatic clients in the form of Muslim terrorists, who need someone to sell their stolen oil for them so they can continue to run amok. There is something about stealing someone else's work and selling it to underwrite their psychotic terrorist activities that gets a person all goose-bumpily. However, if we can blend the low-cost oil from the Muslims with the over-priced oil we got stuck with when the oil market took a dump on our business, we might be able to sell it to the Koreans and actually dig ourselves out of our financial hole.

"Of course, we have to get it into their dark country without anyone noticing the source of said crude. Oh, by the way, we need a way to help them figure out how to upgrade their crumbling infrastructure so that they can burn the damn stuff to make electricity! And you're telling me, the only thing that the fat boy regime wants to know is how he can get more uranium or plutonium so he can barter for food? I'm probably going to have to work through lunch and maybe happy hour to get all of this under control!"

Now it was Marge's turn to be sarcastic. "Oh, my goodness! We ARE the overworked, melodramatic, and under-appreciated snookum, aren't we?

"This is how we will divide and conquer, whiney boy. I'll work on the enriched uranium sourcing. You will find a way to convert the Korean won to something more useful than toilet paper so we can continue to buy. Do you understand your role?"

Mike studied her a moment. "Who said we have to convert it? Why can't we just use it to pay the Muslims? Money is only useful in making purchases anyway, so what if we use it to pay Kashan?"

Marge thought about the possibility for a moment and questioned, "What good would that do? Kashan would have the same problem that we have with their bird-cage bottom liner paper."

Mike smirked and offered, "Yes, of course. But it would be his problem, not ours."

Marge then wondered, "You think you can get him to go for it? I mean, without any more discounting, because of the nearly non-negotiable status of the won?"

Mike retorted, "The Koreans have a sizeable manufacturing industry, and their currency would easily be accepted for purchase of weapons that would not show up on the world stage. We would solve four problems at once leveraging the won as the currency of choice."

Marge puzzled a moment and then asked, "Uh, four problems? I only count three; being paid in won; using the won to pay for the unsanctioned oil; and then Kashan using the won to buy arms made in Korea."

Mike ignored her commentary as he grinned and declared, "I won't have to work through happy hour to make all this work." Marge sported a rather sour face as she replied, "How economical of you. Make your call to Kashan and let me know if he'll go for it."

Kashan disconnected from the call with Mike Patrick but said nothing.

His favorite lieutenant, Achmet, studied Kashan for a moment then asked, "Kashan, you appear to be lost in thought. Is there something about the conversation you just had with the western dog we deal with which troubles you?"

Kashan tilted his head in thought and finally stated, "Patrick called to propose new trade terms in our arrangement."

Achmet, now expecting the worst, angrily ranted, "He wishes to pay us less, is that it? How can these western dogs be trusted when they do not believe as we do?"

Kashan quietly offered, "Actually, he brought us good news and some resolution to our problems, which he isn't involved with. He suggested that for our oil, we be paid in Korean won that in turn could be used to quietly purchase Korean weapons. This would keep our activity very low key and off the global landscape. All very useful suggestions."

Achmet, somewhat taken aback, offered, "He...he made helpful suggestions? Why would he do that? His only interest is in his next profit."

Kashan mused, "That is what I have been pondering. Several possibilities come to mind. He might have a surplus of won which he cannot use in the open market. He might be working multiple deals and this provides greater flexibility for him to deal with those who won't deal with the won. Word is that his company is either the best or most desirable to work with for their connections in the marketplace, or they have some losses to overcome. I am certain he is getting the better end of the deal with the suggestion.

"However, we need to discover his true reasons and exploit them as westerners do. I suspect that he is selling our hard-earned oil to the North Koreans, and if he can use their money to pay us then he can conserve his U.S. dollars. This is all to his benefit, except for one thing."

Achmet puzzled a moment and then asked, "What is your observation?"

Kashan smiled and said, "What if we can determine who is buying our oil. If we can, it might profit us more to deal directly with them and cut out the middleman."

Achmet now grinned at this new understanding. "Yes, Kashan, it would."

After Achmet left, Kashan sent a note to his nephew, Dabir. Kashan thought to himself, time might be on my side in this.

CHAPTER SIXTEEN

Getting the Job Is Everything!

Julie woke up refreshed and ready to conquer the job front. After completing her morning workout, she'd showered and taken special care with her hair and makeup. Young, capable professional was the look she hoped to project. The suit she picked was chocolate brown, well-tailored, sedate, and not too revealing. The goal was to get the job and make friends all at the same time. She'd regretted removing her wedding ring, but a single up-and-coming professional did not sport a large diamond and sapphire ring like hers. This was really the first job for which she'd removed it, and she found it unsettling.

While putting herself together, she'd listened to the morning news reports. The price of oil was fluctuating, a new showing at a local gallery was creating quite a stir, shopping was good, no particularly violent crimes overnight, and the rail was running on time this morning. Her appointment was at one, just after lunch. She had wanted to make it into the area by ten and check out the different shops and eateries available. Observing the people in and around the area would also allow her to blend in even better and seem like a resident rather than a tourist. It was her method of immersing herself into a character very quickly, and it had always proven successful.

Julie's hair, now dyed to almost black, was styled simply. She added some modest earrings and a necklace to break up the colors but not draw attention. Her nails were trimmed neatly with a clear polish. A simple swipe of mascara, light pink gloss on her lips, and a spritz of lavender perfume was the extent of her makeup. The beige blouse blended with the brown suit, and simple leather pumps rounded out the professional look she'd wanted. After she completed her activities, she was very pleased with the reflection in the mirror. She mused what Juan would do with this new her.

She gathered her umbrella, purse, portfolio, and directions after donning her raincoat. The walk to the station was well within her time estimate, and the rail was still running on schedule. Though there were other passengers aboard, it was not crowded as she expected the morning or afternoon commute would be. She found a window seat that allowed her to watch her fellow passengers without staring at them, the reflection enhanced because of the light fog. People were reading, snoozing, listening to their devices, or quietly speaking to their seat companions. Overall, it was a relaxing ride with no drama.

At her stop, she easily walked toward the building designated for her afternoon interview. Luckily, she found a few places nearby for food and beverage which she mentally noted for future activity. Old habits never die as she targeted a coffee shop like one favored by JAC the barista, one of her former identities. The different types of people who wandered by Julie's position in the coffee shop gave her a good sense of the demographics of the professionals, the tourists, the locals completing their chores, and overall mood. Capturing the notes and a few photos with her tablet also provided the foundation for a future report. The tablet was discreet and truly resembled a reading device rather than an information gathering tool, fairly innocuous.

JAC, as she was totally feeling the part, sipped her delicious coffee, feeling increasingly armed and ready for the events of the afternoon. A glance at the clock indicated it was time to pay the check and depart. She liked being ten minutes ahead for professional appointments. It was a quality that business people liked. A modest tip was included in the cash payment. She had credit cards in her current identity, but the mode for this transaction as a local would be cash. After she added a bit of fresh lipstick, she rose and thanked the waitress as she gathered her belongings and proceeded two doors down to the target building.

Outside, the building appeared a little old from an architectural perspective, but the inside spoke of recent renovations. New paint, current artwork, and leather chairs and sofas without cracks were her clues. The receptionist verified her on her list and directed Jackeline to the elevator and the 10th floor. When the doors opened, a mousey looking lady smiled and extended a hand.

"Hi, Jackeline! My name is Laurie."

JAC could not help but flash her megawatt smile as she greeted, "Hi. Yes, I'm Jackeline Cooper, here to interview for the opening. What a pretty building! I'm so excited at the chance of working with ePETRO." Laurie grinned back and replied, "That's a great start." She then turned slightly to her right and indicated, "This way. We're going to talk in the conference room at the end of the hall."

The room contained no windows into the hallway, but there was one that was positioned to look onto other buildings in the district. With the fog thickening outside, it provided almost no view. Laurie indicated she should take the seat to the left of the head of the table so they would be cornered to each other. The room was very quiet and the lighting was good. One side had a wall of whiteboard, but no markers were visible.

After they were both seated, Laurie structured the conversation to verify Jackeline's qualifications and asked strong clarifying questions. JAC seemed visibly comfortable with the questions and answered simply but succinctly. JAC then asked about growth potential in the future and specific learning she might do over time. They were nearing the end of the scheduled hour when she asked what Laurie thought of the company.

Laurie replied, "I have not been here all that long, but I find the people nice and the work interesting. The benefits are good for this area which are important to me. There is even a profit-sharing plan employees can participate in as an incentive to contribute to the profitability of the company. It works well for my situation. I take care of my mum, and it helps with the medical costs when I need to leave to care for her. One of the reasons we have this position open is to help build some backup for some of my duties. Most of the roles in the organization have a bit of overlap just for that purpose. I am hoping the person who fills this role might learn enough to be able to fill in for me when I have to be gone."

JAC smiled and quickly interjected, "I can learn quickly. One of the best ways to do that is to almost become someone's shadow for a few days. Would that be agreeable?" Laurie said, "I think that will work, except for the areas where I have security clearance. It will take a few months before you will gain that status."

JAC beamed and flashed her friendly smile of encouragement. "I totally understand and will work toward that. What's the next step in this process? I would like to start as quickly as possible."

Laurie answered, "We do have some formalities including reference checks and criminal background reviews. But that is not kicked off until an offer is made. You know, privacy and all. Plus, I want to have you meet my boss." Then scooting forward as if they were nearing status of best buddies, she quietly added, "Honestly, if he has no objections, I would like to make you an offer today. Wait here and let me go speak with him."

After Laurie left, JAC schooled her face into a very pleasant expression with only a hint of a smile. Slowly she looked around the room like someone interested in the pictures on the walls, plants which appeared to be silk, and finally spotted the camera. The recording mike had to be close, but it was not easily spotted. When she'd entered the building, the security was evident, but at the elevator it was more subtle. This, she decided, was the floor where visitors and customers came to talk and be observed.

It was extremely likely that she was being observed even now. Her hands rested comfortably in her lap with no fidgeting. She wouldn't grab her purse for a phone or makeup, like many people alone tended to do. The need for many people to fill in time with random activities or habits was a poor behavior when you didn't want anyone knowing what you were thinking. As she continued the mental countdown to the ten-minute mark, she detected movement on the door handle.

Laurie entered with a smile. "Mr. Patrick says he has a few minutes to speak with you. You may leave your things here, and I will bring you back when you are done. I set you up in the best light, Jackeline, so just keep up what you are doing and don't be nervous. He's gruff, but fair."

They walked a short way back down the hallway toward the elevators and stopped at a door. Laurie knocked. "Come in."

Laurie ushered them inside a very expansive office. Definitely one a boss would have. Big desk, executive leather chair, papers stacked haphazardly, a large computer screen, several monitors against the wall providing views into other markets, JAC guessed. The man stood and walked around the desk to shake her hand.

JAC fought the urge to say, '*Wow, Petra said you looked like a pear and she was right*.' She flashed her best smile as she extended her hand and said, "Very nice to meet you, Mr. Patrick. Laurie said you ran a very tight ship at this highly regarded company."

Mike gave this female an assessing look. Professional attire, hair in place, limited makeup, no sex play, and an engaging smile. He thought she might work well with some of their visiting clients.

"Nice to meet you, Miss Cooper. Have a seat." He indicated a chair by a small table away from his desk and closer to the windows. He turned to Laurie and said, "Thank you, Laurie. That will be all for now. While I speak with Miss Cooper, I need to have you make certain Dabir is comfortable with the mailing process. I will ring you when we finish."

Laurie smiled as she exited to Mike's words. "Please, Miss Cooper, what do you know about ePETRO and how can you contribute?"

An hour after the interview with Mr. Patrick had completed, JAC had been made an offer which she of course accepted. She signed some papers which allowed the background check to officially begin. In getting the information from her portfolio and purse, she noticed they had been searched, presumably while she had spoken to Mr. Patrick. This made her wonder if it was their normal hiring practice or just for the role she was filling. She knew she would pass this test too.

Laurie had indicated the process would take two or three days and she might consider Friday as her official start date unless there was a problem. Laurie had seemed sincere when she almost begged that, after JAC's first day, they could go out for a friendly beer or glass of wine down the street.

CHAPTER SEVENTEEN

Deli or Bar...Tough Choice

The arrival of Tyler and Ernesto to La Guardia had been uneventful. They passed through customs with ease, their modest suitcases in hand. The inbound flights of their targets were on time within an hour of one another, only a few gates apart in the same terminal. A modest New York style deli was in the area near the first expected flight exit from customs, so they set up there to grab some food and watch.

While they waited, they reviewed the information Jamie had sent to Ernesto, with Tyler still pondering the picture of the dragons. It seemed out of context with the rest of the shots, so Tyler was convinced it was a critical component. Ernesto leaned toward it being just some street art that had captured the imagination of the photographer. Nothing had been added by Julie or Juan from the camera, outside of acknowledging receipt of it and working on trace evidence recovery. Julie had sent a text suggesting it may have just been an isolated case of information gathering gone wrong.

"Tyler, you keep staring at that picture expecting it to come to life. What about it do you find so interesting?"

"Outside of the fantasy element of dragons overall, it is the fact they seem so docile."

"Docile? What an odd concept for dragons."

"Ernesto, my point exactly. Dragons are legendary creatures included in cultures around the world. For example, these dragons do not fit into the European folk traditions. They do not have the wings common to the six-limbed varieties found from the Balkans and Western Asian myths. As a matter of belief, those reptilian creatures were thought to possess only animal-level intelligence.

"This picture is clearly of what is thought of as the Chinese variety of dragon, with counterparts in Japan, Korea, East and South Asian countries, what I collectively think of as the Asian variety. The deep-seated myths of these serpentine creatures are that they are four-legged and wingless with above-average intelligence. Even though the two traditional varieties evolved in very separate ways they have influenced each other through modern times and storytelling, to a degree.

"The movies have depicted dragons for the most part as fierce, fire-breathing, and huge. The scales are often colored and shimmer in the sky or water. It is the fantasy elements of the beast that has kept the folklore alive for centuries.

"Look at this picture, Ernesto. The beasts depicted seem to almost touch one another with no fierceness. Almost as if they were thinking about something. I guess that is why the word docile came to mind."

Ernesto studied the picture for a while and replied, "I see what you're saying, but I don't understand why they are positioned as they are. What seems to be highlighted in this light are fine lines making it appear more as a drawing of dragons. Look at the care in the lines and how they are drawn, almost like they were traced.

"But we do have more important things to take care of first, like following Penny and Jenny. Let's put this drawing aside until we get the evidence off the camera. For now, since it is so very different from the rest of the shots, I am going with the random shot of a photo or drawing. Interesting, but not likely related."

Ty shrugged and agreed, "You're right. This is likely just a whim by the camera owner.

"Look at the board, the first flight is landing. You're on first with Penny, old man."

Ernesto laughed and got up to move into position before the passengers began to deplane. He watched the doors open and the travel-weary passengers exiting customs and making their way toward the baggage claim area. A herd of people passed until the flow became a trickle of people looking at the signage for the proper exit. These long flights made people a little slower in their movements, so he hoped he had not missed his target.

He nonchalantly spoke into his phone, alerting Tyler he had not yet picked up Penny. Then he spotted her, just coming through the doors, dragging her suitcase like one would a reluctant puppy. He noticed she walked slowly with her sweater buttoned up as if she was cold. She looked around like she was hunting something specific, until her sights landed on the bar across from the deli and moved toward it.

Ernesto watched her without moving. She was young, good looking, comfortably dressed in slacks and at least two tops, but not dressed to reveal. She did not appear to be overweight and moved easily in her sandals. Her dark hair, obviously wavy and thick, was caught up in a giant clasp of some sort to keep it off her neck and out of her face. From a distance she did not appear to be wearing a lot of makeup. She stopped at the bar's hostess stand and with ample gestures made it known she wanted a seat. The hostess escorted her to a table one row back from the front on the edge of the restaurant nearest the main walkway. Ernesto shook his head, disconnected the call with Tyler, and decided to wander back toward the deli, picking up a magazine at the newsstand.

Tyler asked, "Why do you think she isn't gone?"

"She's either very thirsty, since they just brought her a white wine, or waiting for someone. I think we can just stay here and watch, unless you think we should separate.

"She didn't appear to give me even a glance, nor look around other than for that bar. From my view, it looked like she had an 'ah-hah' moment when she saw it."

Tyler nodded and agreed, "We look like travelers so why not stay here. Lots of people around to watch. It's a shame we're on duty because a glass of wine sounds nice about now."

"That, my young friend, is why we are in the deli and she is seated at the bar."

They passed the next hour plus watching the people walking by, trying to decide what their story was based on the luggage, clothing, languages, and so forth. It was tedious but one easy way to watch Penny and stay in their places.

A short while ago, they had almost had a total laughing fit when two flight attendants and a pilot, seated in the middle of the terminal, randomly started rolling quarters out into the walkway. The resulting mayhem was whether the walkers stopped to pick up the coins and decided to pocket them, or look for the owner who might have dropped the coins. Stopping in a busy airport terminal to pick up a loose coin practically guaranteed some pedestrian would collide with them as they groped for the newfound wealth. The three culprits were cracking up at the antics of their victims.

Tyler and Ernesto watched the board showing the incoming flights until the flight Jenny was to be on showed as landed. Tyler moved over to try to pick up his target, ready to follow her while Ernesto stayed with Penny.

When Jenny emerged from the customs doors, she calmly made for the bar as if she were already familiar with it. Penny stood and they both hugged like long lost friends. With a second look though they were so similar as to possibly be related but Penny appearing a bit older. Another wine was ordered as Tyler made his way back to the deli.

When he was seated, he said, "I guess this makes our life easier. We just wait for the guy and duct tape them all together?"

Ernesto laughed and replied, "That might be a bit obvious, but we continue to wait. The male was supposed to be on the same flight as your Jenny. If that was the case and he is with them, we should be able to spot him soon or he'll join their little party."

Tyler shook his head and stated, "I don't think anyone is joining their party! That table is only set up for two.

"Ernesto, these females are behaving like they haven't a care in the world. The only odd thing I have observed is, after Jenny sat, she struggled to open the back of her cell phone and slipped something inside then closed the back of the case. I suspect she put the battery back in, but I can't figure out why."

"I noticed it too but thought I must be seeing things. The only reason one would do that would be to ensure no signal is tracked."

Tyler cocked his head to one side then commented, "Trying for off the grid status? But why?"

CHAPTER EIGHTEEN

Cursed...
and Not Knowing It!

George listened patiently to Summit as he carefully explained his plan. George randomly nodded his head to keep his disbelief in check. Finally, after clearly articulating all their next steps, Summit halted and with a sense of pride asked, "Is this not a good plan? I've never seen you quite so speechless. Therefore, I must interpret this silence as you having gained a new appreciation for my planning abilities."

George strained to keep from clucking his tongue in acute amazement at his friend's naivety but managed to inquire, "You really think that we can waltz down there, dash onto the ship when no one is looking, gain access to their ship's logs, and calmly photograph everything with our special issue phones, and leave peaceably? Oh yeah, and looking the way we do, Mister *I shave twice a day and all my clothes get pressed before I leave to go out in public and after*? We would have a better chance of pulling this off if we were known narcotics officers in drag queen outfits! Looking like a couple of clean-cut boy scouts isn't going to help us blend into the grimy surroundings we are trying to penetrate. Remember, it's not just getting in but getting out too.

"Getting out simply isn't possible if we don't blend in! We don't look like we belong, mister *perfectly groomed mustache,* so let's approach this a different way."

Summit sulked a moment and then conceded, "I guess I shouldn't have shaved this morning, huh? But surely with a little cosmetic action, combined with only bathing once a week, we can modify my grooming habits and downgrade my appearance to more closely approach your more excellent blending with this grimy port area. However, I will draw the line at having to have a disgusting cigarette dangling from my lips like that dock worker over there. Ugh!"

George glanced at the unsightly dock worker, but before resuming his tirade with Summit, he stopped himself and, with a puzzled look on his face, turned back to study the scene unfolding in front of him. Summit quickly turned to look as well. Not seeing anything unusual he asked, "What's wrong? You seemed re-focused on something else rather than your lecture on *dressing for success.*"

George now insisted, "Summit, you know Middle Eastern languages better than I do. That pallet they're unloading…, what does it say? With my rusty command of the Middle East, I think it says furniture, but it's in Turkish. Can you confirm?"

Summit confidently turned to read and then agreed, "You are quite correct. It says furniture Made in Turkey. Have you always had A D D, as a personal-hygiene challenged semi-adult?"

George ignored the comment. "Why would you ship presumably cheaply made Turkish furniture into a country like China that is famous for exporting its own cheaply made furniture?"

Summit moved his vision between the scene of furniture being unloaded and George.

"How about we focus back on our earlier conversation that must have occurred two light years ago in your memory banks? You know the one about getting on board the freighter to record the ship's manifest?"

Almost not hearing Summit and still studying the scene, George absentmindedly commented, "Those two dock workers seem to be squabbling about something and they're not paying attention to the crane operator. Okay, wait for it...and there! Whoa! Nice shot! See? They both got whacked by the pallet they were supposed to be directing to the ground, and...oops! Now the operator is overcompensating and...there she blows! A nice spill of poorly secured goods on the pier! You know, I for one would like to get a little closer to see what is going on.

"As part of my cover, I plan to behave as a concerned passerby just trying to help those two unfortunates. Now you wait here, but keep talking to me as if I am still here or that I care about your poorly conceived planning effort."

George marched quickly to the drama as Summit flared his nostrils in anger at the current situation. George got to the area before anyone else did and promptly helped the dock worker who had received the harshest blow from the pallet. Even though he appeared to be fully engaged with helping the badly dazed dock worker, he was very discreetly taking photo after photo with his special issue phone. One of the boxes had broken open on impact, and George quickly identified brand new semi-automatic weapons stacked in packing grease. He got one last photo before others showed up on the scene.

George quickly put his smart phone away and tried to re-engage his help efforts when one man hollered, "Who are you and why are you in this area? This unloading area is restricted to only dock worker personnel! You don't work here! Leave immediately before I call security!"

George stepped back but couldn't resist casting out the taunting comment, "I was trying to help since there is no security and no one supervising the unloading process. Someone got hurt, dog-breath! As for who I am, I am from the shipping company's management team, and my job is to watch and evaluate efficiencies in handling our cargo. Based on what I've witnessed so far, all I've seen is gross incompetence and a near fatal supervisory oversight!

"I need to see your shipping manifest. These infractions need to be properly recorded so the harbor master doesn't take our port license away for near fatal stupidity! I will assume that, based on your adversarial attitude, you are probably in charge… for now. Escort me and my assistant to the bridge and the ship's logs. Now, is there anything you don't understand about my demands?"

The activity on the pier had nearly stopped during George's explosive tirade, so in keeping with his impromptu rant, he shouted, "And get these men some medical attention!" Then looking in Summit's direction he hollered, "Summit! Bring our evaluation sheets and the computer tablets! We need to file our report on board, so let's go!"

With his mouth half open, Summit staggered forward in near disbelief to obey the command but said nothing. George gave Summit a knowing wink and then bellowed, "Alright, people, let's get a move on! Showtime is over! Get back to work and this time no more carelessness, alright?" The loading area became a hive of activity as they followed the angry and sullen supervisor up to the bridge.

After their work on the bridge and making some bogus ship manifest entries, George and Summit returned to their hotel, via a roundabout way in case someone had taken an interest in their hotel choice.

Summit hadn't said a word all afternoon, but once they got back to the room for their informational review, he offered, "I'm glad my planning paid off for us. Do you wish to apologize now for disparaging my approach to this situation?"

George stared incredulously at Summit then finally qualified, "If memory serves, you recommended that we walk down there, gain access to their ship's logs, and calmly photograph everything with our phones and leave peaceably, looking like a couple of shiny new pennies! Perhaps you weren't paying attention. I saw an opportunity unfold, stepped into a persona that was easily accepted by everyone, and got us on board where we comfortably photographed everything!"

Summit smiled and said, "Yes, that was my plan from the beginning, was it not?"

George's cognitive skills now fully engaged, and he rotated his head moderately to the left and commented, "Well, hell! I have to admit what we did was almost exactly the way you laid it out. What is our next moderate plan that you want to have brilliantly executed, Mr. Summit, the surmiser?"

Summit, now quite pleased with the compliment, responded, "Since you have graciously complimented my planning skills, I should like, as a truly conciliatory gesture, to comment on your impressive display of impromptu actions that skillfully got us in and out of our target. May I say, a hearty well done, George!"

George responded with a smirk, and he felt compelled to ask, "Summit, as you go through life I have to know, how does it feel not to be cursed with self-awareness?"

Summit pondered a moment and then replied, "I will give your question some thought. My planning instincts tell me we should focus on the information we obtained from the shipping manifest. Are you okay with that?"

George, not quite sure if he was ever going to wake up from this surreal series of discussions, nodded slightly and offered, "It's easy to see why you are the senior member of this task team. Yeah, alright, let's get into character. I kind of want to know why they are porting weapons and munitions labeled as furniture and why they detoured to Singapore before docking here. I recommend that we upload all our findings to the company collaboration server so Julie and Juan can see our progress."

Summit reflected a moment and asked, "How did you know that I iron my clothes before I retire for the night, as well as when I get up in the morning?"

George suppressed his smirk as he responded, "I didn't. I guessed again, and you took the bait, again." Summit sulked at George's deftness of obtaining information from someone who should know better.

CHAPTER NINETEEN

Transitions Can Be Subtle or Dramatic

Mercedes watched as Laurie boarded the hopper flight to Gatwick, presumably to check on her family. The background Julie had sent them on Laurie was that she routinely took one of the express trains out of Gatwick to reach her family home quickly. While she sat waiting for her plane to board, Laurie fussed with her makeup using her compact, checked her earrings, added a necklace and scarf, and tucked away her jacket in favor of a nice sweater. The result was Laurie looked more like a hometown girl rather than a city professional. The only thing of note before she boarded her flight was to mess around with her phone. Mercedes wasn't close enough to see exactly what Laurie had done, but the movement was similar to what one would do to remove or insert the memory card or battery, depending upon the brand of her device.

Just after Laurie passed to her gate area, Brayson softly said, "She is off soon then, to her Mum I suppose. Let's pass it along to Julie and get over to our flight to Panama. I was able to change our flight to a more direct one, but we need to move to the other terminal to make it."

Mercedes turned, smiled rather wistfully and commented, "Yes. It was so sweet how she changed her look just a bit, to be more casual. I bet her mum appreciates having her little girl come and take care of her. I only thought it odd that she fumbled with her phone. I got the sense she was changing the battery or SIM card, but I couldn't really see with people crossing my line of sight."

As they watched Laurie wait for the boarding call, a very determined male boldly walked up and promptly sat down next to her. The manner of the male's approach clearly indicated that he knew her and that most probably this was a pre-arranged meeting. For several intense minutes, the young man very deliberately spoke rapidly to her without waiting for a response. Finally, at the end of his intense and rushed delivery, Laurie acknowledged the verbal onslaught and then she did all the talking while the man sat in deliberate listen-only mode. Once she was finished with her side of the conversation, the male nodded slightly and promptly left.

Brayson cocked his head in thought and said, "Let's get to our flight, and we can alert Julie before the door closes on the aircraft." They hurried through the airport and connected to their terminal, arriving at the gate just as the flight was called for First Class boarding. Mercedes paused and breathed a sigh of relief at their great timing. Brayson kept moving then turned toward her.

"Mercedes, come on. They're boarding First Class. Let's go."

"Just when did we get First Class? I thought we were only able to get Coach."

Brayson grinned and replied, "I guess it was during another one of my undisciplined moments when I changed our flight. Don't know what came over me, but I did include my partner in the changes to First Class."

They moved onto the plane and stowed their carry-ons, then Brayson questioned, "Why would someone go to the trouble to transform their look before getting on the plane? What would you do? And what was that impromptu meeting all about?"

Mercedes' eyes widened, and she exclaimed, "You're right. Either she is meeting someone on the plane, or she never boarded at all because that was the meeting she was actually here for. I was so being sentimental and family-focused for a moment, and I may have messed up."

Mercedes quickly placed a call and asked for confirmation from the carrier that Laurie had in fact, boarded the aircraft, and it was en route. She nodded her head at the response and then called Julie.

"Julie, I used my federal marshal credentials to confirm Laurie stayed on the plane. Brayson brought up a good point, which: he is texting, along with a photo he took as she passed through the boarding gate. It might be good to determine the rest of the passengers on the flight and cross-check them with other flights we believe she previously took.

"Also, we watched a weird impromptu meeting between Laurie and some guy who plopped down next to her and started talking.

"No, we couldn't hear from where we were sitting. It seemed more like a business transaction; not like he was a friend.

"Only a few brief minutes. She did all the talking and then he left.

"Yes, and she also messed with her phone, possibly replacing the SIM card or the battery.

"Alright, we will. I need to hang up; the flight attendant is giving me the evil eye."

She powered her phone off and then turned to Brayson. "Good catch. Julie said she would have EZ check the passenger lists. We need to call EZ or Juan if we need anything else, as Julie will be unreachable while on her assignment."

Brayson asked, "Can I get one of those federal marshal approvals too? It might come in handy." Mercedes grinned and replied, "I might be able to hook you up, if you keep the partner attitude going and avoid being that uncontrolled rogue."

Chung-Ho had straight black hair with hints of grey, ragged at the ends, but still above his uniform collar. As is the custom, he had no facial hair but the lines of age crisscrossed his face and spoke of the hard life he led. He was short by Western standards at 1.6 meters and under 60 kilograms, but he was viewed as fierce and demanding by those around him. Known as a fierce negotiator, he used his position for personal gains and no one dared to protest.

He held a command position, making decisions and negotiations for changes needed for his country, as ordered. The demand to expand arms to include nuclear capabilities to threaten the Western powers was his top priority, second only to undermining the gains made by small capitalistic countries like South Korea. The means to achieve these ends included bartering for munitions and moving into modern power resources and technology on the backs of those he forced into service.

Chung-Ho had allowed his son Chung-He to train some in the West. Though Chung-Ho had worried his son would change, he was honored to know that Chung-He had learned well during his time abroad. His son, a bit taller at 1.7 meters and solid muscle at 64 kilograms, had not been influenced by his time in the West. His unlined face would contort to near rage if he was to speak about the capitalists he'd been forced to live among. He remained fully committed to undermining all elements of the free world.

It was fortunate that with the ongoing relationship with ePETRO, Chung-He had a good command of English and Mandarin along with his native language. In the background, during the conversations with what they referred to in private as *the Capitalist bitch*, he advised on points to clarify or products wanted. Chung-He was also trained in hand-to-hand combat and weapons expertise. His passion for slow but deliberate moves, followed by lightning speed actions had earned the only whispered title among his detractors as *Killer Crane*. He was aware of the many steps they needed to accomplish to meet their goals and thus always moved like a crane on the hunt. Chung-He arrived for an early morning planning session and deferred to his elder, who began their discussion.

"Chung-He, I believe that ePETRO has another agenda that does not map to our goals. We asked for oil and we are planning on delivery at Hungnam and Nampo. Are the storage container areas ready to receive the delivery?"

"Yes, sir. The docks have been reinforced to handle the estimated weight of the amount of crude. Product will be transported for some additional refinement for fuel and such. The other items we ordered are scheduled for delivery in Nampo, and I will be on hand to verify that the items meet our requirements. I will also test several of them to insure they are functional."

Chung-Ho looked pleased with the update and asked, "What about the expanded facility for our nuclear testing? Though we have had some successful tests, which we have touted to the Europeans, I want to make certain we are a valid threat if necessary. Our long-range ballistics weapons are still ranging too high in their orbits and are disappointingly inaccurate at low terrain levels."

Chung-He nodded and curled his lip up to the point of a snarl before he responded. "The expansion has been done, but we need the oil and the processed materials for the generators and other equipment to run. The building of other short and medium distance rockets for various payloads continues, and more refinements to our guidance systems are being delivered. Accuracy is a matter of practice, and practice takes more resources.

"There are some chemicals which are being tested by our scientists, however you may recall we lost over two thousand laborers with the last accident a month ago. We are in the process of moving laborers to fill those spots. I am overseeing that to a degree, sir, but have focused on the receipt of the goods."

Chung-Ho almost smiled as he quietly replied, "Good! I have the won secured, ready to pay their courier for the products. Even though the amount is almost triple what we should pay, I take comfort in the knowledge that the currency conversion is not my issue.

"Now, on the personal side, when will I have a new grandson?"

Chung-He frowned as he reported, "I do not know, sir. I beat her this morning for my disappointment of showing in her clothing she was not pregnant, again. We will try again. I reminded her no more females would be tolerated. If we do not have success within a year, I will replace her with a female who understands the correct meaning of fertility."

CHAPTER TWENTY

My Partner...
But Why Me?

Juan smiled broadly on the video conference call as he stated, "Excellent planning and execution on your part, gentlemen. The content of the ship's manifest and transit logs was very interesting."

Summit beamed at the compliment, but George pressed further. "What did the shipping company say about the stop in Singapore? Was it to pick up or deliver goods? And any leads on those weapons? Looked like enough weapons for a good-sized skirmish by a determined insurgency somewhere."

Juan smiled slyly and responded, "Actually, the shipping company had no official record of the Singapore stop. Don't you find that odd? Of course, it could have been an unscheduled stop for some repairs, and the electronic updates haven't made their way to the corporate offices yet. However, the Hong Kong docking event was posted. It is almost like a scripted voyage was planned and filed, but someone forgot to tell the captain."

Summit showed surprise, but George continued his questioning. "Any other correlated yet highly unusual event that can be added to make this even more puzzling?"

Juan chuckled and said, "Ah, now that's the George I know! You keep digging and asking insightful questions. As it turns out, gentlemen, we believe that one of the AIMs you were sent to track went dark just about the time the shipping tanker made its unscheduled stop in Singapore. Our computer systems put the probability at 87% that the AIM was making a prearranged meeting with the ship's captain at the same time."

Summit mused out loud, "I am hearing now that the unrecorded stop here in Singapore was scheduled, but that their headquarters has no knowledge of the deviation of course. Why would that be?"

George then thoughtfully added, "Or they knew and doctored the electronic records to cover up the event. If that is true, then there should be no ship-to-shore communications advising corporate of the unscheduled stop, but rather the communications were conducted by way of the AIM, ensuring no electronic record would exist."

Summit, continuing to think out loud, offered, "However, if corporate headquarters is NOT in on the scheme, then the ship's captain would be acting on his own as a rogue player for another organization, although that seems unlikely. There would be too many loose ends to handle as a rogue in that role, so it's more reasonable to assume that their headquarters is directing the operations, or at the very least is aware of what is going on. With no corporate records to corroborate the deviation by the ship's captain, the corporation can easily claim plausible deniability if everything falls apart. Shipping mismarked weapons would fall under international arms trafficking, and no country wants to be vulnerable to that."

Juan, now smiling broadly, commended, "Again, gentlemen, well done! Several good cyber sleuthing deductions and reasoning in this unstructured environment.

"What would you recommend as the next steps to take?"

Summit confidently offered, "I would like to look for this individual and discover the source of these analog communications, as well as learn the target destination of the weapons. Does that not sound like a good plan?"

George rolled his eyes yet again at Summit's naivety. But rather than stop and deride Summit he calmly offered, "Perhaps Summit should try to penetrate the ship's work team. I can't because of my loading dock performance. With a few grimy lessons we should be able to get Summit undercover and into the thick of things. My best tactic will be to hunt for our newest Analog Information Mule here in Singapore who should be in close proximity to our rogue ship's captain.

"At some point we ought to find out what is to become of their oil. I mean, after all this is an oil tanker, and we were originally supposed to be finding out where the oil is destined."

Juan smiled as he nodded his head and agreed, "Gentlemen, it sounds like you have the situation well in hand. Keep up your regular reporting and good hunting!"

After they disconnected from the call, Summit looked at George and asked, "In this grimy learning exercise you wish to subject me to, do I have to have a cigarette dangling from my lips? Ugh!"

George, now in a teasing mood, said, "Summit, that's twice now you have voiced an objection to smoking. I'll tell you what, let's have you just wear a cigarette behind your ear and that way everyone will assume you smoke but you won't have to. Plus, if someone wants a cigarette, you can offer them one, thus gaining their camaraderie and, dare I say it, become friendly?"

Summit, oblivious to the sarcasm, nodded and said, "You have good operational ideas. Coupled with my vast planning expertise we make a formidable team. Perhaps you can learn from me and acquire the planning skills that you currently lack. This will be a good exchange of skills improvement for both of us."

George, now thoroughly irked but still in command of his annoyance, responded, "How generous. I'm overwhelmed with lukewarm appreciation. Right now, let's get busy dressing you down for your new role, grime ball. Hey, you didn't just shave, did you?"

Summit hung his head down and, unable to look George in the eyes, responded, "Uh, yeah, I did. Sorry."

George heaved an exasperated sigh and said, "Okay, let's go to plan B about your appearance, shall we? If anyone asks why you are so clean shaven and well-groomed, you tell them that you suffer from the non-communicable disease called the werewolf syndrome. You are forced to shave your body twice a day to keep your hair follicles at bay so you don't look like a werewolf with a very bad 5 o'clock shadow. One problem solved.

"Now, about this ironing your clothes twice a day…I'm stumped on that one. Maybe we could say you grew up in a dry-cleaners environment, and you have an addiction to the smell of scorched starch."

Summit, now somewhat a little melancholy, quietly offered, "Perhaps I could just tell them the truth. I was on patrol with my company when we got ambushed by Pakistani partisans along the border of India and Pakistan. They hit us hard and all of our transport went up in flames, along with all our spare clothing, toiletries, food, and extra ammunition…everything you need to deal with living away from base."

Summit paused a moment as he warmed to the story, then added, "The firefight was tough, and we foolishly took cover in a ravine where they had us pinned down for days. Our personal canteens ran out of water. The good news was that it began raining so at least we had water, even if it added to our discomfort. With the water we had mud everywhere and no way to get out of it or keep it off of us. Soaked to the bone, filthy, cold, hungry, and constantly being shot at does something to you. We took heavy casualties, but we finally got out after HQ sent in reinforcements.

"I shall never forget how I looked in the mirror once we finally got back to base. I swore I would never look that bedraggled again! That, Monsieur George, is why grooming is such a part of my make-up. My lifestyle may seem peculiar to you, but sometimes the things you vow to yourself are immutable."

A now chastened George humbly responded, "Well, Summit, I'm sorry I stepped on an old specter. We will call this a well-deserved lesson. I will no longer pick on that wound. We shall speak of it no more. Now, we still need to see if you can blend into the crew scene and gain the information."

Summit pondered the issue for several minutes before he finally suggested, "I could appear as a holy one. They are expected to remain cleaner than mere mortals. We can use various teas and dyes that will stain my clothes, but they wouldn't really be dirty or uncomfortable for me. I would go in undercover as an Islamic teacher or holy one to protect the crew from the infidels of this world, in exchange for passage."

George stood staring and blinking at what he perceived as a 180 degree turn in thinking by Summit. Before he was able to really marvel at the new approach and comment, Summit continued, "George, you should understand that in this part of the world such a man joining the crew would be considered a good omen. I would receive their respect almost immediately, and they would seek a level of guidance. This would greatly affect our timeline, because I would begin from a position of advantage with their trust.

"My story would be that I was sent into the world to work with my brothers and preach the words of the prophet. I would help to guide them in the ways of reaching their destiny as defined by the prophet. They would enjoy many blessings for proper treatment of a holy man. They would also feel compelled to answer any inquiries from me."

George had to chuckle at himself for being so self-righteous and narrow-minded. With a large smile on his face, he bowed, sweeping his arm, and stated, "Then let me help you stain your ironed clothes, add some robes and other appropriate head attire. I will help ready you for your trials and tribulations, my poet master, Moulvi Sahib Summit."

CHAPTER TWENTY-ONE

Recollections Hidden but Not Lost

Jamie and Ernesto had spoken until very late in the evening. They had decided to meet up in the middle of the United States, Dallas to be precise. Jamie had hopped on the bus to make the long trek toward the meeting. As he got onto the bus, a deep feeling of *déjà vu* had him gripping his chest. He ignored the sensation and took a seat at the back. As the bus rolled out of the terminal, the weariness of the last two months overcame him as he drifted into what he hoped would be a dreamless sleep.

The old memories flooded into his deep sleep like they had happened only yesterday. All his senses were attuned to the events that unfolded like the scenes of a play, only he was one of the stars.

Jamie and his brother, Ian, had always been close. However, it was a grimy box of old motorcycle parts that proved to be the cement for their working together. Using all the contents of the dirty box of used parts, plus a few others they purchased with the joint resources of Irish pounds, they reassembled an old DKW motorcycle. After several late nights and dedicated weekends, they almost had it running. The final improvisation to get it to start was to use a 16p nail, in lieu of a proper key, thus completing the truly *franken-cycle* look.

The end of that period had redefined and expanded their relationship into a cohesive team that carried them through secondary schooling. They were mates in most of what they did, though Jamie was almost a year older. The lads were identically built and roughly 1.9 meters with blonde hair and blue eyes that matched those of their Pa, with the smile and singing voice of their Ma. By the time Ian was due to graduate secondary school, they were mates in everything, including a marked preference for dating the lassies who were sisters in the same years of schooling.

Both of them had worked not only for their Pa, but for any local merchant who would hire them for a few hours around schooling. Not afraid of work, both of them had saved up enough money to buy brand new motorcycles when Ian completed his secondary school. Neither were ready for university, so they plotted their trip to Southern Ireland.

Their Pa was indulgent in their quest to push the envelope before they would be forced to settle down and grow up, so he didn't forbid their ill-conceived plans. Ma had always taken great joy in her sons and was well aware that her headstrong boys would not be dissuaded from their adventure. After forcing them to outline their plans, she acquiesced and even gave them a little money for food, an item they had overlooked.

From all Jamie's research, it appeared to be a great tour with spectacular views, unfolding in the heavy mist, making one feel like they were exploring the wilderness alone and untouched. And even though he'd found one report of the area as being plagued with traffic jams caused by small herds of sheep, the delays meant access to local gossip, a cool Guinness now and again, wild Irish music and friendly locals if needed.

By the second day of their great adventure, they both realized how ill-prepared they were for such a long trip on two wheels, despite using Killarney National Park as a base after negotiating a room in the barn of a local sheepherder. On the ride toward Cork, they had not counted on being soaked through by the heavy mist and a temperature drop that chilled them to the bone as they traveled down the road. They should have pulled over at a small inn and let the weather clear. It was a fateful decision to continue down that small two-lane road.

Jamie led while Ian trailed him. It was dusk when two cars approached them side by side. Jamie, while not as naturally athletic as his brother, was just able to get off on the left shoulder, enough to miss the oncoming car. The look of terror on the elderly lady's face was quite telling, but it didn't stop her from nearly killing Jamie. Ian, however, wasn't so lucky. If only Ian had been more focused on the road, Jamie always thought, perhaps he too could have gotten clear of the panicked, elderly driver, frozen by fear.

The hardest thing about the trip that Jamie always remembered was having to call his Pa and plead with him to come pick up dead Ian. The guilt he felt was not enough to get his Pa to speak to Jamie when he collected his son's body. The heavy sorrow that encased his father's attitude kept the two men isolated during the discharge process.

Finally, when Jamie could not take it any longer, he pleaded, "Pa, I'm so sorry! It's my fault that he got killed, but don't shut me out of your life! We both lost him. Please don't shut me out!"

His Pa just looked at Jamie, shook his head, and simply moved past him without saying a word. After the funeral, when his Ma deferred to her husband and closed her heart to her remaining son, he sold the motorcycle for pennies on the dollar. Shortly after this, he found an article about riches in the North and bought a bus ticket to try his luck in the city and never looked back.

About halfway through that bus ride, which eventually took him to the top of Ireland, a brooding female tourist plopped down next to him and introduced herself as Frieda. It took no small amount of badgering to finally get him to open up. He smiled slightly as he savored the early memory of the light of his heart but then went melancholy about also losing her.

Frieda and he had shared so much together. Now that chapter in his life was closed. He smiled sadly, thinking about how all the people he ever cared for had not survived. He awoke and wistfully thought about Timmy, his son. Timmy was safe with Frieda's parents. With gloomy thoughts still covering his now painfully awake mind, he sighed about yet another person out of his life; at least Timmy was safe from his "dark angel" touch. He knew that sleep, a rare and painful occurrence, would not touch him for the rest of the bus trip to Dallas.

CHAPTER TWENTY-TWO

Transformed and Ready to Board, Captain

They had worked round the clock and were weary but determined. By all reports, they had until the dawn tide to get Summit onto the ship. After working steadily since the idea had taken flight, they had located suitable materials for extra robes and a modest headpiece. Summit had indicated the headpiece would actually help secure him a place of honor on the ship as it indicated the level of his beliefs. Though George had scavenged most of the materials, Summit took lead in creating his holy man persona. Avidly reading the prayers and quotes from the Qur'an, he was also committing the key ones to memory. Fortunately, he had located a worn copy which he could take with him, securing it into one of the many pockets he'd built into the robe.

They both debated Summit keeping the specialized smart phone with him, but in the end, he knew that if it was discovered it would result in his immediate death. Summit and George added several different weapon pieces that separately would be innocuous, but assembled would be deadly. The only thing that was clearly obvious as a weapon was a knife, which no self-respecting holy man or Muslim would travel without. A man had to eat and protect himself. The handle of the knife was his only concession to electronics after George repeatedly insisted, "Summit, you are not going on a ship with a crew as hardened as this one without a way for me to find you if you have an issue. Especially with a planned route from here to Sakaiminato, Japan. That is just shy of eleven days at sea."

"George, I can take care of myself, I am a professional," grinned Summit. "Plus, it gives me more than enough time to gain their confidence and keep them on the correct religious path."

"I know you can, but heck, we have a great deal to teach one another on this mission of ours. If you go missing, I must have a way to find you or at least have a starting point. You told me no one would take your knife unless you were dead. If that is true and you go missing, I either find you or kill the crewman that takes your knife."

"Alright, let's put the geo-locator into the handle. Since you will have the receiver, no one will spot it."

"Exactly my point. Good!"

George, continuing in his role as manager, had ventured out of the room they worked in and completed some reconnaissance on the captain, the ship itself, and the crew. He discovered the crew tended to travel the same route on a repeat basis, making at least four confirmed trips in the last twelve months. Rarely did they add to the crew, though they certainly, like all ships, picked up rations and some additional shipping containers to replace what was offloaded, at least from a space perspective. The crew spent some time at the local taverns but did not take advantage of the females available for a few hours of entertainment. George was reminded on more than one occasion of the variety of sex available in Singapore, regardless of one's orientation.

The captain was a different story. He only came off the ship to speak to the Dock Master and once, to try his luck with the working ladies of the night, along with a hearty meal and some ale to wash it down. As the captain was leaving the dockside tavern, a girl approached him and blocked his exit. They held a brief conversation, with the girl doing most of the talking. Then, when she turned to walk away, George captured a photograph. She was the one in the image that Juan had sent. He hurried after the girl, knowing the captain would be returning to the ship. He called Summit to alert him to his discovery.

"Summit, I found our missing AIM. She just approached our target ship's captain. I thought she was a panhandler initially, but when she turned, I took her picture."

Summit replied, "Okay, I know you need to follow her. I'll let Juan know, and if she comes back online, I'll call you back. I am almost finished with this robe. If you're delayed, I'll get on the boat. Do not worry."

George was a bit torn as he moved down the road, keeping the girl in sight. She was rapidly approaching an intersection with far more people. He replied, "Good call. Just make certain you stay their holy one, not chum for the sharks following the ship."

George drew closer to the AIM to minimize his chance of losing her. In the upcoming crush of people, it could be dicey. She appeared young and on the move. As she walked, she had changed a portion of her clothing to appear different and more refined than the first photo where she looked like a beggar. When she gave her cloak to a street urchin, a pale blue dress of silk clearly spoke of money. George heard her soft laugh of delight at the urchin's surprise. Her handbag of leather was also exposed, and it too spoke of money. The girl was clearly practiced and familiar with the area.

She slid onto a bus, and George jumped on through the backdoor. Two stops later, the girl jumped off and flashed her tourist transit pass and boarded the train before it pulled out. George cursed his bad luck at not having his pass and watching his target disappear. He found a taxi and headed back to report his failed effort to Summit.

Summit took the information in stride. He suggested they needed to verify the functionality of the geo-locator. It worked well when they were in the same room, but George wanted to check with some distance between them.

George headed over to the dock to see if he could find out what cargo they were adding and test the geo-locator at the same time. There were only a few hours before the dawn tide, and Summit was ready to go. George timed his arrival just after midnight, near perfect as the crew, without the help of the crane operators, were manually loading the new containers. George squinted in the dim light at the markings on the containers and finally caught a good view as the moon moved out from behind the clouds. The new cargo being loaded was labeled as pharmaceuticals. It bothered him, but he couldn't put his finger on why. He tested the locator then hurried back to Summit. It was time he boarded.

Summit was perplexed as George related the label on the containers. "George, the labels were in English, or could you be translating incorrectly?"

George replied, "Yeah, that's what's been bugging me about it. They were in English and said Made in China Pharmaceuticals."

Summit looked unconvinced and then said, "Typically containers are never labeled that way as it would open them up for being stolen. You know, even over the counter products can be taken and made into something else, like using *pseudoephedrine* to make meth. Unless they are using that for negotiation. It could be why it was loaded in the middle of the night."

George agreed, "That makes sense. Clearly marked negotiable materials. This just gets crazier. I will send all the shots to Juan. You need to get on board."

Summit nodded and then finished the last touches on his headdress as he headed out the door and walked toward the docks. He walked as if he owned the entire scene. George was impressed by the visible transformation in his teammate. The crew had finished their loading and were getting the ship ready for departure. As Summit entered their line of sight, all activity ceased. George was too far away to hear the words.

There was a calm exchange between Summit and three of the crew on the dock. They seemed to almost bow as they listened to him. Several minutes went by before one of the crew scurried up the ramp and returned a few minutes later with the captain, who looked over the side of the ship at the stranger. A conversation between the crewman and the captain ended a few minutes later with a nod from the captain. The crewman scurried back down the ramp and apparently asked Summit to please board. Summit slowly walked up the ramp and disappeared from George's sight. His only link was the spot on the map from the geo-locator.

CHAPTER TWENTY-THREE

Eating, Sleeping, and Grazing in the Digital World

Juan sat immobile, in an almost frozen state, with only his eyes wandering around the room looking for where the voice originated. It was several minutes before he carefully tried to access the computer keyboard again. And just like before, the voice admonished him.

The stern voice reminded, "Mr. Rodriguez, Dr. Quip was very specific about not testing your access rights limits. I believe you are aware that trying to use his login credentials to review restricted materials is inappropriate."

Now alarmed and defensive in his unauthorized access attempt, Juan stammered, "I…I…I wasn't snooping! He said he'd be right back and that was ages ago! I was just trying to keep our progress, uh…moving forward. Uh… you want to tell me who you are to keep such close tabs on me?"

Quip, standing at the doorway took in the scene, clucked his tongue in annoyance as he returned to his seat and said out loud, "ICABOD, I thought we had an understanding on this matter. Remember? No direct communications with visiting dignitaries?"

ICABOD responded, "That is correct, Dr. Quip, except that Mr. Rodriguez was attempting to use your login ID to access the system during your absence."

Juan, trying to justify his action, weakly offered, "Well, when you got that call from your lovely bride EZ, I wasn't sure how long you were going to be. I thought I would try and maintain our forward progress by reviewing the notes that were being displayed on the screen. That's all."

ICABOD then responded, "The lost time amounted to 7.5 minutes while Dr. Quip was on the phone. At your near remedial rate of reading, Mr. Rodriguez, you would have only been ahead by fifteen words if you had waited."

Juan hung his head down and pouted but said nothing.

Quip, now amused, chuckled and said, "Alright you two, that's enough. Juan, this voice that you are losing the argument with belongs to the R-Group's ICABOD, which is our enhanced Artificially Intelligent supercomputer. ICABOD, this is Juan *the rogue* Rodriguez, whom you have helped us rescue on several occasions.

"Congratulations, Juan, on agitating my highly disciplined supercomputer into breaking his prime command of not communicating directly with you."

Juan, now mortified and humbled at the forced introduction, said, "I'm sorry to have pressed your stated boundaries and provoked Mr. ICABOD. And, let me add my heartfelt thanks, Mr. ICABOD, for helping to save my bacon on multiple occasions."

Quip continued, "Okay, class, recess is over, and now that introductions have been done, over my wishes that they not be, let's discuss the research we have so far. ICABOD, now that he knows you can speak, let's dispense with spilling all the info onto the screen and just say it out loud."

ICABOD offered, "As you wish, Dr. Quip. My apologies at being badgered into overriding your instructions. Mr. Rodriguez, please call me ICABOD, not mister.

"Let me begin by saying that determining who these AIMs are was our first milestone. Once we knew who they were, based on their peculiar blackout habits, we then attempted to correlate their movements with what we determined to be Event Anomaly Transactions or EATs. These EATs have a high correlation to the presence of the AIMs of approximately 93.274% of the time. Where we see the AIMs go dark, which is to say they become digitally unobservable, we see an EAT occur.

"If we extend the time horizon of the EAT to then look for Sequential Logarithmic Events Extending in Parallel, or SLEEP, we can attach follow-on events in a serial fashion. Basically, if we group EAT and SLEEP together, we get a cause-and-effect relationship that the AIMs are driving. Consequentially, they are not leaving the usual digital fingerprints we use to examine these goings on. That is to say, no cellular phone usage at the EAT and no definable bank account number at the SLEEP."

After staring at the speaker and monitor during the explanation, Juan turned to Quip and asked, "Is he always like this? I mean, talking about Information Mules EATING and SLEEPING in the underground economy?"

Quip grinned, but before he could respond, Juan interjected, "ICABOD, what is the likelihood that these Information Mules are not only EATING and SLEEPING, but also GRAZING?"

ICABOD responded, "Mr. Rodriguez, you bring up a valid point. Let me cross check this concept with our findings thus far."

Now somewhat agitated, Quip began to fidget until he insisted, "Okay, I have to know! What is GRAZING in the discussion context of AIMs EATING and SLEEPING?! You two are going to drive me nuts!"

ICABOD calmly offered, "Dr. Quip, this would be Geographically Randomized Analog Zealots Involved for Next Generation Goals."

Juan nodded, smiled, and agreed, "Yep, the extra G on the end makes it work better. Good job, ICABOD. And please, call me Juan."

Quip lowered and shook his head as he stated, "I didn't think it was possible to have anyone but Julie cut up with ICABOD. Now, here I am watching the newest member of the Marx Brothers perform."

Quip asked, "These are the pictures that Ernesto got from the camera that you wanted us to look at?"

Juan nodded and said, "This came from Jamie, the young man we moved from Macau to EZ's father's ranch. He's one of those kinds of people who seems to have a bad-luck lightning rod attached to him. You know the kind; trouble is never far away for him."

Quip cocked his head to one side and stared directly at Juan as he flatly stated, "There's a lot of people like that. Okay, let's have ICABOD scan these in for analysis, shall we? ICABOD, view and comment, please?"

ICABOD responded, "Certainly, Dr. Quip."

After a few minutes ICABOD commented, "The initial thinking seems to be correct. A handheld digital camera, photographing nuclear weapon creation technology and images of the unfortunates. My facial recognition programs confirm that the female in the burka died the day after the date stamp on the image.

"There is a high probability that there was an effort to collect all necessary intelligence on nuclear weapon production without being on the Internet where the authorities could trace the queries back to a source machine. It is easy to speculate that the information gathered is not for an academic research project, but a search for practical manufacturing details. Keyword searches on the Internet would attract too much attention in today's world."

Quip looked at Juan and said, "Looks like your man may have stumbled onto something here. I would suggest that you follow up on that lead, even if it means splitting up your ground team in New York."

Juan nodded thoughtfully before he responded. "Agreed."

ICABOD then added, "The first image of the dragon is uncharacteristically included along with the rest of the images."

Quip asked, "Speculation on why the photo of a dragon is there, ICABOD?"

ICABOD offered, "Since there is no indication of a password or passphrase anywhere in the images, perhaps this is a pass-visual that would be used in communications to the next recipient."

Juan mused out loud. "Are you suggesting the next person in the drama wouldn't offer a password, indicating they were the intended target, but might instead show an image for identification purposes?"

ICABOD responded, "Quite possible, Juan. In three-factor authentication it is something you know, something you have, and something you can do, as was demonstrated to gain entry to this facility. The something you have could be a picture or an ornament to properly identify you to someone you have never met."

Juan nodded thoughtfully and said, "Interesting."

CHAPTER TWENTY-FOUR

Check It Out, Settle In

Julie breezed through the elevator doors just as they opened, balancing the two cups of coffee she'd picked up at the shop next door to the office building. The barista knew her well enough, after a week of daily stops, to make the correct lattes without direction. She passed by a few of her new coworkers and flashed her trademark smile with a nod of recognition. Folks were in a hurry to be in their places when their various customers called with buy and sell orders. She made it to her small office, which was next to Laurie's, and was seated just as Laurie passed by. Julie picked up the lattes and walked to the next office to find out her assignments for the morning.

"Good morning, Laurie." Julie handed the latte over and grinned at the look of delight on Laurie's face.

Laurie took a savory sip of the warm brew, then exclaimed, "Jackeline, you are the best helper ever. Not everyone knows how important a morning latte is after a long train ride. Thank you. How'd you do yesterday with the work? Was Mr. Patrick in a good mood?"

"I really missed you being here and was a bit nervous. I hope your mom is doing better since you are back so soon." Then she leaned toward Laurie much as a best friend would and confided, "I think your buddy Dabir missed you too! He came by your office several times and looked in to see if you were back, though he never asked. He did seem to be almost every place I was yesterday. I don't think he likes me. He was watching me like a hawk. Odd."

Laurie giggled and replied, "I am certain he is just seeing if he has to compete with you. He really looked for me?"

"Yes, he did. Maybe he likes you."

"I don't know if I am his type of girl, but I do like him. Let's change subjects. Did anything else happen?"

"Mr. Patrick added a bit to my work. He actually had me type a couple of letters and put together information for a proposal. I placed the file copy of the proposal package on your desk to review before I file it. The only portions I was not able to do were the tasks that needed your special computer program access. Mr. Patrick said he would take care of those portions. Hopefully, I will get good enough at everything else, where you feel I am ready to take those tasks on. I'm trying!"

Laurie smiled as she replied, "You're doing a great job. You learn quickly! To be honest, as quick as you are learning, I plan to ask Mr. Patrick if I can start training you on the systems. Let me work on it for a day or two."

Just then, they were interrupted by Dabir in the doorway. He looked back and forth at the females as if assessing them. It actually made JAC's skin crawl just a bit. The guy was too sure of himself and from JAC's perspective he seemed to be targeting Laurie.

Then he leaned casually against the doorframe and looked directly at Laurie as he quietly asked, "If you aren't too busy training Miss Jackeline, I need to see the reports on purchases over the last two weeks. I am to provide Mr. Patrick with an analysis on the estimated time-to-money ratio, based on the buyers we are working with this week. Something about the distribution of time and transportation costs, which I don't quite understand yet. Can you work with me on this?"

Laurie's checks reddened a little as a smile rose to her lips, simultaneously with the twinkle in her eyes. "Jackeline, I will look at that report after I get Dabir sorted out and on the right track." She cleared her throat and added, "It could easily take us until lunch to assemble the information in the correct format. Why don't you go ahead and file the stack of reports the account managers have accumulated on the cabinets."

Knowing she was dismissed in favor of the male who Laurie had taken a fancy to, she smiled and nodded as she quietly returned to her office. As she passed through the doorway, she heard Laurie's tone of voice grow provocative as she cooed, "Dabir, bring the chair over next to mine, and we can walk through the steps of the process together. I think if I help you, um, from top to bottom, we can clarify any open issues and concerns you might have."

JAC thought to herself, Laurie is in for a fall with that player. He has lots of women, knows the right things to say, and yet shows almost no sincerity. Something about the man caused her concern. He was a mixed bag of suave and secretive with the right words said at the right time. He seemed to be observing Laurie for more than her mentoring lessons. Several times over recent days, JAC felt like he was poking into areas Laurie should be more guarded about. Bottom line was, he needed to be watched.

CHAPTER TWENTY-FIVE

The One Left Behind

It had been a long and taxing flight to Panama. Mercedes was asleep. She had drifted over in her seat and was resting against Brayson's shoulder. He tenderly pushed her hair back off her face and studied her. In her dreamy state, she nuzzled up closer to him and, smiling in her sleep, she said, "Yes, honey."

It was crushing to hear these warm words, spoken for someone else and not by his lost lady. The modest action only served to remind him that Gretchen was gone and that an emptiness was still consuming him.

Brayson looked down on Mercedes and softly said, "I hope one day I will lose this psychological baggage and earn the right to love someone again. Someone like you."

He spent the rest of the flight looking out the window, unwilling to move so as not to disturb her while she napped. He almost smiled at how much better, yet worse he felt with her leaning against him. A melancholy feeling was overtaking him, but he forced himself to focus on their upcoming insertion at the Panama data center. He thoroughly immersed himself in what-if scenarios, until he too fell asleep.

Brayson switched his gaze from the dilapidated, one lane road to Mercedes and then back again. After the fifth extreme chuck hole she'd tried to navigate around, he finally asked, "Are you *sure* this is the way to Santa Fe? I mean, OMG, this looks like we're in a third world country! I see a couple of miserable power lines and maybe a rural POTS line. There's this early model wrecked car that was wrecked again and should have been upgraded.

"It's okay if you've taken a wrong turn, even I, as a man, am willing to ask for directions. Of course, we would need to see a human being again for that to be an option. And why are we driving so fast? Each bump, no strike that, each pit you crash through threatens to shake out my fillings!"

Mercedes, still focused on the road, tersely responded, "You mean, Mister Perfect has fillings in his teeth? Probably from flapping your gums too much. Understand that this is the same road that Juan, Jim, and I came down to get to this god forsaken place. I know where we are, but if this road is too much stress on your bladder, I'll pull over at the next gas station for a potty break."

Brayson clucked his tongue in a very annoyed manner and continued, "I'm telling you there isn't enough power and tele-communications lines heading this way to support a stop light, much less a decent size data center. You require power, you need cooling, you need telecommunications lines, and…" Brayson stopped his rant. As they crested the hill, they saw a single lane bridge crossing over a healthy river as the road continued into a compound area.

Mercedes pulled up short before crossing the bridge and brought up her binoculars to glass the area.

Brayson was now taking in the compound and asked, "What's that sound?"

Brayson sat there a moment then motioned for use of the binoculars. After he too glassed the area, he said, "Not bad. See the turbines in the fast-moving river? Looks like they're improvising their own power supply from the running water here, and that sound, madam, is their diesel generators filling the needed power to operate.

"Just as well, since the power provider here in Panama isn't known for reliable power up time. No wonder there was no power grid reaching out here. They do it themselves. If that's really true, then their telecommunication is probably all satellite. Madam, I give you data center processing in an isolated jungle. If I had to guess, with all the rain and humidity, they most likely water cool their data center."

Brayson turned to study Mercedes who was still surveying the compound and asked, "Do you think Steven's nebulous job offer to you was legit? And, how do you know him again? He's got all the warmth of a Man-O-War jellyfish."

Mercedes swung her head around to face Brayson. "That's sweet, coming from you, Mister Awkward! Didn't you notice how he carried his arm?"

Brayson replied, "I noticed it right off, having served in the military. I wanted to see how he would deal with someone offering to shake his prosthetic hand. Most people with a disability like that will decline, or offer you their other hand, rather than have you freak out when you touch an artificial limb. He didn't flinch so I assume he was hoping to catch me off guard. He even looked a little disappointed that I didn't come unglued. Why did you introduce me as your cousin and tell me to go grab a magazine and some snacks?"

Mercedes considered Brayson's statement then said, "Steven Christopher and I were in the same training class together. I was new and he was finishing up some missed training. He was one of those excessively driven people that could be running the Pentagon by now, if he hadn't been wounded on his Afghan deployment. Word is, he was accidently hit by friendly fire while on a patrol.

"The story I heard was that he was so gung-ho that his squad let him go first and failed to radio in their new location coordinates. I find that hard to believe since most of his squad got hit as well. More likely, it was gross incompetence at the higher echelons because they quietly drove him out afterwards. No commanding officer needs to have a blemish around to hose up their career, so I figured that as soon as they had him patched up, they gave him a one-way bus ticket out."

Mercedes sat reflectively for a moment then added, "Anyway he helped me through some tough issues my first year, and it wasn't to try and get into my pants either. He was a soldier's soldier. He wouldn't stand for any hazing of first year cadets. Although, I will admit, he wouldn't turn down an opportunity to tease you if you had it coming. Boy, did he tease me a lot.

"As for the quick introduction, like family. I wanted to see if he'd talk to me thinking you were a cousin rather than a boyfriend. I wanted to hear his story, which I suspect is filled with hardship, due to his injury."

Brayson nodded and asked, "What was the opportunity he was trying to get you for? Looked like he was giving you a hard-core press even from my distant vantage point."

Still studying the compound Mercedes squinted her eyes a little and responded, "That is something still left unexplained. He seemed different than I recall, which I suppose is understandable with the life he's led since I knew him. He wouldn't quite say what he was doing or what I would be doing, but that I was perfect for the activity. He also added that I'd be pleased with the comp package. I know now why the pitch felt funny: it's almost like he was hitting on me."

Brayson opened his eyes wide as he asked, "You mean he was trying to get the Mercedes vehicle aligned into a suitable drive position so he could manually exercise the stick shift and obtain proper speed through repeated thrust and acceleration?"

Mercedes rotated her head to observe Brayson with her incredulous look and stated, "Brayson, your observation is not nearly coarse or vulgar enough to represent your shallow understand of the female creature, so I'll let it pass for now. At least your soft, caring, romantic side didn't simply blurt out *time to plunge the pork chops* like my brother would."

A surprised Brayson asked, "You have a brother?"

Mercedes smiled slightly and replied, "Thankfully, no. You are quite enough and more trouble than a cousin."

Brayson chuckled slightly. "Not to take away from your personal charm, but the woman he collared at the airport, after you left him, was definitely locked in listen-only mode. It was quick and intense, then they split almost as soon as she said something to him. It took the same duration of time too, like a message being repeated back as a confirmation. That's twice now that we've seen a quick, terse activity between our targets. This time we have a fresh new face all cloaked by the pedestrian noise of an airport."

Mercedes mused out loud, "Hmmm…an exchange between a male and a female that was quick and intense before they went their separate ways. There's a lot of things like that."

Brayson clucked his tongue and flatly stated, "Sounds like someone's gearing mechanism is stuck in the double entendre mode."

Mercedes smirked and retorted, "You started it."

CHAPTER TWENTY-SIX

Meetings on the Fringe

Tyler stated as he nodded his head, "I don't see any way around it either. We will have to split up since they are heading in different directions. I'll stay with Jenny and you keep up with Penny."

Ernesto nodded in agreement and said, "Her route actually works well for me to meet up with Jamie in Dallas. Looks like your Analog Information Mule is bound to Washington D.C. Don't you find it weird that Juan keeps sending us tracking information just ahead of us needing it?"

Tyler mused as he responded, "There's weird and there's useless, wondering about how we are getting this timely and useful information. I tend not to be concerned over useless wondering as it makes me constipated."

Ernesto studied Tyler with a sour look on his face then mentioned, "Well gee, we wouldn't want THAT now, would we? Let's review this material from Jamie one last time before we split up. Now Juan asked us, me that is, to follow up on this Muslim lead to see if there's anything to what Jamie is suggesting. For all we know, it could have just been a school report, and her death was just a coincidence."

Tyler seemed to mull over the possibilities for a few moments. "From what you've told me about this Jamie and what I've read in our archives, he strikes me as a calamity magnet. He is always in the wrong place at the right time for disaster to get him in its sights. He is the type of person who, as a pick-pocket, foolishly targets an off-duty vice officer. He was trying to steal from an automated casino in China run by a civil servant mobster when we fished him out of his predicament. He's one of those human beings who can reliably act as a trouble divining stick. You know, the kind used by charlatans to find underground water supplies for a thirsty wagon train in the Wild West.

"No one should have that much bad luck, but I suspect he has some genetic chromosomal defect that lets him gravitate right to the epicenter of the next disaster. So, yes, I think he's onto something, and you, my friend, need to be wary so you don't become collateral damage while trying to *help* him."

Ernesto cut his eyes back and forth a few times in contemplation and then stated, "You're right, maybe you should go meet him."

Tyler was now trying to suppress his smile and offered, "Oh, c'mon! Everything will be fine if you remember your training and keep your eyes open. Just don't let him drive or pack your parachute before a jump, and I'd make him taste my food first before eating."

Ernesto now projected a little mock concern and flatly stated, "You're right, we shouldn't split up our team. I'll just call him and tell him I moved to the New Hebrides and can't meet with him based on what my urologist turned astrologist advised me to do to stay healthy."

Tyler finally broke into a grin and asked, "You take advice from an astrologist? I didn't know that about you, Ernesto. Just didn't know that about you."

Ernesto said, "Alright, we know where our two AIMs are moving to next. With the time we have left, let's talk over this photo information. Let me be honest here. In reality, all we have is a series of museum artifacts chronicling the making of the first atom bomb. The facts are that it took all the brain power of the known free world three years and 60,000 people to build it, based on then primitive nuclear physics theory. Taking a bunch of photos even with a burka on is not really a crime, even if you wanted to build an atom bomb.

"In fact, just stating it out loud makes it sound even more ludicrous. Even if you had the materials, which, by the way, are not on aisle three of the local supermarket, trying to assemble a device like that would gain the attention of every American security agency. Oh, and to do it right, you would need to have it timed so when it went off you would be somewhere that you could say *what was that*?"

Tyler, always the analytical, responded, "Every project begins with research. This looks like that type of effort. Realize that when you type a question into your favorite Internet search engine, that always indicates to the security folks and watchers what you have in mind. I've got a friend of mine who works in an R&D department at a well-known software company, and they have two simple rules. Number one, waste anything but time. Number two, do NOT use the Internet to search for answers to questions related to your project.

"Asking questions on the World Wide Web with your corporate email identity is like giving your plans to your competitors. My friend was at a forum getting a tech briefing, and they took questions from the audience afterwards. Like a dummy he went up to ask his questions. Except he never got to because as he approached the microphone, he felt someone grab his arm and pull him away. It was two of his developers dragging him to the back of the room. Once there, in hushed tones they reprimanded him, *don't ask them questions because you are teaching them what they didn't know.*"

"I believe that these people have learned that same lesson as well. They aren't asking where they can be heard but instead go see for themselves. Hence the analog mule model for your intelligence gathering."

Ernesto pondered these statements as Tyler continued, "So the trick is to gather all the information readily available, but not get observed in doing so. The mechanical engineering schematics on building the bomb do exist and are often used in advanced engineering studies as examples. Key pieces of information are usually omitted, but that won't stop a highly motivated, semi-intelligent terrorist from assembling them. The activity is contingent upon not having your research efforts be spotted by the security people. As for the raw material, all you really need is uranium 238 and the mechanical engineering know-how to detonate it.

"Uranium is now mined not just for weapons, but also for commercial consumption. Companies get licenses for mining and refining the stuff. All you need is some details on someone's supply chain, then you intercept modest amounts to stay under the radar of the authorities. It would be ideal to also have a well-outfitted machine shop and a nice little quiet place to do your assembly work."

Ernesto took all the information and then finally said, "I'm not sure YOU aren't a terrorist. That's how I feel about you right now!"

Tyler made his characteristic half smile and responded, "Malicious mischief always begins with a thorough reconnaissance of your target without being observed. Once you have your details, then you can act upon them. A terrorist group seems to be following the same type of playbook in this scenario. All we need to do is pick up the threads of the broken information chain that Jamie created and look for the rest of the puzzle pieces. Oh yeah, and not get whacked like what was done to the burka babe."

"The biggest problem we have is that as an information driven society, it is also available for the bad guys to leverage as well. If this terrorist cell really is trying to assemble a bomb on U.S. soil, then we need to intercept them."

Ernesto then solemnly responded, "Perhaps you're right. You should go meet Jamie instead of me."

CHAPTER TWENTY-SEVEN

Confusion is When Bad Things Begin

...The Enigma Chronicles

Steven Christopher scanned the area. When he'd confirmed he was alone, he plopped down in a semi-comfortable chair to compose himself. The flight back from Panama was unsettling for him, not because of the flight duration but because of the effect of the running into the woman at the Panama Airport. He told himself she was only another potential AIM recruit. But he couldn't stop thinking about how the light danced in her eyes, or the warmth of her smile at their chance meeting.

Ever since his injury had forced such an abrupt career change, he'd immersed himself in this new role and lived the memories. The friends he'd lost in the friendly fire mess, coupled with his girlfriend and her emotional meltdown at the sight of his artificial limb, steeled him into believing he'd travel all alone on what remained of his life's journey. Sylvia had seemed brave when she came to the hospital for the first time after the accident. Then the reality of the situation must have kicked in, for soon she was running from the room crying hysterically, never to return. Her parents had shielded her from all contact with him: they even disposed of his letters, he assumed, as he'd never received a response. He eventually accepted that there wouldn't be anyone to join him in his life, and he was left as a shell, cold and empty inside.

It made him shudder as his frozen emotions began to thaw so quickly at the sight of the actual Mercedes in such close proximity. His shortness of breath and completely unfocused stare threatened to have his eyes overflow with tears. She was so much like Sylvia before the Afghan tour of duty. He couldn't stop the emotional processing that now had him fixated on Mercedes.

Christopher recalled the conversations and teasing that had ensued at the academy. He had replayed it all, knowing she had teased back in a friendly way, which with a bit of cultivating could have possibly been more. During that period, however, Steven was focused on his career. He knew that anything more serious would have been poisonous for his future, so he kept his distance at the graduation, very much in the background. It hurt when others had related that she cried when she saw him leaving the ceremony. He wished he had spoken to her directly instead of remaining in the shadows. Steven Christopher had foolishly kept Mercedes out of his life, only to be emotionally eviscerated by his fiancé, after nearly being killed by his incompetent commanding officer.

He actually pondered the happenstance of their meeting. Looking at the last few years, he tried to calculate how often his paths had crossed with anyone from the old days, when they were young and invincible. One bunk mate from training was all he could recall, and that earned him a free beer at a bar in New York, along with some unwanted sympathy. Could it be that the universal world order had ordained he now be given a second chance at a full life? The thought actually made him smile. But deep in his heart, he knew it was a very foolish thought.

Suddenly he wiped tears from his cheeks, facing the reality of the here and now. In near panic mode, he checked his watch to see that his meeting with Marge was almost overdue. With great effort he pushed his disturbed feelings back in their internal containers and slowly got back into character. After a brief stop at the men's restroom to throw up and splash some cold water on his face, he marched to Marge's office for her briefing. Standing outside her door, Steven paused for a moment, dreaming of blowing off Marge and catching the next plane to seek out Mercedes.

The crossroads was decided for him as Marge opened the door and said, "I thought I heard someone at the door. Come in, Christopher. I have been waiting and we have many things to discuss."

Marge had lunch brought in and set up next to the conference table so they could talk and plan without interruption. Christopher had kept to the juice and water, avoiding the food, though it looked delicious. They had passed some pleasantries, and she'd handed him his check for the month, which was very generous. Marge listened patiently to the updates he'd supplied and asked for specific clarification when needed. They discussed the next week of plans and information transfers she expected.

There was a pause as she refilled her beverage and looked at him. He had the same squared posture and set to his chin, but his eyes seemed dull. Finally, she asked, "You seem a little off today, Christopher. Anything the matter?"

Christopher swallowed hard, concealing his inner turmoil, and calmly said, "Apologies, madam, but the flight back from Panama was a bit more taxing than I anticipated. The data center is now on-line with enough processing power to sort and store all the data we will provide. The aggregator problem that the DEATACS had is now under control. The facility is practically all self-service with the power and telecommunications issues addressed. We can now collect all the AIM transactions through our audio/visual portal that I had installed. The transaction currency you wanted in place is also working to our expectations. I completed two test cases for verification before I made my flight back. There were two other deposits scheduled, but I have not checked for those yet."

Marge suppressed a smile of satisfaction then continued, "Now our intercept plan on the uranium shipment, how is that coming together? Our uh…customer is chomping at the bit for his *research project*. Have all the incentives been put in place for the material switch?"

Now completely focused, Steven replied, "Yes, madam, all the financial transactions have been made using our best AIMs. I actually facilitated some of the information delivery myself to keep on our time schedule. The material exchange is to be completed in the next 36 hours at the prearranged point."

Marge smiled as she hedged, "Now, I really don't want to burden Mike with all the details of this project. All he needs to know is that we are securing the required material for our customer, but he doesn't need to worry about the currency or amounts. Am I being clear on this? This is on a need-to-know basis and he doesn't need to know."

Christopher nodded and replied, "Understood, madam. Which brings me to a topic I wanted to surface with you. Mike has asked for AIM support in his project with our other customer. However, his customer has gone to using some free-lance contract labor which has potentially created a breach in security. Mike doesn't seem to be providing all the operational details we normally exchange, as though our efforts are augmenting another project. I am only seeing information flow one way and then reading about the effects of the aftermath. Our listeners, at Mr. Patrick's favorite bar, seem to have more knowledge on Mr. Patrick's activities than we do."

Marge's nostrils flared as she responded, "What are you saying? Has he gone into business for himself?"

"Madam, that is difficult to say at this point. I see resources being reallocated, AIMs being leveraged in non-standard environments, and others listening in on Mr. Patrick's boasting while carousing with the bar maids. He's also had many impromptu meetings with our Muslim customer, both in person and over the phone. All the activity suggests a duality in behavior that I think we need to keep an eye on. At the very least, madam, I wanted you aware of the situation."

Marge considered Steven's comments and then said, "Christopher, let me say that your military instincts are usually correct. To date they have not failed me or our DEATACS operations. I want you to keep a close watch on Mike. I foresee an internal audit being launched on ePETRO tomorrow, and I will be most curious to hear how he behaves when he learns of its launch and more specifically, what he does while it goes on. Do we still have our AIM in place to provide perfect reconnaissance as the audit unfolds?"

Christopher nodded and replied "Yes, madam. Your AIM will be alerted to observe, but will not be told why. That way we should get untainted reconnaissance."

Marge smiled and moved her chair closer to Christopher. While gently touching first his natural arm and working her way up to his neck, she calmly offered, "You know, Christopher, I've always admired people who can be trusted to meet my expectations and return value to the organization." Marge then moved her lips closer to Steven's ear and in a low sultry voice purred, "Perhaps after these two projects are in the bag, we should get to know one another better, hmm?"

Steven, now perfectly into his icy persona, characteristically replied, "If it would please you, madam, I would welcome the assignment wholeheartedly."

Marge, undeterred, pulled back and watched his emotionless face nearly turn to stone. She still smiled slightly as she finished, "Christopher, you are dismissed…for now."

CHAPTER TWENTY-EIGHT

All Looks Quiet, But It Isn't

Brayson had convinced Mercedes they needed to thoroughly investigate the hydro-electric power set up as a part of their stakeout. They had driven to the far side of the river, leaving the car well hidden from the road. From this vantage point they could see not only the top surface and lower entrance to what had been the data center, but also the road used to approach it.

Brayson commented, "Mercedes, if we looked at a satellite image of this area, it would look desolate and undisturbed. The terrain doesn't hold tracks, and the way the water moves over the rocks, along with the scraggly branches of the trees clinging to the shore, makes the hydro-electric generator invisible. Perhaps that is why you guys didn't notice it when you were here before."

"We actually did notice it the first time, and determined what it was. There's also a storage battery just inside the entrance. That door is concealed though." She pointed to the area above the entrance. "See those sticks and rocks scattered on that flat area? Those are the antenna the compound uses to bounce information off the communications satellites to the designated IP addresses and associated devices. The devices then either boost the data information packets and forward them on or save them to their system. That's how we're monitoring the feeds to make certain this data center is essentially dormant."

Brayson grinned, "That's cool and blends totally into the surrounding terrain. We need to take several shots from different angles and compare them to any earlier images that may exist. I'd like to know if there is a signature heat bloom over this area, as I suspect one comes and goes with information processing surges." Brayson pointed. "Hey, is that the bridge where all the excitement occurred?"

Mercedes glanced toward the area Brayson indicated. "Yes, that is where Jim was injured, and the culprit, known as LJ, tried to dive off with his dead passenger." She glanced from one area to the next and seemed to be working out a problem.

"What?"

"Sorry, I was just back in that moment. I had been waiting near the entrance. I bet if LJ had known the power source was right there, he might have vectored the car a little differently. You would have had to have been there to believe the destruction inside the data center itself.

"Come on, let's get some photos taken and then set up the propane stove for some dinner. I am looking forward to eating and looking at the stars tonight."

They spent some time capturing pictures from several areas, when Brayson pointed at some dust in the distance which seemed to be moving. Without a word, they moved their equipment closer to the car, out of sight of the entrance. They belly crawled up to the top of the overlook, keeping behind the few boulders which were there. A few minutes later they heard the groan of an engine under duress. A battered, once tan or maybe red, twenty something year-old Honda Civic hobbled into view and pulled up to the entrance. Brayson was videoing it, and Mercedes was taking stills.

The car stopped and the arm of a young female appeared out of the open window, blond hair taken by the slight breeze.

Moments later the door opened, and a young woman in jean shorts, non-descript tank top, and hat appeared. Only her nostrils and chin were visible, while the hat disguised the rest of her face. Closing the door, the young woman strutted to the entrance and placed her hand on the plate on the wall. They couldn't hear her words but saw her lips move as if she were talking.

Mercedes heard a disgusted grunt from Brayson and silence from his special smart phone. She suspected his battery was drained. She watched the lady and kept shooting photos, controlling the distance of the shot with the ball of her thumb to zoom in as close as possible. Maybe three minutes had passed before the lady stopped talking and turned away from the panel, her long legs gracefully carrying her back to the car. She had just opened the door and turned toward Mercedes' position when the wind caught her hat and pulled up the edge. In that moment, Mercedes took as many shots of her face as she could get. The lady got into the car, the sun reflecting on her pendant necklace. After the car was running, the lady backed into her K-turn and left the way she came.

It was several minutes before either of them spoke.

Brayson commented, "That was like watching someone walk up to an ATM in the middle of nowhere and check their account balance. Any thoughts?"

Mercedes shook her head and said, "That is as good an analogy as any. Let's get these devices charged up and then upload the pictures."

"Mercedes, I'm sorry I let it get so low."

"No worries, but we need to be prepared in case other visitors come to this remote ATM. Then I want to get into the data center."

"Good by me," agreed Brayson.

CHAPTER TWENTY-NINE

Puzzles Have 100 to 1,000 Pieces. What Did We Get?

Juan began the video call as he opened, "Hi, gang! Thanks for joining the call to provide your updates. I'm not sure if Julie is going to be able to join. I do know everyone is hip deep in alligators concerning their assignments, so let's jump right in."

George took the first turn. "Let me tell the team that Summit is undercover on an oil tanker that is traveling from Singapore to Sakaiminato, Japan. Curiously enough, the tanker's original route before he boarded was supposed to take them to Hong Kong, not Singapore, but now they are not even stopping in Hong Kong.

"We caught several pictures of the cargo they were loading up. These depict shipments of weapons labeled as Turkish furniture, so gun running is one of the oddities for this venture. Summit is on-board disguised as a religious holy man with a great chance of getting more firsthand information from the mostly Muslim crew in the ten days it will take the tanker to get to Japan. I'll pick him up there, assuming all goes according to plan."

Juan asked, "Was there anything on the AIM that I alerted you to?"

George clucked his tongue in annoyance. "Yeah, well, she hopped on, then off a mass transit bus, and I lost the lead I had on her. The only thing I was able to get was a quick photo of her stepping out into the rain. I am afraid I got more umbrella in the photo than her."

Juan, not being able to resist a taunt, stated, "Okay, if that umbrella surfaces again, we'll scramble all available resources, whether it's raining or not. I can see it is filled with pastel rainbow stripes which should be easily spotted."

Most of the team members smirked, except George.

Mercedes then offered, "We are still watching the data center here in Panama. It may be more operational than we left it, Juan. Oddly enough, all we have seen so far is female visitors that take this ghastly drive down what can almost be described as a road, walk up to this weird looking portal, and make contact for a few minutes, then leave. If it were anywhere else besides way out in the wilds of Panama, I would swear they were hitting an ATM machine."

Brayson then added, "The data center looks to be almost deserted except for one automated caretaker somehow helping the travelers with their ATM transactions. If we assume that they are all AIMs, then this could be an information repository that is most probably dispensing new assignments as the AIMs swing by. We got several good head shots and not just of their umbrellas either. Of course, at this time of year here, they would be used for shade, not keeping dry."

A few more chuckles were heard on the conference call, but as before George and Tyler abstained from participating.

The team was then surprised when Julie intervened, "Hi, team! Sorry I'm late, but it is a bear here in London trying to find a quiet and private place to conduct a video call without being caught on camera." Juan, now not able to resist yet another tease, asked, "So we should not be too unsettled if we hear a toilet flush?"

Julie rolled her eyes and, being totally mortified, retorted, "I'm not in the ladies' restroom, thank you very much! I borrowed a small drop-in cubicle with no camera. Remind me to cut your recess time on the playground to zero so you can write on the chalkboard a thousand times, *I will not piss off the partner!*"

The team members struggled mightily not to laugh at the Juan and Julie exchange for a few moments, waiting for one of them to speak.

Julie, having regained her composure, stated, "Alright, my activities have me in close working proximity with one of our AIMs here at ePETRO. Mercedes, you and Brayson caught her at the airport with what looked like an information exchange with some male. Kind of odd that this is the only male we have seen in these transactions, don't you think?"

Mercedes quickly offered, "Well, that's not true. We saw another guy at the Panama Airport talking to one of the AIMs we've identified. In fact, the man she was talking to, I knew from my academy days, Steven Christopher. We spoke briefly as he needed to catch a plane, but in that short exchange he wanted to know if I was looking for work.

"He seemed surprised to see me, and we didn't have much time. Brayson was portrayed as a family member and wandered off for magazines and discreet observation. Steven offered me very few details, but it might be worthwhile to look him up, just to see what he had in mind."

Julie asked, "Do you think he was off to another meeting for business or pleasure?"

Mercedes pondered a moment then replied, "I am not exactly sure. He seemed distracted, and we were trying to get moving to our stakeout, so I can't really say."

Juan, trying to distance himself from his earlier comments, offered, "I think you should try to reach out to him to see if there is, in fact, a connection to our AIMs. After all, he was there in Panama, so he may have a connection to the data center as well."

Mercedes acknowledged, "Understood. As soon as we wrap up here in Panama, I'll see if I can reach him."

Ernesto then offered, "The two AIMs Tyler and I were following split up and so did we. I am tailing one of them, who we call Penny, to Dallas, Texas, where she has landed in a no-tell motel near downtown. Tyler has followed his AIM to Washington D.C. I should link up with Jamie, as soon as his bus gets here. I was going to have him tag along with me on the AIM I am tailing while we discuss his peculiar set of events.

"Now Jamie may have stumbled into something that is either quite innocent or quite horrific. Tyler and I believe it is worth exploring and, if nothing else, try to ascertain if Jamie would be a suitable recruit, as we discussed."

After a moment of silence Juan asked, "Tyler, you seem kind of pre-occupied. Anything to report?"

Tyler, still studying the uploaded reports and pictures, absent-mindedly asked, "George, the umbrella picture you uploaded seems to have a subtle design. The stripes separating the colors appears to be drawings of dragons. Would you agree?"

George, still a little embarrassed by the image, replied, "Yeah, that's what I would suggest. Why?"

As Tyler clipped the image out of George's picture and inserted it into a new place on the shared screen of the video call he asked, "Mercedes or Brayson, would you categorize the jewelry piece around the neck of the AIM head shot as a dragon as well?"

Brayson watched as Tyler also clipped that image from the photo and placed it near the other. "Looking at it enlarged and isolated as you have it now, I can easily say yes."

Brayson then asked, "Hey, while you are clipping these images, how about a close-in shot of Laurie that I got at the airport too, huh?"

Tyler zoomed in on the Laurie photo and then commented, "Rather peculiar set of circumstances, wouldn't you agree? They all share the same preference for dragon jewelry which…"

Tyler then pulled in the dragon photo from the camera he had gotten from the deceased Muslim female and, pasting them next to each other, continued, "…is an identical style match to the photo on the camera Jamie sent us."

Before anyone could comment, Julie hurriedly stated, "Uh… I need to go now! The area is no longer secure or private. Juan, I'll check in again in a few days. Keep up the good work, all! Bye for now!"

Juan picked up the discussion and asked, "Tyler, you appear to have hit on something. Do you have any theories?"

Ernesto suggested, "Tyler, it looks like either all our AIM leads buy their jewelry from the same wholesale manufacturer or you may have found a unifying thread that can be used to clearly identify our information mules. I personally hope they're victims of flea-market bargain sellers, so I won't have to put up with your insufferable conspiracy theories. But, to humor you, I will watch our AIM targets to see if the dragon image is consistently there."

Tyler blinked a few times as if clearing his thoughts. "Biting sarcasm being driven by professional envy also makes me constipated, Ernesto, just so you know."

Ernesto studied the video screen with a sour look on his face and then stated, "Well, gee, we wouldn't want THAT now, would we?"

The team members chuckled at the verbal sparring as Juan offered, "Alright, team, let's stay focused and continue to hunt for clues in this highly fragmented puzzle. We may have more connections than we thought.

"George, let me know if Summit is able to check in earlier than the ten days you indicated, alright? Though I know without a device of any kind outside of the geo-locator you insisted upon, it will be difficult."

Before dropping off, George responded, "Understood, but I would only expect him to try to communicate while on the ship if there was an emergency. I'm hoping not to hear from him until the tanker docks, and he can make a call without risk of discovery."

Juan nodded and said, "Copy that."

CHAPTER THIRTY

Lay the Foundation
Before Building Begins

Sunday evenings in London were, in Dabir's mind, designed for relaxing and reflecting on the objectives for the upcoming week. The jazz music that played in his earbuds suited his relaxed mood. He curled up in the doeskin easy chair by the window overlooking Trafalgar Square as he watched the lights of the other homes wink on. The charming and eager young woman who had spent the weekend with him had been most impressed with the flat. It was nice that, if he needed to learn this business and keep his eyes open to all the possibilities, his uncle was willing to set him up in a comfortable location with creature comforts to his liking. In this lifestyle he had no need to fabricate arrogance, it suited him.

The cook who came on Mondays and Thursdays prepared meals he could simply heat and eat with no real effort. Housekeeping was arranged on Monday, Wednesday, and Friday and provided for his laundry, cleaning, dishes, and any other household errands. Other than making his own tea and handling his daily grooming habits, he lifted no unnecessary hands for his lifestyle. Most of the females, which he used for his satisfaction then tossed aside, were delighted to have him at their home, where he could easily extract himself after sex. Inviting pretty Olivia to his place was a rare occurrence. When she left, he'd told her not to return in no uncertain terms.

This was an easy life he knew could not continue as it was but a stepping stone to power and riches. Trained, educated, and now immersed in Western business, he was ready to complete his tasks and move on. There were still a few gaps in his total understanding of the business operations at ePETRO, but his learning curve had spiked more than he had imagined in the past three weeks. His earbuds indicated an inbound call. The ability for this very small bullet earbud to permit multiple audio streams was a luxury he would never give up.

"Uncle Kashan, peace be upon you."

"And upon you, peace, my nephew.

"How is your work going? Are you making progress with the operations and the fawning female you outlined to me last week? I suspect there are no big shifts or you would have informed me."

Dabir smiled at his insightful uncle. The man may have had a different education, but he was not a fool. "Yes, Uncle. I did as you suggested and, with mild flirting, the administrator Laurie is falling all over herself trying to help me gain facts and figures. A simple question from me, and she turns on the information faucet. She has twice used her higher access password for two different programs, so I have that now. The problem is she needs to be out of the office before I access it, as it only allows one sign on at a time.

"I am getting closer to the financial information you asked for and even found a file marked *Special Partner*. I haven't been able to open the file to see the contents or copy them, but I will this week. Your pigeon, Mike Patrick, plays his hand close to the vest. Even Laurie is not privy to all his plans. He works very late hours, staying after everyone else leaves. On Wednesday I tried to stay and talk with him, hoping to gain some additional confidence, but he finally dismissed me, telling me to go home and report bright and early in the morning. As a task master he is difficult to understand, but he is certainly driven in his responsibilities. I watched the outside entrance for almost two hours before he left to visit his favorite pub before going home."

Kashan was quiet for a few minutes before he replied, "It sounds as if you are making progress. The rumors were that Mike was finding his life in the bottom of a bottle. Is that the case or just what he wants his people to believe? That boar he works for, I believe, is still pulling the strings, even though he insists during our calls she is not present."

Dabir replied, "Laurie said, on more than one occasion, that Mike forbids her to share any information Mike doesn't approve. Any requests from Marge are to go through him. I am not certain if she follows those rules, as she always adds an odd grin to those comments, as though I should understand otherwise. I meant to say too, this Laurie seems to be taking care of her ailing mother and travels some to the country to check on her. When she does this, Jackeline is left in charge.

"I don't know her background, but this Jackeline Cooper started when I did, yet seems to have gained a lot of ground in support of Laurie, and the associated access for her keeps increasing. Not certain what to make of that, but it seems a little too convenient. Can you have someone find out a bit more about her background?"

Kashan replied, "I will have Achmet look into it, and if he gets any good data, I'll pass it along. Maybe a look into this mother of Laurie's is worth some cycles. Your thoughts?"

Dabir rubbed his chin as he thought about the potential gains. "I think a little more detail would be useful to me. I find it odd that a parent who requires so much attention is so far removed from her daughter. One would think that an infirmed parent would be kept closer so as to require less travel.

"I have sent copies of some of the files I have accessed along with notes made after overhearing conversations. I'm also sending some pictures of the office layout and the floor plans just in case they are needed. If I cannot get the information needed, we may need to stage a break–in, although a clandestine operation to obtain information would be risky and could compromise our intelligence gathering here."

"Very good, my nephew. Work this week to uncover the rest of the contact information for this other main partner. Go the way of the Prophet, Dabir."

"I live to serve. In Allah's protection, Uncle Kashan."

Kashan disconnected from the conversation. A mobile device and laptop, his most modern trappings, were in stark contrast with the rest of the items in the room. The room came into focus even though it was nearly consumed in shadow. The warm flames flickered from the lamps, reflecting off the modest furnishings, with the boldest in color belonging to large, variable rugs covering the floor. A fierce leader of his people, he enjoyed his modest comfort in low chairs with his feet stretched out on the woven wonders. Even with his bare feet he was warm in his modest robes. He rose and replenished his tea, which had grown cold, and returned, easing himself down in a fluid motion. The short silence allowed him to organize his thoughts.

Kashan looked to his oldest and most trusted advisor and asked, "Achmet, any thoughts on the discussion? It seems Dabir has brought us some new insider information, which makes his time there a good investment. I looked at some of the material he'd sent earlier, and it seems to point to more profitability in ePETRO than I thought. Of course, I did not think the business was on the rocks, but their negotiations are definitely to their advantage. They are a good avenue for us to offload our oil, out of the traditional prying eyes of the West. The prices are subpar, it seems to me."

"Kashan, we do not have many avenues to offload our resources until the embargos are lifted. We do however have additional revenue streams we might take, including arms running and blackmailing. Our arms running has a bit too many moving parts and dependencies, so perhaps blackmailing, with its single focus, offers a better return on investment. Laurie does in fact have an ailing mother, who is also very well off. I am trying to see how the old woman's holdings are to be distributed upon her demise for leverage."

"I think it is time I take a few of my trusted men and get very close to the situation. It permits me to see all that is going on, as well as to step in if needed without delay. Dabir's observations of Mike Patrick are confirming your instinct that he is a self-serving liar, like all Western pigs, even if the boar he serves isn't pulling all his strings. They do have other offices, and her base has always been between Toronto and New York City. That was the intel we received and it hasn't changed."

Kashan leaned back in his chair and sipped his tea. He always thought before making decisions, so he would not have to change them. Achmet had expressed many of the same thoughts as him. He needed to make certain that he converted his resources of oil into more liquid assets. This meant finding the direct link for that oil buyer to improve negotiations, and securing additional funding avenues, to make the Westerners pay for their treatment of his people. So much to do, but which path to take? Then he reached his decision.

"Go to London with no more than three men, Achmet. Make certain to arrive via different avenues so as not to raise any flags. Be sure to use the poor displaced immigrant routine that will garner all the necessary sympathy to reach your destination. Secure new communications devices and weapons, then find a secure place to use as base. You have less than a week. I want you in place and watching by Friday."

"So it shall be, Kashan."

It Never Hurts to Ask

Mike was barely able to contain his astonishment as he thundered, "What do you mean, they're here for the audit!? Who the hell ordered an audit in the middle of our fiscal year?"

Now wishing she could crawl under a rock to let the storm pass, Laurie timidly offered, "Um…the audit that was ordered by the governance board? It has several signatures from the directors on it, so I assumed…"

Mike fought to get his rage under control and get his thinking back on track with this unexpected turn of events. He snatched the memo from Laurie's hand and quickly reviewed the contents. After a moment of scanning the document, he added a quick breath of resignation then stated, "At least they got the right floor for ePETRO this time. Dammit! With everything else going on, these clowns ordered a corporate audit, and now we have to babysit the fresh college grads and the junior accountants they always send in who don't know the first thing about the oil business! I hope they don't send any more like the last two we had to deal with. By the second day they had been nicknamed *Debit* and *Credit*. Crap!"

The reality of the situation began to sink in. Mike started feeling fear and panic methodically replacing his anger. With forced calm he said, "Alright, get Dabir and the new girl, the one with the laughing teeth, in here so we can do the *all-hands-on deck* routine. The sooner we get them moving through this audit, the sooner we can have them out of our hair."

Laurie didn't need to be told twice as she bolted towards the door. As soon as she was gone, Mike quickly picked up his personal cell phone and launched a speed dial to a familiar number.

Marge smirked slightly as she saw the number come across her phone, but took her time answering it. When she finally accepted the incoming call, she flatly asked, "What is it now?"

After a few moments a ruthless smile began to emerge on Marge's face as she replied, "Of course I knew it was coming. Who do you think ordered it?"

Marge had to hold the phone away from her ear, based on the volume of the verbal reply.

Again, she offered, "Mike, I had to order it so it would appear that we are well on our way to proper self-governance in our accounting records. Now, was there something in there that shouldn't be in there?"

The response tone was now at the proper decibel level, and almost all of the exasperation was gone from Mike's reply.

Marge responded, "See? I'm so glad you understand the lay of the land here. I order an audit, the auditor drones come in, they badger you and your staff for a week, but the end effect is that we pass with flying colors, which lets us tell the exchange commissioner to piss off. You've already said there is nothing to worry about, so put up with the inconvenience for a few days, and then we won't have the Americans or the Brits breathing down our necks for a while. It will all be good, trust me."

Marge listened to the deflated response and then soothed, "Now do a good job, and I'll buy you a nice ice cream float with your favorite whiskey, all right? There's a good lad. Must dash now."

Mike held his phone at arm's length in front of himself as he blankly stared straight ahead wondering how all this would play

out. Finally, he sang out loud to no one in particular. "A ditty by
Mike Patrick:

Woe that a foe could derail my cause!

Ah that my destiny would force on me now a pause!

She hath grasped at me with her claws!

Mike's plans are at risk due to Marge's scheming prank!

For my cause all I ever desired was more money in the bank!

But instead let us plot to run her over with a tank!

Mike sat there momentarily as a small sense of satisfaction
changed his scorn to a wry smile. His thoughts were interrupted
as Laurie, Dabir, and Jackeline barged into his office.

Even though Mike strove to maintain a businesslike atmo-
sphere as he faced the reality of the pending audit, he could not
suppress the sour faced look that spoke volumes about his feelings.

He said, "Laurie, you know the drill. Get them access to
whatever they ask for. Dabir, you see to it that any copying or
office supplies that they ask for are filled promptly. Jackeline,
you get these auditors into a conference room and see to their
needs, but no whiskey and soda, please."

JAC smiled but instinctively knew this was a cover up exercise
on many fronts.

After a few moments of inactivity, Mike insisted, "Well, let's
get cracking, team! Don't let them bother the regular analysts
or account managers. They just love to hover over someone's
shoulder and ask *what's that you're doing*? Oh, Dabir, can you
hang back a minute, please? I have a special assignment I want
you to do. Thanks all."

After JAC and Laurie scooted out of the office, Mike's tone became rather somber as he confided, "Dabir, usually I have all my personal accounts up to date, but I've let them slip a bit. I need you to discreetly retrieve them and put them in my car. I'll take them home tonight and update all the journal entries at home. They'll be ready for the auditors by the end of the week.

"This is a bit embarrassing so I'd prefer that you not mention any of this to anyone. It wouldn't look good to be the only account manager who has let his journal entries fall by the wayside."

Unconvinced but in an obliging manner, Dabir offered, "Yes, sir, of course. I will see to it the records are moved to your car right away. I will place them in the boot so they will not be noticed with any casual walk by your vehicle."

Mike forced a moderate smile and pitched Dabir the keys to the Bentley. "No scratches, and make sure she is locked up when you are done."

Dabir, with something of a mischievous grin, asked, "Should I get the car to load it quickly by the elevator or should I use a hand cart to move all the files to where you parked it?"

Mike gave him his most challenging *you must be kidding look*. With no other contextual clues, Dabir smiled widely and stated, "It was worth the asking! I sense; however, you would prefer that the files be taken to the Bentley rather than the other way around." And with that he scampered off.

CHAPTER THIRTY-TWO

Speaking With
and Without Words

Brayson scrutinized her facial features, which showed no emotion and then asked, "So, how did it go?"

Mercedes thought a moment and replied, "He seemed pleased. Maybe a little too pleased that I had reached out to him. He wanted to come meet me. I told him that I was finishing up some personal business in Panama and asked when he would be back in the states so that we could meet. He sounded surprised at my knowing he was out of the country. I don't know why I said that.

"Anyway, he recommended New York, but I got him to meet me in Washington D.C. like you suggested. How did you know that we could piggyback off the satellite transmissions here? I mean, it was nice not having to go into Panama City for a 3G/4G wireless signal to make a call."

Brayson rolled his eyes slightly with a smirk. "I figured this far out in the middle of nowhere, they wouldn't expect people to casually be trying to camp onto their Wi-Fi networks that tie directly into their satellite uplink communications. They simply had not changed the default password which made it easy to hack their network. Much like the buildings near our headquarters where I use the Wi-Fi all the time. There's one cute gal that uploads some saucy pictures to attract her part-time evening playmates. Her favorite singles/mingles/and tingles website is one called…"

Mercedes, now in full disapproval mode, interrupted, "I just asked you how you knew to camp on to the site's communication link, and you launch into your lurid, voyeuristic diatribe observations obtained when hacking into someone's private life. I do not need another TMI episode from you."

Brayson feigned a mock pout and weakly offered, "You asked." He waited for more and finally asked, "Where are we to meet him?"

Mercedes gave him a disapproving look. "WE aren't meeting him anywhere! I've arranged to meet him in D.C. so I can have Tyler back me. He is already there, or close to there, watching his AIM. I don't want to take any chances of you getting spotted with me."

Brayson, somewhat taken aback and not hiding his hurt, wounded look, asked, "You mean I don't get to go with you? I can be stealthy and secretive!"

Mercedes stared at him with her incredulous look #2 and blurted out, "You did a direct oral assault on Laurie in the airport, then you did the *'let me shake your prosthetic hand so I can have my facial recognition attributes burned into your memory banks'* as a way to hide in plain sight! You have *flirted, agitated, annoyed, and recursively troubled* people on three continents, which makes you a *FAART,* so I don't believe you can be stealthy or secretive!"

Brayson slowly lowered his head and meekly replied, "That hurt! I thought you were so cute when you snuggled up on my arm on the plane ride here." Then he dejectedly added, "Of course, you did call me Jim."

All of her annoyance and irritation melted at the little boy routine, so she grudgingly admitted, "Brayson, you are going to make a fine catch for some lady someday, just not this lady, understood? Let's split up, so we can get maximum coverage on this project. If Tyler hadn't been in D.C., I would have asked you to back me up. Just so you know. Besides you can scope out the babes that seem to come in here on a regular basis. That should keep you entertained for a while."

Brayson suddenly brightened up and smiled as he asked, "Can I have an ice cream too, big sister?"

Mercedes, now in a mock sulk, spoke as if she were speaking an aside to the theater audience. "I hope that the lady that shows up for Brayson, in this theater of the absurd, knows what she's in for."

Mercedes took a defensive but coy posture as she sat, stirring her drink with the straw. Her mood was neutral, neither rejecting nor embracing the statements from Steven Christopher. She knew something was wrong with his pitch, which is why she knew she was on the right track.

After listening patiently, followed by a few moments of contemplative silence, she finally asked, "When would this unstructured job begin? I have to admit that I am in between careers, so to speak, but if I take your job proposition as offered, then I'm off the job market. I could miss something better. Would a trial effort be something we could discuss? You know, if it doesn't work out, then we go our separate ways, no foul, no blame."

Before Steven could respond, Mercedes flatly added, "I'm only here for business, clear? A job that has lots of travel will keep me on the move and away from any more personal family entanglements, like the damaged goods you saw me with in Panama."

Steven, now somewhat disappointed but still hopeful, replied, "Of course, Mercedes! Clearly understood. The ground rules are clear. It is a six months minimum commitment." Seeing her nod in agreement, he continued, "Alright, let's begin our new business relationship with something special." Steven then removed a small box from his pocket and, after opening it in front of her, took out a silver dragon pendant. Grinning like a cat that just swallowed the finch, he asked, "As a show of our good faith, this is a necessary part of the job as it is your communications signal. It is not a show of affection if that's what you were thinking. Please wear this always while working for us. Trust me, it works better than business cards."

Mercedes reluctantly accepted the dragon pendant and slipped it over her head and let it ride outside her clothes. She allowed a small smile of pleasure at accepting the gift, but Steven struggled to keep his emotions in check, hopeful that she might be won over at some point.

From his vantage point several tables away, Tyler quietly clucked his tongue and under his breath commented, "I didn't need to read anyone's lips to know what was going on in THAT transaction. I wish I could see her full facial expression."

CHAPTER THIRTY-THREE

Watching and Delivering

Mercedes had left her meeting with Steven and returned to her hotel for some downtime. Tyler received her text message and decided to resume the monitoring of his target AIM Jenny until his next contact with Mercedes.

In a very dissatisfied tone, Tyler idly remarked, "Well, this is just great. I'm following two attractive females who should not be able to see me. This routine is probably how Jim Hughes got the nickname Stalker. They only call you that if they catch you, and so far, I've never been caught."

Tyler scanned his cell for any updates from Juan on Jenny's new location. Not finding anything, he sent a message to Juan who immediately returned the call.

Juan began, "No, Tyler, I don't have any new updates on your target Information Mule. She needs to either resurface on the 3G/4G cellular grid via her phone, or if you can get a better close up face photo, we might feed the image into the computer system for a try at facial recognition."

Tyler made a sour face and replied, "If I'm keeping my distance from her so I can tail her, how could I ever get close enough to get a proper front facing photo? Riddle me that, oh clandestine caped crusader."

Juan, sensing Tyler's annoyance but unable to resist teasing him, replied, "Boy, for someone with a new girlfriend in the making, you sure are grumpy. You mean to tell me you haven't done the Brayson maneuver of taking her photo while conducting an oral assault on her lipstick?"

Tyler, in his normal deadpan way, replied, "She doesn't know she is my girlfriend yet."

Juan thought to himself, *one of these days I'm gonna get a laugh out of him. Doesn't look like it today though.*

"Alright, I'll let you know. Hey, wait a minute! It looks like she just surfaced on the grid a few blocks from where she disappeared after leaving Dulles International Airport. The signal is stationary so high probability is she has a flat nearby …and likes to have pizza delivered. You are in luck, my boy. Let me text you the address, and you can continue your surveillance."

Tyler promptly reminded Juan. "I am also monitoring Mercedes in case she needs backup. My concern is if one of them goes somewhere, I won't be able to watch over both ladies."

Juan offered, "Let's deal with that scenario when it occurs. Right now, you've got two ladies who can't see that you are stalking them."

Tyler thought for a moment and then asked, "You still want that up close photo of Jenny? Because now I think I know a way to get it."

Juan, somewhat taken aback, answered, "Sure, it'll help firmly identify her. Whatcha got in mind?"

The pizza delivery driver had trouble finding a parking place at the address for delivery and had to circle the block in hopes of finding something opening up. It was the same again the second time around. Annoyed, the guy double parked his car on the street and was ready to get out when a friendly comment came in through the window from someone standing outside.

"I wouldn't do that if I were you. This street has a lot of grumpy folks living here, and they have paid to have some off-duty officers to sit in a car at the end of the block and hand out tickets for just this kind of thing. I know 'cause I got one myself just yesterday. The jerks!"

The pizza delivery guy, now thoroughly frustrated, asked, "How the hell I am going to get this pizza delivered? Sit here and honk until she comes out for it? We got rules that if I don't deliver it in under 15 minutes, the price is on me!"

Tyler, suppressing his smile, offered, "Hey, let me run it over to her, get her to sign for it, ask for a handsome tip, and bring it right back. You stay with the car, the fuzz can't tag you, I get my revenge on them, and we all win! Except of course the off-duty rent-a-cops."

The driver suspiciously asked, "Why would you help me? How do I know you won't just grab the change and run, even if you do deliver the pizza?"

Tyler smiled confidently and admitted, "Because I want to deliver her pizza just for a chance to meet her. I've been trying to strike up a conversation with her for over a week now, and this seems like fate. I deliver your pizza, return with your change, and I get to meet her. Oh, and we get to hose off the ticketing goons. You will owe me a favor someday."

The driver grinned, looked at his smart watch and agreed. "Okay, you got a deal! My delivery time is almost up. You would be doing me a big favor. Here." He handed over the pizza and his ball cap with the company logo on it. "You gotta wear this, another rule. Just get her to sign the charge slip and don't forget to ask for a tip!"

Tyler slipped on the hat, took the keep-it-warm portable oven, and quickly marched to Jenny's door. As soon as she opened the door, Tyler boldly took her photo causing her to recoil in surprise.

Grinning, Tyler cheerfully offered, "Madam, thank you! We are running an area contest to see how many pizzas we delivery guys can deliver in an evening. The company is offering $500 to whoever delivers the most pizzas in one night, but we need a photo to prove it for the contest!

"Again, thank you! Oh, can you please sign the receipt? Hey, and add a handsome tip on there, in case I don't win!"

Jenny, amused by Tyler's antics, signed the ticket and turned to close the door, but not before Tyler hollered, "Wow! Thanks for the tip, Suzy Q!"

Tyler scampered off to return the receipt to the driver who was starting to panic that he had been scammed and that his signed receipt wasn't coming back.

As soon as Tyler returned, he took the bag and looked at the receipt then exclaimed, "Whoa! You really did deliver the goods, bro! I am gonna remember this gal from now on! She's the one with the big tips!"

Then the driver hollered out into the evening air as he drove away, "Thank you, Miss Suzy McMurtry! I love your big tips!"

Tyler was still chuckling at the comment about big tips as the driver sped away. He had a satisfied smile on his face as he remarked, "Yes, thank you, Suzy Q!"

CHAPTER THIRTY-FOUR

Honky Tonks Still Exist!

Ernesto had followed Penny to Dallas, where he had a rental car and driver reserved to cover the options. The driver seemed like the best choice so he could keep an eye on her. When she picked up her car from the preferred customer slot, she confidently pulled out of the rental lot and headed downtown like she had been there many times before. She ended up in South Dallas where she rented a modest motel room. Once he determined where her room was, he headed for the front desk, marked by a fluorescent arrow under a flickering vacancy sign.

The area was clean but definitely outdated with once white paint peeling in the corners above cracked vinyl chairs. He noted the rack of brochures for local attractions was bent and out of order. The woman behind the counter eyed him head to toe a couple of times and grinned. Her distinguishing characteristic was her hair which was curly to frizzy and the color of cherry red soda, bright against her pale white skin. Her jeans and tee shirt were non-descript and her jewelry was plain and mostly silver. He pegged her for mid-thirties and single as no ring was on her finger.

He approached the counter and she leaned forward as she said, "I'm Tammy, how can I help you? I know everything about Dallas and Fort Worth, and I can tell you all the best honky tonks. Heck," she batted her eyelashes. "I can personally show you if you want." It was subtle, but the southern drawl came through in her words.

She seemed like a friendly type and went on for several minutes on the things to see, places to go, and what to do. Finally winding down, she asked, "How long are you in town? We rent by the day, the week, or the month. The price is such that if you are staying at least four days, it's cheaper to rent for a week, like the lady, Ms. McMurtry, did a little while ago. She comes here usually once a month for a week, sometimes with her sister. The best part though is the week rate; gets you a nicer, quieter room with a bit of a view of the pool and even some of the city because you are up higher, rather than just the parking lot. We do get lots of repeat business. It's clean, convenient, and not too expensive. There are even some places that deliver food, if you want. Mexican is my favorite, how 'bout you?"

Ernesto smiled at the myriad of subjects she raced through and replied, "I prefer Italian, myself, though Mexican is a good second.

"I am so glad you clarified the rate for me. I think I'll start with a week, though I may extend it. My nephew is coming to town soon to see the city, too."

Tammy grinned and asked, "Is he as good looking as you? I don't mind showing you both around, if you want. My family owns this place and we always trade shifts to cover each other, so I can pretty much take off when I want."

Her flirting was, he decided, just a part of her southern charm, though he suspected she did like to dance and have a beer or two. When she handed him the key, he noted on the floor plan that it was just a couple of doors down from Penny on the same floor, but on the wing which allowed him a clear diagonal view to her door and draped window. Tammy explained all the ins and outs, what to see, how to order food, and even gave him some extra coffee with a wink and a smile. After he promised to bring his nephew in to meet her, he left feeling confident that Penny, he supposed McMurtry, would likely stay put for a couple of days. Ernesto went to the waiting driver, knowing the fare would be high after all this time. The driver agreed to take him back to the airport to secure his reserved rental car.

Later, after he returned to the motel, he noted that Penny's room light was on and she had received some food delivery. It reminded him he was hungry so he ordered a pizza. It arrived piping hot and full of his favorite toppings with a crust that was spicy and plumper than his normal thin crust choice. He ate with the light off, watching until her light turned off as well.

Up early, grateful for extra coffee, he watched in silence until she exited her room around 9:30 in the morning. He followed her at a discreet distance as she walked to a nearby donut shop, ordered a couple of pigs in a blanket, and ate while reading the morning paper. Ernesto picked up a variety of donuts and some juice then returned to his motel. He noted she returned roughly an hour later and went into her room.

A short time later she left the room in her swimsuit, with a towel and book in hand. She positioned herself for optimum sun exposure and looked settled in the sagging lounger. The pool looked maintained, and the automatic cleaning device was making its lazy circuit around the pool. Using her mobile phone, she must have placed another food order as a sandwich and soda were delivered right at the pool. The short conversation between Penny and the delivery boy made Ernesto think this was not their first meeting.

Never even sticking her toe into the pool, she returned to her room around the dinner hour and turned on the television, evident by the flickering images he caught through the window.

Like the previous night, another food delivery was received, and the lights turned out around the same time. Ernesto wrote up his notes and sent them to Juan and copied Tyler. He'd decided that whatever she was doing in Dallas, it involved waiting. No visitors or deep interactions, other than the short time with the food delivery people.

Day two was identical to day one, with the exception of the type of food she ordered. None of the behaviors the other AIM watchers on the team had noted were present, like the jewelry or short bursts of face-to-face conversation. Finally, after the third day of pizza for dinner, his phone rang.

He answered, "Hey, Jamie, good to hear from you. Are you close?"

"I am almost to the bus station. The driver announced we would be there in just under an hour. I gather you are in Dallas," said Jamie.

Ernesto chuckled and clarified, "I'm here and I have the poshest accommodations and a real pretty girl I need your help watching. I also have some additional details on what you sent me. I will head out now."

The trip to the bus station was trouble free and fairly close to the motel. It was strangely busy at the bus station, which surprised Ernesto for this time of night. Looking like he hadn't slept well in a very long time, Jamie, with scraggly hair and several days' worth of beard growth, was the last off the bus. He carried a duffel bag and grinned as he caught sight of Ernesto.

After he settled into the car, Jamie said, "Glad you made it, my man. And I get to help you watch somebody? Is this a paying gig or just hanging out?"

Ernesto watched the road as he started back toward the motel. "I'd say this is a mix of the two. It turns out the job I'm on has a surveillance on a pretty lady I am currently calling Penny

McMurtry. But there is a local gal at the motel, Tammy, who wants to meet you and take us to the local honky tonks."

"I only brought a couple of pairs of jeans and tee shirts. I don't have any dress suits, Ernesto."

Ernesto laughed and remarked, "Oh, you'll fit right in."

The remainder of the drive back to the hotel, Ernesto updated Jamie on the local job, leaving out the big picture portion and the information from the camera Jamie had sent. Jamie seemed pleased that he may have found something useful to do for the folks he owed. They spoke a little about how they might work together on this job, and then Jamie showered and hit the sheets.

The next morning, after a good night's sleep, Jamie offered to tail Penny to the donut shop and retrieve their breakfast. Jamie sat eating his food and noticed she didn't speak to anyone at all as she ate and read the paper. He noted it wasn't like she was anxious, or waiting, or anything which struck him as unusual female behavior. Penny was really pretty though, with her dark wavy hair. She was attractive without deliberately drawing attention to herself. He watched until she looked almost finished with the paper, and he departed.

Ernesto was propped up with a view of the window, talking on his smart phone as Jamie entered the room. Ernesto nodded at him.

"Juan, you're telling me that Tyler is keeping track of both Jenny, aka Suzy McMurtry, and Mercedes? What happens when they move in different directions? …

"According to the manager of this motel, Penny typically stays a week. …

"Yes, she has been using her cell consistently to order food for delivery. I am monitoring her geo location with the mobile device…

"No, I have not seen it go dark, and I had Jamie write a routine to notify me if it does…

"Yes, Jamie is with me and helping…

"I did explain about the information he sent to us and what we think it might mean…

"Thank you, Juan, I think he would be valuable as well…

"Agreed!"

Ernesto disconnected the call and looked at Jamie. Then he grinned a little and said, "How is our little beauty doing this morning?"

"She was doing exactly like your notes said. Definitely a creature of habit, budrow. While you were talking to Juan, she reentered her room and if she is true to form will go to the pool shortly. Can't say as I'd mind watching that. She dresses to be ignored, but I suspect there are some fine curves on her."

Ernesto nodded then stood to refill his coffee as he suggested, "Jamie, how'd you like to call me boss instead of budrow and come work for us? The work is varied, pay is good, and the team is a fun, diverse group. We could consider this an in-training exercise, which would allow me to fill you in on additional details."

Jamie's surprised yet doubtful look was not what Ernesto expected. He seemed about to turn and walk away when instead he asked, "Even after all my mess-ups, you and Juan want me on the team? Really?"

Ernesto smiled and reassured, "Yep, you have some great talent and experience the rest of us don't have. The things you don't know, we can teach you. Of course, you'd have to slow down on the independent wheeling and dealing, though that skill applied correctly is one Juan mentioned was as valuable as your programming skills."

Jamie grinned and nodded acceptance when Penny placed another call to a number not used since they started monitoring. Jamie reached for the laptop and did a quick search to find out who she was calling.

Jamie showed the location to Ernesto and then commented, "I think we have a change in the pattern, and it's time to pack up."

Ernesto decided not to check out of the motel. He had a few days remaining on the prepaid week. They left by the back stairs with their belongings, just in case, and loaded up the car. Ernesto pulled it around where they could observe the front of the motel. It was mid-week so there was little activity, until two vehicles pulled up. A man with slacks and green shirt purposefully walked into the motel office, stayed for a few minutes, then walked out and left in the other car. Jamie looked up the license plates and noted the owner of the vehicle, per the registration.

Several minutes later, Penny walked to the motel office with her satchel and purse in hand, got into the vehicle left by the man, adjusted the settings, and turned the car toward the exit and the freeway marked I-45. Ernesto was glad he'd filled the tank on the way back to the motel after picking up Jamie.

They followed at a discreet distance using a few cars for separation. Ernesto briefed his new team member on what had unfolded so far in Tyler's and his assignment. He discussed how they had separated to follow their two characters and all the additional details of their efforts to date. Ernesto had Jamie log in and look at the data the collective team had assembled to possibly gain some fresh perspective. As the miles stretched out, they talked about how all the different areas might be interrelated. After Jamie had a chance to look at the pictures from the camera and the rest taken by the working teams, they began to speculate on how the actual pictures from the nuclear exhibit might fit into the puzzle.

Jamie reflected out loud after he'd completed his review. "Looks like someone figured out the fundamental flaw of the digital age. Just don't use it and your communications won't be compromised. After all my efforts to be fluent in the digital world, here I am up against the misfit of our information age, the analog adversary."

Ernesto nodded without comment.

CHAPTER THIRTY-FIVE

It's About Damn Time

George had steadily kept track of the geo-locator signal before he boarded the flight from Singapore to Sakaiminato, Japan. He wanted to get settled at least a day before the tanker was expected to arrive. Through multiple flights and half a day of total travel, George continually checked the geo-locator before each departure and after arrival. He opted to carry on all his luggage due to the multiple airplane changes. The first flight to Tokyo was the longest, and the service on the commercial flight was impeccable in First Class. He'd eaten and enjoyed a dreamless rest during the flight.

The next two hops were a bit more interesting with older aircrafts and local travelers. These legs of the trip had a single class of seating, and he'd been seated next to someone's grandmother on the first leg and a teen with very loud music on the second. He was actually amazed that it only took two flight changes for a total of a single day to make the trip. He was able to take a taxi and secure his reserved room at the Sakaiminato Marina Hotel. He had wanted to get something relatively close to the docks with accommodations Summit would appreciate after living on a tanker for over a week.

After checking in, he turned on the geo-locator, expecting the tanker to be within sight of Japan, only to discover there was no signal. He immediately phoned Juan to make certain his signal was being transmitted correctly, while his stomach churned and his anxiety tripled.

Juan answered, "George, did you finally make it to the Sakaiminato hotel? I expected you to call hours ago." George replied, "The flight delays were longer than anticipated, but I am here and at the hotel. The problem is the tanker is not, and I don't show a signal."

Juan's tone changed to concern as he replied, "Uh oh. Let me check for you, George. I have been working on some other issues and really thought this was tracking just fine. Don't panic yet!"

George mumbled, "Too late!"

Only the sounds of fingers running a keyboard was heard for what seemed like hours. Finally, Juan replied, "George, I have the signal showing he is about a day out of Sakaiminato, maybe a little less. You may need to reset your device. All of the flight changes may have confused the signal, but my signal seems strong. Not certain why the time at sea lengthened from the original timing. I can't see any weather issues for the last two weeks in that region, but I am certain Summit, if the criteria he outlined was good, is en route."

George breathed a sigh of relief as the signal did appear to him after rebooting the tracking program. George admitted, "Sorry to bother you, Juan. I should have tried that first. This has been one crazy trip so far."

Juan agreed, "I suspect it will only get crazier. I loaded up some information to our case file you might want to familiarize yourself with, in case you find something similar. New photos and new players. Mercedes is planning to get totally on the inside track, though the actual start date has yet to be confirmed.

"Let me know when Summit arrives, and we can set up a call to debrief."

"Sure thing, Juan."

George went down to the docks and noted all the ships due to arrive over the next three days were displayed on a board near the dock. The hotel concierge had indicated this was the practice to help provide locals with information on potential work loading or unloading the ships. He said it had been that way for a very long time, as his family had worked the docks in addition to having a couple of fishing vessels of their own. From that point on, outside of a quick meal or two in the hotel, George stayed in his room and monitored the signal presumably coming from Summit. He planned to go to the docks in the morning about the time the tanker should be docking.

George had been reviewing the information on the team's cloud file, looking for connections. The dragon jewelry had been an interesting find and did seem quite relevant. Mercedes' apparent infiltration would likely provide the best intel, though having Tyler watching two females seemed a challenge. He also looked forward to meeting the newest member of the team, Jamie. He'd heard about some of his background, but not enough to feel he knew the man. He made his updates and noted some opinions or considerations that he'd garnered from the information.

George rechecked the tanker location once more and calcu-lated the time for docking. Then he fell asleep and experienced some of the most outlandish nightmares he'd had since being on special ops patrol. The only difference was the members of his unit were his current teammates, and nothing went right. He woke in a panic after Mercedes was blown up, giving him a lousy start to his day. He could barely hold coffee in his stomach as he headed toward the dock. With the night filled with doom and destruction, he really wanted to see his teammate disembark, so they could move on.

The dock was busy with lots of workers either moving cargo or trying to get hired on to assist with the next ship. George kept his distance and took everything in. He saw the tanker, not too far out, making its way toward the pier it was assigned. He noted that additional people were gathering at the docks, including possible families there to greet the ships.

The tanker maneuvered into place, and the gangway was lowered. A couple dozen men from the tanker walked down the gangway and then waited on the pier, almost in line. Then he watched as Summit slowly made his way down the gangway moving his hands and his lips like he was performing a soliloquy. The men gathered stared intently at Summit, taking in every word and gesture. George noted the captain made his way off the ship and walked in the opposite direction from the men lined up. A lady approached the captain, and he briefly spoke to her. George tried to visually follow her to see if he could get a direction when she vanished into the crowd. He'd only had the presence of mind to take a few photos of the interaction.

His focus returned to Summit passing slowly by the men in line. When Summit reached the end of the line, he faced toward the east and went to his knees. The men followed suit, and for the next thirty minutes the prayers of Summit the Teacher were heard across the docks as the remainder of the crowd provided quiet for the ceremony. It was a mixture of piety and showmanship that had the men and the crowd totally engaged in the ceremony. Summit ended and rose, as did the men. He bid them farewell and slowly walked toward George. He made no contact as he passed George, but he heard the hotel name George murmured.

George quickly made his way to the hotel and watched Summit until he melted into the shadows. George kept walking until he reached where the parking garage area headed into the shadows. George continued but kept to the shadows on the side. He figured Summit had ducked behind one of the pillars and was rewarded when his teammate emerged without the robes and headdress on, carrying a tightly packaged bundle under his arm. Summit walked a bit further, until George appeared next to his side.

George quietly said, "No one is in here, and you were not followed. There are some back stairs just over here where we can go to our room unseen."

Summit nodded and they moved quickly up the stairs. The room George had secured was only a few doors down from the stairs, and no one was present on the floor. He opened the door to the suite, and Summit rushed into the bathroom and closed the door. The next sound was the water running in the shower. George knew it would be a while and took him some clean clothes which he set on the counter along with an iron and spray starch. George then sent a text to Juan.

Summit is here. Will call you soon with the update.

Juan responded quickly.

Good, get a flight booked to Turkey to find the furniture source. Post Summit's update from the airport.

Summit finally emerged clean shaven, freshly dressed in starched clothes, and hair combed. It looked like he'd even trimmed it. Summit saw the lavish foods George had ordered via room service and raced over to the chair without a word.

George let him eat for a few minutes and then demanded, "What the hell happened? You're two days late."

Summit looked at him like a lost brother and somberly announced, "You are not going to believe it, but that tanker made an unscheduled stop at Hungnam, North Korea. They knew the captain. It was not his first visit by any means. The crew unloaded the furniture marked crates, and the weapons were distributed to the soldiers on the dock there. The head of the greeting party, who must have been a ranking officer, provided a few bottles of local wine to the captain, then we left.

"It was the strangest experience! The men made certain I acted as if nothing was unusual about the docking and cargo unloading. I, of course, assured them it was not my business and went into a session from the Qur'an. I must admit I was suddenly very scared I would be lost in this bleak place no one will claim."

George was astonished. Of all the things he had thought might be the reason for the tanker delay, that hadn't made it to the list. "Summit, this is huge. Obviously, this is something far bigger than we thought.

"Eat up! We need to head to the airport and make our way to Turkey to see if we can tie up some loose ends. I will help you write up your report and fill you in on what has been going on since you left.

"Glad you made it, Summit. Your plan was a success."

CHAPTER THIRTY-SIX

Highway to Somewhere

Jamie commented, "I've never been to Texas, but it seems to just continue on. How long until we reach the Gulf?"

Ernesto laughed and replied, "It is a very large state, and we are nearly out of gas. I hope she is keeping an eye on her gauge. She has to be getting low, even if it was dropped off full to her at the motel."

Jamie said, "There are a lot of big trucks on this road. Many more trucks than cars, in my opinion. The transport of goods within the U.S. is often done by trucks, as I understand it."

Ernesto nodded and then added, "Yes, and each kind of truck has markings if they are transporting something that is kept cold, or dangerous, or even gas to fill up the stations we've passed. I sure hope she stops soon, or we're going to have to stop to avoid pushing this to a station. I think we're running on fumes; the low gas light has been on so long."

"Look! She's pulling off at the next exit," Jamie informed. "And she's pulling into one of those huge truck stop places. I hear these drivers stop to rest, eat, and even shower. There is lots of traffic, so hopefully she won't spot us following her."

There must have been close to thirty pumps on one side of the station for passenger vehicles and then fifteen longer pump areas offering diesel for the transport trucks. Both of them added the ball caps Ernesto had picked up, supporting the local football favorite. Jamie took in all the different types of trucks, like a kid that just wanted to play with his toy cars. Ernesto chuckled at the amazed look on Jamie's face as he also kept one eye on Penny while she pumped her gas. Over the course of her drive, she had let her hair down and added a shirt. When she turned a bit to respond to another motorist who asked some sort of question, he spotted the dragon necklace.

Ernesto asked, "Jamie, see if you can catch her when she turns around. I think she's added some jewelry which may indicate some sort of a meet, now or soon. I don't think it was the motorist. He looked like he was hitting on a pretty lady, nothing more."

While Ernesto topped off the tank, Jamie took a few photos and nodded to indicate he'd accomplished the goal. They got into the car and pulled out of the way where they could readily observe. Penny finished a few minutes later and cleaned off her windows too. She started up her car, but instead of taking off back down the road, she circled to the back of the station where the truckers were lined up for short-term and long-term stays. She lined up next to a truck with some chemical symbols that suggested dangerous and hazardous materials on board. Jamie took as many shots of her and the truck as he dared.

Penny exited the car and walked into the station. They decided not to follow her, but with the large glass windows they easily tracked her path. She picked up a couple of sodas, some chips, and must have ordered something from the deli. She waited.

Jamie commented, "I sure would like a fresh sandwich myself. How about you, Ernesto?"

Ernesto lamented, "Yeah, but the second we do she'll spot us and take off, or we'll lose her. We have enough in the ice chest. You need to go run to the men's room and hurry back, so I can as well. I don't think we're done driving yet."

Jamie took off for the side door as Ernesto kept an eye on his target. A few minutes later the guy behind the counter handed her a wrapped package and she stood in line to pay. She sauntered back toward her car, set her food items on the trunk, and leaned back, facing the open parking spaces behind her. Not seeming to be in a hurry in the least, she unwrapped her sandwich and ate her modest meal. Jamie returned and Ernesto made a hasty retreat inside. He'd decided to pick up some of the ready-made sandwiches he saw on the way in. He felt confident she was waiting for something or someone.

Five minutes later he headed back and noticed Jamie was covertly taking pictures. He looked over and saw another truck had pulled up in the short time he'd been gone. Two men walked, one with a two-wheeler, to the back end of the truck she'd originally parked near. She turned and walked a bit closer toward the main store of the station and kept a close eye on the crowd inside.

Ernesto finally reached Jamie and asked, "How's it going, my lad?"

Without taking his eyes off the targets, he continued to take photos and replied, "Another truck showed up. These two guys got out and walked up to Penny. She had a one-sided conversation for just under two minutes, and they scampered back to their truck and started what you are seeing. Honestly, it was like she was issuing orders of some sort. They said nothing, and it looks like she is watching out for the owner of the first truck."

The guys had somehow opened the rear of their target truck and lowered something on the back end in a practiced, methodical manner. A tall man with a worn, black cowboy hat had approached the door, still speaking to another fellow who stopped at the register for another purchase. Penny quickly moved in the direction of the convenience store, loosening her top buttons on her shirt and strutting as she got closer. Before the man in the cowboy hat could finish his conversation, she had pulled open the door and blocked his path.

Penny was easy on the eyes, and Ernesto had seen her smile before. The man was mesmerized and checked her out from one end to the other. He must have made some sort of comment, and she tucked her arm into his and pulled him back in toward the deli. As they turned, she looked at him like he was the man of her dreams.

Jamie quietly snickered and said, "She's good. He never saw it coming. I'll bet she keeps him talking until she figures they are finished loading. Her phone is totally not signaling, so this must be the task she came to complete."

Ernesto replied, "Yes, and these guys are almost done. They're moving at least two containers marked with radioactive symbols to their truck and unless I'm mistaken, they put two bogus containers in their place. I think we need to stay with both the truck and Penny, though I am not certain how we divide and conquer in this instance."

Jamie suggested, "After they are finished, what do you think will happen? I would guess the guys would go one way, and Penny would return to the motel."

Ernesto mulled that over for a minute and replied, "That could happen, or she could go someplace else and fly home. She seemed to take all her belongings from the room and spent some time in the motel office. We picked her up in New York originally. Perhaps that is where she will head, or she might have another assignment and could go anywhere."

Jamie had his hands flying over the laptop and after several minutes of searching grinned and said, "A valid point, budrow, valid point. You said her last name at the motel was McMurtry, right?"

"Yep."

"There is a Corinth McMurtry scheduled on a flight late this evening out of Houston International to New York La Guardia." Jamie's fingers continued to search for different things in rapid succession.

Meanwhile Ernesto said, "That does answer one question. Good job!

"Now it makes sense for me to follow the tanker, and you to follow the pretty lady back to New York and track her next destination. The only issue is …"

Jamie interrupted, "There is a rental car company relatively close that will drop a car within two hours, maybe sooner. There are also limousine services available to take you anywhere. Oh," Jamie grinned, "and if you give me your credit card, I can confirm a seat on the flight she is scheduled for, but only First Class is open."

Ernesto handed his card over and laughed, "Remember what I said, lad, and no more cowboy stuff. Take that card with you. I'll get it back later. I think the limo would be fitting. Now get out. These guys are about buttoned up, and I want to stay with them."

Jamie grinned and promised, "I'll stay with her. You take care and keep in touch."

Marge planned to start the call with Chung-Ho from a point of strength. She had aligned the shipments so they would be willing to not only pay a bit more, but also give her the few extra weeks needed for the shipment to reach them. She was well aware that a misstep on this portion of the negotiation would open the door to a competitor, or worse, to Mike taking over the negotiation. Mike had insisted on being bridged into the conversation.

She'd considered returning to London for a look at the office, but with the audit she decided this course of action was more suitable. Plus, if she needed to mute or disconnect him, she had that control.

The clock ticked slowly toward the appointed time, and she had her agenda completed. She dialed into the conference bridge, and Mike joined a few moments later. Finally, with the expected ten-minute delay, something Chung-Ho had always done to clarify that she'd wait on him, he joined the call.

Marge greeted with a tone of deference, "Comrade, so grateful you could join this call for our status update. How are you and your family fairing, sir?"

Chung-Ho waited a moment, then replied, "We are doing fine and making progress toward our place in the world."

His refusal to ever thank her for the efforts ePETRO did on his behalf always rankled her, but she swallowed that bitter annoyance and replied, "Good to know you are making progress. I heard in the news that the other world leaders were beginning to listen more closely to what your leaders publicly offered. I am certain it won't be long before you are on equal footing with those leaders. We here at ePETRO are doing our part to help support those efforts.

"Which reminds me, I hope the recent shipments met favorably with the expectations of the military heads and perhaps we even surprised them with a few extra items provided in the shipment."

Mike provided a desk-to-desk instant message (IM) with a thumbs up to her dialogue and a reminder that additional funds would be appreciated with the shipment arriving within the week with more furniture. She had placed his line on mute so that he could not inadvertently comment, but her IM window was up to show she and he were close partners.

Chung-Ho acknowledged, "Yes, the general who received those items found them to be much more state-of-the-art in design and range. These are different than our normal stock, but we are working on reproducing them here as we speak."

Marge smiled to herself and replied, "Good. I can get more of this grade of ordnance and make some available on the next shipment, but the costs are higher than the other. Costs would increase by at least sixty-five percent if you want them included with the upcoming shipment."

She paused for effect. The deference to his position and rank as well as the drawn-out negotiations was an area she truly excelled at. Mike was burning up the IM window telling her the steps and to hurry before he went to another subject, but Marge ignored his IM comments. Marge had not fooled herself into thinking the North Korean males had any more respect for her than other business leaders she successfully worked with. They did, however, defer to a degree based on her age and experience in the business. Chung-Ho and she had met in person a couple of times and agreed neither of them could be trifled with. Chung-He, his heir apparent, was not quite the same, although Chung-Ho was teaching him. She was aware that Chung-He had studied some in the West, and she knew he was also in the background offering thoughts and opinions. Like most Asians in business, age had some relevance over gender.

Marge continued, "If you do not believe that is a price increase you can deal with at this time, I do have another buyer in the region interested in these items."

Chung-Ho remarked, "I did not mean to draw out my response. I was merely calculating if I would be able to absorb the outrageous increase, even for such a valuable weapon. I believe that by the time your next tanker arrives, the additional funds will be available. If not, I will advise you before they drop anchor."

Marge wanted to interject the possible delivery of the key product, but not with Mike on the line. She reached over and disconnected his line, then quickly said, "Comrade, I am fine with that arrangement. I would however remind you that the other item on your list is also being secured and will be in your hands within a month. I hope your ability to deal with the 238 is in position. I know the original quantity was miniscule compared to your expectations. That will be corrected within the month."

Mike's call came back in, and Marge added it and immediately muted the line as well. Mike had been sending messages via IM to alert her the line had been interrupted but that he would rejoin. She had messaged back apologies, hurry and rejoin, and that she did not know what had happened.

Chung-Ho sighed and then said, "Madam, I think we have no problems with the additional funds for the ordnance coming to our port along with the oil. We are making strides on using more advanced ways of powering some of the key infrastructure. My Chung-He is seeing to it personally. Keep me advised on the shipments, madam."

He abruptly disconnected. Marge smiled. Mike sent a thumbs up message.

CHAPTER THIRTY-SEVEN

Trial by Fire

Brayson seemed a bit distracted as he used his macro lens to get the close-up photo of the next female showing up at what he was now calling the *Photograph Outpost Catering Exclusively to Babes and Dragons,* or POCÉBAD activity. He smirked at the POCÉBAD acronym which got him thinking about building a mobile app for it so others could wander around aimlessly in the forested areas of Central America, staring at the output of a smart phone.

Brayson then gave a dejected sigh as he saw yet another vehicle approaching the data center compound. He quietly commented to himself, "Boy, what I wouldn't do to trade this photo session for some real action. I'd better get this one photographed and uploaded so the others can review it too. I wonder what Mercedes is doing? It's quiet around here without her nagging at me. Hmmm…if I were somebody else analyzing those statements, I would suggest that I miss her. Well, not really miss her, but prefer the verbal fencing we always seem to engage in. Oh great, just what I need! Another impossible female that has been imprinted on my subconscious! The next thing you know I'll be trying to get a date with the Mona Lisa!"

Chiding himself, he counseled, "Come on, Brayson, let's stay focused on getting these AIMs photographed.

"Hey, wait a minute! I think I've already photographed her." Paging back through his digital pictures, he stopped on one from four days earlier and stated, "Yep, I was right. There she is. Now, if we are picking up the same females…"

Brayson picked up his smart phone and quickly established a link between the digital camera and the Wi-Fi network he was sponging connectivity from and uploaded the photos. His text to Juan read:

> Juan, run these through the computer system to see if they are the same. If true, then maybe we have the full inventory of AIMs and I can move on.

Juan's return text stated:

> You need to hold the course for the time being. Besides, Mercedes has Tyler watching her back and can take care of herself. I know stakeouts are like a chartered air flight to a pilot. Hours of boredom only interrupted by just a few minutes of panic and terror called take-off and landing. One more day, then let's get you on the way.

Brayson clucked his tongue and in an annoyed tone bemoaned, "The only thing worse than a boss that doesn't understand you, is one who does."

The morning had a lazy start to it, but Mercedes forced herself to get up anyway. While lingering over her second cup of coffee, she received a text message that read:

> Mercedes, we have a short window of opportunity to do a trial run in your new role. Quickly meet me at the plaza so we can get started. I need you there in 16 minutes so we can meet all the deadlines. Steven.

Spilling her coffee, Mercedes jumped up and quickly sent a text to Tyler, alerting him of the new fire drill. A sense of uneasiness overcame her as she typed out a quick message. As soon as it was sent, she dashed to put on street clothes and the dragon necklace.

Tyler quickly read the text from Mercedes indicating that her first trial with Steven Christopher had been called to start in sixteen minutes. Not able to make the rendezvous schedule, Tyler asked that she stall Steven until he could get into place. Mercedes sent a text back saying:

Let me see what I can do.

Moving as quickly as he could to get to the target destination, Tyler raced to get into position so he could observe Mercedes and Steven without being seen. The rush to get to her location had put Tyler off his game. He made the destination out of breath but was able to visually identify both Mercedes and Steven where they seemed to be loitering. He started to relax a little as he made like a tourist, taking selfies with his phone in the area they were in. It didn't change the outcome of things.

Two Middle Eastern men in military grade jackets moved up close on either side of Tyler before he could react. He quickly felt their weapons sticking him in the ribs as one in a low voice announced, "If you move to escape, we will shoot. Move to alert her, we will shoot. We will now walk to the SUV parked over at the curb. Remember, if you do anything…"

Tyler, now extremely annoyed with them and himself, interjected, "Yeah, I know, you will shoot."

The two men stopped at the side of the SUV and turned toward where Mercedes and Steven were. They waved to Steven briefly then trundled Tyler into the vehicle. Tyler just had enough time to see Steven pointing them out to a now alarmed Mercedes before a black bag was pulled over his head. Now he knew that they had both been compromised, and he was going to be used as leverage in making Mercedes do Steven's bidding. Or worse.

Tyler felt sick at having let her down and falling into these people's hands, but it didn't last long. They clubbed him hard as they shoved him in, knocking him unconscious.

In full view of Steven and Mercedes, the two thugs took Tyler's phone and dropped it on the pavement in front of the rear wheel where it was sure to be crushed upon leaving.

Mercedes whipped her head around to face a cool, collected Steven who sternly asked, "Any idea why he was following you? And by following you, I mean following me."

Mercedes struggled to keep from trembling and haltingly asked, "Why are you accusing me of being followed? I don't know who that was or what your game is, buddy. Am I starting a trial engagement, or are you going to display some more unfounded paranoia? It's not like I haven't EVER been followed by a male."

Still in his icy mode, Steven asked, "If you don't know him, then you won't have any problem with what happens to this photo-taking pizza deliverer, correct? If that's the case, I guess we can simply chalk it up to him having a fixation on females that are in my employment. We will see to it that he does not trouble you again. We take security for our people very seriously. You must take our interests to heart to be on the team."

It was now Mercedes' turn to feel sick.

Steven smiled an icy smile and said, "Time to start your training, my dear."

CHAPTER THIRTY-EIGHT

Winners at Losing

Christopher took the quick train to meet with Marge. "We have all of our AIMs fully engaged in operations on just about every continent. In fact, we have more required activity so I am interviewing potential AIMs to obtain more capacity. The DEATACs operation is at full capacity in accordance with your plans, madam.

"I'm unclear on these new instructions concerning the uranium. I have been queried by Mr. Patrick for more details. I sidestepped his questions because I assumed you are withholding those details from him for a reason. However, may I be privy to those plans so I can facilitate or offer better disinformation?"

Over the length of their relationship, Steven had speculated on which of his attributes was the erotic driver for Marge, his business-like iciness or his prosthetic arm. She continued to sit close enough to him at their usual meeting table so she could stroke the artificial appendage almost to distraction. Anyone with normal human emotions would have been undone by the affectionate touching she continued to provide to something that was artificial. She brazenly smiled at him, knowing he couldn't feel anything, but then neither could she.

After a last stroke, Marge raised her stare to look Christopher in the eyes and stated, "The North Koreans not only want oil but uranium as a part of their bargaining position on the world stage. We are transporters of goods from suppliers to buyers, and the NKs are our buyers. Not many people like them and not many people deal with them, which creates a void in the supply chain. We fill that void, but not all governments share our enthusiasm for the supply/demand model for uranium.

"To protect my…associates, I don't burden them with unnecessary details that might put them in the cross hairs with my overall vision for our business model. This also prevents any mishap if they're asked…sorry, if they are *ordered* to testify. People can't comment on what they don't know. Consider that I'm protecting Mike from some inconsequential business details. I keep the holistic picture of the business, and Mike focuses on the oil aspects, which are his strengths."

Christopher nodded and said, "Understood, madam. A very commendable attitude to those that work for you. It is easy to see why you are held in such high regard by Mr. Patrick."

Unsure if the comment was sarcastic, but unwilling to challenge the statement, Marge continued, "Yes, of course. In any event, I appreciate the interception and redirection of the shipment to Houston for transport on one of our ships. They are waiting, and I need to make sure that the new cargo is discreetly loaded and that the tanker sets sail as soon as possible."

Christopher then asked, "May I know if the ePETRO oil tanker will be allowed through the Panama Canal with changes to their cargo manifest?"

Marge wrinkled her face at the question but politely offered, "You see, this is yet another area of concern that I don't want our people to have to deal with. They have too much paperwork to deal with, it hardly seems fair to burden them further with trifling details. Now your AIMs are how we keep everything nice and tidy from a transaction perspective. Goods are picked up, monies are discreetly awarded, and everyone gets what they want. Isn't commerce wonderful?"

Christopher commented, "I can see where the provisional governments in each location our ships dock might not subscribe to this type of commerce, but I do see the wisdom in this approach, madam. May I know the destination of the oil tanker? I don't believe you would order the tanker to head straight for North Korea, so it makes sense to first dock at a country that subscribes to our brand of commerce, for a fee of course."

Marge smiled and offered, "Christopher, you are a quick study indeed. Almost anything can be had for a fee. I need the tanker to make a quick stop in the Philippines before heading to Hungnam, North Korea. And yes, we will need to make some campaign contributions while in the Philippines before the tanker can continue. We do have legitimate oil deliveries to make there.

"The tanker will then travel to NK where we will unload oil there at Hungnam, as well as the uranium they have been waiting for. I won't have an AIM there due to visa delays to that area. We'll complete the funds transfer in Hong Kong as usual. Understood?"

Christopher nodded and said, "Understood. She will meet their contact at the usual rendezvous so we can receive our payment, correct?"

Marge smiled and, taking her hand to smooth back Christopher's hair over his ear though it was too short to warrant it, responded, "Correct. Now once we have this project in the bag, as the Brits would say, we really must have that drink together and celebrate. Agreed?"

Without the slightest amount of emotion, Christopher acknowledged, "Agreed, madam. Now I must be going to begin training my new hire. Good day, madam."

After Christopher left, Marge smiled wistfully and remarked to no one in particular, "Good day to you too."

Trying not to be rattled by the penetrating question, Mercedes coolly answered, "I had made a mistake. After a couple of failed relationships with some low value men, I was determined to travel south and just be by myself. You know, get away from it all and not be pestered. I can take care of myself, or so I thought. I get on this train in Mexico, but I didn't pay for a premium seat, figuring I could save a few pesos by riding back in the non-tourist section. Big mistake.

"As it happens, a bunch of Mexican soldiers are also in the same section, and even though it was a hot day, well, I shouldn't have worn that tank top. It wasn't long before they decide that I'm back there to be used as shared property by their platoon. I'm putting up a fairly good fight for almost fifteen seconds and hollering for help from anybody on a moving train. This big American boy, the one you saw me with, stuck his head into our car to see what was up, thankfully. Well, long story short, since he was a strong strapping lad, several Mexican soldiers got off the train while it was moving, and I didn't need to surrender anything to them. Then I told you he was my cousin, because that's about how much he meant to me in the end."

Steven almost smiled as he realized, "So your shining knight and benefactor became your escort from then on?"

Mercedes gave a sigh and said, "Yeah, and with that was the implied demand that I offer up exactly what the Mexican troops wanted to take over my protests. Anyway, it wasn't a bad trade, just not what I wanted to sign up for. He wanted me to come home with him, and I didn't want to, so I said goodbye to him at the Panama airport, then took another flight out in case he came back to debate it with me. Like I said, I'm in it for the money and that's all. Can you tell me the job now, or are you going to ride me again about that lost puppy that was following me?"

Steven, now back under control of his business persona, responded, "I'm not sure I understand your outlook on life, but

I can certainly understand why you easily attract male attention. Now in our line of work that will be an undesirable attribute, so I'm going insist you wear a burka to help cloak some of that female charm that apparently seeps out when you aren't looking."

"I have a modest trial run that will include working with a few other individuals so we can see how you carry out your assignment. Sound good?"

Mercedes flared a little bit and said, "Hey, wait a minute! I don't wanna dress like a Muslim piece of property! I'm trying to get out of being owned by some male, and you are setting me up to do it in another culture! What kind of gig is this?"

Moderately amused, Steven responded, "The gig, madam, is to work disguised so as not to attract attention. The work assignment you are to perform must not attract undue attention if it is to be successful. Now are you in or out?"

Mercedes feigned that she was suppressing her annoyance and after a few moments said, "Alright, I'm in and on your terms. What do I need to do, and how much are we talking about?"

Steven finally smiled and handed her a sealed envelope.

Mercedes hefted the envelope, tucked it into her fanny pack, nodded with a slight smile and said, "I will be here tomorrow, then."

With a puzzled look on his face he asked, "Aren't you going to look inside? What if they are all dollar bills?"

Smiling, Mercedes turned and said, "If they are all ones, then this is the last time we see each other. If they are all tens, then it will all be spent before midnight, and I'll keep looking for a place to punch a timecard. If they are all 100's, then I'll see you tomorrow."

As Mercedes turned to leave, Steven called, "What if they are all $1000 bills?"

Mercedes offered a wry smile and responded, "Then I'll bring a friend."

Better Watercooler Relationships

Dabir had worked so hard during the week as he responded to each of the auditor's requests. He knew the information the auditors received was perhaps not quite current with operations. He had been so stuck between his desk and the copy machine that he had run home every night to work out and get the kinks out of his body. At least he'd had the satisfaction in seeing that Jackeline had no more relief than he did. The difference was that Laurie hadn't asked him to work overtime, but Jackeline had last night.

Laurie was back and forth from one area to another. Every time Dabir went to the copy machine to fill another request, he looked into Laurie's office. On at least two occasions she had left some screens open where he garnered a little more data and background. He really wanted untethered access to the backend systems so he could copy information, but it looked like that would have to wait until after the audit was completed. He didn't think that Jackeline had access to those areas, but it appeared that greater trust was growing between the two females and it irked him.

Laurie had been so busy with the auditors and answering questions that she started to push more responsibility on Jackeline. Though Laurie missed drooling over Dabir, Jackeline had demonstrated not only a willingness to take on new tasks and learn, but she was quick and accurate. She'd been grateful for the cheerful help, and especially for the perfect latte she frequently found on her desk in the morning or handed to her when Jackeline returned from afternoon break. Jackeline was becoming the sister she'd never had, yet always wanted. Maybe in a couple of weeks when the dust settled, Laurie could introduce her to the others she worked for and share the work as well as the extra income it produced. On the few occasions when they had shared a drink after work, Jackeline had alluded to the need to work and earn her keep.

Mike was becoming increasingly demanding and asked her to specifically move some funds between several accounts after work. Laurie knew these were special accounts reserved for his use, but per her primary directive she memorized each and every transaction so it could be related when needed. She had not been called upon to take any trips, which was very helpful during this audit. It had not gone unnoticed by Laurie that the parameters of the audit had shifted a couple of times as if being redirected based on information found, almost like a complex puzzle of some sort. But that was Mike's problem, not hers.

It was growing late in the afternoon when Laurie decided she needed a break. It just so happened that Jackeline stopped by her office and asked to accompany her for a latte. Laurie agreed, and they took the elevator to the ground floor.

Laurie commented, "I am so glad you asked me to come with you. I feel like I haven't been outside during the day for months rather than just a week. I guess working all last weekend didn't help."

They entered the line in the coffee bar and glanced at the menu. The fresh scones looked amazing and Laurie eyed the one with strawberries, while JAC seemed to almost ignore the choices. She really watched the empty calories since the twins had been born and felt her heartstrings tug at being gone so long.

JAC replied, "I'm right there with you, though I haven't worked the overtime you have. Do you need me again tonight? I don't mind helping, I have nothing else going on."

Laurie held up her finger while she placed the order for her latte and added the scone to the order. "Jackeline, order for yourself, my treat this time. And yes, if you can work tonight, that's great."

JAC ordered a tea and skipped the scone with a quick prayer for Juan and the twins. "I'm good with just tea right now, thank you."

They walked back toward the office and at JAC's suggestion decided to take the stairs up. They talked about several items of work, and JAC gently probed about taking on some additional responsibilities to give Laurie a break. Her willingness to help Laurie was so touching.

Laurie remarked, "You know, you are really taking on a great deal. I like being able to count on you completing your tasks quickly and near perfectly. Tonight, I will show you a few of the back-office files and see how you do, alright?"

They opened the door to the office, not noticing Dabir standing in the shadowy alcove. He looked almost angry at the conversation he'd just overheard.

Dabir was angry when he returned to his desk and even angrier when Laurie said she would not need his help that evening. She had, however, softened the blow when she reminded him that after this audit was finished, she wanted to help him work with some of the back-office files, especially since Mike seemed to increasingly rely upon his help.

He stopped on the way home to get some fish and chips along with a bottle of fine wine. He was beginning to see Jackeline in a new light, as a friend and confidante to Laurie. Perhaps he had been looking at a way into the information from the wrong perspective. He needed to think about the short and long-term implications of a change in direction.

The moment he opened the door to his flat he knew someone was there. The air smelled and felt very different. He wasn't worried when he identified the scent.

Dabir moved toward the kitchen and turned on the light, then said, "Achmet, it is an honor that you would visit me."

Achmet replied, "I see you still have the senses you were taught. Your uncle sends his greetings and hopes you are making do here in London. I think by the looks of this place you are doing well. Is that what I should relate to Kashan?"

Dabir opened the wine and poured two glasses. He handed one to Achmet and responded, "Please tell my Uncle I am fine and look forward to continuing to serve his interests."

Achmet hesitated to take the wine but then smirked and said, "When in the land of the infidels, behave as one!"

Dabir smiled and agreed, "Yes of course. Once we return to our normal ways of Islam, we will not have such access to this corruptible drink that compromises the faithful."

Dabir and Achmet sat and watched as the lights flickered on, softened by the fog. They sipped the fine wine, and Dabir relayed all he had learned so far. He talked about some of the files he had retrieved and the key people at ePETRO he had met with, along with impressions of their strengths and weaknesses. Achmet was impressed with the knowledge of the business Dabir shared and how he indeed had grown in the last year into a mature man able to take on additional responsibility, though a bit spoiled by Western ways.

Achmet suggested they meet again soon, and perhaps Dabir could find the names he needed for some of the bargaining Kashan desired. As Achmet bid his farewell to return to his undisclosed location, he handed a burner phone to Dabir and requested that additional pictures of people and files be provided.

CHAPTER FORTY

Never Let It Be Said

The museum was busy as expected, which made it relatively easy to move around within the crowds without attracting too much attention, but under the burka head cover Mercedes felt like everyone was looking at her. She had refused to wear the full robes, as she insisted that some western style clothing permitted better blending with the general visitor landscape.

Mercedes had practiced a little before coming to the Smithsonian for her research project. Nevertheless, she felt the stares of men, women, and children alike. It was a sign of the times. Even though she kept her head down and stayed close to the edge of museum areas, she still seemed to attract unwanted attention.

She muttered under her breath with a frustrated tone, "Great! I need to maintain this charade in the hope of helping Tyler. I am being watched on federal cameras, trailed by the jerks who hired me, and sneered at by the non-Muslims! I get one more uppity Western woman asking me why I believe that the contemptable Sharia Law should be obeyed by women everywhere, and I'm gonna choke the living…"

She was annoyed with the ruse she was having to play and, with her head down, she plowed right into another museum patron which only added irritation to her mood. However, once she stepped back to look at the person she had collided with, her heart stopped.

When the man turned around to see who had run into him, she was shocked to be standing face to face with her boyfriend, Jim Hughes, who had no idea what she was doing. Her eyes grew wide with fear and anxiety at bumping into him, of all people, while she was operating undercover. Jim read the situation quite correctly and stopped himself from saying a word or adding his normal affectionate greeting. They had always been attuned to one another when they worked together, which had only improved as lovers. Though he'd not heard from her in a week or so, he hadn't been concerned. She'd always been very self-reliant.

Jim discreetly scanned the area and, bowing slightly with his right hand over his heart, offered, "Peace be with you, my Muslim brethren."

To her great relief Jim did not say anything else and slowly walked away to admire another item on display further away from her.

Trying to get her breathing and heart rate under control, she almost imperceptibly scanned the area to make sure that her tail was not unduly alarmed by the encounter. Then a practiced signal between them indicated that all was fine, and she proceeded on.

Once inside the archives area, she requested the historical documents she had been sent for and waited for the volumes to be brought to her. She managed to get all the volumes over to a quiet area where she could use the digital camera to photograph certain pages. As she was discreetly copying them, she kept a sharp eye out for her tail and anyone else that might be too curious about her actions.

She found it curious that she had been instructed to photograph some pages, but not all in sequence. Mathematical computations and quantum physics theories were the high value targets of this exercise. She had been instructed to only work for an hour and no more with the volumes. She speculated that multiple people coming in making quick copies before leaving was less suspicious than one person coming in and camping out for days. Still, all the high touch requests for the same series of books could make somebody curious, unless there were different volumes at different times.

As she approached the end of the hour, she closed the volumes and gathered them up to take back to the helpdesk. When she looked up and through the bookshelves, she saw Jim watching her through the glass of an ancient tomb on display. She quickly scanned for her tail and not readily seeing him, she shot Jim a longing glance that left no emotion uncommunicated. He smiled slightly and winked at her, knowing that he had said everything he had wanted as well.

As she left the building holding the camera she had been using, she briefly looked up to see Steven Christopher in the van ready to pick her up as planned. She lowered her head and continued to walk in the predetermined direction.

Steven smiled as he turned to the tail that had been assigned to her and remarked, "She was identified by the Feds as we expected. She did good!"

Achmet stared in disbelief at the images of the two women. Dabir, puzzled at Achmet's response, repeated, "Achmet, these are the two Western females that hold the most trust at ePETRO. Mike Patrick has them do everything for him, but I cannot say for sure what all that entails. Mike warned me against any entanglements with Laurie, but nothing was stated about approaching Jackeline. Frankly, Jackeline is more interesting, but far more standoffish than Laurie. And Laurie has the passwords and the keys to the high security areas, so I need to stay engaged with…"

Achmet interrupted Dabir's monolog. "The raven-haired one you call Jackeline. That is a false identity. I have seen her before, and now I suspect a ruse, a trick is in play here at ePETRO."

Dabir, now caught between his loyalty to Achmet and Kashan and his growing desire to bed Jackeline, placated, "Give me until the end of the audit to find the truth of it. Any disruption in the workflow of the audit will derail our progress. Let me get Laurie to allow me access to the restricted files.

"Understand that the auditors should be completed with their work tomorrow, and our efforts will warrant a celebration of sorts. I will invite both to a celebratory drink that Laurie most assuredly won't turn down, and then together we can insist that Jackeline must accompany us.

"We can capture them Friday after work and take both of them to a place for questioning. We will have two full days to extract the information you need to either confirm or deny this Jackeline is not who she appears to be at ePETRO. She is very skilled in office procedure and well-liked by the staff."

Achmet was about to protest the delay when Dabir added, "Taking them now will only ruin what I have built here so far. Please, my uncle's trusted advisor, we have come too far to be impatient now. Just a little longer, then we can hunt for the truth."

Relenting from his position, Achmet refocused on Dabir's eyes and said, "You have the wisdom of your Uncle Kashan. It should not be said I have no patience. We shall make it so."

CHAPTER FORTY-ONE

The City Bridging
Two Continents

George stopped at the check-in counter and picked up the tickets. Summit met him at security, and they started the tedious process of passing through customs. In general, Japan was reasonably efficient with their process, and they ended up at their departure gate with time to spare. It appeared as if the flight was nearly full. The gate attendant called them and informed them that they were upgraded to First Class on this flight.

As they returned to wait for the boarding call, Summit commented, "You know, George, we may have to travel all over and we get into some rough situations, but have you noticed the travel and accommodations for the most part is top drawer? I think I like being a part of this team."

George agreed, "It seems there is at least some good balance with the risks we take.

"I want to board and relax for a bit, then think about how we are going to approach finding the furniture makers. Juan provided a couple of leads based on the photos taken of the crates and other research he was able to complete. I think after this is solved, we need to make certain Juan and Julie get away for a while. With all the work Juan is doing for us and the rest of the teams, I doubt he gets more than a couple of hours of sleep a day, or maybe every couple of days."

Summit said, "I think that's a good idea. Perhaps we should all get together and give them a getaway gift. They have both been very supportive of us.

"Alright, I uploaded all the new information from what I hope is my one and only trip to North Korea. I also downloaded some additional updates from the other teams for our review. I am looking forward to seeing Istanbul. Did you know it's only city that actually connects two continents? It was considered the most important city for Christians for more than a thousand years. I have never been, have you?"

George replied, "I traveled to Istanbul once before on a trip with someone I was trying desperately to impress. At the time, I hoped she would be my future wife. I promised to show her the world. She was mustering out of the service, so I took a month's leave. I figured with all my language skills she would be very impressed. Turns out she was more of a love 'em and leave 'em kinda gal. It was a good trip, and we saw a lot of places. At our final destination, we made mad, passionate love, then she left in the middle of the night with no forwarding address, not even a note. But I did get back the custom-made pendant I had given her. Discovering it on the nightstand the next morning pretty much said goodbye without a whole lot of debate." Staring off wistfully, George gave a slight sigh of remorse.

Summit was stunned at the revelation and quietly offered, "I had no idea, George."

Just then First Class was called and the moment was lost. They were greeted by the flight attendant, Azra, as they boarded. They easily located their seats and ordered some juice. George slipped off his shoes and asked the flight attendant for a blanket when she delivered their beverages.

George stated, "It is definitely ancient history. I'm not even sure why I mentioned it. No worries, Summit. I am going to take a short nap and we'll start planning once we're in the air and well on our way."

Summit, only too happy to find a different subject to focus upon, said, "I will think of a few plan variations to discuss. I've had all the best plans so far, right?"

George leaned against the window and replied, "Yes, you have!"

A few hours into the flight, George awakened to find Summit busy flirting with the flight attendant. He stayed quiet, so as not to alert Summit, and listened to the exchange. Apparently, she had stopped to offer a choice of dinner, and they had started a conversation. From the parts George was hearing, it was much more about where she lived, what she liked, and what cities she flew to and when. After several more minutes George decided he needed to stretch.

Not missing a beat, the flight attendant asked, "And you, sir, would you care for the lamb or the beef? Our chef made both dishes with the flavors of Turkey in hopes that the visitors would appreciate the subtle flavors of the region. The rest of the First-Class passengers are still resting, so I am happy to serve you first."

George grinned and replied, "I think the lamb would be a delightful change of pace. I don't get it often. I'd like a ginger ale as well. Summit, may I please get out while you continue to chat with Azra?"

The flight attendant looked pleased at his recall and pronunciation of her name. She moved so Summit could stand. After George walked forward and stretched out the kinks in his back, he glanced back and noted they were thick as thieves in their discussion. He thought, what the heck, the man had been on a tanker preaching for days and deserved a break.

George returned to his seat a bit later, almost disappointed to find that Summit was alone. Summit grinned as he moved out so George could get back into his seat. As Azra brought their meals and drinks she winked at Summit and began assisting the other passengers who were starting to awaken.

George sipped his drink and began to butter his roll when he asked, "How are you and Azra doing, my friend? She seems quite taken with you. And that wink, well, it was very direct."

Summit chuckled and then announced, "George, I think you will be most pleased with my plans this time. Azra grew up in Istanbul and knows the area very well. She has friends in four of the five best furniture designer houses and has offered to be our guide while she is off for a few days at home with her family.

"I explained to her how you had your heart set on adding some furniture to your loft and had seen some pieces at the friend of a friend's house during a party, and someone informed you they had been unpacked just before the party. Being the creative, resourceful man you are, you took pictures of the delivery crates. We are hunting for that brand while here on business.

"Azra thinks the markings on the containers are one of two places. But, if we don't find what we need at either of those, she can take us to the others. Then she graciously agreed to allow me to take her to dinner while we are in town. She is quite lovely, is she not?"

George shook his head. Summit looked almost hurt and asked, "You don't think she's lovely?"

George laughed and replied, "I think you are a far better planner than you think, Summit. And, yes, she is. I will make certain we have separate rooms at the hotel."

They landed and deplaned. After they cleared customs, they went to wait at a bar Azra had suggested. George was doing his usual people watching while Summit ordered them some drinks.

Towards the end of the flight, they had reviewed all the new information posted by the other teams and speculated on how things fit together. It certainly seemed like the AIMs being watched were somehow transferring information and staying under the radar.

Summit had refined his notes and added their thoughts, which he was uploading now. Their plan was to meet up with Azra and have her return to their hotel. After they checked in, Summit planned to take her to dinner, her choice. They did not have a car reserved, which Azra said was the safest. The drivers here were all crazy in her opinion.

The drinks arrived, and they continued to watch when George tapped Summit on the shoulder without really looking at him. "Summit, take a look at the female in the green jacket and short green skirt. Looks to me like she is wearing one of the necklaces. Can you get a shot while I follow her?"

George rose to go in pursuit when he noticed another female stop directly in front of her. He couldn't believe they had a ring side seat not forty feet away. The second female was dressed in jeans and a leather jacket with a blue silk blouse and a necklace just resting at the top of her cleavage. Her mouth moved for almost two minutes, and then they side-stepped one another. George went to pursue and noticed the female in green walk through the customs doorway. When he turned, the female in the jeans had been swallowed up by the crowd.

He returned to the table looking dejected and stated, "Well, I thought I saw something, but now I'm not sure."

Summit replied, "I think you saw an exchange, and I captured it on video. Good heads up, partner."

CHAPTER FORTY-TWO

Return the Original

Juan woke up with a start from a very fitful sleep. He had been staying in the data center ever since the team began to uncover more and more areas of concern in this increasingly complicated assignment. Being a pilot on demand, he could always sleep anywhere. But with the team engaged around the world in multiple time zones, he was getting less and less sleep trying to help coordinate everyone's efforts. The constant feeling of dread that had settled in his stomach had really put him on edge, like nothing he had ever experienced. The ghastly dream he had just woken from, where Julie told him goodbye for the last time, only served to promote an emotional instability he'd never experienced.

Still breathing hard from the nightmare, he tried to talk himself down by repeatedly saying *it was only a stupid dream.* He got out of his sleeping chair still somewhat stiff and marched into the communications room of the data center where he and Quip usually met for their planning discussions. He'd become more effective in working with ICABOD to a small degree.

Juan practically shouted, "ICABOD, I know it is against protocol, but I want to send a text message to Julie's burner phone asking her to call me now. I know it sounds stupid and my brother Carlos would laugh at me for saying it, but this time it is my Yaqui Indian senses that are tingling madly.

"I want…no, I NEED to speak with her to know she is alright. I'll let her chide me for being foolish about the direct contact."

ICABOD did not respond. A few moments later, Quip arrived in the room as if he had heard all the commotion and had been filled in on Juan's request by ICABOD.

Quip offered, "Juan, you know that she is undercover, and any direct contact could compromise her position. Don't you think that …."

Juan, now a little more forcefully, insisted, "You know how to get through to that phone even if it is turned off. Understand me, I am asking to get her on it!"

Quip now quietly explained, "Um, Juan, her phone has stopped transmitting and signaling. This suggests that it is not merely turned off but…"

Juan practically yelled, "Quip, what do you mean it stopped transmitting? Julie always checks in and is ALWAYS reachable, even from a burner phone! I haven't heard from her since the last team meeting, and this is simply not like her! Now you and your *Digital Immersion Blender* need to help me reestablish connectivity with her! Comprende?"

ICABOD stated, "I won't object to you using shorthand notation of calling me a DIB in your emotionally charged state, Mr. Juan. However, with the phone out of commission, we have no discreet lines of communications to reach her."

Juan, now starting to hyperventilate in his overly tired state, began to reason, "Okay, we know where she is in London. London has more video surveillance cameras per capita than any other city in the world. How about using that colossal brain of yours to…"

Quip interrupted, "Juan, we've already been doing that! Don't forget, she's part of our family, too. We even called the front desk at ePETRO and asked that she be paged, but no response. She is either unwilling or unable to respond. We are hunting in all the last known areas we believed she's been in. Part of this hunt for her will use art as well as science."

A sick fear started crawling over Juan and he began to speak random thoughts with fragmented sentences. "I saw her in my dream…I can't believe she would leave me…the children…I can't call the kids until…I have to know she is safe…they would hear it in my voice…we have to find her…don't you understand? She cannot…I won't let it…I'm going there …must find her…no way out…she can't vanish…trouble maybe…but never…it can't end like this…she has come for me…I will…for her…"

Quip now sensed that Juan was on the verge of mentally shutting down and tried to calm him, "Whoa, slow down! You are sleep deprived after all the work you have been putting in to be on your game. We need a little more hunting time, with EZ also on the case, to get some solid leads. You need some sleep, buddy, because right now you aren't making any…"

Juan turned to face Quip like a cornered wild animal ready to lash out. Quip instinctively backed up. He knew he was no match for Juan's karate expertise, and he had just witnessed his failure to talk him down from his overcharged state of mind.

Just before the situation became explosive, ICABOD intervened, "Gentlemen, I would like to point out that even though we don't know precisely where Miss Julie is, we will be better served by having Mr. Juan on the ground at the last known position, looking for clues. I would observe that while we can continue to probe the digital landscape from our vantage point, a highly motivated sleuthing detective looking for analog-based clues at ePETRO might improve our efforts enormously."

Juan said nothing as he headed for the door with a level of determination that no sane person could have hoped to stop. Before he reached the outer door, ICABOD stated, "Mr. Juan, the jet is being fueled as we converse. It will be ready for takeoff as soon as you arrive. The car outside has been alerted to your destination, and fresh clothes are being loaded onto the plane you will take to London. The flight plan is already filed and cleared, but you will not be the pilot in your current condition. The resources of the R-Group are there to help you, not let you be reckless. I recommend that you use the time to rest while you are in flight so you can have a fresh outlook for your hunt. May we have your assurance of cooperation, sir?"

Juan turned at the door to stare at the computer monitor and Quip, then replied, "Gentlemen, thank you."

After the car pulled away from the building with Juan, Quip said, "Thanks for interceding on that one. I do hope he finds our little Julie, because I liked the old Juan better than this Juan."

CHAPTER FORTY-THREE

Turnabout is Fair Play

Ernesto had followed the truck down the highway for hours. It was coming up on dawn, and to his left the sunrise was glowing from faint orange to dark pink as it bounced off clouds that seemed to go on forever. Ahead he could make out the change in color as the land melted into the Gulf of Mexico. He thought about the different ways this truck could efficiently pass through the port authority and reach their target ship. He deftly skirted the area but kept an eye on the truck as it found its place in line with many others. The port authority operated like a well-oiled machine, despite it appearing to be a busy time of day.

The driver presented some paperwork to the port authority guard, and a conversation between the two followed. It seemed like the guard and the driver had some familiarity with one another as they appeared to laugh and carry on. Eventually the port authority guard flagged the truck through and Ernesto watched as the truck navigated through traffic to what appeared to be the target pier and a tanker in the process of being loaded.

Ernesto took some shots of the tanker and made sure the markings were clear for identification of the particular tanker and its registration later. Then Ernesto parked as close as he dared and donned a jacket and hat which seemed similar in style to some of the dock workers. He picked up an unattended dolly as he worked his way toward the tanker.

The guys from the truck had gotten out and leaned against the back of the truck, either waiting for someone or their turn for loading. There seemed to be two trucks in front of theirs in the process of being unloaded. Additionally, a large crane was being operated and transferring large cargo containers onto the tanker. It was a busy, noisy process with all the workers focused on what they were doing. Ernesto commented to a couple of the other workers and helped out here and there, effectively blending in with the rest of the workers. As long as the process continued, no one spent much time chit chatting.

Ernesto discreetly took shots of the containers and dock workers, making certain he was not spotted in his efforts. Finally, the two trucks pulled away onto their next destination. The target truck and one other that had arrived a few minutes before were next. He focused his photo taking on the driver of the new arrival as he walked up to the two guys at the target truck. The three of them had a conversation, which lasted a little while, until the two guys finally threw up their hands and stomped back to the truck. Both trucks were started, and they slowly made their way down to a pier with a different tanker.

Ernesto looked around, thinking about the easiest way to be inconspicuous, and finally walked up to a forklift in idle. Ernesto commented, "Hey, bud, have you ever had one of those days when you simply cannot please the boss?"

The guy in the forklift chuckled and said, "Yeah, and this is one for me too. What's up?"

Holding up his smart phone, Ernesto lamented, "I just got a call that I need to move some cargo down at another pier, and we don't have any free forklifts. I am going to be late moving the cargo, and you know the saying 'time is money'? I sure do, because it was just yelled in my ear."

The guy looked at Ernesto with sympathy and asked, "How long do ya think it'll take to move what ya gotta move? I just started my morning break, waiting for my next work order to start in 'bout an hour. Does that give you enough time? You can borrow my lift if you give me fifty for a beer later and get back in about an hour."

Ernesto tried to keep the absolute delight from his face as he handed over a hundred-dollar bill and remarked, "You just saved my ass, man. Have two beers and I'll bring it back safe and sound."

They traded places and Ernesto headed off to where he'd seen the trucks park. He saw they had just begun unloading both trucks, and the third man watched as the first two began to move the canisters toward the ship. Ernesto took some quick shots of the markings on the tanker and the guys as they worked. He located some pallets and asked the dock workers if these were the pallets that needed to be loaded. The workers looked surprised but nodded as they handed him the papers, which would be required. Ernesto went to work, grateful for his experience with this kind of work while in college.

The ramp for the pallets and forklift was different from the one being used to walk up the canisters. Ernesto navigated the ramp easily with the pallet and handed off the paperwork to the chief at the top of the ramp while he received directions on where those pallets should be placed. He placed the pallets into an area that was nearly full. Taking a chance, he parked the forklift and made his way to view where the other containers from the truck were being placed. After a few turns, he identified where the containers were being placed and worked his way back to the forklift.

He made another trip down the ramp where a mild traffic jam had formed. As he made his way back up with the second and final load, he noted the guys were returning with empty dollies and no more canisters were being loaded. He watched as the guys got into their trucks, taking a few more quick shots as they drove away. He dropped the final pallet and noted the din of loading was definitely diminishing. He parked the forklift and quickly made his way to the canisters, finding four with the warning symbols. To be safe, he applied an RFID tag to each of the canisters out of sight, near the base. Someone would really have to hunt for the tags to find them. He turned them on, straightened up, and headed back toward the forklift.

A large man with a scowl and deep voice bellowed, "What the hell are you doing here? This ain't your area. I sent you and your forklift to deliver pallets to that section over there."

Ernesto instinctively knew this man was not to be trifled with. He reached into his pocket and was rewarded with the cigarette butt he'd picked up on the way past where the two trucks had first parked. He'd snagged it in case some DNA evidence might be gathered from it. He showed it to the burly man and stated, "Chief, I saw smoke wafting up from this area and wanted to stop a big problem from occurring. I know smoking in a cargo area on these tankers is a dangerous game. I put it out and pocketed it to get it off your tanker. I can show you exactly where it was if you want, but I promise there is not a spark left. I made certain."

The large man's facial features softened, and he replied, "Now that was good thinking. Thanks, man. Now git off this tanker. We are getting ready to weigh anchor in twenty. Unless you want to go to the Philippines, you better get a move on."

Ernesto grinned, nodded and quickly made his way to the forklift. Driving it back to its destination, he handed the driver another hundred-dollar bill with his thanks.

Jamie had just boarded the plane to Washington D.C. to align with the ticket change Penny had made at the airport. He hoped Ernesto wouldn't be too angry at the fees for changing flights. Ernesto had updated his earlier notes that he had eyes on the tanker and would call when he finished tagging it. He wasn't certain that he'd speak to Ernesto before the flight attendant insisted all phones be turned off, so he sent a text with regards to the change in destinations.

Ernesto had taken some time to upload the photos he'd taken to the team share point and then phoned Juan. There was no answer, which surprised him, so he left a message. He stopped at a nearby gas station and fueled up. He read some emails he'd received as well as the texts from Jamie and Juan. Jamie was en route to Washington D.C. Juan was out of reach and would update the team later. The entire team was copied, but no one had replied. Ernesto thought it was about time Juan slept a bit so he did not text back.

He looked at the flight schedule out of Houston Intercontinental to Washington and could only get on standby. He would have a relatively short thirty-minute drive to the airport, and his flight was four and a half hours away. Taking advantage of the secure session he was connected to on the CATS network, he decided to work on his laptop. He was reviewing the comments and uploads made by the other teams when his smart phone rang. Ernesto answered, "Hi, EZ, what's up?"

EZ replied, "It's crazy here, Ernesto! Things are good and bad. I just read your uploads and started to track on the devices you set. The ship you spotted is a tanker currently leased by ePETRO, so these folks are up to their eyeballs in something. The manifest suggests it is headed to the Philippines, as you noted. The photos are being reviewed, but the driver that arrived at the docks looks to be identified as Steven Christopher. He is someone Mercedes was working with on the inside.

"Jamie's text says that he is headed to D.C., which is good for us. Now that I have matched his smart phone, I can send some instructions and keep him updated. He is good, right?"

Ernesto looked confused and said, "Yeah, he is good, but I am on my way to meet up with him, so I can take care of sharing the information."

EZ sadly countered, "No, I will. I need you to head to London. I will send you an address and the process for getting access to a flat there. Julie missed her check in with Juan, and we have no signal from her devices at all. Juan is on a flight to London and focused only on finding her. I decided you need to give him some back up, regardless of whether he wants it. George and Summit are in Turkey, so you're the handiest."

Ernesto was stunned and asked, "Okay, so Mercedes is on the inside. That's good, right?"

EZ cleared her throat and stated, "Except Tyler is missing as well, and Jamie may be his greatest hope. Mercedes was spotted by her boyfriend who works for the U.S. three letter agency. She looked alright but had some very ugly handlers who were guiding her every move. I'm going to have Jamie keep an eye on your Penny and hopefully locate Jenny. I'm counting on Mercedes being able to handle herself.

"I need you to help Juan. I will track the signals and alert U.S. customs about these containers. We think the contents may be uranium, based on the markings in your photos. We are trying to tie up the purpose of stealing them and redirecting them to the Philippines."

Ernesto digested the information. "I'm worried Jamie may be in a little deep, trying to watch the AIMs. I could go to him for a day and then get to London."

EZ demanded, "I know it is tough, but we are short on options. You trust Jamie, we'll see if he can help. Juan needs back up.

Julie needs to be found, and you can be the voice of reason with Juan. He left in a horrific mood and won't even speak to me via phone."

Ernesto placated, "Alright, EZ, I get it. Breathe slowly in and out. Is your new husband close by?"

EZ sighed and replied, "Yes, Ernesto, he's helping me. He has some great talent for finding things and good contacts. He agrees with this approach, too."

Ernesto said, "I know Juan was working some with Quip on new data access. I am glad he is with you. I am headed toward Houston Intercontinental Airport and I will get a flight to London as soon as we hang up. I will text you as soon as I get all the flight information."

EZ chuckled and replied, "I will text you your modified flight information, and there will be a car on the other side to meet you. Leave your rental at the airport parking garage, and it will be handled. Thanks, Ernesto. I knew I could count on you!"

CHAPTER FORTY-FOUR

What's Missing and Where Is It?

It had been the classic romantic evening. The bottle of Beaujolais wine Quip had chosen with such care was mostly vinegar. The carefully crafted homemade soufflé dinner turned into crispy tacos that had to be removed from the flat in order to get the smoke alarm to stop. Quip had run late from work and completely missed the window of opportunity to pick up a dessert from the local bakery which, of course, was now closed. But somehow the plan B items worked, and before long they were laughing at the failed perfect dinner event.

Their lovemaking had reached a feverish pitch. EZ was riding him so aggressively that her red hair was flying in all directions and forcing her to take one hand to smooth it away from her face. Quip thoroughly enjoyed not only her driving herself down on top of him, but also the frenzied movement of her whole body. Her sexual exertions had given her body a moist glow with a sexual scent that fanned both of their passions.

Just as they were about to both reach the pinnacle, EZ's cell phone chimed, with that special ring tone of 'answer this now,' causing a disastrous psychological disengagement from their lovemaking. Quip looked up in horror and dismay as EZ dismounted him, leaving him high and dry, as it were, so she could answer the call.

Quip stared incredulously at her as she said, "Even if you never stop running or looking over your shoulder, I'll make sure you pay for disturbing me and my husband at this hour!"

After a few seconds of listening, her shoulders slumped down, and with a very sour face she put her robe on and acknowledged, "Alright, alright, I won't kill you this time. Yeah, I get it. Let me log on and start hunting."

EZ disconnected from the call and fastened her robe up in a very agitated manner and proceeded toward the door.

Quip bellowed, "HONEEEY?! You can't leave, not now!"

Lovemaking forgotten and almost fully into her unified communications persona, EZ absentmindedly threw him the keys and announced, "Sorry, honey, but we've got MIA personnel I need to try and find. Be a dear and unlock your handcuffs while I get coffee going and get logged into the system. We'll play ride 'em cowgirl another time, real soon."

Now annoyed to near lethal proportions, Quip finally got the handcuffs undone and, still fuming, stomped off after EZ, determined to finish their session. While the coffee was set into motion, EZ sat down in her chair to bring up her machine and launch her hunt program. Moments later, an undeterred Quip, in all his glory, was standing right next to her, still breathing heavy from their aborted lovemaking.

After logging in and launching the hunt program, EZ turned and, with a feigned surprise look, exclaimed, "Oh, my goodness! Look how swollen you look, honey! Does it hurt? Here, let me kiss and make it better…and lick…and maybe some of this… and…"

She took Quip's manhood into her mouth and gently stroked his male pair while she continued to lavish attention to his manhood. Quickly forgetting the previous indignant interruption, Quip stood there, now building again to a satisfying climax.

However, EZ's program alerted her of a location match, and she abruptly refocused her hands and face to the screen. Oblivious to Quip's yet again incredulous gawk, she addressed the computer screen. "Oh, do come along! Seriously, another false positive? No, now do it again, dammit, and this time ignore that data location set."

Now with more time gained from the search algorithm, she gathered up all of Quip's manhood and reengaged the oral activity that held so much promise of satisfying him. Again, Quip was on a build that would probably have him collapsing momentarily, but once again the computer program returned something. This time it was far more interesting.

As EZ disengaged from pleasing Quip and stared intently at the monitor, she sweetly but distractedly murmured, "Um, honey, will you hold this for me while I boost this query to track some other vectors? I think that this location prowl holds some promise."

A rather dejected and irritated Quip now pulled over a chair and sat down to look over her shoulder at the search results. After a few moments of resigning himself to a terribly broken I didn't want to mention it earlier, but it's Tyler. He got grabbed and they were smart enough to crush his phone before they left the area. Luckily, they weren't smart enough to destroy theirs.

"I mapped all the phones near Tyler's just before it was destroyed, and I have something to trace. Assuming they are still holding Tyler, then we have his location by proxy. Of course, like anything, timing is of the essence."

A very sour Quip replied, "Tell me about it!"

EZ shot him a sideways glance and chastised, "Let's get this info off so they can try to find where these two clowns are, and maybe Tyler can be retrieved.

"Aren't you cold sitting there with nothing on? Don't you want a robe or something?"

Something changed in Quip's mood. He smiled with pride, leaned over toward her face, gently kissed her forehead and said, "You are an amazing woman. I am so glad you are in my life. I'm going to get you a cup of coffee so you can find Tyler. I mean, we need to find him, so I can hear the rest of the story about how his hypnosis session at a party once went terribly wrong."

EZ, now puzzled by the half of a story, stopped Quip and asked, "Okay, so what did he tell you? I'd like to hear at least the part you know."

"The shortened version is that on a dare at a party he hypnotized one of the ladies there into genuinely believing she had lost or misplaced her nipples."

EZ appeared stunned. "I didn't know they were removable."

"As far as I know, they are either in an on or off state. But what I want to know is, how does a lady confirm that they are in fact gone without some third-party corroboration?"

EZ nodded. "I can see where this would turn into a show to confirm the poor lady was or wasn't intact. What a hoot!"

CHAPTER FORTY-FIVE

Information Now, and I Mean Right Now

Jim Hughes stormed into Eric's office without so much as a glance at the secretary he usually greeted. He was in no mood for socializing or stroking the ego of Eric's right-hand man. The thought that Eric might be in a meeting was banished as insignificant while he had ridden up in the elevator. Rarely did Jim Hughes, aka Stalker, ever lose his cool. But he wanted answers, and he wanted them now. As he reached the inner sanctum, Eric waved him to the old, well-worn government chair. Nothing but the best furnishings, circa 1954, for his boss.

When the phone had settled into its cradle, Jim launched his case without even a greeting. "My mission at the Library of Congress had its good side and bad side. Yes, we have some questionable reference materials on atomic fusion, chemical reactions, and uranium constructs being reviewed by some people that aren't exactly historical students or chemists looking for background materials. The views are short with specific references being requested. There appears to be a very methodical routine to gather bits and pieces over time and then assemble the parts later.

"Eric, if we take this activity and combine it with the material sent to you from that informant in Washington State who witnessed the photographing of the atomic bomb processes in the museum there, it could mean we have a group planning to assemble a bomb. The bomb construct could either be in their homeland and they are just here gathering information, or it is being built right here on our U.S. soil. They get flagged if they do Internet searches of these subjects, but this way is more subtle, unless someone brings it to us.

"It is really hard to say how much has been gathered, over how long a period of time. I would also like to have us consider that the information may be on the seller's block to the highest bidder. The critical point now would be to verify that all our uranium is accounted for."

Eric looked at his longtime friend. Jim Hughes had been his best and most formidable operator for years. He had unquestionable loyalty, completed some of the toughest assignments, and added good value, always. They had a comfortable working relationship and rarely did Eric feel the need to pull the boss card. He sensed that Jim was not even close to finished but decided to interject.

"I think that makes a lot of sense, Jim. I am glad you took the time to assemble the information summary for me. I look forward…"

Jim tersely interrupted, "I'm not even close to finished, boss! A funny thing happened on the way through the library, which, by the way, was also being observed by some known Muslim parties-of-interest. I was able to capture some license plate numbers, vehicle descriptions, and I already turned the video footage over to the guys downstairs for analysis. I used a tag of first priority, with your authorization code."

Eric shook his head, knowing if Jim was this amped up, there was even more. He decided to not offer his information, but to wait him out.

Jim stood, started pacing and continued, "I digress. On the way through the library, I was really surprised to bump into one of your former operatives, who just happens to be my girlfriend, browsing through the books on nuclear fusion. She was wearing the oddest costume, and it isn't even Halloween. By the way, I resent that any material created by our government which is not considered classified is public domain.

"You know, I have seen this woman shoot a man at 50 yards and cleanly clip an ear, or a hand or knee. I have seen her read briefings for projects, background on targets, and even some smut novels, but never have I seen her interested in nuclear fusion. Plus, the panic in her eyes when she thought I might acknowledge her was palatable. Of course, she might have been hiding the fact that she was cross-dressing as a Muslim or covertly photographing pages from the archives, but we didn't speak.

"After she finished taking photos on the sly, she quickly exited and vanished into a vehicle with a man that I swear had a stopwatch on her. Plus, I haven't heard a peep from her!"

Eric volunteered, "She has her own assignments, Jim. There are assignments and roles she is required to do with her current employer. That is not yours or my business unless she breaks some law in the U.S., which I feel confident…"

Jim growled, "Hell, I know that, Eric! I want to know what she's doing and who's manipulating her. She is under someone's control, or she would reach out to me and at least talk naughty. Now, call your European contact and see if they might share some information. Either that, or give me some numbers and I'll call!"

Eric's eyes darkened as he was rapidly growing tired of this conversation. "Are you finished? I might be able to share some information if you would sit down and listen. Or you can keep acting like a three-year-old, pacing around. Your call!"

Jim was pulled up short with the comment and sat down. He didn't look happy, but he didn't speak. He then took a breath and nodded for Eric to proceed.

"The call I was on when you entered was from a previously contracted contact, Quip in Europe. He informed me that Mercedes was on a specific assignment when she lost her teammate and was electronically taken off the grid. The SIM card from her phone was removed and has not gone back online. She is somewhere in the Washington D.C. area and is believed to be infiltrating an organization that operates only in an analog manner. As more information is available, he will provide updates and asked that you be notified. If you hear from her, he asked that I let him know. He also suggested that he has some additional resources he will be redirecting to this area.

"Quip also wanted to inform me that one of his team believes that they witnessed the transfer of radioactive materials onto a tanker. The good news is the individual secured a tracking device to the container so that we might be able to find the signal. It is currently expected to be inside U.S. waters, like the Philippines, which means we can intercept. It's our decision on the appropriate action to take."

Jim digested the information and took a deep breath before he commented. "Let him know that mid-day yesterday she was certainly walking under her own power, but I believe she is being handled.

"What do you want me to do, boss?"

"I want you to find out the identities on the video and match them up to our wanted for questioning list. I think we have a couple of things in play, and I want us on top of them, now!"

Jim stood and approached the door, then turned and said, "I have no intention of apologizing."

Eric grinned and replied, "Not expected, but don't ever barge in here again and bark at me like a junkyard dog. I will keep you in the loop! She is good, and she will return. Of that I am certain."

CHAPTER FORTY-SIX

Catered Events

She'd decided it felt like humidity, thick and dense like a blanket on her skin, almost oppressively holding onto her as she dreamily watched, mesmerized by the light dancing off the water. Oddly disconnected thoughts drifted through her mind as the uneven ripples through the water charmingly distorted the light patterns. It was almost like being in suspended animation.

Unexpectedly she was released from this oddly surreal suspension, and in a flash her muscles responded to her need for oxygen. She instinctively shot up through the surface of the water desperate to refill her lungs with that all-important ingredient of life. The air she rapidly gulped in also included some quantities of water. She was alternately gasping for breathable air or choking and retching to expel the water from her lungs, fighting for a whole breath. Reality rushed back into her mind as she realized she was still in the holding tank. She grappled to hold herself up on the side of the tank, trying to stabilize her heart rate while evening her breath. She had to be aware enough to focus on her surroundings.

An eerily calm but loud voice with a heavy Middle Eastern accent interrupted her focus.

"Ah good. You still retain life. I thought we might pick up our discussion again. This time I might recommend that you keep the western-female insolence out of your responses. We know you have just been hired into ePETRO Oil. This alone is not an issue, but your endless questions and the unusual clinginess you have had to Laurie seems a bit too suspicious. I want to know why."

JAC, almost able to breathe normally, quickly tried to assess her surroundings and recall what had occurred before. Her brain was so fuzzy and she wasn't sure if she was dreaming or not. Instinctively she knew the hunters had her.

The unfamiliar male voice continued, "If you are curious about the focus of your questioning, she is over there to your left."

JAC turned slightly and locked her sights on Laurie, who was lying on her back but with opened eyes that stared straight up. No movement whatsoever confirmed there was no trace of life left in her body. Laurie's death-pale form both frightened and hardened JAC. She began to recall some fragments of her capture, though they were jumbled. She realized she was truly a captive in a life and death scenario.

"My name is …I don't recall. I don't know that woman. Where is the man, I was meeting? Perhaps he knows her." She wasn't sure if her words were clear or not as she was pushed back down into the water. She closed her eyes and tried to figure out where she was and who she was, when she was roughly jerked up by her hair. When her mouth rose above the surface, she simultaneously gulped air and spewed water out of her mouth. A piece of the puzzle clicked into place, but she was still so confused.

Catching her breath, she mumbled, "JAC is my name., I was to meet a man when I fell. Where am I?"

JAC tried to steel herself before speaking again, so she wouldn't sound frightened as she recanted her story while in London. At least, she thought she was in London last.

He interrupted, "Liar, I don't believe you. How convenient to have memory loss. Who are you really?

"It is funny that a few months ago, I received a picture over the Internet posted by someone in Russia looking for a woman. The woman could be your sister, only with somewhat different hair and not near the shape you seem to have under those wet clothes. This look alike is the only reason you are not as cold and lifeless as your friend. If I hadn't noticed your face in the pictures our intel sent, I might not have been personally involved in your capture and questioning.

"The woman in the picture may have taken part in the elimination of an enemy of mine. Have you ever gone by the name of Natasha?"

JAC coughed and choked up some water to try to align the confused puzzle pieces in her brain. *Why ask that*, she thought. Then she slowly replied, "No, who is that?"

He studied her with a menacing set to his jaw before he clarified. "There is some evidence to suggest that a very clever female, named Natasha, the subject of the picture sent on the Internet, engineered the untimely demise of my most hated foe, Dmitry. He was a former powerful cyber overlord in Russia. It was gratifying to hear that he had been executed by his own people. Even more so because he was responsible for the death of my nephew, Salim. That is what I am interested in finding out if this Natasha was involved and maybe Dmitry too. We know someone engineered his capture."

JAC choked up some more water before she asked, "If I was this Natasha, who whacked an old enemy of yours, is this your idea of thanking me? It makes me wonder what do you do to the people you aren't thanking."

The man's voice held a bit of a snarky tone as he responded, "It is clear your temper has helped to control your fear in our discussion. You should understand that young savvy people can be an asset if properly vetted during an interrogation, but extremely clever cyber actors are difficult to confirm. It is possible you are this Natasha who engineered the downfall of Dmitry, since everything we found on you so far was mostly fabricated. I suspect you are a liar like all females, but you are welcome to enlighten us."

JAC swallowed hard as she tried to set her game plan through her fuzzy memory and, with all the courage she could summon, calmly asked, "You mean to say you grabbed me, worked me over, and killed Laurie, because I might be someone you want to say thanks to? It must have occurred to you that there might be more than one Natasha on the planet of seven billion people.

"If I tell you, one more time, I needed a job and was trying to learn as fast as possible by asking questions of the person who I thought could teach me the ways of the office, and that I don't know anyone named Dmitry, will you let me out of here?"

One of the captor's sentinels leaned into her line of vision over the edge of the tank. The smell of his body odor threatened to make her retch again. She assessed that, with his slight build, she could easily take him out with a quick jab to his throat. She feared she really didn't have the strength.

The man stated, "Achmet, it would seem that four episodes in the tank were not enough to quell her female insolence. I volunteer to perform the administration of another teaching to this female."

A swarthy, ungroomed man entered her line-of-sight at the edge of the tank. His torn, sweaty shirt threatened her gag reflex. The fragments of time she had spent here rapidly pieced themselves together in her mind. This was the leader and would not be as easy as the other to overcome, with his broader build heavier weight.

Achmet ignored the comment as he lifted up a treasured photo of her children into her line of sight and responded, "There are far easier ways to gain obedience from people unmindful of their position. Send word to our operatives that we need them to secure," he flipped the photo over and read the annotation on the back., "Gracie and Juan Jr. Ahh, we can have leverage on our mystery guest."

JAC panicked at the threat to her children and frantically offered, "No, wait, not them! They are innocent babies! I've told you everything there is to tell! Leave my children out of this!"

Achmet smiled a chilling smile with a foregone conclusion etched in his snarling lips as he stated, "You're right! A fifth time should be the charm."

Before they grabbed her for yet another near-drowning experience, JAC deftly spun out of the tank and landed a side kick squarely in one man's groin and then hit the other in the solar plexus with a perfectly placed spin kick. Both sentinels were down for the count as JAC spun around to face Achmet, who held a gun on her.

JAC saw her chances of escape dwindling by the moment so she played her last card, "My congratulations on your detective work, Achmet. Yes, you do owe me a debt of gratitude. I will collect that now if you don't mind. Allow me to leave unharmed, and we can call it even."

Achmet pondered her statement a moment then said, "I have pictures of your children, and we can find them for leverage over you. I also hold a well-used weapon on you. Since I have all the cards, I will take that other piece of knowledge you hold now."

JAC smiled like a feral predator about to pounce on a prey and calmly offered, "I took out your two henchmen, and I will do the same to you by putting my right foot hard against the soft nerve sector in your neck, and there is nothing you will be able to do about it. But before I do, I wanted to let you know how Dmitry actually got ahold of Salim for his vengeance. You should know, those children are only a part of my cover for my work at ePETRO. They are useless as leverage over me. They provide good cover when deceit is required."

Achmet's manner immediately shifted from all smiles and he demanded, "How do you know any more about Salim? What do you know about his capture by Dmitry?"

JAC, playing the female taunting routine to incense Achmet, calmly said, "Salim was a bargaining chip. I delivered Salim to Dmitry for a favor in return. I was fairly sure it was Salim's last useful transaction, so I received a very good price for him.

"I learned later his torturers treated him like a fondue pot, stabbing him with forks until he expired. A bit much for my tastes. Dmitry must have relished the event based on the graphic pictures he sent. He claimed to sleep forever soundly after that incident." JAC looked up as if for a divine vision then chuckled as she added, "I don't know which one suffered the most, Salim at his own dinner party or his psychotic partner Oxnard, who ended up as tiger food. Somewhat comical, don't you think, one being *at* their last supper and the other one being *the* last supper?"

Unable to control his rage, Achmet clumsily closed the gap between them as JAC had hoped. She was focused as she delivered a perfectly executed spin kick to the nerve center in Achmet's neck, stopping him cold. Without wasting a moment, JAC retrieved the gun and his phone as well as her ruined handbag and the precious photo before she turned and ran barefoot, looking for an exit.

CHAPTER FORTY-SEVEN

Seized and Squeezed

A self-satisfied Marge listened while Christopher recounted, "Madam, the diverted uranium shipment was securely loaded on our tanker in Houston and, according to my sources, is en route to the Philippines, per our previous discussions. The records were doctored per your instructions. I have scrambled an AIM to meet the tanker as soon as it reaches the Philippines. With the altered shipping manifest, we expect no issues going through Panama. Therefore, the plan is in flight."

Marge studied Christopher a moment and then asked, "With so much going according to plan, why the distracted attitude? Do we have a problem to discuss?"

Christopher was tersely silent for a moment as he tried to structure his thoughts and then said, "Madam, our primary AIM at ePETRO has gone missing. I was to receive a briefing on the actions and attitudes of everyone, including Mike Patrick, but she has not returned to work or responded to several communication requests. Therefore, I have nothing to report on the ePETRO audit, and more specifically, I have a missing Information Mule who was in a key listening position."

Marge considered what Christopher had stated and then queried, "Speculation as to what happened? I mean, the audit is complete and everything came back with a clean bill of health. Why would she up and vanish?"

Christopher now chose his words carefully as he speculated, "Madam, it is entirely possible that her role as an observer and AIM was compromised. At the very least, she was likely captured to be squeezed for insider information. The worst case is she became scared and went to law enforcement, using information for protection. Since no such activity has surfaced through any of my sources in local law enforcement, I am ruling out a run-of-the-mill robbery gone bad or homicide. More likely than not, she was seized for interrogation."

Marge was getting more agitated by the moment and angrily commented, "Okay, let's say she vanished as part of a planned abduction. My comrades in North Korea are anxiously waiting for their uranium, which is en route. My sanctioned Middle East partners are selling their oil under the table through us and using the money to finance their weapons purchases. This suggests that we have happy customers, so who are we looking at?"

Christopher, still reluctant to put all his thinking on the table, responded, "Madam, I do not have enough information to make a valid statement. I only have suspicions, and those are always less than useful."

Now at the point of losing her temper, she demanded, "I asked, who do you suspect?!"

Christopher calmly said, "Mike Patrick, Madam. Our AIM indicated that some special assignments were given to a new person in the office named Dabir. The scope of that activity was kept from her. This shift by Mr. Patrick during the audit suggests a duality in purpose.

"Thus, ePETRO passed the audit, but special circumstances seem to have occurred to help facilitate that outcome, and now our AIM is missing. With her abrupt departure, so close to these events, I can only speculate that she saw or heard something that Mr. Patrick didn't want anyone to know."

Marge sat with her nostrils flaring at Christopher's suspicions, but before she could say anything, he regrettably added, "Madam, you did ask what I thought."

Marge reeled in her anger for the moment. "How do you recommend that I approach this with Mike? If I call up asking about a missing staff person, I would have to explain why I had our AIM there to watch him, which won't work."

Christopher suggested, "You could begin with asking about the audit and his impressions of how it went. You might ask if there are any loose ends that need attention. It might be easier to get into a discussion about the new people he had just hired to assist Laurie to see how they are doing."

Marge questioned, "New people? I don't recall hearing about new hires working directly for him besides Laurie."

Christopher offered, "Laurie was quite clear that two new people had been hired almost at the same time, but only one of them had gone through standard hiring procedures. The other one, Dabir, just showed up, and Mike simply had him start. All of that suggests that it was a pre-arranged new hire, perhaps as a favor to someone."

Now irritated again, Marge snapped, "With all the things that have gone right these past two weeks, something is now wrong. Is that what I'm hearing?"

Christopher nodded then ruefully added, "It is beginning to look that way, Madam. How would you like me to proceed?"

Marge bristled at the possibility of her plan failing. She had worked so hard and covered all the bases. It annoyed her to no end to think it might be for nothing when success was so close. "I will look into it. You just stand by for instructions."

Mike looked at the number and, answering in a rather dispassionate tone, asked, "What is it now?"

Marge, feigning a humorous, upbeat tone, responded, "Is that any way to answer a congratulatory call on a successful audit?"

Somewhat taken aback with the unexpected comment, Mike said, "Excuse me, who is this and what have you done with the real Marge? And now that I think about it, where is my whiskey ice cream float you promised?"

Marge, now losing traction on the upbeat tone to her side of the call, said, "Hey listen, stupid, don't give me attitude when I call to congratulate you. You got it, buster?"

Mike almost smirked and responded, "Oh good, you are the right Marge. I always hate it when you call up with a pleasant-sounding voice, since it typically means you want something."

Now allowing her normal speech patterns back into her voice, Marge said, "Let's just get down to it. I called to commend you and the team on a job well done. I got back a note giving us a clean bill of health so I called your administrative assistant. She isn't there, nor is her backup. What happened? Did you give everyone time off for an audit well done? Not really like you to be so compassionate with the people who work for you. Little bit too…you know, warm and fuzzy."

Mike, now a little irked, snapped, "No, I didn't give everyone the week off! I don't know where Laurie or Jackeline is, but I still have Dabir here who is…" Mike's voice trailed off as he wished he hadn't mentioned Dabir to Marge.

Marge, now smiling because Mike had slipped as she'd hoped, casually asked, "Dabir? I don't remember us discussing any of these new hires. And this Dabir one? Tell me, dear boy, are you so overworked that you needed two more personal assistants?"

Mike, now seeing that Marge was going to box him in, took to the offensive. "As a matter of fact, I am overworked! Laurie has been going off to attend that confounded mother of hers so frequently that I needed admins for the admin. And it was a good thing too since you ambushed me with that stupid surprise audit! If it hadn't been for them…"

Marge, pleased with how Mike was responding, interrupted, "And that is why I'm calling. Get them all on the speaker phone with you so I can give them my thanks."

Mike swallowed hard and conveyed, "Um…Dabir is the only one here right now. Laurie had to go attend her mom, and Jackeline had scheduled the day off. Perhaps another time, Marge."

Marge smirked at how easily Mike had been outmaneuvered on the call. She could play him like a pair of cymbals, just clang them together like his two brain cells. "Ah well, no matter. Get him on the phone with you so we can talk real time. I'll hold while you summon him. By the way, before he shows up, tell me some of his background."

Mike, now experiencing the beginnings of a good-sized anxiety attack, tried to dissuade Marge. "Dabir was brought in as an intern at a very low entry level salary. I owed his family a favor, and they exchanged that minor debt for a near free, university graduate, six-month internship. It's helping to grease the skids in ePETRO's business dealings. Nothing more."

Marge pressed further. "His name is Dabir? May I assume he is of Middle-Eastern descent? And what family asked this of our company that you felt the need to comply with them?"

Mike closed his eyes and shuddered at the direction of the questioning, because he knew where it was going. He offered, "Dabir is the nephew of our prime oil source from that country which must not be named on an open mobile device call."

Marge, appalled and outraged, stormed, "You mean to tell me you hired a nephew of that Muslim bastard to work in the most strategic office of ePETRO?! Have you gone insane?"

Mike, now in a full defensive fighting mode, shot back. "He is only a step-n-fetch-it gopher here with no security access to anything! Laurie is the only one with clearance! And anyway, we passed the audit with his help, so calm down."

Marge stewed a moment then asked, "Then who is doing all the work with the two admins lost in time? It can't be you since you said you were overworked! If you tell me, it's this Dabir who has no access rights, you are dumber than I give you credit for. Now tell me about damage control for this situation!"

Mike, presently devolved to full angst mode over the way the conversation was going, weakly offered, "Marge, it was a favor to get favors and keep our negotiating position with them intact. If I trash the kid now, what do you think the repercussions will be? We will lose our low-cost source of oil, which will punish our bottom line! Besides, the kid doesn't have the keys to the kingdom, so there is no damage he can inflict on us. I've got this!"

Marge was fuming but sensed that the conversation was at a stalemate. "You better hope so, bright boy! If those Muslim bastards have one of their vermin in our shop, then we are vulnerable! Don't you think it's a little strange and all too convenient that your admins are missing, but the interloper, a potential terrorist in training, is still in our inner sanctum? I want all the passwords changed now, and don't tell him that it's being done, got it? If anything goes wrong there you will soon be introduced as the eunuch, once known as Mike Patrick!" She abruptly disconnected.

Being the only one on the call Mike remarked, "Now looks like a good time to do that planned diversification and spin up of Mike Patrick Incorporated." Smiling, he added, "And may I say thanks to Marge for awarding me that long overdue bonus! Why, yes of course, it won't be any trouble to write myself the check. Happy to!"

CHAPTER FORTY-EIGHT

Pain is Better than Death

Tyler could feel the jarring of the rough road long before he gained any of his other senses. His head pounded terribly, the blood pulsing right behind his eyeballs. Sensations of cold echoed from head to toe, with the shivers to match, and was accompanied by a dread that centered in his gut. At least the restraints on his hands were in the front, but it seemed less than a blip in the plus column. His last memory was having something pulled over his head, then darkness.

He felt stickiness from the seat he was lying on but nothing else covering his cheek, and maybe he even felt a slight bit of air. Perhaps he'd imagined that there was something on his head. With no idea where he was headed and no knowledge of time to reconcile how long he had lost consciousness, he felt disoriented and almost paralyzed. The noxious odor of unwashed humans was nearly as painful as the jarring caused by what felt like the worst road possible.

Even with the constant vibrating as the van traveled down the road, his brain functions slowly returned like a replay of a movie trailer. Multiple scenes flashed, and he realized he had no idea where Mercedes was, let alone where he was. Had he let his teammate down? How had he been spotted and by whom? In his mind, he saw two men, scruffy, with black hair and swarthy complexions. He'd heard them speak English but couldn't recall the words before his head was bashed. Taking inventory of his injuries, he guessed he was lucky to have survived.

One man's voice penetrated his thoughts. "How long before we get to the warehouse, Najih? We have a schedule to maintain."

The other man, Tyler presumed Najih, replied, "We are very close now, Rajir. We need to extract the information before we kill him. You are correct, timing is critical. I need to see to the next phase of our disruption to the U.S. pigs.

"How long have you been in America?"

Rajir's tone held disdain as he said, "Too long. I was promised that after this mission the cell would be disbanded, and I could go home for a visit with my family."

Najih ruefully replied, "May your family be blessed with your presence. I have been close to death at the hands of these infidels so many times. I know we will succeed this time."

At least Tyler knew the score. As the vehicle pulled up to a stop, his head hit the side of the door and he yelped.

Rajir stated. "ميتواند، كافر..."

However, Najih stopped him and sternly reprimanded, "Remember, while in this country we only speak their primitive, coarse language so as not to be identified with our home country."

Rajir began again. "Good, he's awake. Let's get him out and into the warehouse. The sooner we get our answers, the sooner we can report back and move on."

"The place is deserted like always. I am glad we found this cluster of condemned buildings. It allows us a meeting and staging place for our operations. You did well in securing this, Rajir."

Tyler forced himself to open his eyes to hopefully gain some hints as to his location. The vehicle was nicer than it felt, riding in his trussed-up position. The two men acted like hardened criminals, and from their comments, they would not be push-overs. They roughly dragged him from the vehicle and had him on his feet between them. They partially dragged and prodded him into the doorway after one of them unlocked it. One man had a worn white shirt with a brownish vest and jeans, which concealed his gun. The other man had a long grey jacket and jeans, presumably hiding his own weapon and the keys he'd just used to open the warehouse door. Though it was sometime around noon, based on the position of the sun, the muted light streaming through nearly opaque dirty windows scattered along the back wall inside the warehouse made it seem closer to night.

They shoved him onto a chair not too far from the door they had entered. The building was a vast, empty space. They removed the zip ties from his wrists and then attached his arms to the chair arms. His legs were wobbly at best when they'd dragged him, so they obviously didn't consider him a threat, as they cut the zip ties from his legs. If the feeling ever returned to his arms and legs, and his head stopped spinning, he might be able to put up some sort of defense.

The man, whose voice he now recognized as Najih, roughly grabbed Tyler by the chin and demanded, "What were you thinking, following that slut outside the museum? Were you trying to protect her, you weakling?"

Tyler tried to focus and replied, "What woman are you referring to? I was not following or watching any of the many women there. I was simply enjoying the weather and the architecture."

The man he now presumed was Rajir caught him with a blow to his right cheek which turned his head and almost loosened his teeth. Rajir screeched, "Liar! You were watching her and taking photographs."

Tyler took a breath and mumbled, "No, sir, I was photographing the archways on the building. People were there, but they were not the subject. Give me my phone and I will show you the photos. You will be able to clearly see the subject."

Najih spat and continued, "The architecture was the focus as well two nights ago at the townhouse, where you knocked on a door and pretended to be a pizza delivery guy? All you Americans are liars and deceivers. You cannot be trusted. Now tell me again, what are you doing stalking these sluts?"

Tyler tried to wrap his head around how long he'd been followed. If they had tracked him in both places, had they been following the AIMs too? Tyler quickly tried to calculate how to get time back on his side. He needed to focus on his situation rather than what happened to Mercedes. He couldn't help her if he didn't get out of here alive.

Najih demanded, "Why were you at the museum? Who were you tracking if not the slut who walked up to a man? Even in her burka, I am sure she was propositioning him. Rajir said he heard her. Is she one of the whores you run, little man?" He slapped Tyler on the other cheek for good measure and received a wince for his efforts.

Tyler waited a moment, regained his composure and maintained, "I was there to study the architecture. I did not focus on the people in the area. Why would I lie?

"Please, I need a sip of water. Please, just a sip to rinse out the blood in my mouth?"

"If I give you a sip of water, you will tell me the truth, you pig? You will stop lying and tell us who sent you to watch the women!"

Tyler wanted to get both of them just a little closer if possible, and without any further pain. He had some feeling coming back into his feet and legs. Enough that he wiggled his toes, as well as tightened and relaxed his thighs and calves in turn, to encourage the circulation. Tyler cleared his throat as he mentally finalized his plan.

"Alright, you guys got me. I was there watching someone, but not the women."

Najih demanded, "Who then? Who were you watching?"

Rajir looked like he might deliver another strike, and Tyler begged, "Man, don't hit me again! It's not my fault he sent me. He told me to watch the man and take pictures of every place he went and everyone he spoke to. I was promised a big payoff to capture him in action."

Najih looked at Rajir and said, "Watch him, don't touch him. I need to make a call."

Najih stepped outside leaving the door ajar. The cavernous walls carried his words back into the warehouse.

"But he said he was watching a guy…

"No, not the women or even your current woman…

"I don't know who yet…

"Are you sure that's a good idea…

"If you're compromised, what is the alternate plan…

"Alright, but it might take some time…

"Yes, he whines. He's a pig."

Najih walked back where he'd started and indicated, "This man needs a drink of water, and let's zip tie his hands back together rather than to the arms of the chair."

Rajir looked confused and asked, "Why don't you let me just start peeling the skin from his arms or legs. He'll talk. He'll tell us why he is watching the women."

Najih stated, "Because if he was watching the man, I want to know who told him to and how this man can be reached. For this, I am willing to start over a bit and see if we can come to a better understanding."

"Now, who is promising you a big pay day? Is it the government?"

Tyler looked up at his captors with dark blue eyes portraying openness and honesty as he related, "I don't think he was with the government, no. He had a couple of guys with him who were dealing crack while he and I spoke. He also said it was a contract job to find out the movements of this guy. He showed me a picture, which I took a picture of, and gave me a couple of addresses where I might find him. Then I was instructed to follow.

"Hey, can I have a drink? My throat is getting dry, and my mouth tastes, well, awful."

Najih opened the water bottle and dribbled a little into his open mouth. Tyler eagerly swallowed then licked his lips. He realized he needed to be a bit more dramatic to get both of them close enough.

"I picked the guy up at the second location I watched for a whole day. Then I followed him to the house where I did pay the pizza driver ten bucks to let me deliver the pizza, because the man had stopped there. I had the picture from when he had been there, and I needed her picture to send to the buyer. I uploaded it to the number the guy gave me on my phone. If you'll give me my phone, I can show you real fast. No games."

Then Tyler started to wheeze like he was having trouble breathing. He was raggedly gulping air, then he looked like no air was going in at all.

"Najih, he's looking bad," Rajir said, "Maybe he's sick."

"I don't think he is sick. I just think he wants another sip." Najih tipped Tyler's chin up and dribbled a bit more water into his mouth.

Tyler nodded and seemed to catch his breath, but then his breathing slowed. Suddenly, without warning, he slumped forward pushing all the air out in a huff and leaned motionlessly against his knees.

Both men reflexively reached for him at the same time. Tyler's joined hands hit Najih in the jaw with a satisfying connection and he heard the sound of teeth banging hard enough for hopefully a broken one or two. At the same time, his right foot came up at an angle and caught Rajir in the throat, in an attempt to crush his windpipe. The man grabbed for his throat and started to turn blue. Najih tried to counter, but Tyler gained his footing and kicked him hard in the knees. Najih fell to the floor, screaming in agony. Not wasting a second, Tyler grabbed the keys and hobbled to the door of the warehouse. He hopped out and awkwardly closed the door. The third key he tried matched the lock and he turned it home. After a few breaths, he hobbled toward the vehicle, swearing he would work harder the next time Juan held a training session.

Rajir had frantically tried to breathe but finally succumbed to the loss of air and crumpled into a dead mass on the floor. Najih looked at his comrade and mumbled for him to go with Allah, as the pain in his own knees intensified. He wasn't certain if both kneecaps were shattered. He only knew the pain was excruciating. It was so bad that he'd forgotten about the pain in his jaw, but he had survived. Najih had always carried painkillers as a matter of practice, so he reached into his jacket and took two pills, washing them down with water. At least he had water. He also had his phone. After waiting for ten minutes or so for the medication to take affect and the pain to lesson enough for him to speak, he dialed a number.

After several rings, the scratchy sounding male voice on the other side responded in a clipped manner. "Where… are… you?"

Najih replied, "I think your Steven Christopher has been spotted. We held a man for him, trying to find out who hired him, then he fought like a wildcat. Rajir is dead and I am not certain I can walk. Can you send someone, Achmet?"

The silence grew longer when Achmet finally replied, "This is not a good day for Allah, when both of us are overcome, but we are alive to fight another day. Where are you?"

Najih provided the details, and they discussed the various options that might be pursued.

After several minutes, Achmet stated, "Your job is to finish your project and instigate the disruption. Paint a story for Mr. Christopher and have him send someone to extract you. Tell him he's the target. We need to know who hired the man you have.

"I have a bitch to find and punish. Let me know when you are finished with your job. Go with Allah and be strong."

CHAPTER FORTY-NINE

Stiff Upper Lip and All

Juan had arrived in London, worried and filled with a sense of emptiness. His stomach had been in knots, and though he had tried to rest as Quip advised, it was in fits and starts. The horrible images of his imagination wouldn't stay quiet. As promised, a driver had been waiting at the airport and collected his luggage without comment.

The man was an older gentleman, nearly 1.8 meters, trim, with greying hair neatly trimmed, not a hair out of place. He carried a stiff upper lip, and was dressed complete with the cap and suit typical of his profession.

Juan had never been one to put himself either above or below anyone. He stuck out his hand and curtly greeted, "You can call me Juan, none of that mister stuff. I am hoping we can get out of here quickly and go to this flat." He passed a paper which identified the destination.

James kept his expression even and unruffled. The worn, wrinkled face spoke a bit about his age, and his experience was reflected in his tone. "You may call me James, sir. Do we need to retrieve any bags?"

Juan held up the duffle and stated, "I have a change of clothes in this and a few items to keep me from looking homeless. At some point, I may need to get a few more things. I have no idea how long I will be here."

James glanced at the paper then indicated with a hand gesture and movement forward that they could depart. As they walked to the car, James outlined some of his support with the decorum only an educated English gentleman can deliver. "The car is this way, sir. This is the address I had received in my contract. I can be with you continuously, or you can page me and I can commit to being no more than ten minutes away at any time, unless you send me on errands. I can provide you with laundry services, additional clothing from the sizes provided in the contract from your administrative assistant, Eilla Zan Waters, and I can get you anywhere in this region."

Juan broke from his emotional anxiety at the commentary and laughed a bit, then clarified, "EZ is a lot of things, many of which I totally admire, but she is no one's administrative assistant. Thorough is a good description of her. James, I think we will get along well. If I was remiss when we met, thank you for being here. I need to find my wife, so I am distracted."

Unruffled, James opened the door to the limousine and said, "I understand, sir, and I will help you in any way I am able."

Juan refused to get into the back of the car and said, "Let me ride up front. It will be easier to talk, and you can tell me a bit about the area. I also want to go by the building where she works."

"As you wish, sir," commented James. "The other address is near the business district, which is on our way to the flat. Would you like to drive by there now?"

Juan nodded and they easily flowed into traffic. Juan thumbed through the messages showing on his phone's screen. He frowned at the last one and commented, "James, it looks like you may have to run one of those errands sooner than I expected. Another man from my firm is arriving to the airport early this evening."

He then mumbled more to himself than to James. "I don't need a babysitter."

Apparently, nothing was wrong with James' hearing as he remarked, "Oh, sir, I thought you had two very small children that required a babysitter."

Juan looked over with a very annoyed face and said, "Yes, I have amazing twins who are with their nanny at present and having a ball building caves and forts. The comment I made was something else entirely."

James drove them slowly by the building and paused so Juan could take in the people coming and going. It was a workday, so several people walked with purpose and obviously a destination in mind. Juan noted the coffee bar and almost visualized Julie there with her endearing smile.

"Very good, James, let's go to the flat now."

James maneuvered back into the traffic like a practiced professional. Juan had no idea how he had lucked out with such a good driver, but he suspected after he found Julie, he would be doling out the thanks to several folks, and maybe a very smart machine.

The flat was nothing special in a neighborhood that seemed to be quiet at the moment. Juan took the key EZ had provided and easily opened the door. Nothing was amiss inside the flat. It was neat and tidy as Julie was with all her living spaces. The refrigerator had a few items, but nothing appeared moldy.

"James, I don't know where you were planning on staying, but this clearly is only a one-bedroom flat, not that I plan to sleep much."

"No problem, sir. There are two Chesterfield sofas in sitting room, which will suffice quite nicely. Far better than my cot at home, sir. However, if you prefer, I not stay here I can still make the contract commitment of remaining within ten minutes of you."

"No, it is fine, James. I need to take a shower, set up some equipment, and check in with EZ. I'm finally ready to eat, but my wife eats like a bird. Is there something fairly close that could be brought back here for us? And if you could secure a cold cerveza or two, that would be nice, plus whatever you want." He handed James some Euro.

"Of course, sir. No allergies to worry on?"

Juan smiled slightly then sadly shook his head. The only thing he was remotely allergic to was being without Julie.

Juan was able to take a shower, and as steam filled the bathroom, he picked up Julie's scent in the air and then again on her towels when he dried. After he finished, he checked the wall safe. He found what Quip had indicated would be there, along with a few notes and her wedding ring. Staring at the lonely ring she so cherished numbed him to his core. He refused to doubt he'd find her. Next, he placed a call to Quip and EZ, which he kept short and to the point. He expressed his annoyance regarding Ernesto joining him before he disconnected the call. James returned a short time later with the local brew and some surprisingly good, hot food.

While James went to fetch Ernesto, Juan continued to pour over the videos in and around the ePETRO office area taken several days before the Friday they suspected Julie had actually disappeared. He paused a few times in segments where she appeared, a couple of which included her with Laurie. Julie's enchanting smile and graceful movements made him tear up until he forced himself to move on, looking for other clues or insights.

The bright spot of the evening had been a call with the twins excitedly recounting the adventures they'd had and places they'd been in their magical tent. Maude had told them stories inside the tent and then had them act out a portion of each story. They couldn't wait to show him and Mama their adventures. They had built a section where the whole family could fit. Juan wanted dearly for this whole family to be together again.

He turned as he heard the door unlocked, ready to defend when Ernesto and James entered. James took some groceries to the kitchen and then slipped back out the door, remarking he had to move his vehicle.

Ernesto said, "Juan, I know this is tough, but I am here to help. I looked at all the information and thought perhaps we should …" Juan stood and moved so the space between them was nearly gone. "Cut the crap, Ernesto. EZ and Quip don't think I can focus, so they sent you to babysit. There is no trace of her. I'm not giving up; I don't care what the odds are. When she is committed and thinks she is right, she sure as hell doesn't give up."

Ernesto knew Juan well enough to realize that being nice wasn't going to cut it. "Look, Juan, I never said I was giving up, nor would I. Why the hell would I waste my time coming here?"

Juan had just passed his last straw metaphor when he shoved Ernesto hard and said, "I sure as hell don't know. Why did you come here? I didn't ask you to. I'll find her without you."

He shoved Ernesto again, and then Ernesto snapped. It was going to hurt to get Juan over this hurdle. Ernesto unexpectedly shoved him back and then did one of the kicks Juan had been working with the team on, executing it perfectly. Juan was over-tired, stressed and missed the moment when he could have blocked the kick and took it in the stomach. He became infuriated and then lashed out with almost no restraint. He simply wanted to beat something up. Ernesto knew that was the case and spent the next ten or so minutes blocking most of the attacks, until Juan wore himself down and sat, holding his head in his hands. Ernesto said nothing but remained ready to defend.

Ernesto solemnly offered, "You are throwing senseless punches in anger, as my CATS team instructor would advise me. And as that wise man would also tell me, *channel that energy to your thinking side.*"

Several minutes later Juan looked up, his face etched with a look of helplessness and defeat. "Ernesto, I'm sorry. I had no right to lash out at you. I…I am just so frustrated. Nothing has worked. I only caught a few segments on video. It's bad, really bad. If you want to leave the insane man to his own fate, I wouldn't hold it against you. I hope I didn't hurt you too bad." He returned his head to his hands, clearly trying to avoid eye contact.

Ernesto grinned and quietly replied, "Heck, you didn't hurt me at all, but you needed to get it out of your system. If you need to go another round, let me know. I'll bet that James can find us a gym. I'd hate to mess up this nice flat. I got your back, just like you've got mine and everybody else on the team. We don't quit, man."

Juan looked up much more composed. "I'll let you know when I need another round. You're getting better.

"What ideas did you want to pursue?"

Ernesto explained, "I suspect from what I reviewed that she was kidnapped for something she knew or saw at ePETRO. I think we need to widen the search area and start going to every hospital and care facility. Maybe we visit the local law enforcement to speak to people. I also sent EZ a note to locate any recently rented buildings or deserted warehouses so they might be checked." Ernesto glanced at the frozen screen with Julie smiling. "If we want to move forward, we need to think out of the box, boss."

Juan nodded in agreement and looked encouraged. "It's worth a shot. James does know the area well."

CHAPTER FIFTY

The Woman Smiled like an Angel

The modestly priced hotel must have been the best kept secret in Istanbul. Their balcony suite allowed a clear view of the port area where all types of ships were busy arriving or departing. With the patchy fog drifting over the water, the Bosporus Strait was a mesmerizing world treasure of activity that retained an ancient, even mystical feel for the weary traveler. The hotel décor reflected many traditional Turkish motifs, from the exquisite tile and the detailed iron balcony to the furnishings and artwork. It made one feel comfortable, wrapped in both the ancient history and modern culture of the country. Between the blue of the sky and blue of the waters was a strip of land with homes, mosques, and businesses scattered from the sea to the top of the hill.

George was contemplative as he took in the view and sampled the rich bold coffee. He felt relaxed as he reviewed the tasks before him. Summit had gone to check out the rest of the facility and complete his workout before Azra arrived. She was expected around ten, so they could scout the furniture makers. Summit had secured a car for their use, but Azra promised she would drive so they might also enjoy the sights.

Summit returned to the suite looking like he'd run a marathon. He nodded at George, who held up a cup of the aromatic coffee, but he declined and disappeared into the shower. George had risen much earlier, as was his custom, and had taken a short run, scouting the inner city as it was just awakening. By mutual consent they had agreed to take Azra to breakfast in the city instead of taking advantage of the hotel cuisine. Summit emerged from the bathing area groomed and dressed in casual slacks, along with a lightweight shirt, similar to George. He grinned as he helped himself to some coffee.

"George, I have never seen anyone who seemed more like a coffee connoisseur, outside of a Peruvian grower I met once."

George smiled and replied, "Some men seek the perfect omelet, others the perfect wine; I am just partial to a great cup of coffee. The Kona from Hawaii I get shipped to me is the best so far, but this is right up there." He held up his cup with an appreciative grin.

A knock sounded at the door, and Summit walked over, opened the door and stared. George was concerned when he heard no voices. He stood and moved to see what had left Summit standing speechless. Azra was petite yet stunning. Her dark hair, which yesterday had been tightly controlled in a bun, was actually long, flowing over her shoulders down to the middle of her back. The teal blue sundress was perfect against her flawless olive skin, and her fine bone structure was accented by the natural light reflecting on her cheeks. George suspected Summit was stuck on that beautiful smile with plump, begging-to-be-kissed lips and white teeth. Wearing no makeup, she looked like a vibrant teenager.

Azra happily greeted, "Good morning, Summit, George! Do you like the hotel I suggested? I think the view is amazing. I had friends who visited and enjoyed it very much."

Both men agreed, and Summit offered her a chair and some coffee. They sat on the balcony for a few minutes and reviewed the plan to visit the furniture makers. Azra had asked her Papa

if he recognized the markings from the photos, and he had
pointed them to the first two establishments they should visit.
After their plan was settled, Azra suggested a charming place
to eat breakfast, not far from their first destination.

Breakfast was divine at a small place overflowing with local
charm. Their meal was made up of feta and kashkaval cheeses,
black and green olives, freshly baked white bread with a fragrance
that permeated the entire area, cold meats and a generous supply
of local honey. The best part, for George at least, was the ample
supply of dark, rich coffee. The service was superb and Summit
and Azra traded comments about the cuisine in a mildly flirty
fashion.

Near the end of the meal, Azra outlined their route to the
furniture makers they would visit. Summit indicated he had a
low tolerance for shopping and would prefer looking around at
the people and the area, rather than being inside the shops. Azra
smiled brightly and said she would be happy to act as guide and
interpreter for George. She also said she knew all the tricks to
the local negotiation practices to secure the very best prices. She
explained that her negotiating skills had greatly improved since
she'd started flying to various destinations.

The owner of the first shop greeted them warmly and showed
George and Azra around while detailing the methods he and his
sons used to craft the furniture, which had been passed down
for several generations. Several minutes later, six of his sons
arrived and took a great interest in Azra but treated her like a
gem to be adored but not touched. They asked about her family
and what she did, and she responded in rapid Turkish. George
had picked up a few key words and recognized the conversation
as non-confrontational. He moved over to a few of the pieces
on display and inspected them thoroughly at the joints and the
finish. He nodded and smiled at the owner.

Azra paused and realized she might be perceived as rude, so she shifted back to English. "Gentlemen, I am sorry, but my guest is not familiar with our native language. I would not want him excluded, as he is the one searching for the furniture."

The owner replied in English, though it was evident that it was not his first language. "Of course. Sir, apologies if we offended."

George shook his head and commented, "No offense. I wish I had learned more of the language before coming here. It is I who begs forgiveness.

"Your furniture is truly well made. The joints fit like they grew in that manner, and the finish is as smooth as fine Turkish silk. And the tile work, wow. Do you also make the tiles?"

The owner beamed at the comparisons and then bragged, "My eldest son," he indicated to the one with a contented grin, "Bayram is the tile expert. His designs are frequently sought after, and he receives many orders. He learned from my grandfather and is teaching his son to assist. We have a very large family, and we all work very hard for quality products."

George recognized good workmanship. He actually liked three of the pieces very much. Summit walked into the conversation like a man who was tired of waiting outdoors and signaled George, so subtly no one else noticed. There was no evidence in the area that this shop was the one they wanted to locate. George ordered the three pieces and asked if they might be shipped in a month to his Luxembourg flat. The pieces would help to fill in his rather sparse interior. After the transaction, they moved on to the next shop.

Summit asked, "Do you think you will have room for more furniture, if the next shop has more items to your liking?"

George laughed and then happily replied, "I appreciate fine craftsmanship in wood, woven fabrics, and the tile they create in this region is amazing. I have room for more if we get so lucky. Azra, thank you for a solid win at the first shop. Onward we go."

"You are welcome, George. This next shop has good quality, but they, as you might say, subcontract out many of the materials. My Papa said they have so many vendors they purchase from it is hard to believe the results are so good. But the family is not as large as this one and mostly daughters. The products are good, though, and the requests from abroad for shipping makes them popular with Europeans, according to Papa.

"After this next shop, I have another old family friend who has some furniture, but really specializes in silk carpets, what you would refer to as Turkish rugs. These are not exported often and tend to be sought after by wealthy regional people."

"Lead on, Azra," said George, delighted with her suggestions.

Summit added, "After this next place, please let's consider lunch before we shop for rugs. I have a feeling it will take you some time to decide the pattern you want, George."

They pulled up to the next shop, and one truck was unloading in the back with another in the front waiting. The men doing the loading and unloading were very different from the family Summit and George had just seen. Azra parked a bit down the street to avoid interfering with the deliveries in progress. The shop was inviting with the tile work around the doorway and had some reinforced iron work around the garden area, providing a different look that was still artistic to the tourist eye.

As they walked in, the displays of furniture were very different from the prior shop. The sense of warmth and pride was missing. The pieces appeared well crafted, but George noted a layer of dust on almost every piece. A petite woman appeared from what was marked as an office door and greeted them. She mechanically recited information about the pieces, prices and the general shipping times in response to inquiries George made, which Azra then translated. The woman, who Azra informed them was named Ekin, was not friendly, nor did she push the sale of anything.

Summit sauntered in a few minutes later with his phone in hand and marveled over the pieces, casually snapping several photos. He focused on one bench seat that was very different than every other item. He bent down and, under the side, apparently located a release button which caused the seat bottom to flip up.

Summit commented, "George, look at this! It has a storage area. I bet you could put your free weights in here instead of storing them on the floor for visitors to trip over."

George inspected the piece and turned it over, scrutinizing the latch mechanism. He moved the piece a little closer to the light of the window and closed the lid, then reopened it. He quietly noted the stains in the bottom. Then he measured the inside of the piece, calculated the weight of twenty rifles, and cheerfully agreed, "Yes, you are right, Summit. This would easily fit my weights. Heck, it looks like it is wide enough to store several things."

He turned to the shopkeeper and asked, "How much weight can this hold? My weights are upwards of ninety kilos, maybe more."

The woman looked at George with a new appreciation of his broad shoulders. As she spoke, Azra translated, "Each of these benches can hold upwards of ninety to one hundred kilos. But if you stack them in here, they would be difficult to remove. We could build a custom piece with shelves. Building custom benches to support various contents, like your free weights, is one of our specialties. We shipped out almost two hundred last week to a buyer in Korea and the week before in China. They are very popular and resell well. It would, however, require a deposit and a couple of weeks to build."

George inquired as to the price for two, which was a far cry from two hundred and likely not subject to a quantity discount factor as the other sales she'd mentioned. Azra negotiated it back and forth with the shopkeeper, getting the price reduced three times. George smiled but said he'd need to think about it. He'd be back to let her know and thanked her for her help.

Outside, Summit said, "Azra, let's find a place to eat with Wi-Fi. I forgot to check in with my boss."

Ernesto had risen early and brewed coffee. Juan was in the bedroom, finally crashing very late the night before. James had left and returned with some scones and a container of fresh whipped cream. James and Ernesto had been busy as they mapped out a route for day two of their wider face-to-face searches and discussions with people. They had received a small tip the previous day suggesting an area which had some significant renovations in progress, but with some hold up in permitting or ownership transfer. The woman couldn't be certain.

Ernesto connected to the team's encrypted share area and downloaded the current material. He smiled at the progress George and Summit were making in Turkey and made notes of the highlights he would share with Juan. He read some of the other reports and noted that Jamie had arrived in D.C. and sent him a quick text to just do his best. Then he reported some of what they were doing in London. After running through these updates, he pulled down the document Brayson had provided, which marked all the sightings they'd had of the ladies with the dragon pendants, correlated to the time, and noted repeats by the photos of each lady. Ernesto smiled as he studied the statistics, he decided Brayson must be very bored in Panama, but he appreciated the effort. It did allow a different perspective of the AIMs.

James had turned the telly on to the news channel with the sound turned low before he had left. Ernesto finished with his review and switched his focus to the news while savoring the fresh scones, covered with a huge dollop of cream, and sipping his coffee. The current weather, like much of the time in London, was partial fog with sun expected to show up in fits and starts randomly throughout the day. The global political news remained fairly standard, while the financial markets continued to be what he referred to as psychotic.

Commentators then turned to local interests, noting the opening of a new bookstore, a Good Samaritan helping an older woman in need, followed by a lengthy special appeal from local authorities for identifying a woman in the Harley Street surgery. She had been brought in unconscious a few days ago, apparently attacked, robbed, and left for dead. The authorities were looking for family or friends who might identify the victim. The photo of the woman looked more like that of a corpse than one in critical condition, her dark hair in stark contrast of extremely pale skin. Ernesto tried to get up close to the picture to see if he could see any details which would suggest it might be Julie. He decided he couldn't take a chance it wasn't and noted down all the information the station provided.

Ernesto walked into the bedroom, hating to wake a man who deserved his sleep. He knew better than to get close enough to startle him. Like most males who had been in combat, care had to be taken when waking them. Ernesto quietly sat to the side, then with an insistent tone spoke. "Juan, I think you need to get up. Nothing certain, but I think we may have a lead."

Juan shifted a bit in the bed but failed to open his eyes or acknowledge the request. Ernesto more loudly insisted, "Juan, I need you up, man. We may have a lead. I need you to look at the picture on my phone."

Juan sat up with a start and refocused in seconds. "What did you say?"

"I think we have a lead on Julie, but I need you to look at this picture. I took it off the telly screen, so the quality isn't very good. Didn't she change her hair for this job?"

Juan snatched the phone and looked at the picture. The woman was so pale it didn't resemble his Julie, but there was something in the shape of her face and lips that made him so want to believe it was her.

"You know where she is?"

"Yes, and I called James and asked that he return immediately. I had sent him home to shower and change. You shower and get dressed. By then, James should be back."

Juan nodded and then added, "Send the picture to my phone and the details of the telly station. I'll be out in a minute. You better have some coffee left and in a to-go cup."

CHAPTER FIFTY-ONE

Are you a Turtle?

Jamie had laid out his approach during his flight to Washington. Initially the First-Class seat he'd selected had been a lark, but in hindsight it was the best way to board the plane before Penny as well as get off in advance of her. This had allowed him to stay hidden and track her. When she had taken a cab from the airport to the apartment complex, he'd followed her with a cab of his own. In addition to the photos of the AIMs he was to locate and track, he also had a photo of Mercedes. In the back of his mind all were critical, but he sensed the team was most concerned with getting his eyes on her.

While he marveled at the credit card Ernesto had given him, he was a little uneasy being an operative for a company that could re-program a credit card remotely so it correctly matched Jamie's identity. It had made the travel purchases easier of course, but the thought occurred to him that he might be out of his league with the team.

As instructed, he focused on tracking Penny and taking new photos that seemed relevant to his surroundings and uploading them to a text number he was provided. Ernesto had sent him some tips and thoughts and had responded to his questions. Other texts he'd received from EZ, whom he was told to follow and trust, even though he had no idea who she was. He chuckled slightly as he recalled being told *EZ was someone to be obeyed.*

He uploaded photos to her, especially on the place where Penny was currently parked. When it appeared the lights in the apartment were out for the night, EZ provided some quick instructions on where he could retrieve a rental car reserved for him. Round trip to retrieve the car was a scant forty-five minutes, and all seemed quiet after he'd positioned the vehicle around the corner and walked back to the place, he'd selected to continue his observation. He was able to stay concealed in the shadows far enough away from the front door, which faced the street in the quiet neighborhood, to avoid unnecessary attention.

In the hour just prior to sunrise, he noted a man stepping out from the shadows across the way to greet another man who had entered the neighborhood on foot from around the other corner. He watched as they exchanged a few comments and then exchanged places. The second man melted into the shadows. Until that moment he thought he alone was keeping vigil. Something in his gut cautioned him they were all watching the same quarry. At least he knew where they were, so he could stay out of their view. He hadn't needed to rest because he'd caught some sleep on the flight, but just to be certain he wouldn't fall asleep on his feet, he'd set his phone alarm to vibrate once an hour.

A few hours after sunrise, the neighborhood had become more active. Quietly snacking on one of the many granola bars he'd purchased at the airport in Houston, along with the water he sipped, he felt refreshed and alert. Shortly before noon, Penny and another female he identified as Jenny both exited the apartment donning burkas as they walked. Jamie was taking photos like crazy. They stopped at the edge of the sidewalk as if waiting for something. The watcher from Jamie's predawn observations moved from his spot. He put on a blue ball cap and slowly walked around the corner, presumably to his car.

Jamie figured the ladies were either waiting for the man and his car or some other ride. He moved equally slowly in the opposite direction to his car. He started the engine and moved slightly down the road for a better vantage point. He was rewarded when a taxi stopped and the ladies entered. As the taxi was pointed toward his street, he waited until it passed, as well as the next two cars. He slid behind the second and noted the first SUV, directly behind the taxi, contained the man with the blue ball cap. Jamie kept at least one car length, sometimes two, behind the SUV. Luckily, the taxi was also reasonably easy to keep an eye on.

The route took them to the Library of Congress. Jamie watched the ladies exit the taxi and work their way into the library along with a throng of other people. The man in the blue ball cap parked and took up a position near the door with a newspaper in hand. Jamie watched as another man walked up to him and seemed to ask for a smoke. A short conversation occurred. Jamie sent all the new photos, as well as a quick note about where he was. A text was returned a scant minute later:

> The building has two entrances. Use the back one. Don't get too close, but observe what you can. Do not follow them outside

Jamie followed the instructions, with slow careful loops through the aisles. He located the ladies on the second floor, standing by a librarian's desk. As he watched, the librarian came back with two large tomes. Penny signed a sheet the librarian pointed toward on the counter. They took the volumes and located a table to the side with two rows of shelves between them and the librarian. There was a display case Jamie thought would afford him a reason to be a bit closer to the ladies. Penny began to turn the pages as she referenced a piece of paper. Jenny waved her hand with a device palmed over each page Penny paused at.

They spent nearly twenty minutes in this activity. Penny retuned the tomes to the librarian and then signed the sheet on the counter. Both ladies quickly walked toward the stairs and down, while Jamie watched over the second-floor rail.

He sent a quick text to EZ, uncertain as to what to do. She quickly replied.

> Go ask the librarian if you might be able to see the diaries of George Washington. See if you can identify the volumes the ladies reviewed. Then leave and go stake out the apartment again

Jamie walked over and added a bit of Irish brogue as he made the request and smiled at the librarian. The petite librarian, with her wavy brown hair and glasses, was professional as she explained that the diaries were available online for viewing. It wasn't even necessary for him to come into the library. She offered to write down the access information and a few tips for viewing. While she turned to get some paper, he looked at the sheet on the counter and nearly choked at what he read. The noise drew her attention.

"Sir, are you alright? Do you need to sit down?"

Jamie caught his breath and replied, "Not feeling so good. Can you point me to the men's room, please?"

She indicated the directions and Jamie quickly left the desk. Once inside the men's room, Jamie sent a text to EZ.

> The volumes were two on nuclear bomb assembly from the 1940's, pictures to follow of the titles

He sent the photos he had snapped while he distracted the librarian and then made his way out the back exit and to his car. During the ride back to the apartment, he tried to speculate on how this event might tie back to what he had witnessed while in Hansford, Washington. The lady in that museum had appeared to be of Muslim descent. These ladies did not. But the man shadowing them could be.

Jamie stopped and grabbed a burger on the way back to his post. It surprised him how hungry he was, so he went back and added fries too and had finished his meal before he arrived. After circling the block once to see if the SUV was in the area, he found it sitting where he suspected it had been earlier. Driving past it, he noted it was empty and the windows were up. Once he was on the block he had occupied earlier, he changed his parking position and car direction, just in case. Then he worked his way through the shadows back to his position.

As the sun moved toward the horizon and scattered colors about the neighborhood in the hour after he moved into position, an SUV pulled up in front of the apartment. It was stopped for several minutes before the door opened, and a different lady exited. She too had on a burka, but once she was outdoors, it quickly came off as she walked toward the door. She stopped as if someone inside the vehicle made a comment and turned to listen. She commented back, paused, and then headed back to the door. She knocked and was admitted by Jenny.

Jamie waited for the SUV to leave and was surprised when a man came out of the shadows and approached the SUV, leaning in the window. A few minutes later the man returned to his post. Jamie scrolled through his pictures and paused. It was as he'd suspected. Mercedes was the face he'd captured when she turned to face the vehicle. Now he was really confused, but he sent a text out with the photos.

The strength that he always counted on had almost returned, except for the numbness in the right foot. It had been his determination that had allowed him to reach the vehicle. Annoyingly, his wrists secured with zip ties, even though in front, made trying to manipulate the door to the SUV a challenge. His hands were tied in such a way that they behaved as one short movement with limited finger control. Tyler had made it this far with his powerful legs and feet, but now he was thinking about how he might actually drive the vehicle in his current circumstances. Having the keys and hobbling this far wasn't even half the battle in his mind. The door gave in to his persistence, and he climbed up into the seat. Using only his left leg and foot, he reached over and grabbed the handle with his toes. Then, lying over toward the right seat, he pulled it closed.

He was breathing hard with the effort but was unwilling to stop. The keys were held in his mouth while he tried to get them between his fingers to press the door lock button. It took four attempts, but he'd finally succeeded as he heard the comforting click. He didn't think the terrorists would be out anytime soon, but he wanted to at least remain out of reach. Though he tried several times to get the key into the ignition with his hands, his continued failure resulted in his giving up in frustration. The angle was impossible the way his hands were bound. He might not even be able to turn over the ignition if the key was inserted.

Reviewing his options, he finally moved to the passenger seat to gain better leg room. He was glad yoga was his friend when he was able to get his foot up to his hands. It seemed to take forever to position the toes of his left foot and the key at the correct angle.

His mind traveled to the Claw Crane carnival game where the player manages the crane and positions it over the toys. Once the toy got snagged it moves over the shoot to be dropped to the player, but looks can be deceiving. Few people ever win with that game, but they keep trying. When it failed to align, he groaned, but he did not drop the keys. He felt encouraged. At least he didn't have to add more coins to keep playing. After what seemed like hours, but was more like minutes, the alignment was perfect and the key slid into the opening. After that, only a slight tap with his big toe was required to make certain it was in all the way.

As he caught his breath, his eyes rested on a mobile phone one of his captors must have left. He carefully used his right and left feet to grab it off its resting area in the passenger cup holder. Then he dropped it into his lap as he worked his body down in the seat. Amazingly, the tied hands were able to hold it. He was not familiar with this type of phone, so turning it on took time. He slowly turned the device over and tried various buttons. Finally, he was rewarded with a screen. It so happened it was a touch screen with large buttons. He sighed happily and found the screen to enter a number. Painstakingly slowly, he entered Juan's number, and after it connected it rang incessantly and dropped to voicemail. He left a short message and then tried to phone EZ.

It connected after four rings and she said, "Hello, who is this?"

Tyler tried to enable the button for speaker, and while he struggled, he shouted, "EZ, it's me, Tyler. I stole this phone. I'm all tied up but I think I'm still somewhere in the Washington D.C. area." Finally, the button enabled.

He heard as EZ asked, "Are you a turtle?"

The question brought him up short. He muttered to himself for a moment and then finally it hit him that this was the go code question Juan had taught everyone to use. It was an old fighter pilot gag that was always played on the new flyer to the squadron. Invariably, the new guy would go to the officers' club, and the first thing that would happen was you would be challenged with the question *are you a turtle*? If you answered with anything other than *you bet your sweet ass I am*, you had to buy the house a round of drinks. It was this pilot custom that Juan had adopted for the team to use in the event you were ambushed and forced to make a call. If you answered the challenge with anything other than *you bet your sweet ass I am,* then it was assumed you were in trouble and someone was listening to the dialog. Any other response would be accepted by those holding you hostage, but the wrong response meant you were in danger.

Tyler flashed on the Juan training. He smirked and promised, "You bet your sweet ass I am! No one is with me. I'm tied up, so I need to drop this phone and pray the call stays up so I can get this vehicle moving."

He slid the phone back into the cup holder and the screen ended up away from him. He shouted, "Can you still hear me?"

"Yes, I'm trying to get a lock on the signal, Ty. It may take a few minutes. Just keep talking, so I know you're okay."

Ty used all his strength to slide back into the driver's seat. Once there he said, "I need to start the car. Then once I get it on the road, perhaps I can give you some hints on my location, outside of the fact I am in a warehouse district somewhere. The guys that brought me here are behind the warehouse doors, but they have a phone too. I don't want their backup catching me sitting here."

"Understood, Ty. Is Mercedes with you?"

Tyler groaned, "Nope, is she lost too? I was hoping the bastard Christopher got tired of her. Heck, I'm not certain how I was spotted."

He reached through the steering wheel with his hands and was able to get to the key. He applied pressure to turn the key, while his right foot was holding the brake. The SUV's engine roared to life.

EZ cheered and commented, "I think that was well done. Why does it sound like you're struggling so much?"

"My feet were tied. Now they aren't, though the nerve in my right foot must be damaged because it is very numb. My hands and wrists are zip tied in two places making it impossible to grip things easily or totally operate anything I usually take for granted."

Without describing the process to EZ, Tyler held the brake with his left foot and put the car into drive. He then shifted feet and used the left foot to help steer as he slowly drove out of the parking lot and onto the street. Very few cars were on the road, and he hoped his slow speed would encourage cars to pass around him.

"Alright, EZ, I have the car on the road. A street sign is coming up. I am going to pull as far to the right as far as I can, then stop to read it.

"It looks like it says Technology Park, but the sign is faded. The buildings around here are industrial, EZ."

EZ replied, "I think I have your signal. You seem to be in Maryland. It looks like you are in an industrial park and within it there appears to be an area being renovated.

"If you are okay to drive, I need you to go three more miles and make a right on Junction, and then two miles ahead on the right is a motel that seems to have a large parking lot you can fit behind. I am sending Jamie to help you."

Tyler suddenly felt like relief was within reach. He pulled back on to the roadway to follow her directions. He was a bit upbeat as he asked, "Jamie is here in Washington? Great! Is Ernesto here as well?"

EZ was quiet for a moment or two. "Jamie is there to help you. I redirected Ernesto to help Juan locate Julie. I will explain after we get you untied. By the way, how are you driving?"

Tyler chuckled and replied, "One foot on the gas and brake as needed, and one foot on the steering wheel, with two hands helping to control the wheel. It is not a pretty picture."

CHAPTER FIFTY-TWO

Bruised and Battered, Inside and Out

Juan and Ernesto arrived at the hospital. After showing passport information, they were allowed to go to the unit where the woman in the coma was being monitored. The room itself was being guarded by a constable who seemed very alert and not to be messed with. A nurse was at the desk where Juan and Ernesto had been told to go.

The young nurse looked up from her work when they approached and offered, "May I help you?"

Juan asked, "I think the woman that was on the telly this morning, presumably behind the door where the Bobby is standing, may be my missing wife. She disappeared at least four days ago. I am not certain exactly which day because I was working in Zurich. She hadn't contacted me in a few days and was unreachable, so my associate and I came to hunt for her. I would like to…"

Juan felt his phone vibrate, and as he glanced at it, he read the text. The nurse rolled her eyes as if he should not have stopped speaking to look at his phone. He had sent a request to Quip to see if he could track down any more information from the newscast to gain confirmation while they had been en route. He closed his eyes and offered up a prayer as he read.

Just finished reviewing the frames from the telly stations original video. 98% certainty it is Julie. Provide status as soon as you can. Glad she is found. Doing what I can from here – Q

"Sir?" the nurse questioned.

Juan showed the text to Ernesto then leaned away from the nurse to regain his composure. Ernesto smiled broadly and moved to get closer to the nurse.

"Madam," he started, "the woman you have in the room is very likely his wife. He is very distraught, as you can see. Can you provide us with a status, or can we speak to her physician? Please, he needs to see her immediately."

The nurse looked confused and concerned. She picked up the phone and placed a call. When the party answered she said, "Doctor, it seems we may have a relative, husband in fact, of your comatose patient. I will let the Bobby escort him in to verify there is no funny business going on, considering what the authorities suspect happened to the poor dear. Can you come down and speak to him and his, er…associate?"

The nurse walked over to the Bobby and told him what was happening. He stepped to the side and opened the door. Another Bobby walked into view from inside the room and was briefed. He nodded and indicated, "Sir, please come in and verify this is your wife. She is pretty banged up, but if it is her, you'll need to speak to my superior before you can stay with her."

Juan nodded and walked inside the room without uttering a word. He looked at her battered face. Now that he was close to her, he recognized the shape of her mouth, the extra piercings in her ears that most women don't have, and lastly, he gently grasped the hand he had held so often. He put his head on the rail of her bed. If someone had looked, they would have seen tears streaming from his eyes.

Juan swore to himself and vowed, "Sweetheart, someone will pay for doing this to you. I am here until you wake up. Don't leave me."

The physician came in and requested Juan step outside. He was an older man, about the same height as Juan, twinkling blue eyes, and nicely groomed salt and pepper hair. His manner was gentle as he explained to both Ernesto and Juan his patient's condition and the stages, he expected her to follow. He couldn't speculate on the verification process, but explained that once Juan was cleared to visit by the authorities, he was welcome to stay. They shook hands and agreed to meet first thing in the morning.

Ernesto asked, "Juan, do you want me to sit with you after the authorities clear you, or may I continue on with the plan and find out if someone saw anything? I spoke to the Bobby earlier, and he pinpointed the area she was found in. Once you are cleared, he promised to send the pictures."

"Ernesto, see if you can track it back to where they held her and get any descriptions. Text me any information you think is relevant, and I will take a look. I don't like to use my phone in a hospital, but a text should be fine.

"Now that the authorities know her name, I think they can verify when she entered the country. That will lead to who her husband is, so I should be fine."

"Alright. Do you want me to bring back food when I report the findings?"

"I'll text you if I get hungry. Right now, I'm enormously relieved."

James waited at the hospital entrance when Ernesto appeared. He didn't smile but nevertheless looked pleased that Julie was at least found.

"Now, James, I want to go to the area where the authorities indicated they found Julie and start our canvassing there. I want to drive around a little bit to see if there is a likely building to search first." Ernesto handed the sheet to James, who scanned it and looked up at Ernesto.

"Sir, this is very close to the area that woman mentioned yesterday. Perhaps the odd duck really did know something."

They walked to their vehicle and were on their way in minutes. They arrived in the area, where James slowed the car to a crawl and pointed out the location written on the paper Ernesto provided. There was very little in the area. A few very old homes were scattered on both sides of the street for most of the block's length, with a couple of older commercial buildings interspersed. James' speculation allowed that these buildings might have been used as storage over the years. He paused the vehicle right in front of the area where Julie had been recovered. He pointed out two staircases that lead down to two entrance doors, one of which was secured with a gate as well. Both appeared to be padlocked.

Ernesto got out of the vehicle and went to the first door and verified it was locked up with an older padlock. He walked over to the other one and found the gate in front of the door was not secured. When he tried the door handle, it opened and he readily gained access. James turned off the vehicle and locked it so he could assist Ernesto.

An older workman walked toward James. His cap and jacket were nearly as worn as the industrial uniform pants he was wearing. The man barely nodded to James as he passed by and went into the second house after the building. James made a mental note to let Ernesto know then proceeded down the steps and into the building.

James noted the walls in the below ground area were a light grey, almost yellow, as if they'd been abused by decades of tobacco smoke. The marks and mars along the walkway and floor suggested carts were used, probably banging into walls as careless drivers pushed them through the halls. Certainly, it had not seen any sort of cleaning in a long time. As James continued to walk, there was an increase in the twists and turns of the hall-way, almost like a maze. He also picked up a growing odor of rodent waste and possibly rotting flesh of some sort. There were a couple of doors, and he tried each of them in turn, even though he knew that Ernesto had probably done the same thing. The stink increased the further he walked until he located Ernesto. Ernesto was trying to use his phone but apparently could not get service because of how deep they were inside the building.

"James, don't go any further. I just found a dead woman in that room. I need to get a signal and call the authorities. Her eyes are still open, staring at the ceiling, and it appears she has been made meals for several vermin. It is not pretty. I took a few photos, and I may recognize her from a photo I saw, but I need to get away from the smell. Plus, I don't want to disturb the scene. I am sure the forensics team will have a field day. There is a huge tank, almost like a cistern, which contains some very cloudy water, possibly blood."

James nodded and preceded Ernesto back up to the street. Ernesto called the authorities and described the situation and the body. Before he disconnected, he promised he would wait for their arrival. Then he sent a text to Juan. He added to the text that he thought the dead woman might be Laurie and sent along the pictures of her face only.

Juan sent back a note that he would take a look. He also said he had been cleared and was in with Julie now. No change in her condition.

CHAPTER FIFTY-THREE

Regrets and the Grateful

Mike Patrick was finally home after a long day at work and the pub. He'd spent too much time drinking to his brilliance and success. The door would remain locked, until someone with a key, or someone who was reasonably sober, unlocked it. After several attempts to fit the key into the slot, he reared back to gather his mental acuity and with a heavy slur stated, "Come on, you old drunk bastard! Don't make me repeat what the basketball coach used to yell at you when you missed the shot, right?

"He'd say, Patrick, imagine there's hair 'round it! But I don't think that's gonna help here, since I'm so crocked…"

All of a sudden, a pair of helpful hands took the keys from him and promptly opened the door to his flat. Weaving back and forth somewhat, he turned to give his thanks when the helping hands became an assailant's hands, shoving him hard into the darkness of his flat. The push definitely gave him more movement than his body could deal with, so he ended up stumbling and slammed into the small hallway table, then he crashed to the floor.

This action, rather than causing him to pass out, helped bring some of his cognizant thinking back, along with his foul temper. The hall light had been switched on, and he could see that not one but four men stood inside his hallway as they were closing the door.

He bellowed, "You bastards! What was that for? I didn't need your help, and I sure don't need any of your crap! You stooges get out before I call the Bobbies to come get your stinking bodies! You're trespassing!"

The leader smirked slightly, and he winced with a groan of pain. Then with no small effort, he announced, "Patrick, we are here to discuss…your skimming techniques which we know you use…with Kashan."

The halting statements, made with a Persian accent, immediately sobered up Mike. A sick feeling of fear now gripped him as his mind raced to get the situation under control. If these men were here for Kashan, then this wasn't going to be pleasant. He quickly recalled that the last oil executive Kashan had dealt with, who cheated on their arrangements, was never found intact. There were just hundreds of pieces of him scattered to the winds. Mike and Marge had offered up their services as soon as their competitor's demise was discovered. A stray thought occurred to him, *when dealing with terrorists, at some point you might also experience terror.* That thought didn't make him feel any better.

Mike slowly sized up his chances against the four of them and decided the best course of action was to attempt to reason with them. "No, you are mistaken! It was not me. It's Marge who uses deceit! I don't have the access codes to do disbursements, only she can do that! You can't skim if you don't have access rights! I'm telling you, if there are shortages, then she is the one stealing! Not just from you, but from both of us!"

Achmet smiled slightly at the trembling man, totally at his mercy. In a voice that masked his pain, he stated, "You are an oaf and a pig. You steal from those you call friends. Your own records verify this. You were foolish to not understand, we have eyes everywhere."

The heavy drinking and the fear from the intruders now had Mike ready to throw up, but he swallowed it back. "You're referring to those bogus records that I let Dabir have? What do you think, I'm stupid or something? I always keep a set of phony books around for just such an occasion. You don't honestly think I'd let some copyboy handle important documents which would incriminate me, do you? Is he here with you, so I can laugh at his accusations?"

Achmet slightly smirked and winced again, then slowly offered, "Dabir is a bit too…delicate for some parts of…business. However, this is unimportant as we now have full access. We don't need you."

Mike went cold inside at the statement. Before he could plead with them, Achmet continued. "However, some gratitude will be shown…if you tell us where to find…Natasha."

Scared, angry, and confused, Mike demanded, "Who the hell is that? I don't know a Natasha!"

Achmet bristled a little bit and painfully responded, "She is the one…and I want her back to finish our business." The pain was increasing so he stopped and struggled for a few seconds before he continued. "She escaped…before telling us why…she was spying…she did damage to my men and attacked me." Achmet gestured to his neck.

Unwisely Mike smirked and replied, "Well, now, ain't that something? I still don't know who she is. But if she fought her way out of your clutches, she must be a brute! If that's true, then a big strapping male ought to be able to mop the floor with you!"

That said, Mike lunged at his assailants in one last desperate effort to turn the tables to his advantage.

Mike slowly opened his eyes. He thought he had cleared the dizziness so he tried to take in his surroundings, but nothing made sense. It could have been minutes or hours since he was conscious, but he couldn't pinpoint it. The only thing he was certain of was he was in awful pain. He hurt everywhere.

He became aware that his arms and legs were immobile, yet he was sort of sitting up. He tried to swallow, but his mouth seemed too swollen to cooperate. As his eyes began to put things into focus, he could just make out his image in the mirror that faced him. He could see why his arms ached so badly. Both arms had been forced backwards at a terrible angle to secure him to the chair. He sat at such an odd angle that he could see the dislocated shoulders on each side of his naked body.

Mike's eyes and brain began to focus much faster as he processed his true circumstances. He could now see the chain that was looped through the carefully torn hole in his upper lip, which was desperately agonizing. In trying to lift his head to an upright position, he pulled the chain through his lip taut. He reviewed what he could see in the low light conditions and the mirror as he visually followed the chain down between his legs to whatever it was fastened onto.

Mike refused to believe the image reflected in the mirror. Even in the low light, it was impossible to doubt what his eyes saw. He was frightened so much that he started to cry. They had secured him naked to a chair, with a hand grenade strapped to the seat. The grenade pull pin was connected to the chain forced through his upper lip. If he raised his head any further, the chain would pull the pin out, and he had absolutely no way to leave the blast area except in bits of blood, meat, and bone. The sobbing was causing him to breathe too heavily, applying unwanted pressure to the chain and the connected pin.

He forced himself to calm down as he tried to think of a way out of his circumstances. With everything hurting so much and all options gone, except one, he did something he had never done. He regretted his life's choices and wished he could unburden himself by confessing. Through all his suffering, he resolved that he should dictate his last will and testament even though there was no one to receive it.

The emptiness he saw as he stared into the mirror made him want to recite his penance aloud. He offered what he could through his thick swollen lips. "Honey, like you always said, I got everything I deserved. I'm sorry I didn't give you any children like you wanted. You were right to leave when you did. I wish I could at least leave something of me with you. I finally understand why it was so important.

"Here sits that ruggedly handsome roughneck you wanted kids with, dictating his last will and testament to… his reflection. Like I always said…what did I always say? Does it even matter now?"

Mike took one last look at himself in the mirror. He watched the tears running down his cheeks. Then he smirked at himself in the mirror. He was unable to pronounce the letter R when he mumbled through his swollen lips. "Supplies! Supplies! I'm going out with a whimper AND a bang! Now before I take my last action, let me give all my worldly goods to…" At that moment his heart began to spasm due to all the physical abuse his body had endured. The heart attack caused him to gasp for air, thus wrenching his head back, which pulled the pin out of the grenade. Mercifully the horrific pain in his chest was such that he didn't have time to worry about the impending explosion. Nothing like a lot of pain to distract you from worrying about being blown to bits.

Out on the street below, an elderly lady was walking her dog when the explosion ripped through Mike's flat, sending building material, furniture, and body parts out the window several stories above her. Once she had recovered from the noise and falling debris, she looked to see if her beloved pet was okay and noted with horror that a full set of male genitals had landed on her poor dog. The lady promptly brushed the organs off into the running water of the curbside ditch where they were quickly washed down the drain. The four-legged rats living under the city were grateful for the unexpected bounty. At last, it seemed someone was grateful that Mike Patrick had come to dine with them.

CHAPTER FIFTY-FOUR

Negotiations

Chung-Ho marveled at the casual tone of the male caller. His voice sounded like they were old friends catching up on shared acquaintances. The disbelief was quickly picked up by the others in the room with him.

After a few minutes of idle chat from the caller, and enough time to have the shock wear off, Chung-Ho finally asked, "Who am I speaking with? Actually, I must amend that to who am I listening to, because since I answered the phone, you've done nothing but talk."

The man chuckled lightly and promptly offered, "Apologies, Chung-Ho, but I thought a direct approach would make the most sense in these circumstances. Allow me to begin again with introductions. I am called Kashan, of Persian descent. I am also the source of the oil that has been coming to you on a regular basis. I am reaching out to you so we can do business directly without ePETRO as the middleman. I assumed that you would welcome a lower price per barrel, or am I mistaken?"

Chung-Ho stared hard at his son Chung-He, along with the others. They sensed his annoyance, but when he broke into a smile, they were able to breathe again. Chung-Ho responded, "It is unlikely that this is what westerners call a prank call, since this number is only available to a handful of trusted people. Better stated, useful people. Not knowing for sure who you are, I must assume that you have obtained my number and some detailed notes on past discussions. For some reason you decided to try your luck. Am I right?"

Again, Kashan chuckled briefly and said, "Allow me to be a little more transparent with my motives, which I suspect are very close to your own. I and my constituents are dissatisfied with the low price per barrel that we are receiving. Unless I missed my guess, you are dissatisfied with the high price you are paying for oil. The leap of faith discussion I am proposing is what if we could give you a 10% discount on your price of oil? Same terms as in the ePETRO contract, and we will continue to accept payment in North Korean Won. All you have to do is agree to source it directly with my organization."

Chung-Ho, being the consummate negotiator, paused then replied, "Perhaps you could share a larger discount with my country, say rather like 15%. I am at something of a disadvantage, not knowing what you were being paid for your product. I am frugal enough to ask for a higher discount."

Kashan grinned and said, "It is said that wise negotiators always give themselves some room to navigate with seasoned professionals. Alas, I am but a poor uneducated Middle Eastern man who never learned that lesson. I was always taught to share one's bounty fairly.

"It would please you to know, my new associate, I have already done that in this case. ePETRO representatives were taking a 20% markup on our product and giving you their story, *this is my best price when dealing with the likes of you.* I propose we split the difference, you get a drop in price and we begin getting what we were cheated. That is how I like to do business. Our offer stands at a 10% discount effective immediately upon your agreement."

All the meeting attendees closely watched Chung-Ho as he smirked slightly and offered, "I must admit there is a certain amount of freshness to your approach. We will consider after a discussion here. Am I to assume that any counter offers from ePETRO should be ignored?"

Kashan smiled and stated, "We are but humble merchants, my new associate, and would never presuppose to dictate to our buyers. I would leave you to be guided by your own counsel and trusted advisers. I look forward to our next conversation. May I call you in two days?"

Chung-Ho responded, "Make it three. Good day."

After Kashan disconnected from the call, Dabir asked, "Uncle, the ePETRO documents clearly show a 25% margin. Did I not make that clear?"

Kashan smiled and reminded him, "It is said that wise negotiators always give themselves some room to navigate with seasoned professionals. Never give your best price first. You will learn, nephew."

Marge was very pleased with how her plans were proceeding. Sipping her special black tea, she made the intended call to her North Korean contacts to boast. Chung-Ho answered the call promptly. "Madam, it is good to hear from you. Tell me, what news of our special package? When can we expect it?"

Marge was pleased with the greeting but sensed something was off in his tone. She guardedly answered, "Chung-Ho, comrade, you must be having a very upbeat day to sound so cheerful. If that is the case, let me add to the positive things in your life. The special package is in transit and should be there in ten days with a slight stop in the Philippines. You understand the precaution of routing through another country to avert suspicions."

Chung-Ho smiled slightly and responded, "Ah, very prudent of you, madam. We shall wait for the promised shipment then. Now allow me to change subjects and dialog on another topic."

"Of course, comrade!"

"I would like to discuss the price per barrel of our next shipment of oil. With the additional expenditures for the special project, my organization is going to need a price reduction of say 10% on our next shipment. I trust your people will understand and appreciate our request."

Marge snapped out of her smugness with a jerk to her hands that threatened to spill her tea. After a few moments of fumbling with the mute button and trying to regain her composure, she regrettably explained, "My dear Chung-Ho, we are operating at razor thin margins already, not to mention risking the wrath of the Western authorities by supplying your country the oil it needs so badly. Would that I could grant your request, but we have no such margin excess to offer. We will hold up our end of the bargain at the present price to meet our operational needs and your country's sake. I hope you understand my position."

Chung-Ho smiled at all the silent listeners to the conference call but then replied, "Madam, I quite understand. I trust you will not hold it against me for striving to get a better deal for my poor country."

Sensing that the crises negotiations were going in her favor, Marge breathed a low sigh of relief and said, "Of course, comrade, I quite understand. Rest assured that any discounts that can be obtained in my sourcing will be passed on to your noble country."

Chung-Ho smiled again and said, "Madam, it does give me comfort to have such trusted business associates as yourself. We will make the necessary disbursements as soon as the special shipment arrives. Until then, I bid you a good day."

After disconnecting the call, Marge turned to Christopher and asked, "Can't you find that Patrick jerk? I need to discuss this last request from the NK vultures. Christ, they want further discounts. The only way to do that is to squeeze the Muslim vermin he deals with. I want one more percentage point from them, so I can pass that through to these other jerks! See if you can locate the bar, he's in and get him to work this issue."

Christopher mused a moment and then offered, "Madam, if I may point out, we have several variables at play here, including missing personnel which now includes Mike Patrick. Making aggressive moves when we don't have all our chess pieces accounted for is…well, unwise. My counsel is to proceed slower until we have a better picture. The discount you seek can always be given after the fact, and the goodwill gained will be just as valuable. You might consider the slight margin reduction and give them a percentage point to keep them from looking elsewhere."

Marge was unsuccessful at suppressing her smile. "You know, it occurs to me that Mike, if we locate him, has outlived his usefulness in our business dealings. You, on the other hand…you appear to be an excellent candidate as his replacement. Unless you have any ethical objections, let me put a few more things in play to make that so. What do you think?"

Christopher gave as much enthusiasm as an emotional cripple could give as he said, "Madam, I will apply myself to any issue you desire."

Marge smiled in a conniving way and replied, "A male worthy is a male found."

CHAPTER FIFTY-FIVE

The Key is the Shipper

George and Summit were pleased with the discoveries they'd made with the knowledgeable support of Azra. They agreed to divide their efforts and continue to gather information. Summit was assigned to Azra, with her families' knowledge of the local craftsmen, and the recent changes in the economy. George was assigned to continue to gather additional information from the local workman.

George and Summit both felt the motivation for these particular craftsmen was focused on money, rather than family, which for some people changed their outlook. Case in point, Bayram the tile maker was proud of his work and boasted of his family's talent, where Ekin was vacant and mechanical, with no pride. The Turks were a proud and happy people which made Ekin's store stand out as a target.

For two days, Summit and Azra had spent a great deal of time together, seeing the sights of the city and enjoying one another. Summit was taken to visit her family, who welcomed him with local lore. They also gossiped about the best, worst and strangest of the community. Time spent becoming accepted often allowed for defenses to be dropped, as well as more sharing to occur. Summit found Azra a delightful companion, but he was careful to be respectful and reasonably chaste with only a stolen kiss or two. Summit drove her to the airport for her next four-day trip. They promised to keep in touch, even after he indicated he would not be in Turkey for much longer. On the return drive, he mentally cobbled together a timeline of events that might become relevant.

George had been busy watching the target store front from different positions. He had documented the comings and goings of different people as well as the number of deliveries and pickup times. There was definitely a rhythm to the deliveries and the pickups. The coarse looking characters came and went, usually at dusk or later, lasting sometimes until early dawn. Many of these men reminded George of those from the docks in Singapore. These questionable delivery trucks often parked behind the building and used several people to help load or unload during the night The other set of deliveries were from dawn until about dinner and appeared to be more like the local craftsmen, happy and cheerful at selling their products. He captured a couple of photos of the products being unloaded, which were predominantly the special benches with the spring tops.

George took a few breaks each day to eat, rest and upload photos and his impressions of the activities. Summit reviewed George's findings, added his gathered information and thoughts, and updated the findings. Once completed, Summit uploaded the information to the team's share site and looked for any comments made by the others. Brayson made the most comments, usually by asking thoughtful questions. The questions he posed always had Summit thinking a little differently and consequently he left comments for George. While Azra was in town, he added other questions for clarity should they get a chance to speak in person.

One of the photos George had captured contained new labeling they had not seen before, SCS. Deciphering these new initials became like a game on the share site for those who checked in. The only thing that was reasonably close for the data they collectively had was Steven Christopher. That was scoffed at for being way too obvious; surely no one was that arrogant! However, once that had been posed, a blast of other words for the letters included Scoundrel, Shithead, Sabotage, Surely and so forth, but nothing fit. It did put a bit of levity into the mix, which the team needed. The favorite one to date was So Clearly Stupid, submitted by Ernesto on the fly.

When Azra had left on her next trip, Summit filled in with the observation time at the store, so that George could start to follow some of the late-night pickups to their next destination. The first night George lost them off one of the side streets. The next night he and Summit decided to get ahead of the truck. Toward the end of their vigil, Summit dressed in typical Istanbul worker garb and walked in the alley behind the storefronts, appearing to search for cast offs from the various businesses. His goal was to get close enough to attach a tracking device to the underside of one of the trucks as it was being loaded.

A burly, rough-looking dock worker coordinating the loading of the trucks spotted Summit and shouted in Arabic, "What are you doing back here? You don't belong here."

Summit, in his best Arabic, replied, "Looking for a few hours work. Just a few Lira. I will work hard."

"No, go away. You are too scrawny for this work. Look how small you are next to the rest of my men. Now go!"

Summit advanced toward the man with pleading in his eyes as he begged, "Please, sir, a few hours. My family is hungry, my children cry, my wife complains." Pushing it even further, Summit did the unthinkable and grabbed the man's shirt.

The response was immediate and as expected. He was pushed hard and fell against the truck, sliding down to the rear wheel near the axle. He quickly affixed the locator device as he struggled to gain his footing. Once upright, he bowed apologies without saying a word.

The man shouted, "Now get out of here before I tell my men to deal with you. Scum!"

Summit walked away. Once out of sight he removed his top robe, revealing black clothes underneath, which helped him to remain concealed as continued documenting the worker's progress. He gave a thumbs up to George, who was headed down to where he had lost the truck the previous night.

George tracked the vehicle to the docks and was able to capture additional information on the vessel itself and the crew. George had captured all he could from the dockside and decided he needed to see if any more information might be available. He found a dockside bar where the inhabitants were already several glasses deep.

After buying a round for the house, in his rough Turkish, he announced, "I believe that the captains and crews of the long-range vessels are underpaid and overworked. Their love for the sea put them into this work, but they are being exploited. I would like to do a news piece on this to open the eyes of ship owners all over the world. I am willing to pay for a few minutes of time, with no names ever mentioned." To make his point he held up a few Lira.

The men ignored him for the most part, but as the barriers were already lowered with their inebriated states, a few wandered into the corner where George had positioned himself. Over the next three hours he heard snippets of stories of where crews had gone, sometimes where they should not, and the cargo they often carried. One man said this was his last trip on the tanker, already identified by George, because the trips were arduous and the pay was in fact very poor. The food and drams onboard this vessel were better than most long voyages. None of the captains were willing to speak and slowly drifted out of the bar.

George paid each man he had spoken to and bought another round for the house before he made his way out the back door. As he made his way back to the hotel, he thought about the insight he had received into S Christopher Shipping. That name had been provided by two of the older workers who suggested it had been brought into the market along with the improved trip rations nearly a year ago.

CHAPTER FIFTY-SIX

Timetables

Marge struggled to maintain her speech patterns at a civil level but failed as she demanded, "Any luck finding the Patrick weasel? I've got oil orders piling up, and no one to run things at ePETRO! I should probably just install you now to pitch our new business model to the Muslim vermin."

Christopher contemplated a moment and offered, "Madam, I can see nothing but difficulty with that approach."

Marge, now in a short-tempered mood, retorted, "So what are you saying?"

Christopher coolly answered, "Consider how this will look from their side. Their trusted conduit goes missing, for whatever reason, and the freshly installed newbie is demanding a 10% price reduction beginning with the next shipment. If that was shoved at you, how would you respond?"

Marge managed to tone down her response, but still she bellowed, "Dammit, I've got these jerk-weed Koreans wanting a 10% discount before they take another shipment! I show our tankers stacking up ready to load, but no one to sell to! What am I supposed to do with them?"

Christopher mused a moment and suggested, "I would recommend that you cut them free and not take any more oil from the Muslims. After all, we currently have no buyers."

Marge began to calm down, mulled over Christopher's suggestion and, in a more civil tone, asked, "You know that if I can cut those tankers free, I can't just go reengage them if the Koreans change their minds."

Christopher nodded. "That's true. It will take some time to find available tankers, and it will disrupt the flow of product to their country. May I point out that when product flow is disrupted prices tend to go up as a consequence."

Marge now tracked perfectly with Christopher's thinking as she smiled and responded, "Yes, prices would be forced up. You know, Christopher, you remind me of how Mike Patrick used to conduct business."

Marge continued, "Then, what do we do with the idle tankers?"

Christopher responded, "I seem to recall that your shipping contract was for volume to be shipped, but I don't recall that there was a time deadline. May I suggest that we politely discharge them until we have more oil to ship? That way they can freelance for a while until we either clear up the contract price issue or until you find Mike Patrick. It will also put pressure on the Muslims to accept a reduced price, if we don't accept any new shipments."

Marge, now feeling a bit emboldened, offered, "I've decided I need to have you take over the reins there at ePETRO to get things under control. Even if we find Mike Patrick, there is no guarantee that he will function to my expectations. You, Christopher, have earned that privilege. And, since Kashan will not deal with me because I'm female, you are the most logical choice. How soon can you leave?"

Now put on the spot, Christopher considered the possibilities for a moment. He answered, "Madam, I am not an oil man, and therefore could not simply step into that role without a huge learning curve. I must therefore decline your request. Besides, with all our missing people and operations in play, you need me focused on these other operations. My best value-add for you is to work in the shadows, not in the limelight. I suggest that you move in and take over yourself, until we can get some of these loose ends under control."

Marge was unsettled and annoyed with Christopher's refusal, but his logic was sound. The problem was that she too didn't want to be in the limelight for what was going to happen. She'd set up Mike to take the fall should the operation go sideways, and that time was fast approaching.

She tried one more time. "Christopher, it wouldn't be a permanent thing. I just need someone to step in for a short period of time, while I can find a suitable replacement for Patrick. Besides, you could still have Dabir to do most of the grunt work. Just don't trust him with any passwords."

Christopher replied, "Madam, I can see that you won't accept my decline. At least allow me to complete some unfinished business in the D.C. area before departing for London. I need a few days to complete our DEATAC operational issues. Then I could be your interim ePETRO caretaker. I will need five days. Surely the operation can function a few more days without someone in that role, particularly if you make some pointed calls to allow the oil tankers to be set free to operate elsewhere."

Marge smiled at her small victory. "I can deal with that. I will set the stage for your entrance and will stabilize the operation with a few calls. However, if you can leave earlier than five days, then do so. Call me to let me know if you can accelerate the timetable."

Najih's knees still plagued his mobility, and they made him even more agitated than usual. He stopped for a moment to down a few more pain killers before re-engaging with his workers, who seemed to be moving in slow motion.

Najih was frantically trying to get everyone to move faster and hurriedly stated, "This is taking far too long! You must move everything into the trucks faster! We must leave before they get here. Don't you understand?"

One of his henchmen seemed reluctant to move very quickly. When Najih roughed him up a little, the man groused, "We just got this place all set up! Now you want to move everything in a hurry to somewhere else! We cannot assemble the sensitive components for our uranium weapon under these conditions!"

Najih threatened to backhand him. "I have been running and surviving on my wits and intuitions for months in this wretched country. I know when it is time to move so our operation is not captured! Do not be such a lout as to question me or my decisions!"

Even though the henchman was unconvinced, he reluctantly nodded and continued to help move equipment onto the waiting truck.

Najih's phone delivered a call which he answered with a snarl. "Steven, where is my shipment? I was told it would be here already, but it looks like another false promise!"

Steven, taking the statement in, asked, "It looks like you are moving your base of operations. Why now and where to, would be important details I need!"

Irritated at being questioned, Najih shouted, "I move when I feel something is wrong, or like in this case, because everything seems too good! As to where I am moving, I will let you know once I have the promised shipment! Where is my shipment?"

Not ready to back down from the verbal onslaught, Steven countered, "If you're going to move your location every time you have a premonition, how can I be expected to deliver your uranium?"

Najih, always adversarial, responded, "You have it for me then?"

Steven almost smiled as he started to reel in his prey. "Of course, I do, Najih. Have I not always come through for you in your campaigns? You wanted weapons, I have gotten you weapons. You have asked for personnel to collect your necessary engineering; I have gotten you personnel. You wanted uranium, I have procured uranium for you.

"There will be, of course, the matter of payment and where we can do the exchange. That event is now up in the air with this move. Please call me when you are settled so our transaction can be completed. Oh, and I have to leave the country on business in three days, so I recommend it be before then."

Najih, now furious, shouted into the phone at the disadvantaged position he now found himself in. "What? I can't get this place moved before then! You must give me more time! I must have the uranium!"

Steven calmly suggested, "You could just stay there long enough for us to make the transaction and then make your move."

Najih now sensed his plans must be altered. "When can I have the shipment? We need to leave this area, as I sense it is not safe!"

Steven offered, "I can have it to your current location the day after tomorrow as planned. It is just crossing into the state, and the handling has all been arranged. If you move your operations, then all those pre-arranged plans must be altered, and none of our arrangements are done over the phone, but in person per your insistence. Your choice."

A brooding Najih was silent for a moment but then covered the phone. He yelled out to his team. "Everyone! Stop what you are doing! We must hold here for two more days to collect the last shipment! Find a stopping point for today. We will finish packing up tomorrow. Plan to leave as soon as the last shipment arrives. Stand down for tonight, but keep a vigilance!"

Najih uncovered the phone and continued his conversation with Steven. "We will wait for you at the original destination as agreed, Steven. Do not delay." He then disconnected from the call.

CHAPTER FIFTY-SEVEN

No Time to Rest

The battery on the phone died shortly after he reached the parking lot of the hotel and confirmed the location with EZ. Tyler was free of his captors but so frustrated with his current condition. He had worked on the zip ties on his hands until his wrists were bloodied and too sore to continue. Resolved that he would have to wait, he decided to make his way to the back seat and perhaps try to at least lie down where he could work on flexing his foot, which was still mostly numb.

He retrieved the keys out of the ignition with his toes and transferred them to his mouth while he made his way to the back seat. What should have been a comfortable leather seat was found painfully stuck to the portions of him that were bloody and sweaty. It was a long and tedious process but he finally ended up in the back seat, though he was less than comfortable. Following a bit of contortionist activity, he was able to move the keys to his paddle hands and press the lock button. Then, as he started his assessment, moving his legs and feet to help his circulation, he noticed a lump the size of a golf ball on the outside of his right foot. At least that explained the pain and numbness.

With his feet elevated and moving, he slowly drifted off with the warm sun relaxing him. Images flickered across his mind in his dreams. He saw Mercedes being mishandled, his captors baiting him, and always Christopher with a snide look and evil eyes. His restless slumber was broken by an unfamiliar voice yelling and alternating between attempts at opening the door and banging on the window. Before he opened his eyes, he readied himself for death. Then he decided he was not giving an inch and kept his eyes shut, playing possum. If they opened the door, he was certain he had at least one shot with his feet.

The banging resumed, and he heard the muffled words inside the SUV. "Tyler, Tyler, it's me, Jamie! Open the door, man. Don't be dead on me. Come on, man. EZ said you were okay and safe here. Just unlock the door, Tyler, and I'll help you. I have a medical kit with me. There's also a clinic not far away." Jamie's pleas finally penetrated Tyler's defenses. He opened his eyes and saw a man he recognized from only a picture.

His hands tried to locate the button on the key fob several times without success. Finally, it connected and the lock on the front door released. Jamie opened the door and released the back locks, then he rushed around to open the door. Jamie quickly inspected the zip ties on Tyler's hands and snipped them in just the right way. Being on his back had helped Tyler's circulation so they weren't as swollen as one would expect with ties so tight. Jamie quickly cleaned off the wounds and applied some antiseptic.

Jamie offered, "Tyler, we need to get you really cleaned up, so I can treat these wounds. Can you make it about twenty minutes to my motel, or do you want to go to the walk-in care place I passed on my way to this complex?"

Tyler nodded and then tried to form his words, but the dryness of his mouth and throat interfered. Jamie offered him a sip of water and helped him rise to a sitting position. Tyler struggled to keep himself upright, as he was so tired and suddenly cold with the door open.

"Jamie, I stink like five-day old rotten fish, and a shower is needed. Can you crank up the heat in your car? I would like to minimize the whole shock thing that I fear is now setting in. Your place is fine, and we can assess the damage from there."

Jamie grinned and said, "Yeah, I smell ya. Let's get you cleaned up, and you'll feel better. I have blankets and ibuprofen ready for you. Let me help you to my car. EZ will be so glad to know you are okay. When I first arrived here, you looked dead so I warned EZ that it could be bad."

Tyler managed a chuckle and replied, "It is bad, Jamie, but let's get EZ relaxed while we determine the damage. Tell her I'm fine, so she'll stop worrying. Crank up the heat and update me on what has happened since I've been gone."

They got Tyler settled into Jamie's vehicle. With the heater blasting, Jamie began, "After I update you on everything that's happened, I would like to hear how you drove that car here. EZ said it was almost five miles. Between that ankle and your hands, I'm dying to know how you pulled it off."

Tyler replied, "No problem. Start with Mercedes and where she might be. I'm out of danger, but she is not."

Tyler had cleaned up, was treated for most of his wounds, and was finally relaxing. While he rested with his legs up on the wobbly coffee table in Jamie's motel room, Jamie explained more about what he had been doing since he arrived in Washington. He also shared the information he had learned while in Texas with Ernesto and how he was asked to come and keep track of Penny and Jenny.

He had set up a fairly good routine, in Tyler's opinion, for watching the ladies as well as learning of the other pair of eyes watching those same ladies. That Mercedes had entered the townhouse the ladies lived in helped to fit a few additional pieces into the puzzle being formed in Tyler's mind. The burkas were a bit odd, unless it was to simply confuse anyone watching or to chalk it up to Muslim activity.

The pictures that Jamie had captured and uploaded showed some men Tyler hadn't seen. However, when he searched the rest of the photos on the team files space, he was able to identify his captors to EZ. They spent some joint time tagging their photos to physical locations and any that appeared in multiple locations were noted as well.

Once EZ had photos of Tyler's captors, she had Quip turn the warehouse location and the images over to his contacts in the U.S. three letter organization to clamp down on where Tyler had left them. Unfortunately, the infiltration team found nothing.

Tyler was glad he was free, but he wanted to make certain they maintained eyes on Mercedes. Jamie indicated he was willing to return to his post to keep watch. Tyler agreed but wanted to also provide Jamie with backup. They spent some time fashioning a disguise which they both felt would prohibit the known parties from identifying him again. There was also the matter of the location of Steven Christopher.

Jamie was certain he had been visible in Houston and then vanished as he followed Jenny back to Washington. Tyler explained that Christopher had been handling Mercedes when he had been taken. The time difference would have allowed him to fly to Houston, but from there his destination was unknown. Mercedes might be inside with the ladies and not able to access the outside world. Perhaps the other watchers were there for insurance that she remain indoors. She had essentially been escorted to the location.

CHAPTER FIFTY-EIGHT

The Weakness of Hurrying

In his usually icy manner, Steven Christopher politely asked, "You had asked about oil tankers? As it turns out, I am able to source some for you. Enough to handle your next shipment. Can we negotiate a deal?"

Kashan studied a moment then asked, "How is it that you knew we would need oil tankers?"

Almost smiling, Steven responded, "The same way that I knew you had approached the North Koreans to sell direct. Information is my business, as it is yours. Are you prepared to discuss terms?"

"Terms? Why would it differ from the current ePETRO terms, unless you want something else? You are yet another Westerner looking to take advantage of a position of leverage. Tell me what's on your mind."

If he had any appreciation for humor, he might have chuckled, but he flatly stated, "You misunderstand. I ask for no additional monies, just a simple favor. Surely you are in a position to grant a small favor in return for all the services I've provided."

Kashan suppressed his smile and asked, "Very well then. What did you have in mind as a modest favor?"

Sensing his goal was within his grasp, Steven politely asked, "My employer has deemed my services irreplaceable over my objections. It occurs to me that if she were to resign her role in ePETRO, then we would be able to continue business unimpeded. Would this not benefit us both?"

Kashan hesitated a moment before he drew his conclusion. "Marge terminated?"

Steven responded, "I can see you are a man who can quickly grasp the obvious. If she were to abruptly resign, then our business association might proceed much smoother. Would you agree?"

"I see the logic of your *favor*." Stated with a smile, Kashan thought of what the future could potentially include. "I presume that timing is of the essence for this action?"

Again, unable to show any human warmth, Steven stated, "I'm glad you grasp the concept of Western time keeping."

Kashan thoughtfully asked, "And what of my associate, Dabir, there at ePETRO? What do you foresee his role to be there?"

Steven smartly responded, "I see no need to alter his role there. In fact, I had assumed that he would continue to provide some continuity during the *changing of the guards*. I trust you will find that satisfactory?"

Kashan nodded to himself. "Quite!"

Steven added, "Oh, and I will need 50% up front for the cost of the oil tanker leases. It's the disadvantage of being the new player in the oil supply game."

Kashan bristled and protested, "You're asking me to prepay?!"

Steven calmly replied, "Since I don't have the business relationships that ePETRO enjoys, I am forced to provide a retainer of good faith on this initial contract. I was assured that if everything proceeded accordingly that future transactions would be the usual payment upon delivery."

Kashan steamed a moment then offered, "I can only provide 25% up front. You must fill the balance to get our product moving."

Steven studied the situation a moment and said, "I am not in a position to fill in the balance, but perhaps I can use the arms shipment that I have on the way to you as collateral."

Kashan mused, "All your funding is tied up in other areas on our behalf? Is that what I'm to believe?"

"Correct. In order to get the weapons your group requested, I had to make advance payments, which is why I cannot cover the 50% prepay figure. If you are willing to wait until the delivery of the weapons has completed and the funds have been collected, then I could…"

Kashan cut him off. "I am not willing to wait for the oil tankers! Alright, westerner, you shall have your prepayment funds! Make sure that those tankers are in position tomorrow and that my weapons make the delivery point in Istanbul!"

Steven nearly smirked. "Yes, Kashan. All is staged and the usual courier should arrive there to complete the prepayment transaction within the hour."

Kashan studied the situation for a moment then asked, "For your courier to be so prompt you must have anticipated the outcome of these discussions. What if I had said no?"

Steven soothed, "I admit it was a calculated risk. If you said yes, timing would be critical to maintain balance, so I gambled on a yes answer. If you had said no, I could have simply recalled the courier. I suspect it is no less than you would have instructed your people."

Kashan was somewhat vexed with the situation but was unable to refute his logic. "Keep me updated to all the events." And then he disconnected from the call.

Trying to contain her annoyance, Mercedes responded, "Yes, Steven, I have it. Now that is the third time you have asked me to respeak the message, and every time it has been correct. When are you going to be satisfied that I can remember the contents of the message and its importance?"

Steven seemed to brighten a little as he stated, "I believe you do have it now, madam. Don't be too angry with me, but this transaction is of the upmost importance. I would have used one of my senior couriers, but she is unavailable at present. Since this is a time sensitive assignment, I am going to have you do it, but a little reassurance helps my state of mind. Apologies if I have questioned your abilities. I no longer have doubts about you, Mercedes."

A little uncomfortable with Steven's gaze on her, Mercedes asked, "Alright, I get it. When do I get my phone back? I am not used to being without a phone. What if I want to take a selfie on this trip? What am I supposed to do?"

Steven tersely replied, "We've talked about this. You will take the cash given to you and buy a burner phone once you get to the Philippines and reconnect there. Part of our courier service is that communications are designed not to be picked up on the digital landscape."

Mercedes, still irked at the situation and the close tracking she was under by Steven, smiled as she commented, "Okay, but can you at least give me a little space while I go to the ladies' room before getting onto this flight? I hate the little cramped airplane facilities. You don't need to monitor that too, do you?"

Mercedes added a slightly taunting smile to take the edge off the comment that again produced no noticeable change in Steven's features. Steven acknowledged with a nod, and Mercedes quickly headed for the restroom. What she really was doing was looking for an unguarded cell phone she could borrow to alert someone on her team. As luck would have it, one of the female patrons was just putting her phone away as she was gathering her stuff to leave the restroom. Mercedes deftly lifted it out of the outside purse pocket as they passed at the doorway.

The first empty stall quickly became her operational headquarters, and after defeating the simplistic password on the device, she was able to access an SMS texting program. It had been agreed upon that EZ would be the text target for impromptu communications, and as such she had an easy to remember number that could be quickly entered. Mercedes smirked as she entered the calling number by saying the memorized phrase 'EZ as π'. The team had protested the exercise, but Quip and EZ maintained you could always look it up if you forgot.

Mercedes was in a hurry to complete the task and hunt the female down to return her phone. She did not want to draw too much attention to the event. She quickly typed out a brief message, hoping that EZ would research it further. It read:

> EZ this is M. doing an AIM mission for Steven. Air from D.C. and need exit from flight 4096 after takeoff. Use G.I. escape protocol Stalker

Then Mercedes quickly gathered her few belongings, deleted the message from the user history, and left to try and return the lifted phone. Ordinarily it would have been difficult to locate the owner of the phone in such a large airport, but the highly vocal hysterics of the female made it quite simple. She handed the phone to the sobbing woman and calmly said, "I believe you lost this, madam. I spotted in on the ground as I left the ladies' room." She then quickly turned to locate Steven, only to discover he was right behind her.

Mercedes was nearly undone by him being so close and that she may have blown her cover. She lightly offered, "If she's like that with her android device, what is she like when she loses one of her own children? If I ever get that way, will you warn me?"

Steven only nodded, and Mercedes moved on to board the plane.

CHAPTER FIFTY-NINE

Standard Procedures
are Very Overrated

Questions came first from the Bobbies, then the detective, and continued for several hours with Ernesto and James, both separately, and then together. The coroner arrived and estimated the woman's time of death at several days ago and suspected drowning as an initial cause. With all the bite marks, bloating, and partial decomposition, it was going to be a long autopsy, at the very least.

Ernesto and James both kept to the same story, we were looking for our co-worker's wife. She had not called in for several days which caused concern. Ernesto displayed his consultant credentials, and James was only the local hired driver. As a consultant, Ernesto did ask if he could be kept apprised and perhaps get a view of the video camera footage from receptacles in and around the area. The request was considered and, though not approved or rejected, Ernesto was allowed to shadow the plainclothes detective assigned to the case, because he could identify where he believed she had worked. By keeping that information with the detective only at this point, Ernesto was at least temporarily considered as contributing to the investigation.

Ernesto contacted EZ and alerted her to the video feeds in the target area well before the Bobbies and detectives had arrived at the scene. The plan was that EZ would start the review from her side, and Ernesto could compare the findings from his side. Next, Ernesto sent a very lengthy text to Juan.

> We located Laurie. She has been dead awhile. I think Julie was being held in this location. She may have been tortured by near drowning. We have video feeds of the area under review. You may want to get her some significant psych help, Juan. It looks very harsh from this side.

Some time passed before a response was sent.

> Good to know. Maybe she simply doesn't want to wake back up if that was the case.

By the time Detective Collins, Ernesto and James arrived at the police station, the in-house technology guru, Warren, had the feeds loaded up and ready for viewing. Warren showed them how to start and stop each of the feeds and the tool for marking or making notations along the way. Warren indicated they had confiscated five days' worth of film from the days before and after the woman had been found on the sidewalk. Every camera in the area was to be reviewed in the hopes that it might allow them to get a view of the standard and non-standard traffic flows.

Ernesto suggested, "It might be helpful if we set up two of these stations with the feeds and do a little divide and conquer. Happy to assist if I may."

Warren looked to Detective Collins who nodded his approval and quickly set up another station with limited access to anything outside of the videos and the tool for notations.

Ernesto conferred with James briefly, and James left to handle the request. Ernesto and Detective Collins started the review. It was going to be a long night at this rate.

EZ had asked Quip for help with the videos while she went back to tracking down the location of the text supposedly sent by Mercedes. It was so short, no questioning for verification, and from a totally unknown number. EZ began the process of triangulation of the signal by the device, timing, and compared the wording in detail back to Mercedes' profile. She had to be absolutely certain that the text came from Mercedes before she acted on the information. The flight number was one that was set for departure later that night from Washington Dulles to Ninoy Aquino International *Airport*, Philippines. Why would Mercedes travel to that country for any reason? That is, unless she was being forced to, but why there?

EZ was about to take her findings to Quip for his input when he arrived at her office with a face that looked as if he'd lost his best friend. EZ went from asking her favor to near panic. "Quip, what in heaven's name is the matter, honey? You look like the system crashed big time, or your lunch is totally disagreeing with you. Whatever's gone wrong, we can handle it, but please don't keep me in suspense."

Quip, not usually evasive with EZ, seemed terribly tongue-tied, which was not a Quip trait she had ever witnessed. "Quip, honey, talk to me. Whatever it is, we can fix it together."

Since Quip was still not forthcoming with the answers or the questions, EZ decided he just needed time and felt explaining her problem would get his mind away from the dark place it was in currently. "I received the text supposedly from Mercedes, but not from her device or in a way that I can verify in any manner. I tracked the flight number as a destination to, of all places, the Philippines. Why the Philippines, do you think?"

Her monitor received a notice of communications from one of the systems working in background mode. She opened the attachment and read it.

> Tanker container being tracked has been diverted from
> original course and now is en route to Philippines, Port of
> Manila per their transmission of course change. They are citing
> medical issues for the change. Expected to reach port within
> two days at the current speed. We might notify The U.S. before
> it reaches port.

EZ stared at the message in absolute disbelief. She turned and saw Quip reading the notice over her shoulder. He nodded then took his smart phone from his pocket and selected a contact.

"Eric, Quip here. That vessel we talked about earlier has now changed course to Port of Manila. You might want to complete the intercept if your teams are in position…

"Yes, I can provide the signal frequency for your team to track…

"No, I don't have that answer yet…

"Possible flight interception needed in Washington. Will send you the flight number shortly. You might want to delay it until after the doors close and it taxis…

"Yes, I will send shortly…

"I can believe that…

"Happy to help…

"Cheers!"

Quip reached down and squeezed the top of EZ's shoulders in a reassuring manner. She wasn't certain if she was being reassured, or he was.

She was patient, but he was really pushing her to the limit when he opened with, "Sweetheart, you have known me long enough and seen enough to realize that I just don't believe in coincidences. There are logical outcomes from a myriad of inputs, but no real coincidences."

"Yes, I do know you that well, Quip. So?"

"So, my darling, when Julie pulled that great switcheroo on that Russian leader sometime back, she actually posted information on the Internet along with photos."

"Right, I remember. Again, so?"

"Do you recall how she looked in those photos, her hair, makeup, and so forth?"

"Sure, of course. I helped her do some of the photographs as well as photo-shopped some of the backgrounds to align with the regional clothing she wore. Why?"

Quip looked up at the ceiling and gathered his thoughts before he replied, "The Russian she helped eliminate previously had a real problem with a Muslim terrorist who had contributed to a bombing in Paris, among other things. The Russian killed him and advertised the method in great detail. Known relatives and friends of the terrorist likely saw the postings in social media channels."

"Quip, why do I feel like you are taking me through the bakery to build a watch? Get to it, will you, honey, or you just might find yourself on the couch tonight!"

Quip nodded his head, but the look on his face was so sad. "If that were my only problem, I would be able to deal with it, honey.

"The videos that we received and have been scanning with facial recognition programs have identified one of the former terrorist's relatives, an uncle named Achmet. He entered London under an assumed name. In the video feeds from the area that Ernesto and the local authorities are reviewing, he is seen several times over the course of a few days, entering and exiting the building where the woman's body was found. From the evening period after Julie was taken to the hospital, it shows what I believe is his last exit from that building. He is being helped by others, whom we are still running through Interpol files on known terrorists in London. There was also what looked like bodies being removed in the last trip out of the building by these men.

"I think he was holding Laurie and Julie for information of some sort. We know that Laurie was involved in sharing information. Julie could have been caught in the crossfire, or he recognized her in some manner and thought she was involved with his nephew's demise. I am hoping his walking out injured speaks to the efforts Julie may have made during her escape.

"I then found a segment an hour or so before of what we believe is Julie, exiting the building and being hit by an as yet unidentified male outside. Possibly a guard. It looks like Julie tried to defend herself and was hit and kicked in such a way that she slipped and fell hard against a streetlight pole, cracking her head. She crumpled to the ground, and when the male tried to inflict additional damage, it looks like someone in the street interrupted the action and called local authorities.

"No one bothered to check out the building where she was found crumpled on the street, and the spectator likely did not see her exit, only the brutal attack. I am hoping the local authorities can identify the passerby as I know Juan and Julie will want to thank him."

"I have no doubt. Is there any way to know where this Achmet is now?"

"Still checking, but it's going to be some time before we go to bed, honey. And, no, I have no intention of sleeping on the couch."

CHAPTER SIXTY

The Good Fortune

Najih awoke with a start. He sensed some movement, and then heard the familiar sound of a lifeless body cascading to the ground. He'd been dozing in the late evening, but was now on high alert, preparing for the new scenario. Slowly and quietly, he brought his weapon closer and strained to see any activity in his area before trying to move. His first thought was that his uranium shipment had arrived, and it was being unloaded in the dark. It turned out that his first thought was wrong.

He then heard a very distinctive *phapp!* quickly followed by two more…*phapp! phapp!* The *phapps* were followed by the sound of bodies as they landed on the ground. Rather than a shipment delivery, he suspected his compound was under a stealth attack. No one had sounded the alarm which meant that the incursion was not from the local police authorities. Najih's men abruptly came alive with the realization that they were under attack. Several men started firing wildly at the unseen assailants, causing a rain of bullets around them.

Two stray rounds ricocheted close to Najih, so he hollered, "Hold your fire! Look for targets, don't just blindly fire!"

During the momentary silence that followed, Najih's phone began vibrating, indicating an incoming call. Almost simultaneously, several powerful search lights came on, bathing the inside of the dilapidated building in white light. The pandemonium caused by the inconvenience of the call's timing combined with the blinding light permeating the area gave him an immediate need to determine who it was creating the maddening scenario. He answered the call in an arrogant tone. "What?'

Outside the warehouse perimeter where the call was being placed, the authorities planned their final assault to complete taking control. The calm voice on the other end of the call to Najih insisted in a firm tone, "You need to throw down your weapons, put your hands over your head, and walk out into the search lights. I will guarantee your safety, but only for the next five minutes. This will be the only call. Don't bother trying to slip out the back or through the ceiling panels. You're surrounded."

Lee looked first to Carl, then to Jim Hughes, before he asked, "How'd you get that bastard's phone number? I mean, talk about polite! We usually blare out our demands over a bullhorn, so this personalized service you three letter agency boys use is …well, a bit too delicate for my taste."

Jim and the Commander smirked, then Jim answered, "We got a tip this was where they were, from someone I trust. It seems she was right, because here they are. Her text message showed us exactly where they were and when they were expecting a high-grade uranium shipment. Too bad we couldn't have gotten both. I'd rather have these vermin in the bag. I feel confident we can also find the uranium."

As he studied the building and listened to the team check-in commentary, Carl said to Lee. "I'm seeing movement. I sure hope they aren't going to surrender peaceably. I'd love to play out a scene from that movie we saw. You remember? When those two cowboys came busting out of that bar ready to give hell to the Mexican army waiting to shoot them to pieces."

Lee smiled and agreed, "Yeah! Let's hope we get to reenact that scene."

Jim got an inbound call from a number with the caller ID reading *Jim, answer my call.* As soon as the perplexed Jim Hughes answered, EZ said, "It is EZ and Quip. I saw the text message from Mercedes's phone, but she doesn't have control of it. Someone else does."

Quip quickly added, "Jim, if you're acting on the text message, please take care. It's likely a trap!"

Jim thought for a moment before he responded, "If so, that someone sent us to bag the really bad guys. I might as well tell you, we were sent to the right place, and while it might be a trap, it is our trap. Our team has been looking for these psychotic killers on our home soil for months. Why do you think we were sent here? Who's giving us this favor?"

EZ answered, "We have a lead, but I don't have anybody free at the moment to hunt him down. What does your schedule look like?"

Jim rather pointedly asked, "What's the scoop on Mercedes? Is she alright?"

EZ replied, "That's one of the issues we are working. Do you have anyone who might be able to intercept if needed?"

Frowning, Jim replied, "We're kind of busy at the moment. I trust you to have some fresh ideas to keep things moving while we are indisposed for a bit…"

At that moment several hand grenades came sailing out of the building and exploded, destroying a couple of the search lights. Then a serious fire fight began between the opposing forces.

Najih screamed, "You'll never take me alive!"

Lee and Carl smiled at their good fortune.

Marge was focused on staying on task and not rushing. Tasks were taking too long and in no time caused her fury to boil over. After her third screaming tirade at yet another inanimate object, she decided to switch tactics to bring her temper under control and tried to settle herself with a quick bath. She always enjoyed sipping wine and luxuriating in her enormous lavender shaded bathroom. The fluffy bamboo towels soaked up the moisture from her ample skin, and she was easily able to assess herself with the two walls of mirrors available. The bath settled her to a degree. She found smoothing on the scented lotion calmed her feelings of uncontrollable anger.

Finishing her after-bath routine and taking a few deep breaths, she quietly insisted to herself in the mirror, "Alright, Marge. Get a grip here. All the corporate funds you have steadily drained over the past two years have been quietly parked off-shore. The final fund transfers you are waiting for will occur as soon as the uranium shipment is in the hands of the NK boneheads.

"Mike may be MIA, but that is actually a good thing since you also emptied his private stash of cash he had tried so carefully to hide. What are you so panicked about, old girl?"

The gentle, pleasing sound of her own voice with the warm scented air should have been adequate to calm her mental stress. However, she had been so long down this path of biting and clawing her way to success, it actually had the opposite effect.

The internal anger expanded again as she looked at her misshapen body protruding from the oversized towel, which missed covering her hips in full. She angrily countered to the face in the mirror, "That's just fine, coming from you! I have to hang around here listening to your drivel about how everything is wonderful, but it's not, chubbins!

"While you have been powering down the fat-girl comfort food, I've had to deal with the North Koreans AND the miserable

Muslim monkeys through a proxy who couldn't step up to the plate in the global series!

"Finish with the lotion and your makeup. You need to be on your way before the fricking authorities show up wanting to investigate something! If you don't get your butt up and out of here, it won't matter how much you have stashed offshore, because you won't be able to get to it! Then you can get on that fitness spree."

Marge's breath was ragged from her shouting. She again tried to reel in her heightened emotional state by deeply breathing in the warm, scented air, and adjusted the towel to provide the most positive view of her reflection. She appraised herself and knew she was a bit fleshy. But her hair was lovely and well-styled, her makeup always applied just so, and her peaches and cream skin was soft and supple, even if there was too much of it.

After the calming routine of applying her makeup, she tried again. "Now, my girl, is that any way to treat yourself after all that money she spent on those anger management classes? Let's try and recall what they taught you, shall we?"

Marge spiraled into the abyss of a psychological emotional split as she wound herself up to new levels of anger and countered with this emerging second self. "You know perfectly well why I am in this mood! I crawled to the top of my world, seducing whoever I needed to so I could get ahead. Here I am on top, and I can't even buy a decent man!

"Look how Mike turned out! He was banging his assistant instead of me! I tried another one, but Christopher has as much warmth as one of my appliances! And now I have you. You are a rotten bitch telling me to calm down, so you listen to me, fat girl…"

Marge's psychological meltdown was interrupted by the ring of an incoming call. Her mental crisis seemed to recede as she read the name of the incoming caller.

Almost as if a switch had been thrown, she calmly answered, "Hello, Christopher. Where are you with the task list you were working?"

Christopher blandly offered, "I have the go-codes assembled for you, madam, but I will be unable to personally deliver them as discussed. My attention is required here in the D.C. area to complete the last of our transactions."

Marge flexed her jaw muscles, which helped to keep her anger under control, but said, "Aww darn! That means no celebratory drink here at my place. What a shame! I was so looking forward to closing out our position and launching our next project together."

Christopher mechanically responded, "Madam, the shortage of trusted personnel has created an unexpected shift in my workload. You should know that I did learn what happened to our top AIM courier, Laurie. She was discovered in an abandoned warehouse and is no longer a viable AIM candidate, based on her decomposed composition. However, I believe I identified a suitable candidate here in the D.C. area whom I believe will meet my…our needs. Our new AIM is en route to complete the special delivery transaction with the North Koreans as discussed. As for the celebratory drink, I don't think it will go to waste."

He used his monotone voice and continued, "I will reach back to you as soon as the fund transfer is complete, madam. I will get the go-codes to you as soon as possible. Good day."

Marge absentmindedly dropped the phone, and a new emotional tremor launched that resumed her open tirade.

She shouted, "See? See how they do? You buy them out of their poverty, but then they hunt for a young slim whore and turn their back on you! Dammit! As soon as that ungrateful jerk gets here, his drink will be less that celebratory, but nothing less than he deserves!"

Marge's rational side came forward again and evenly announced, "Perhaps it is better this way, Margie. Look at your good fortune in this matter. You'll have enough money to buy and dispose of suitable males on a regular basis, way before they aggravate you like these two have done." Marge's contorted smile added to her edge of growing insanity. "I always like it when you and I fight, because afterwards we have sex."

CHAPTER SIXTY-ONE

Competition for Life

Brayson protested, "Come on, EZ! This is ridiculous! I'm stuck here watching the foot traffic come and go with no goal in sight! There's got to be some action that I could get into, rather than just counting the number of flies I've killed! At least ask Julie or Juan to disengage me, so I can return to a useful existence, for crying out loud!"

EZ, now growing tired of the badgering from Brayson, sternly insisted, "Calm down. We've got lots of people in motion, and several problems being worked with Julie and Juan indisposed! Right now, I don't need one more agitating prima donna demanding to be coddled!"

Brayson was annoyed but now showed concern as he asked, "What's in play, madam? How can I help? Your tone of voice suggests people are in trouble?"

EZ pulled herself up short in her tirade. "As a matter of fact, we do have some touchy issues in motion, and right now you are at the bottom of my worry bucket! Just hang there until we get some things under control and stop trying to be a cowboy."

Brayson, unwilling to let it go, hotly responded, "I said I could help, dammit! Now what needs doing?"

EZ argued, "You know, with as many things going sideways as there are, no one, not one person, has asked *can you please get Brayson here*? What does that tell you about your personal aura?"

The comment stung Brayson and left him speechless.

After a few moments, EZ regained her composure and, in a more civil tone, offered, "Brayson, no one wants to count you out. But right now, no one believes that they can count on you. Without confidence in a team member, who, by the way, is always brooding …well, they are inclined to struggle on their own without your help. I have to be honest Brayson, I'd like to have you finish your chore in Panama and move you closer to the action, where you could be valuable again.

"At present, Julie is unconscious, Juan is incommunicado, Mercedes is lost in space, we just got Tyler out of the clutches of abductors. We have a newbie who needs guidance. If I could count on you, you need to follow directions. What do you say?"

Brayson was chastened by his reprimand and swallowed hard before he offered, "I'm sorry, EZ, for my current attitude issues. I would like very much to help, even if no one believes that I…" EZ cut him off, "That's exactly what I'm talking about! You wear your feelings on your sleeve, rather than jumping into the fight! I'm shorthanded, so here is what I want you to do.

"We are going to upload some code to the team web site. You need to download it onto a server in the Panama data center so it can replicate itself throughout the servers, and then I want you to contact me so I can determine where you are needed the most. I don't need you to get crossways with anyone! Oh, and I need this done yesterday."

Brayson was irked but in control of his annoyance and responded, "You know we could have simply jumped to this portion of the conversation right up front so we could be farther along our action curve."

EZ smirked a little as she responded, "What? And miss the opportunity of dressing down a putz? Not likely! Now get a move on, soldier. I've got another little boy to deal with. Your target instructions will be texted to you momentarily."

After EZ disconnected, Brayson muttered, "I just hate ripped apart by a drill sergeant who looks the way she does. Plus, I hate the thought that she could probably be right."

Brayson was still mulling over the statements from EZ as he reached out to start repairing some of his credibility with the team. He had some challenges accessing the data center as the access methods had changed since Juan and Mercedes had been there. He wished he had tried to gain traction with Mercedes when she had been there. He sent a plan to EZ on how he thought the access might be accomplished, which she was evaluating and promised to get back with him on the plan or changes.

In speaking to Summit and George, he seemed to have cleared the air. It was obviously one of the easier conversations he faced. Tyler was still hurt from his ordeal, but it didn't stop him from taking an adversarial role with Brayson when he answered the video call.

Tyler stated with a hint of annoyance, "Well, that's just great! We needed some honest to God help before Mercedes went missing. Are you planning to pout until we give you a group hug?"

Brayson held his temper in and said, "I was told that a team member and a newbie needed some help. Which one are you? Still haven't learned to avoid taking a beating, I see!"

Jamie, who had been standing over Tyler's shoulder observing the call, studied Brayson's facial expression for a moment before cautiously asking, "You seem a bit on edge with your teammate, Brayson. Actually, he seems a bit annoyed with you. I would observe that there is something gnawing at you, and it's keeping you somewhat distant."

Brayson was irked at the newbie's penetrating statement. He didn't know this guy, so he only nodded. Jamie, taking Tyler's place on the video call, continued, "Let me guess, you lost someone close to you, and you can't forget her or forgive yourself. Right?"

Brayson continued his silence and only nodded again.

Jamie brightened and commented, "Hey, me too! Oh, and let me guess, her death was your fault, just like mine. Right?"

Brayson now studied Jamie intently but maintained his silence at the statement. This time he didn't nod. Jamie, unwilling to stop the emotional onslaught, related, "How about leading your brother headlong to his death on a motorcycle? Have you got one of those stories to tell, 'cause I do."

Brayson continued to study Jamie intently but made no acknowledgement of his statement. Jamie, working himself up to laying his soul open and displaying his pain, visible for Brayson to understand, continued, "And how about your only child, confiscated by your love's parents after she dies in child-birth, so you can't watch him grow up? Or get help with her loss…" Jamie was quietly in tears at his own hurtful statements and stopped while Brayson looked on.

After a moment, Jamie wiped the tears from his face and quietly admitted, "I am an outcast from everywhere and anywhere. No one wants a damaged human being like me to be around them or in their lives. Consequently, I have drifted here and there, always on the outside.

"Now, I find a team of likeminded people, dedicated to a just cause, who just might take me in. I'm actually terrified that they won't want me to stay. Maybe you don't see the irony of your situation, but I would give anything to be wanted on this team, like you are. I just don't understand why you push them away. I guess it's true what wise men say, *people will give up anything but their own suffering.*"

Brayson couldn't bear the scene any longer and tried to turn away from the camera only to see Tyler studying him closely. Their stares were locked momentarily before Tyler offered, "No one wants to see you continue your suffering. With a damaged mental outlook, I see you as a danger to others, but mostly to yourself. I would like…let me restate that, we all would like to have you stay, because you want to. Please rejoin us. I believe it is your best destiny."

Jamie had pulled himself together and was now again in Brayson's field of view.

Brayson gave a small smile and softly asked, "You think there's hope for me then?"

Tyler, in his usual deadpan manner, responded, "Naw, we're just tired of your crap!"

Jamie was the first to crack a smile, and then Brayson smirked slightly before they all chuckled at the coarse statement.

Brayson then offered in a conciliatory tone to Tyler, "Now THAT I can believe."

Tyler, now smiling, stated, "Gentlemen, we need to reengage with EZ to verify our next steps to getting Mercedes back. I personally want to find Steven Christopher, and I think I have an idea on how to do that."

CHAPTER SIXTY-TWO

To Have and To Hold

... The Enigma Chronicles

Ernesto texted on the latest information he had. The doctor had made an extended appearance the previous morning and had updated Juan on the recent battery of test results Julie received, including the spinal tap. The doctor was pleased that the swelling on Julie's brain was receding. One by one the various intravenous tubes of medicine, save one for her hydration drip, and had been removed. The doctor and the nurses encouraged Juan to talk to her, hold her hand, and remind her of all the reasons to rejoin the world. There was nothing at this point physiologically preventing Julie from coming out of her coma. As with many of these cases, it could be hours or weeks.

Juan was disheartened and refused to leave Julie's side for even a minute. The primary care nurse finally insisted Juan at least go home, change clothes, and eat something besides hospital food. She encouraged him to bring back some things Julie might recognize. The nurse promised someone would be with her at all times. As torn as he was between going and staying, he knew that he needed a shower and a little time away. Ernesto finally convinced Juan when he agreed to stay and watch over her, along with the nurses.

James drove Juan home. The first thing Juan did was retrieve Julie's wedding ring from the safe. With her out of danger, he intended to make certain she either wore it or had it close. While Juan was in the shower, James went for some food and a few cervezas to help Juan relax. Juan felt better after his shower, but he really improved after he spoke to the twins. He hadn't called them while he'd been in Julie's room watching her. He decided to record some of their antics as they laughed about how much fun they were having building forts and caves. Juan Jr. was trying to boss Gracie around, but she wasn't on board for any of that and made it known.

He spoke briefly to EZ and Quip, getting updates on some of the more pressing issues. He repeatedly thanked EZ for her efforts in taking on the additional responsibility. When Julie came home, together they would find something special to reward EZ's efforts. After the call, Juan leaned his head against the back of the Chesterfield sofa and slipped into a fitful slumber with crazy dreams. He was startled awake when James touched Juan's shoulder. Fortunately, he'd had enough rest not to launch into his usual defense mode, where he could have hurt James.

"James, I'm one of those people whom it is unwise to touch to wake up. More effective if you stand on the other side of the room and call my name."

"Sorry, sir. I know you wanted to get back to the hospital before sunset. I made you some coffee to take along. When I spoke to Ernesto, he said there was no change. He suggested you might want to bring some lotion for her hands and feet as her skin seemed dry after the nurse gave her a sponge bath."

"Good thought. Let me grab that and my own pillow and we'll go." He scarfed the food and coffee. "Thanks for the food and drink. It was far better than the hospital tray." Juan looked away as if lost in thought, then turning back to James saying, "I am looking forward to you meeting my wife. She has the best smile." Then he stood and went to the bedroom to retrieve the lotion and his pillow. He nodded to James, who locked up as he went out the door without another word.

The trip back to the hospital was uneventful, and Juan remained quiet. James dropped him at the entrance. "I'll wait here for Mr. Ernesto, unless you need me to run errands."

"I'll send him down. I'm sure he could use a shower and food. Take him back to the flat, and both of you get some rest."

"Yes, sir."

Juan spoke briefly to the nurse and then entered Julie's room. He sent Ernesto downstairs and told him to come back in the morning. He set up the tablet to play the recording of the video call he'd had with the twins and their laughing antics. Even though he saw no response, he replayed it several times. In between listening and watching the video, Juan massaged her feet and legs with the lotion she loved. It did help make her skin much smoother. Then he moved on to her arms, taking extra care to rub her hands. At any other time, it would have been a delightful prelude to making love to his beautiful wife. Inwardly, he resolved they would do that again soon.

He stopped playing the video when the nurse came in to check Julie's vitals one last time for the night. With the help of the nurse, he found a smooth jazz radio station, with the first song being one of Julie's favorites. The nurse left, promising to leave them alone until morning, unless he rang the call button. He plumped her pillow and continued to stroke her skin as he told her how much he loved her and wanted her to come back to him. He slipped her ring on her finger and watched it sparkle in the muted light.

Her face was so relaxed, yet different from how she normally appeared when she slept. Perhaps it was the lack of mobility or the pallor of her skin from the days of medication she'd endured. He spoke to her of how they would train together to regain her strength, and how he would never leave her side ever again. Giving in to the urge to hold her, he put his pillow next to hers on the opposite side from her IV and laid on top of the covers next to her, wrapping her in his arms. Juan explained all the things they were going to do, until he finally drifted off to sleep.

A continent away, Mercedes boarded the flight that would take her to the Philippines. At least she was by herself, as Steven had remained at the gate. Up until that moment she was uncertain if he would be joining or not. Steven hugged her briefly when the flight was called. He promised they'd meet up soon and thanked her for being such a big help. Then he assured her that her reward at the end of this assignment would be three times the money they had agreed to, plus he hoped she would consider possibly working on a more romantic relationship with him. Surprised at that statement, she merely smiled and nodded as she turned to board.

Once the boarding was completed and the door shut, Mercedes glanced out her window, where saw Steven watching from the terminal. She smiled and gave him a thumbs up, and he curtly turned and left to wherever he was going. The plane began to back up, and the flight attendants started their normal announcements of safety and features of the specific aircraft. They turned and began the drive toward the runway.

Mercedes teared up a bit as she'd had no way to contact Jim and reassure him she was alright. The flight attendant noticed her distress and returned with tissues and a cup of water, along with a smile. Mercedes thanked her and sipped the water as she thought about how she'd gotten into this mess. The plane seemed to be doing the long drive toward the runway.

"Folks, this is captain Eberly. We have a small issue with a light up here. We will need to return to the terminal and get it fixed before we take off. We apologize for the delay, but our policy is safety first. Our flight attendants will come though when we are parked for a free beverage while the maintenance is completed. The ground crew is alerted and ready to board to correct the issue as quickly as possible. Thank you for your patience."

Mercedes leaned back in her seat and, using the earbuds provided in First Class, tuned to the onboard radio. She closed her eyes and thought of all her options as the plane came to a stop. Several minutes later she felt the air shift as if the door had been opened. Some new voices were heard near the cockpit area. She felt a familiar hand on her shoulder and opened her eyes in disbelief at the man dressed in maintenance coveralls, who was anything but an airplane maintenance jockey.

"Jim, what are you doing here?"

"Right now, you're getting off. We'll discuss the details later. Come on."

"How did you know I was here?"

"We'll discuss it later. But after I watched you board without your handler, I knew it was safe to pull you out. He vanished in the crowd, though we are trying to find him. Are you wearing any tracking devices?"

Mercedes shook her head, undid her seatbelt and grabbed her satchel from the overhead bin. "Let's go. I have some research to do."

"Not without me, sweetheart."

CHAPTER SIXTY-THREE

Fate Ordains,
While Destiny Delivers
...The Enigma Chronicles

Over the next several days, the thin layer of control Marge normally maintained was quickly dissolving with the continued rapid-fire receipt of bad news. In the lull between the barrage of bad news bulletins, Marge sat at her home-office desk and stared numbly out the window, watching the sunset colors as they dissolved into darkness.

She slowly closed her eyes and shook her head, as yet another call came into her new ruggedized smart phone. The last two devices had not stood up to the irrational beatings and treatment, so she hoped that this new rhinoceros hide encasement might allow the device to last longer.

She finally accepted the call and dejectedly asked, "What is it now?"

Christopher hesitated for a moment but finally calmly stated, "Madam, if this is a bad time, I can always..."

Marge snapped, "What makes you think any other time will be better?

"I just got off the phone with our corporate counsel, who was contacted by the U.S. justice department about the undocumented uranium confiscated from our oil tanker just off the coast of the

Philippines. They want to know why the ship's manifest showed it was bound for North Korea by way of the Philippines when we had commissioned it for a route to Japan and three ports there."

Her temper continued to build as she added, "Then, I got a call from the Chung-Ho bonehead, who already knew that their shipment of uranium had been commandeered by the U.S. Navy. He screamed about losing his precious shipment and asked what was being done to fix the situation! Like I'm going to take on the U.S. Navy for his unsanctioned uranium! For a criminal mind, he is truly as dumb as a box of rocks!"

Marge was slowly building into a psychological detonation as she continued in an even louder tone. "Then some building superintendent called to get monies for the damages to the corporate apartment in London that used to house Mike Patrick! Seems he had something of a problem with a hand grenade, and now they want funds to repair not only the apartment but the structural damage to the surrounding building as well. Apparently, there was an obscure clause in the lease about not playing with unlicensed hand grenades! I, of course, had cosigned with Patrick because dumbbell didn't have any credit, so now I'm libel for the damages! It almost cheered me up to learn he had been vaporized!"

Now seething, Marge finally insisted, "Now it's your turn! Gimme some more good news, man!"

Christopher swallowed hard then allowed, "Madam, it would seem that our positions have been compromised in several areas. I am now en route to your location with the go-codes for access to the data center, so we can terminate it if need be or set up shop in some other endeavor. My...I mean, our new AIM courier was picked up at the Dulles airport before she could arrange the funds transfer for the specialized shipment. The good news is we don't have any prints on the failed transaction. However, there is a high probability she is in the hands of the U.S. authorities. My recommendation is that we terminate all our activities and leave for warmer climates."

Marge was all set to explode, but instead a sinister smile broke out across her face as she calmly asked, "You're on your way here? Well then, I can arrange for some private air transport to whisk us away as soon as you arrive, hmm? Oh, and of course, please let's have that farewell drink before we leave for the jet. I'll be all packed by the time you get here."

Christopher breathed a little easier and responded, "I should be there in a few hours, madam. Happy to leave with you."

Marge smiled as she disconnected from the call and mumbled to herself, "Yes, we will be leaving, but not together."

Marge then turned to see herself in the mirror and coyly suggested, "Come on, sweetheart, we have enough time to play in the *harness* before we have to pack it up." She began undressing as she moved towards her play area.

She was almost finished packing when Marge heard the pounding on the apartment suite door. Eager to see Christopher before heading to the aircraft, Marge promptly opened the door without checking first through the peephole, committing mistake number one.

The four men on the other side of the door quickly poured into the suite and closed the door behind them. Marge was almost too startled to comprehend what was going on, but she finally managed, "Who the hell are you? What do want?" Mistake number two.

Before Marge could really get wound up, the assassins were on top of her with cable ties. She was rolled over and trussed up like a pig, ready for a spit, before she could put up a decent fight.

The only thing missing was the apple in her mouth, rapidly remedied by a wadded-up paper towel that was roughly shoved into her mouth to the back of her throat.

The leader of the group stated in a low halting voice, "Check the rooms…make sure we are alone."

They all nodded silently, save one who acknowledged, "Yes, Achmet."

Moments later one of the men came back and explained, "She looks packed and ready to leave, except for a strange leather item suspended from the ceiling. I am uncertain what it is used for, Achmet."

Just then another man returned and added, "It appears she is expecting someone. She poured two glasses of champagne. We should hurry, so as not to be discovered by the guest."

Achmet returned from the bedroom and smirked, "The leather item is a pain/pleasure harness for decadent western erotic pleasures. Put this pig in it, and make sure she enjoys all that it can deliver."

Marge struggled to get free, but she was no match for their combined strength. Soon she was laced into her harness with the choking apparatus fully engaged. The self-release pulley had been removed. She was able to enjoy what the harness could deliver, but she wouldn't survive to share or relive the adventure.

All the assailants watched and even enjoyed the tortured ending that she faced. Achmet wandered over to where the champagne had been poured. He took one of the glasses and came back to toast to Marge's struggling end.

He raised his glass and said, "Time for you to leave." He tipped up the nicely fluted glass and drank down the bubbly beverage.

Still engrossed in watching the grim spectacle of Marge choking to death, he retrieved the second glass of champagne and would have tipped it up too if his muscles had cooperated. The glass slipped through his fingers as his breathing became sporadic. His henchmen all looked at him as abject fear became plain on his contorted face. The spectacle of Marge's gasping end no longer held any interest.

His men raced to catch him as his legs buckled underneath him. As he clutched at his heart, his henchmen panicked. With one on each side of him, they rushed out the apartment door to the stairs in hasty retreat.

Their concern over their leader had left them sloppy in their exit. They ran right into the federal SWAT team that was waiting to enter. Without a plan or a viable leader directing them, they were quickly subdued. Achmet was loaded into a security vehicle and pronounced dead by the team leader.

Spectators who had gathered outside the building took pictures and commented on what had caused the commotion. A tall, quiet man asked one of the SWAT team if he could enter. Before the officer could respond his radio transmission relayed a gristly scene which needed to be handled before anyone would be allowed to enter or leave. The man turned and headed back down the street.

CHAPTER SIXTY-FOUR

Lost, Found, and Lost Again

Even though the building superintendent had let them in p eacefully, they still charged in ready for a fight. Jim Hughes backed them up with his service weapon drawn, ready to intercept any problem that might occur. Jamie boldly led the charge, only slightly ahead of Mercedes and Tyler. Jim was trying to hold Mercedes back a little out of his concern for her welfare, and Tyler was still favoring his left foot with the persistent swelling in his right. They pushed their way into the rundown flat and came to a halt in a shabby, dank room. It was likely once considered a living room, only you would be hard pressed to see it that way now, and what they saw drew them up short.

The elderly black woman was neither surprised nor concerned by their presence and not even Jim's weapon produced any emotion in her face. After a few moments of sizing each of the intruders up, the black woman rather blandly stated, "Name's Connie. I had no idea that you all were coming to take over my watch. Since I don't see no food, how about you watch him for a spell, while I get him something to eat?"

The team's disoriented state continued to build. Connie read the confusion on their faces and sensed a bit of sport was in order. "Oh, not to worry, young'uns. I've already bathed him, applied talcum to his bottom, and put on a fresh diaper, so he'll be alright for a few hours. Now, he don't say much, but he loves to hear folks talk. I kin tell by the way his eyes move. I should be back in about half an hour, so if you want to wait…"

Connie moved forward as she put on her light jacket. It almost fit around her generous girth, and she moved to the door and almost opened it before they stopped her.

Mercedes was the first to break the silence. "Madam, Connie, we are looking for Steven Christopher. He is wanted for questioning by the authorities. Our information sources suggested he was here. Is he here, perhaps in another room?"

The rotund lady, now a little indignant, snapped, "You barge in here like you own the place. Now you act like you're wet behind the ears, like you ain't even done your homework.

"Steven Christopher is right in that wheelchair with the blank look on his face! Now just 'cause you don't have no manners about introductions, let me begin and show you how it's done!

"For YOU rude people, my name is Connie!" She waited a full minute then snorted before she added, "It be your turn now, go ahead and speaks your name." Then she pointed to Jim's weapon and sternly ordered, "And put that away! Didn't yo' momma learn you no manners?" A now sheepish Jim almost followed her orders, but he caught himself and kept it in his hand as he slipped it under his jacket.

The team was now completely dumbfounded. Mercedes retained some presence of mind and walked over to Steven in his wheelchair. Kneeling down to look into his eyes, she quietly asked, "Steven, is that you? It's Mercedes. We trained together. Do you remember me?"

For a brief moment, Steven reached back into his isolated mind for old, dear memories, and a flicker of a smile crossed his face as he gently replied, "Mercy."

Mercedes choked on the revelation that he was the real Steven Christopher. It quickly explained why something had not felt quite right with the Steven Christopher she had been working for. Her eyes filled almost to overflowing as she gently touched his face. Steven's smile faded, and his eyes lost a bit of light as he again retreated inside his broken body.

Connie commented with a face, "There, hon, you got more words out of him than I ever did." She spied the concern on Jim's face and saw that his expression reflected the jealous worry a man has for his woman. Unable to resist the teasing, she stated, "Mystery man, looks like you might be moved back to second string. I kin offer you a few openings on my dance card until my Mister Right comes along. Whaddaya say, handsome?"

Jim swallowed hard in an effort to cover his blushing. Tyler intervened, "Miss Connie, my name is Tyler, and I want to thank you for making Jim blush. We all wondered if he had the ability. Would you mind if we took Steven's picture? I need to upload it to, uh…people so they can see who we found.

"Please, forgive our poor manners, but the Steven Christopher we were looking for is very mobile and frankly into something that we need to intercept before people are hurt."

Connie studied Tyler a moment and then in another burst of brassiness asked, "Man, you look like something of a catch as well! If Mister Tongue-tied can't get over Sugga-britches, my dance card could be in yo hands, if you play yo cards right."

It was now Tyler's turn to be tongue-tied. Before Connie could give any more flirtatious offers, Jamie slid his arm into hers and, with his best Irish brogue, quietly seduced, "Now, lass, you have been very coy with the other lads, and, well, I'm feeling a little left out. My name is Jamie. I'll tell ye my dance card is just aching for a splendid session around the dance floor with a full-figured lass like yourself. First though, can you tell us, how is it that ye came to be here?"

Connie giggled and, after a quick peck on Jamie's cheek, gleefully announced, "There now, that's how a lady likes to be courted!"

Connie retrieved her arm and, in a now businesslike tone, offered, "Steven Christopher was on patrol when they came under fire. Some say it was friendly fire, some say otherwise, but it doesn't really matter. He was hit and several others in his platoon, including my son. Steven and my boy got far enough away to survive and helped each other until they were evacuated to a medical facility."

She drew a breath and continued, "My boy believed that if it wasn't for Steven, he never would've made it. I'm not sure what Steven believed since he ain't never spoken of it. The Army released him and gave him some money. I think they wanted him to go where they wouldn't be reminded, they didn't take care of their own. My boy had too much mental issues, and…well, he didn't want to stay and face them…"

Connie's voice trailed off. She couldn't offer any more.

Tyler filled in the silence. "You take care of Steven because …well, because."

Connie nodded her head as she wiped a tear from her face. The emotion in her stirred up a question. "He called you Mercy, didn't he? And you said you two trained together, right? Are you that girl in his keepsake letters? I'm lookin' at you and seein' somethin' of the gal in the faded picture."

Mercedes, startled by the questioning, replied, "I never expected he would keep those letters! How do you know…"

Connie cut her off. "Hon, there ain't much to do around here. Some of them was pretty good reading. I even read them out loud to Steven to see if they would help him open up. Why, even that fellow from the VA who turned up a couple of years back thought they would help. Heck, he even took a few photos of them letters, but I don't hardly believe they went back to Steven's official file. He was kind of an oily feller, if you ask me."

Mercedes eyes got wide. "What did this man from the VA look like?"

Connie smirked and snorted, then replied, "Hon, he looked a lot like Steven here, size wise, and even most of his face, except he was talking all the time and didn't have poor Steven's injuries.

"I mean to tell you; it was worse than listening to me! If youse around talking folks all the time, it gets you to listen once in a while." She scoffed, "He was always asking questions about Steven's past and any family detail I might know. Ya knows, thinking on it, the funny thing is that should have had all been in Steven's file. All his annoying questions and reading or photographing Steven's stuff, it put me off, so I finally told him to leave. Never seen him since."

Tyler quietly took Steven's picture with his smart phone and sent it along with a text message to EZ that said:

> We found Steven Christopher, only it's not the one we were looking for. If this is the real Steven Christopher, then who are we really after?

Then Tyler faced his team and suggested, "Have we been chasing a shadow or a lousy identity thief? What now?"

The Turkish officer was finishing up the paperwork from George and Summit's interrogation, which had been conducted entirely in Turkish, leaving George out of the conversation. Every now and then, Summit would translate into English for George's benefit. However, it wasn't often enough to keep George's annoyance from showing a little.

The duty officer had sensed the growing irritation from George but continued in his native language. As the last entries were made in his electronic document, the officer stood up to shake their hands.

As they stood there, George asked Summit in an annoyed tone, "Did I get any credit for turning over our detective work on the arms smuggling, or was I simply categorized as your man-servant? You know, you could have translated a little more frequently, so I could understand what was going on."

Summit was caught unawares by George's comment. He awkwardly shifted his gaze between the officer and George, unable to decide on a fitting response. The Turkish officer smirked slightly and said, in English, with only a slight accent, "Sir, it was easier for me to record your collective detective work in Turkish instead of English. I'm sorry you have no knowledge of our rich and flowery language, so I would recommend you make that effort. But be that as it may, I have a riddle for you before we part."

George, somewhat startled, stammered a little then offered, "Uh, okay. Tell me your riddle."

The officer smiled ever so slightly and asked, "What do you call someone who speaks three languages?" Not completely engaged with the question, George shrugged his shoulders to which the officer responded, "A tri-lingual."

He continued, "What do you call someone who speaks two languages?" Still unable to process the questions, George again shrugged his shoulders to which the officer responded, "A bi-lingual."

The officer again slightly smiled, obviously coming ever closer to the punch line as he asked, "What do you call someone who speaks only one language?" George was now flustered but felt he was being set up to provide the wrong answer and said, "I don't know."

The officer, now smiling broadly, stated, "An American!"

Summit was the first to begin laughing and was quickly joined by the Turkish officer. George fought the urge, but he too quickly surrendered to a good laugh.

Once outside the station, George said, "Summit, let's get back to base headquarters. This situation is under control by the Turkish authorities. Unless we are being misled, the SCS is going to have some explaining to do."

Summit nodded and said, "Agreed. Once we get back to base, we should plan to get you some language lessons. I can help you plan for that." Thinking back to the Turkish official's joke, George retorted, "Now, if I learn another language, I can still be an American, yes? I won't lose that status, correct?"

Summit nodded thoughtfully and replied, "I don't *think* they revoke your citizenship just because you learned another language. But I will research it." George simply shook his head in disbelief at his partner's thought process. He suspected that Summit had forgotten George was fluent in three other languages along with English.

CHAPTER SIXTY-FIVE

When to Cut Your Losses

Kashan began the cellular conversation. "Nephew, the steward-ship of ePETRO is now drifting like sands across the desert dunes. Mike Patrick is no longer a problem for us, since he resigned. The other leader of ePETRO, Marge, has also resigned her position, but the cost for that was my loyal comrade and lifelong friend, Achmet.

"I was made to understand that Steven Christopher was to be installed to run ePETRO as the next in line, but he too seems to have vanished. Several activities he has been involved with remain unsolved. You should know we lost one of our best cell operatives in the U.S. You would be pleased to know that he fought like a tiger before he went to join Allah."

Kashan let his words sink in before he continued. He wanted the impact to be meaningful. "I'm inclined to bring you back to our underground location, to help rebuild our organization after so many of our soldiers have fallen. It would be for your own protection, as much as for our rebuilding efforts."

Dabir swallowed hard at the thought of leaving the lavish lifestyle he had embraced so completely. The contemplative loss of his revolving door of females and the thought of living under-ground in his uncle's primitive hut, with basic electricity only available on a sporadic basis, sickened him. His breathing became short and hurried as he desperately tried to think of a way to remain in his decadent western surroundings.

Fighting to hold back the panic from his voice, Dabir offered, "Uncle, I must protest this decision! While it may be true that we need to rebuild our organization, we must also market our oil. This seems to be the best, if not the only vehicle, we have. If we, meaning me, abandon ePETRO, how will we be able to get our oil to market? I can better serve our cause by continuing to use ePETRO as a front for selling our oil, to continue the funding for our principled causes. Please do not discard such an important advantage we now have! My safety is unimportant, Uncle."

Kashan waited a moment before he responded, "I don't need you at ePETRO to market our oil. That can be done from anywhere since we have every oil broker's contact information."

Dabir closed his eyes in disbelief at his miserable prospects of returning to his uncle's hovel. His terror was mounting by the moment. He then hurriedly added, "I have Marge's proxy statement, which I can use to continue to run this operation!"

Kashan again waited a moment then said, "I saw the document as well, but it names Steven Christopher, not you, as the principal operator of ePETRO. If you are suggesting that it be altered so your name is there, then that is a fool's errand. The success you have enjoyed so far was because of others in power.

"You could have remained in the shadows for a while, then perhaps moved up. Without Steven there to ease the transition, the whole effort will look suspicious to anyone watching. Additionally, I have no trusted associates to help protect you now with Achmet gone. No, it is best that you drop everything now and return here so we can rebuild our organization. I could not face my sister if her boy were to be compromised…"

Unable to contain his anxiety at the fearful request, Dabir screamed, "I will not leave! I cannot return to that…that…hovel you find so comfortable and dear! I will remain here and engineer it to be in charge! No one need know Steven Christopher has vanished! I will keep up that masquerade but run things through his proxy statement! You will see, Uncle! I will turn my presence here to our advantage! You will thank me one day soon!"

Kashan began to understand he had lost Dabir to the Western culture, but implored, "Nephew, I know your fondness for the wonderful lifestyle you have enjoyed, but understand, that life is now gone. I need your help here, not there in London. I have no protection for you, and you have no leverage any longer without Marge, Mike, or Steven. I cannot subsidize your extravagant lifestyle with all our mounting losses. For all these reasons, you must return."

Dabir now lifted his chin and sniffed in defiance, as he made up his mind. He then calmly stated, "I will not be returning, and if you will not fund my position here, I shall engineer that as well! Good day, Uncle!" Kashan watched as the cell phone call dropped, and he simply shook his head after a heavy sigh.

With a renewed vigor, Dabir began organizing his thoughts as to how he would persevere without his uncle underwriting him there in London. A fresh outlook came over him as he detailed all his expenses and reviewed his income in an effort to reconcile the two. The two numbers weren't very close, but not that far apart either.

It occurred to him that if he could entice one or more of his ladies to come live with him, he could get the cost-of-living difference from them. Then after a few months of engineering things at ePETRO, he could arrange a raise for himself by simply forging Steven's signature. Once he had sufficient funds coming in, he could dispose of the interim bill-paying lady and resume his revolving door of females. He had even drawn up a timetable of how long each step would take. His confidence soared with his plan. Then there was a knock at the door of his flat.

Puzzled by what he saw through the peephole, he cautiously opened it. The detective put his badge away and he, with two other officers, marched in without saying a word. Dabir, uncomfortable with the intrusion but not willing to deny them entrance, asked, "What can I do for you, gentlemen?"

Still standing, the detective flatly said, "We need you to come down to the precinct with us to see if you can clear up a few things. We, ah…have some questions about ePETRO that apparently only you can answer. It seems everyone who was in contact with you has vanished. We are investigating several illegal oil transactions that have been brokered and also found ePETRO corporate funds have gone missing. We would like to know how and who is behind it."

Dabir stammered as he protested, "What am I being accused of? I've done nothing wrong!" The detective smirked a little and snidely remarked, "If that's true, then we should take you into custody for your own protection. Two females you worked with were abducted, and one murdered, as was the head of this office. The replacement you were going to work for has probably been killed. If you get whacked, then we can say you were targeted as well. But since you are the only one left standing…well, you can understand, I am sure, why the Crown is curious about the business dealings at ePETRO. For now, let's just say we would like to know more about Dabir's good fortune. Shall we?"

Dabir quickly assessed the new turn of events and gambled everything on his next foolish move. In an extremely clumsy attempt, he bolted for the balcony window in an effort to flee down the fire escape. The two policemen intercepted him before he even had taken three steps. He was roughly handcuffed and then partially escorted, partially dragged downstairs to the waiting vehicle.

Christopher had decided it was time to move into his next role before he arrived at his apartment. With each item he added to his suitcases, he grinned with the smugness of a man who had gotten everything he'd planned for. Chuckling to himself, he poured a glass of Pinot Noir from a freshly opened bottle and promptly toasted himself. He told himself he was in a hurry, but he couldn't resist the luxury of a little wine after all he had pulled off.

His thoughts drifted to the early days where he was still nickel and diming his way as a predator through the VA ranks of broken or injured veterans. It had irritated him at the time that he had lost his job for stealing, but that was also when he hit on the idea of stealing someone else's identity. Once he had concealed his past by assuming the identity of a soldier who would never find out, his fortunes had really taken off. That fateful meeting with Mike and Marge one night in New York City had opened the doors to a future he knew he would master.

The second glass of wine had him smirking about fleecing Kashan and Najih for their oil and money, yet delivering nothing. The smirking grew into loud laughs as he imagined in his mind the looks on Marge and Mike's faces, had they lived to discover he had pirated their hidden stashes of offshore money. His smile faded as his mind drifted towards thinking about Mercedes.

He sighed heavily and wondered if the money he had spent to intercept her in the Philippines was going to be a waste. Part of him said write her off, but the other side wanted to continue to woo her. He wasn't sure which way to go, but she was beautiful and perhaps worth fighting for. He felt he had earned the right to a bit of happiness. He would explain some of his deceit and the good reasons behind it. He had the funds now. By her own admission, she loved money. He almost smiled as he started to figure out the best ways to implement that plan.

He got up to begin scrubbing the apartment and get ready to flee. After packing was done, he was in a position to finish erasing his existence from the last few rooms. As he used up the last of the bleach, his old personal cell phone rang.

A guarded Steven Christopher cautiously answered the inbound call on the special phone that hadn't rung in months. It was on his list to drop in the river on his way to the airport. "Connie, is that you, madam?"

Staring straight ahead like she was reading from a teleprompter, Connie responded, "You told me that if anyone came by, or if Steven Christopher's condition changed any, I should contact you. I was going to try the VA, but you had left this direct number, Stu." Steven, a little less guarded but still wary, said, "I'm glad you are still his caregiver, but I'm no longer with the VA. I am, of course, interested in what has changed that prompted you to call me."

Connie blandly continued, "Someone stopped by this morning and said they were looking into some irregularities regarding Steven. They said he had done things that just weren't possible for him to do, so I said they were mistaken. I let them see Steven and even talk with him, but of course he never replied, Mr. Chesterfield.

"It was funny I thought, that after you were here, his monthly allowance was reduced by half. But it worked out okay. We simply decided to make a team. I watch him and think of my son, you know. I tried to fix that once, but the folks at the VA said his family had made the change. I didn't know he had family, did you?"

Steven swallowed hard and said, "I think he might have had a brother somewhere, but I have forgotten. Did you want me to call some of my old friends at the VA to help you?"

Connie replied, "If you know someone there who is your friend, that would be nice of you, and I'd be right grateful." She cleared her throat and added, "You recall, when you gave me this number, you said if I didn't tell any of the visitors about you that you would give me a bonus of five thousand dollars? I ain't one to ask when I don't deserve, but after those visitors this morning, I felt I was due, so I called." Connie, emboldened, continued, "I am hoping that you can give me that small fee you promised for saying I don't know how to get ahold of you. Living is kind of tight on what I'm being paid and, well, extra money sure would feel good about now."

Steven's anger was held in check as he tersely asked, "If I send the five thousand, you won't help anyone fill in the puzzle with the missing pieces that only you know, is that it?"

Connie smiled and slowly replied, "You're a right sharp fella, Stu, or should I call you Steven?"

Steven coolly replied, "Not smart enough it would seem! My fortunes could well spare a modest retainer fee for your discretion in this matter. I will send it out by courier today to Steven's apartment." Connie, now seeing her payday looming close at hand, enthusiastically replied, "Oh, that would be great, Stu, I mean Steven! I will call you when I get it. Thank you!"

After he disconnected from the call, Stuart pulled apart the phone, removed the SIM card, and ground it under his heel. Then staring at the useless cell phone, he promptly hurled it to the floor and repeatedly crushed it with a chair. Once he was done indulging his anger, he remarked to himself. "Steven, never hold on to your past no matter how sentimental! Damn phone almost cost me everything."

Still seething but now refocused, he added, "Time to finish and close out this position."

At the other end of the line, Connie disconnected from the call and looked at them individually and asked, "Just like that?"

Jim smiled and replied, "Just like that, madam." Jamie and Mercedes grinned and nodded. Tyler seemed disappointed but nodded as well.

They left the apartment and Tyler commented, "Not enough time for a lock on the call, but I suspect he is leaving town."

Mercedes added, "The VA has no record of any Stu or Stuart Chesterfield anywhere. We lost him again, damn it!"

CHAPTER SIXTY-SIX

Regrets and Second Guessing

Through the fog of sleep, Juan heard the noises from the hallway of the hospital beginning to come to life. He felt warm and comfortable as he recognized the peaceful form of his love sleeping next to him. He'd lain by her side all night, arms gently wrapped around her body to help her and himself feel more secure that they were together again. The rise and fall of her breathing matched his. They had always seemed synchronized when they slept together, with his warm breath gently kissing the side of her face as she remained on her back. Pleased he had not moved since he had climbed up beside her, he kept his eyes closed and envisioned how it would be when she and he were at home.

In his mind, she was waking up with a slight curve to her lips, always thinking she might wake up first. She often tried but rarely succeeded in that endeavor. She was a very strong athletic female, and he knew it would take some training for her to feel like herself again. One of their passions was working out and then working as it were. His mind drifted to a particularly passionate episode. The whole injury and hospitalization thing had always been reversed with them, except when she had the twins. It was disconcerting, but he knew he wanted and needed to be here. Thoughts of their children crept into his mind, and he struggled to stay focused on the here and now. They both had such a long way to go yet.

He felt an odd intake of breath by Julie, quickly followed by simultaneous arm flailing, like she was fighting specters, accompanied by terrifying screaming. Without thinking, Juan jumped out of bed, ready to fight whatever had entered into her room and scared her in such an earthshattering manner. Julie had never screamed to that level, and it terrified him. He looked around in a readied fight mode and saw nothing between himself and the door. Juan turned to see if someone had bypassed him. Julie had her eyes wide open and was still striking toward the air and gasping for breath, but now with no sound at all. Her eyes were not focused on anything in the room or on him.

Distressed beyond belief, Juan tried to hold her arms down and soothingly murmured, "Julie, sweetheart, it's Juan, honey. You are safe. Everything is going to be fine."

Trying to restrain her only resulted in a renewed effort to flail and swat at Juan with unbelievable strength. One of her punches clipped him in the mouth, and he tasted blood.

Julie raised up her head, gasped for air, eyes open with a wildness in her stare, and begged, "The children, don't hurt the children. They are a cover. They did nothing. They do not need to be involved." Then she stopped fighting and took big gulps of air, her eyes beginning to clear as if awakening from a horrible nightmare.

Juan stroked her arms gently, rather than trying to restrain her, and reaffirmed, "Sweetheart, you're in the hospital. I'm with you. The children are fine at home, I spoke to them a little while ago.

"You can wake up now. You were hurt badly, but you're safe now. Our children are fine, honey. I'll show you the video I played for you last night so many times. Honey, please!"

Julie stilled her arms and closed her eyes as she tried to take deep, slow breaths.

Juan continued his stroking on her arm and pressed the call button for the nurse. "Julie, I'm calling the nurse so she can see you're waking up, honey." Juan rambled, "You've been asleep so long. Your brain healed. You have some bruising, but you will be kicking my butt soon in our workouts, honey. You still have some powerful punching in you. I am so proud of you. We think you took out some of those kidnappers as you broke away and ran outside. I am so glad you were prepared, sweetheart. Of course, I will never let you out of my sight again." Juan was thoroughly choked with tears that were sliding slowly down his cheeks as he tried so desperately to get through her fog.

The nurse entered, looked at the situation, and then took a few of Julie's vitals. She nodded toward Juan before she commented, "I think she is coming back to us. Keep talking and I am going to call the doctor to also come and check.

"Julie, come on, dear, your husband is here with you, and he promised me I could see your breathtaking smile. Don't make a liar of him, dear. Men are so fragile, aren't they now?" The nurse helped Julie take a sip of water then rushed out to alert the doctor.

Juan felt his efforts were helping. He so wanted her to know he would wait forever for her to come back to him. He took a deep breath and pulled some extra strength to willingly share with her and kissed her gently on the cheek. Juan stroked her arms and begged, "Julie, honey, open your eyes. I want to have you see me here. I want to show you the children and their wonderful fort they have been building with blankets and pillows. They built a spot in their fort big enough for us to all sit together and tell stories. Come on, honey."

Julie did flutter her eyes and then opened them. She blinked several times as if trying to focus or avoid the bright lighting.

"Do I need to turn down the lights, Julie?"

She shook her head slightly and slowed her eye blinking. The heavy humidity she had felt a few minutes ago was gone, and her body wasn't floating. Julie was stronger than this, but she felt so lost. She moved her eyes around the room, trying to take everything in. Her hand reached up to briefly brush his tears away.

Juan felt a few more tears sliding down his cheeks as he saw the light slowly start to return to her beautiful eyes. She seemed to get her fill of the room, until her eyes landed on him. Julie licked her lips like she was trying to swallow, so Juan reached for the water and helped her get a sip. Her eyes never left his face while he helped her take a drink. After she had a few sips, he noticed a slight upturn in her mouth, as she searched his face for something unknown to him.

Juan solemnly offered, "That's right, honey, keep staring at me. I need you to focus on me. I love you sweetheart and need you with me."

"Juan," her slightly scratchy voice stated just above a whisper. Then a few moments of silence followed as she searched his eyes. She swallowed more gently as her breathing was far more even. "The children are safe?"

"Yes, honey, they are fine. Maude is playing with them and making certain they are fine, though they miss both of us. Do you want to see the video I took of them?"

She shook her head gently as a few tears slid down toward her ears. She looked terribly upset at the memory. "He threatened the children because I carried their photo. I never should have done that. I put them at risk, Juan. I am so sorry."

"Honey, they are fine, not at risk. Do you remember the man, honey? Can you describe him? What do you remember?"

Her eyes grew big, and she started to gulp air again. "It was so bad. They killed Laurie. They tried to drown me. It was awful. His name was Achmet, but others were there with him. He was evil. He mentioned Dmitry. He'd seen a picture of Natasha on the internet."

Julie closed her eyes at the memory and then reached for more water. Juan assisted her, and she continued, "I think I was able to hurt him and maybe killed one of the others. Laurie was swollen, pale…staring at the roof…with…dead eyes. No one will help her mother now. She just wanted a friend. She liked Dabir, but he didn't like her. She wanted to tell me about her mother, but she never got the chance because we were captured. Dabir, he started when I started. Mike Patrick hired him, she said. You told me not to go there. You were right! You have every right to be mad at me. Do you hate me, Juan?"

Juan stroked her hair and leaned over to kiss her cheek. "I love you, Julie. I could never hate you. You and I are like one whole being. I knew you would be okay, even when you were missing. I never doubted you'd come back to me. I want to tell you how…"

The doctor interrupted the discussion as he entered with the nurse trailing right behind. He moved up to the bed and retrieved the chart to look at the numbers as he commented, "There you are, madam, back with us, I see. You are looking so much better. I bet you are tired of lying around. Your husband informed me you are quite the busy woman, wife, mother. By all accounts, you're a warrior."

Julie smiled a little as some color rose to her cheeks. He checked her over briefly then asked Juan to leave so he might do some further examinations. Juan hesitated, looking for Julie to stop him, but she inclined her head and smiled a bit more.

Juan left and quickly called EZ. "EZ, Julie is awake. She sounds good. She said the man who hurt her was someone named Achmet and mentioned Dmitry. No description yet, because she is in with the doctor. She only has the IV for fluids at this point, so perhaps after he checks her over, we can talk about release."

EZ was almost giddy as she replied, "Woo-hoo! That's so awesome, Juan. I am glad she's awake and that you were near. I will let the others know. They will be relieved. All of them wanted to be there to help. We are doing great and close to wrapping up most of the investigations.

"George and Summit are finished and, on their way, home from Turkey. They will meet up in the office tomorrow with updates but have mostly resolved the issues. Mercedes and Tyler are back with Jim and Jamie nearby. Brayson is finishing up in Panama, and Ernesto is with you. If Ernesto is finished helping you now, send him back home to help George and Summit with the reporting.

"Every team succeeded in their missions, and I think you will be proud. Only one small issue, but Mercedes and her team are on it. Don't worry about a thing, Juan, just take care of Julie and come home. Achmet is dead. I am going to stay with Quip in Zurich unless you need me at the office."

"Okay, EZ, sounds good," confirmed Juan, "but the one small thing is likely a bigger problem than you are letting on. Fill me in later. I want to see if the doctor is finished."

The nurse came out and motioned to Juan to rejoin. He rushed to the bedside and took Julie's hand in his. She attempted one of her megawatt smiles and kept her other hand on top of his. The doctor announced, "I want to keep Julie overnight and make certain nothing else happens. I want her to eat several small meals throughout the day to make certain everything is functioning as it should. She is now untethered from the hospital devices, so it is up to her how rapidly she regains her strength. I would like her to start walking around with your support. She needs to be able to walk and digest her food before I release her. Understood?"

Julie flashed him another smile and replied, "Yes, doctor. I will follow your orders, but I want to go home tomorrow."

The doctor ignored her directly as he looked at Juan and replied, "Sir, she does possess an amazing smile. So glad I was able to see it. Also, no flying for at least five days. I meant to say that before. With the head trauma it is too risky."

Juan nodded and agreed, "No problem, doctor. We have a flat here and a driver. We can stay, and she can get stronger before we fly home."

The doctor and nurse left, and Juan commented, "I think I like that you can't fly home yet. I can have you all to myself." Julie smiled and replied, "I like that too. He also suggested I speak to someone professionally in case I have nightmares. You don't mind, do you?"

"Whatever you need, we will do. I love you, Julie!"

CHAPTER SIXTY-SEVEN

What is My Place in the World?

The visitor activity to the PRIMP, or *Panama Revolving Information Mule Portal*, as Brayson had fondly tagged it, had increased with several females passing through who were not currently in the alumni album. For the past several days, business had boomed with steady arrivals in the morning through early afternoon. As a result, late afternoon before sunset was the only time for Brayson to try to gain entrance to the data center as EZ had requested. Nighttime was not an option with the levers and locks that needed to be simultaneously activated. Nothing he tried had worked, and he had followed the exact method that had previously worked for Juan. He had contacted EZ, who had provided several suggestions, but there was still no real success. EZ cautioned him not to destroy the entrance and raise suspicions to the never-ending stream of visitors, which he agreed with.

Brayson planned methodical sequences for access while winding down in his sleeping bag at night. He typically fell asleep imagining the correct sequence that would get him in the subsequent day. After trying several of these combinations, he was convinced that at some point the access sequence had been altered by whoever had set up the process these females used.

The only things that seemed consistent were that the females all were attractive, and that the dragon pendants they all wore seem to be a conduit for the portal or gateway to partially open.

To date, none of the team had secured a dragon necklace except Mercedes. Now that Mercedes was finally rescued, EZ had mentioned in one of their quick exchanges, perhaps she could return to Panama with the pendant for a try together. He had sent that request to EZ while he watched the AIMs deliver their special brand of information. He also promised to look at the team information posted later that day. The text from her said it was important, but she gave no details.

Shortly after the noon hour, the second female had finally left. Brayson watched for over an hour as the dust from her car on the road slowly dissipated in the distant horizon. Brayson gathered his accoutrements to go to the entrance and try a few more combinations. He hated the idea that a stone doorway and some crazy lever system could defeat him so completely. Access to the entrance was a tedious hike that provided cover most of the way and left no visible trail from the entrance area or the direction from which the vehicles approached. He had almost reached the entrance when he noticed a new plume of dust growing bigger. Distances were hard to determine, but this one was moving fast.

He muttered, "This is ridiculous! Just when I get a pattern down, they change it." Wasting no time, he scrambled back up the path toward his modest campsite to deposit his tools and retrieve the camera. Then he worked his way down to the over-hang, which allowed him a great view of the entrance but hid him completely from visitor eyes. Perhaps it was some unrelated vehicle and wouldn't get close. This was the latest he had seen anyone approach the area, because leaving this place after dark was a huge risk unless you knew the rocky, hilly terrain.

The vehicle, which he finally identified as a jeep, made its way down the final approach. The vehicle choice at least indicated why the driver was moving so fast. Brayson surmised it was a repeat visitor as the driver seemed to know the precise turns as it barreled along with no hesitation. The jeep pulled to a stop up very close to the entrance. It appeared as if this driver was a male by the arm exposed on the door of the driver side. Brayson sighted, focused and enlarged the view of the camera on the man who was emerging. Initially it was an up-close view of the back and side of the man, until he turned after closing the door and reached back in through the open window for the bag he'd forgotten.

Brayson nearly shouted out when he realized it was Steven Christopher. Now this was interesting. Perhaps Christopher could solve Brayson's problem. The idea of ripping this man apart was the only thing running through Brayson's mind, but his training to quietly and patiently wait until the right moment kicked in as he watched, almost not breathing. He knew exactly how long and how many steps it would take to reach the area where Christopher was right now. He started to plan at what point he would start. Christopher approached the portal with confidence. This attitude alone convinced Brayson to stay still, but he kept wiggling his feet so he could move when needed.

Christopher had turned slightly at the left side of the portal, blocking some of his movements from Brayson's view. Something small was in his right hand as he raised it toward the wall. Brayson couldn't see exactly what it was. Christopher moved two of the levers in a bottom-up order with his left hand. Brayson had messed with those levers in different ways. It appeared, however, that the lever lowest to the ground was ignored, Brayson noted. Then Christopher took both hands and pressed them against the area the PRIMP visitors had faced. Like magic, the opening door slid to the right, disappearing like a soffit door in an expensive home.

Seconds later, Christopher was swallowed up by the darkness. Brayson knew what to expect inside from the previous descriptions given by Juan and Julie, knowledge they had gained from their original visit. Not knowing how long Christopher would be inside, Brayson pocketed his camera, then scrambled from his position and went to the jeep. He looked inside and was rewarded for his patience, finding the keys still in the ignition, which he quickly retrieved. Brayson smiled with the certain knowledge that one way or another Christopher had to now deal with him before he left. Trussing up Christopher like a calf in a rodeo was what he had in mind.

Endless darkness beyond the opening beckoned to Brayson. No sounds came from the inside, though he knew there were several turns and twists to what had been the operation floor of the underground data center. There were also living quarters and meeting rooms scattered throughout the maze of catacombs. Juan had drawn a rough map of the corridors and rooms, which Brayson had reviewed with Mercedes when they'd first arrived, then memorized. Using his hands and the memorized steps from Juan's map, he headed toward the operations center. His hope was to accomplish the activity EZ had assigned as well as to locate Christopher, whom he expected to be in that area. This time the CATS team was ahead of the game.

With the latest right turn, he began to see the low light increase and bounce off the dark walls like shadows. The muted lights were likely caused by the lights of the various servers operating and any lights Christopher may have used. The brightness increased as he slowed his approach to the main area. Reflections, which Brayson suspected were due to Christopher's movements, added to the surreal qualities of the grey glow. Stopping at the entrance to the operations center, he peered into the gloom but didn't see Christopher. The racks of servers were straight ahead. It appeared a console area on each side was activated with the screens lit, but he saw no one and the drone of the server fans prevented him hearing any sort of typing.

He crouched very low to the ground and started a crab walk to the left, pressing his back against the wall. His careful steps produced no discernable sounds, even as he listened carefully, trying to identify any movement. Christopher had to activate the screens, so he was likely somewhere in this area. He had reached the back wall when he heard a couple of clicks, like eject buttons from a server, and deliberate minor noises of a slide moving, then stopping, and steps moving away from him. Brayson stepped further to his left to get a view down a row of server racks and caught the movement of Christopher as he went toward the console. In his rush to reach Christopher, Brayson caught his foot against one of the feet of the end rack, and the noise was loud enough to be heard. No longer having to move silently, Brayson moved in and called, "Christopher, stop right there. I think we need to have a chat, man."

Christopher stopped what he was doing, grabbed a piece of gear sitting next to him and rushed away without finishing his keying into the console. Brayson moved toward him, stopping to glance at the screen on the way by. An upload of something was in progress. Brayson quickly keyed a command to stop the routine without really seeing what it was doing and resumed his chase. Christopher had gained some significant distance and obviously knew the maze far better. Brayson could see him paused outside the entrance and doing something on the panel. Christopher looked up to see Brayson headed at a dead run now and grinned.

Christopher taunted, "Too late, old man. Oh, and she is soon to be dead, you know. She has cheated me for the last time with you being here."

The entrance began shrinking as it was closing. Christopher disappeared from Brayson's sight, probably headed for the jeep. Brayson poured on the afterburners and launched himself like a runner toward home plate with the last chance in the World Series. Face first, his dive slide picked up momentum on the smooth rock floor, and he knew it would be close. One of the tricks his baseball coach had taught him was to pick up his feet and not let their drag slow down his momentum. He only just cleared the entrance with a final snap of the closure catching on the sole of his shoe. He sighed in relief as he wiggled his shoe out of the grip of the door.

Christopher had apparently discovered the keys were gone. He was leaning over the seat rummaging through a duffel bag. He retrieved a long ceramic knife, which gave off a menacing glint in the sunlight as Christopher turned to face Brayson. The jeep was squarely between them.

Christopher's face contorted with his scorn and anger. "Why the hell do you people keep getting in my way? We need to end this. I have what I came for, now I have to waste time dealing with you."

Brayson grinned and replied, "Worse yet, Christopher, I have your keys. If you come quietly, I will let you ride in the front seat, tied up, back to the authorities, or I could just tie you to the back bumper. Oh, and just to set the record straight, Mercedes was pulled off the flight and wants first shot at getting your confession. If I don't get one first!

Christopher's eyes burned with rage as he moved in on Brayson. Brayson moved to one side of the jeep, and instead of retreating, Christopher met him head on. He had the advantage of the knife, but with his prosthetic arm, Brayson felt his balance and agility would be hampered. Obviously, Christopher had some sort of training or at least street smarts as evidenced by the way he moved with the knife. Brayson was in no mood to be sliced, regardless of how much his opponent increased his attempts. Brayson was not one to necessarily fight clean, but he had to fight smart, as he feigned one way then the other, working to move them both away from the jeep and toward the river.

Christopher's thrusts became wilder, almost erratic, and Brayson saw his opening. He landed a great right-hand punch to Christopher's chin, knocking him on his ass. Christopher scrambled to a pivotal position on his prosthetic arm and kicked Brayson's legs out from underneath him before regaining his stance. Brayson rolled after being kicked to the ground. He managed to come up to knock the knife out of Christopher's hand, and it slid toward the river's edge. Christopher threw a stunning nerve punch into Brayson that made him stagger, then followed up with two well executed sidekicks to Brayson's chest.

Christopher growled, "I don't need the knife to finish you off!"

Christopher clubbed Brayson hard upside the head with his prosthetic arm, knocking Brayson flat to the ground. Brayson now realized he wasn't a match for Christopher's strength and tried to crawl quickly to the knife's location, but Christopher repeatedly hit Brayson's rib area with punishing kicks. Just before Brayson could reach the knife, Christopher delivered a powerful hit to the back of his neck, driving Brayson to a dead stop.

Christopher smirked as he circled the still figure of Brayson, then raised his eyes to where the knife lay. Christopher was all set to retrieve it when Brayson spun around on the ground, this time knocking Christopher's feet sideways. Even though Brayson had taken a heavy beating, Christopher was now dazed, and the initiative became Brayson's. But rather than jump for the knife,

Brayson kicked it away and delivered his own punishing sidekick, knocking Christopher to the ground.

Their struggle devolved into a drunken brawl as Brayson jumped on top, and they began wrestling, throwing punches, rolling one way then the other. Both men were around the same weight and height. The plastic fingers on the end of the prosthetic arm moved but seemed unable to grip. Christopher heaved with all his strength and pushed Brayson to the side. Once free of the threat, he reached around his body for something. Brayson assumed it was another weapon when the prosthetic arm released and quickly became a club-like weapon. The surprise made Brayson back up, but Christopher didn't press his advantage. Instead, Christopher turned, presumably to look for the knife, and slipped on the loose gravel at the edge of the river. With no warning, the slide continued as he fell off the edge with no time to even scream.

Brayson, knowing how slippery the gravel could be, rushed to firmer ground to look over into the river. Christopher was face up, eyes open, on top of the hydro-electric generator. He must have cracked his skull as Brayson observed blood flowing down the generator, no other injuries visible and no movement whatsoever. After he caught his breath and still holding his sore ribs, he made certain Christopher wasn't going to magically rise. He got up and went to the jeep where he found the duffel bag in the rear seat and what appeared to be a server drive with terabyte markings on the outside.

Brayson suspected the information on the drive would answer many of the questions they all had. He looked around and located a silver dragon pendant on the passenger seat and pocketed it, figuring it was needed for the return trip inside the data center. Then he retrieved his phone and called EZ.

EZ answered, "How's it going, Brayson? Did you finally get inside the data center?"

Brayson grinned as he explained, "Sort of! Wasn't me though. It was Steven Christopher who showed up with the keys to the kingdom. Mercedes is safe, right? He said she was dead. I taunted Christopher into an anger driven fight. Remind me not to do that again."

EZ panicked and exclaimed, "Brayson, he's very dangerous. His real name is Stuart Chesterfield. He is an identity thief, swindler, and likely at the heart of the conflicts created at ePETRO. Mercedes, Tyler, and Jim Hughes tried to track him, but he slipped through their fingers. I will send the authorities to help you. Mercedes was going to catch the next flight to bring her pendant, but the flight won't depart New York for another couple of hours. Just watch him, Brayson!"

Brayson chuckled and offered, "I could watch him, but it would be like watching grass grow. Nothing to see here, he's dead. You knew his arm was really fake, right? I was so surprised when he came at me with it. I guess I should have read the team uploads this morning, right, Boss?"

EZ sounded relieved as she replied, "That might have helped you realize we had found out who the bad guy really was. Do you think you can get into the data center, or does Mercedes need to come help?

"And, I don't hear you whining, Brayson."

Brayson thought about that a moment then explained, "I don't think you'll hear any more whining out of me. This has really helped me get out of my doldrums and back into living. I was in the data center already when I followed Stuart inside. He was retrieving some information which he brought out on a terabyte drive, which I will bring home. I stopped a program he was executing while I chased him out, so I will try to get back in and finish my assignment. Then I'd like to come home, boss."

EZ laughed a bit then said, "I am not your boss, just a fill-in project manager. Finish up and get on home. The rest of the team are headed there as well. You can read the updates on your way home. Make certain you post yours before your flight. Do you want me to get you booked for tomorrow morning?"

Brayson replied, "Yes, late morning. I would like to get out of here as soon as I set the routine in the data center. I will alert the authorities to the body as a tip from the departing gate. Thanks, boss!"

CHAPTER SIXTY-EIGHT

Is it an Odd or an End

George and Summit arrived in the office at dawn. They started the tedious process of itemizing all the elements by category. The property and tankers' leases directly tied to ePETRO took up most of the time. Summit added his color commentary on the crew and captain of the vessel he traveled on, along with the stop made in North Korea. He was able to identify three of the men on the docks as known antagonists for what was now a lost cause.

George focused on the furniture makers and gunrunners identified in Istanbul. With some extra research, he determined that the weapons were bought, and sometimes stolen, from multiple sources all over the world. The random and small thefts and purchases had not raised the level of multinational concern. The summarized information for this portion of the investigation was uploaded to the team file and flagged for review and potential forwarding to the appropriate countries impacted.

Finally, they stopped working and enjoyed a late lunch. During their conversation, Summit volunteered to pick up the team arriving shortly from the U.S. George was glad he didn't have that duty. He decided to take advantage of the time to get in a full workout. Before he'd had a chance to shower off and change, Ernesto called in on the office line. George answered, "Hey, Ernesto. I see Julie has been recovering and resting for a few days in London before flying home. How's Juan doing?"

"George, I think Juan is just relieved that she was located. From looking at the place where she was held and tortured, it will be a very long time before Juan will let her out of his sight. I think the suggestion they made to add more people, before we split up on this unbelievably intertwined set of cases, is going to happen. I'm at Heathrow and will be arriving later this evening. If there's nothing planned, I want to go home and rest for tonight.

"Also, I don't believe you've met Jamie, but I think he's going to make a good addition to the team. Do you have some other contacts we might consider adding? The reason I ask is, I've been thinking about who I might trust to add to our group." Ernesto sighed at the last statement.

"Ernesto, as wild and crazy as Summit and I have been, I hadn't given it a thought, but I am anxious to meet Jamie. I understand he's had a tough road, like all of us. Where did you want him to stay until he finds a place? I have the room but only the floor to offer until some of my new Turkish furniture and rugs arrive. He, Mercedes, and Tyler should be back in an hour or so. It would be nice to know where to direct him, or we can keep the lad in limbo?

"As far as new teammates, I think any new additions should be multilingual. Summit was so funny when he said I needed to learn some languages because Turkish wasn't on my list. He forgot I have some others. But I think that needs to be one of the criteria we use. Military training wouldn't hurt either. A couple like Mercedes or EZ would be nice and likely improve our flexibility for assignments. Let's talk about it when you get back and have a plan ready to present to Juan and Julie when they arrive."

Ernesto commented, "I like the idea of having a plan ready. I'll think about it on my flight back. I downloaded some new material to read from our team's virtual storage drive as well. Overall, we did really well. I liked partnering with Tyler and Jamie. I learned quite a bit from Tyler. I can't wait to hear the story behind driving while zip tied, though I suspect we will need to ply him with generous quantities of Bushmills to get the whole story.

"Jamie can bunk with me for a while. I have the extra cot, and we did some good bonding on a very long Texas drive. We need to get together and get something for EZ for all her efforts too, after Juan set off to find Julie. Juan said he simply left her in charge and walked away. He felt bad about dumping and running, his words, after he found Julie. Heck, I would have been just as focused if I were him with a sweet lady like that. Hey, they're calling my flight. Let's all have a sit-down and rehash tomorrow night. I think everyone will be back by then, though EZ will stay in Zurich with her man. I understand he helped use some of his computer processing power for our collective benefit."

George chuckled and replied, "Sounds good. I will work on the party. Fly safe."

George was just coming out of the gent's locker room, following his long shower and having changed into fresh clothes when he heard the muted conversation and laughter from the conference room. He followed the sounds and leaned against the doorway, watching the team interacting, with wine in hand and an enormous tray of cheese, crackers, and fresh fruit carefully offset with an open bar. Summit was the first to notice him as he looked up, smiled, and then raised an empty glass in George's direction. He nodded and located a chair to join the conversation after selecting his adult beverage of choice.

Like a slow starting party of professionals who were also friends, the back-and-forth story telling had several dialogs going on at the same time. Each person was contributing snippets of their exploits but was also eager to hear from the others. If the entire team had been in the room, it might have been tough to get in a word.

Mercedes and Jamie helped Tyler hobble into the room and parked him in a nice chair where he could prop up his right leg that was now in a walking cast. Mercedes insisted on playing bartender for him and delivered a nicely capped brew, insisting he take it easy. Tyler smiled at the attention but didn't bother to resist. It had been a long trip back.

Jamie seemed a little reserved at first. Mercedes took note of Jamie hanging back and promptly made introductions in a highly spirited way, sprinkled with a little bit of gentle teasing. Her playful nature helped to put Jamie at ease, and before long he was filling in team members on his epic journey. Of course, Mercedes made sure that he was amply plied with a nice creamy Guinness brew, fully laced with fine Irish whiskey shots in the bottom of the glass. She said these were called *depth charges* yet couldn't recall who had provided that name for the near lethal concoction that put everyone at ease, according to Jamie. She smiled as she watched the group embrace Jamie and praise his support during the whole assignment.

The team almost stopped talking as Brayson finally found his way into the party. Sensing the uncertainty of the others, he tried to smile but ended up wincing as he tried to greet everyone. Tyler read the scenario correctly and invited Brayson to sit over close to him to see if they could get Mercedes to play bartender for him too.

A smile broadly crossed Brayson's face, but before he sat, he went right up to Mercedes to see for himself that she was alright.

She poured up a nice Chablis for him and mentioned, "EZ told me what happened. Thanks for worrying about me and thanks for closure with that psychotic thief. How are the ribs?" Brayson drew a ragged breath and offered, "They're fine, as long as I don't breathe too deep or too often. The tape helps them stay aligned, but, boy, what I wouldn't give to be healed. The doctor promised it wouldn't be too long, but the twenty minutes after I checked out of his office was already too long.

"I'm glad I had a chance to work with you, madam. I learned a lot on this assignment. Mostly what I learned is that I want to be with this team. Thanks for helping me see that."

Without thinking, Mercedes beamed and gathered Brayson into a nice hug, immediately amplifying his pain. Realizing her error, she carefully helped him into the chair next to Tyler and rushed to refill his glass of wine with a promise of no more hugging for a while.

Tyler smirked and quietly offered, "Admit it, you deserved that!"

Brayson studied Tyler a moment and asked, "You want me to rap that sore leg of yours?"

Jamie wandered over to them to see how Tyler was doing and Tyler watched him approach. Before either of the men spoke, Brayson boldly stated, "Jamie, thank you for your much needed help and support. Most importantly, for helping my fallen team member here. I understand that we are looking to add some new team members. I would like to think you could join us, but it is important to ask, is there anything keeping you from making a commitment to the likes of this motley crew?"

Jamie adopted a crazy grin and stated, "It has been suggested that you folks might have some openings but that you are only looking for motley people, so I might have a shot at it. And no, I don't have anything keeping me from joining. How about you? Are you going to stay after that dressing down, I provided? I probably should apologize for how I spoke to you, so we can clear the air between us."

Brayson gave a wry smile and said, "Dude, your comments were spot on. There is no need for any apology from you. I am the one who needs to apologize to almost everyone here.

"In fact, this is as good a time as any."

Then in an effort to get everyone's attention, he pinged on his glass until they all stopped talking and looked in his direction. With a little discomfort and wincing, he raised his glass and stated, "My teammates and…well, my friends. Thanks for not giving up on me! I would like to apologize for my past indiscretions and flawed behavior to one and all. I promise never to fall into that emotion pit again, nor let any of you want for other support if mine is available. I would like very much to stay and work with you, if no one has an issue."

Mercedes, now having served everyone and well into serving herself from the bar, lifted her glass in a slightly inebriated motion and loudly stated, "Here's to Brayson's return from putz-ville! May he no longer be a colossal jerk, but instead do…uh…be… well, whatever the hell he purports to be! So anyway, here's to good ol' Brampton!"

The team members suddenly realized their little sister Mercedes was snockered and all raised their glasses and in unison toasted, "Here's to good ol' Brampton!"

Brayson, somewhat mortified, quietly eyed everyone and responded, "I have so missed the brutal sarcasm from the team. I'm tempted to think going home is a good idea, but instead let me thank you from the heart of my bottom!"

The rest of the evening passed with sporadic chuckling from the different team members, until finally they drifted back to their own quarters. Everyone promised to come back in the morning and help clean up. Tyler and Brayson had to help Mercedes back to her room, each making sure that the other didn't stay, which was very easy when Jim waltzed into the living room with a raised eyebrow for his female's condition.

Jim quickly promised, "I've got her from here, boys. She'll be back in the office late tomorrow morning. Goodnight!"

Better, the Same, or Just Different?

Julie was awakened from her dream, less intense than the last, but still dreaming of being smothered. She could sense she had made progress against the psychological damage she had sustained. Hopefully she had not squirmed too much before recognizing it was a dream. She refused to open her eyes as her senses picked up on her current world. Before she had left the hospital a scant day and a half ago, she had spoken to the resident psychologist. She had recommended Julie see someone when she got home. In the interim he suggested when she had a bad dream, she might tr to control the outcome. This was why she did not open her eyes until she could smell her lotion, the scent of Juan lying next to her, and the warmth under the sheets and blankets. The noises were also familiar, and she was grateful to have spent time in the flat before the trauma.

Julie replayed in her mind the afternoon before last when she had been released into Juan's care. James had welcomed her like a long-lost daughter. Before he had picked up the happy couple to take them to the flat, he'd procured enough food and beverage to let them hold up comfortably. He had laughed when Juan said he could stay and have their evening meal with them, begging off by saying his cat missed him. Julie had flashed him a smile, and he immediately understood why Juan was so in love.

James had parted after he promised, if he'd been thirty years younger, he might have been tempted to woo her away from Juan. They only had to call if they needed anything or a ride anywhere.

Julie recalled the first evening away from the hospital with her updating her information to the team files. Laurie had provided some offshore account numbers for both Marge and Mike in a roundabout way, as Julie had earned more responsibility. Julie and Juan had been on a call with EZ and Quip and had been briefed on the newest developments. Julie didn't know if her information would be of any benefit. During the conversation, she had started crying, and Juan had ended up cutting the conversation short. Though Julie was slightly embarrassed with showing her vulnerability, Juan had promised he would help her over this rough patch. Then he'd taken her for a luxurious shower. Knowing her bruising was all but vanished with no serious physical injury to slow him down, he gently scrubbed every inch of her, then smoothed her favorite lotion all over her until she'd drifted off to sleep. She loved to be spoiled by her husband, who had this uncanny ability to both excite her with body massages and totally relax her. She vowed to return the favor soon.

Then yesterday morning when she woke with a start, Juan had been lying close and simply watching her. She knew she must have looked a little wide-eyed when she awoke, but he quietly murmured, "Ah, my darling, I was wondering if you would wake any time soon. I love watching you sleep. I love you in my life. Thank you for coming home to us."

That simple statement and the kisses he applied to every bare space of skin pushed the worry of the dream far away as he spent time stroking her breasts until her nipples ached to be tasted. Juan stroked her thighs while taking first one nipple and then the other, forcing her response of kissing and calling his name.

His hands trailed down over her hips, then between her thighs, and she pressed into his hand and asked for more. There was no shortage of excitement for either of them as they gave into their passion.

Juan masterfully pushed her onto her back, and his eyes darkened as his passion deepened. After her responses had rewarded him twice, he picked up her hips and slid quickly into her wet heat. The pulsing of her recent climax, coupled with having her home where he so desperately needed her, gave him a quick release of all the passion he'd held in reserve. Taking great care not to crush her, he'd turned them onto their sides and held her close.

Once he recovered his breathing and realized he might be holding her too tightly, he softly admitted, "Sweetheart, I missed you. I love you so very much. Thank you for being with me."

They'd spent the rest of the day lounging, making love, eating a couple of meals, sampling some wine, and only talked business when she brought it up. They at least agreed they should expand the business and start looking for new recruits along with their training. Juan suggested she be the one to do the interviews, since she had done that when hiring their current team. Julie was suspicious that his motives were not just driven by the desire to grow the business, but his desire to keep her out of the field. However, the evening had ended on a positive note when EZ sent a text that Julie's information had been enormously helpful.

Juan was hovering over her the entire evening, trying to second guess her needs. After their shower, he waited until she fell asleep with another body massage. As she roused herself further to the morning, she decided they needed to get something straight between them. She opened her eyes to see Juan watching her. He often woke and watched her, promising it was a thrill to just see her in his bed next to him, but she also saw a new intensity, or perhaps it was fear.

Julie flashed him a smile and sweetly questioned, "Honey, did you get any rest, or did you just watch me all night?"

Juan hated lying to Julie, because he was always caught, so he replied, "But I love watching you next to me. It makes my mind wander, and, well, I simply must make love to you, just one more time, darling."

Julie laughed and immediately made a move atop Juan. She pinned his shoulders in a way that he could easily defeat but wanted to make certain he knew she was serious. "Juan, I love you, but we need to get something straight between us."

His eyes flashed, but she continued, "I'm serious. I am a very capable female who has defeated many a difficult situation, just like you. I get that you worry. I've been there myself with some of your situations. We can each be strong, but I will not be kept in a jar to be loved and admired, just to let you have all the fun of getting bad people put where they need to be. I will not have you looking at me in fear that I will disappear. We have our babies and our love, and we will always find a way. Right?"

Juan smiled and responded, "Yes, honey, I agree with you, but it will take me time to work through this. You're going to have to help me."

Julie replied, "Yes, we will help each other." Then she leaned down and give him a soft exploratory kiss.

Juan murmured, "What was it you were saying about getting something straight between us? I think I am up for that."

CHAPTER SEVENTY

Paper Currency – Irony in our Digital World?

Quip concluded, "We received the terabyte drive that was shipped to us from Brayson's haul there at the Panama data center. The contents of this drive are going to be time consuming and tedious to break into. So far, the only thing we have extracted is a name: Matthias. We are still not sure why this was the only thing out of the data center that our identity thief wanted."

Juan launched into his team debrief. "Julie and I have combed through all the team notes trying to make sense of this puzzle. By all accounts, Stuart Chesterfield started off as a petty thief preying on veterans, something of a detestable livelihood. Along the way something happened to morph him from a petty thief into a psychotic identity thief. It would seem his damning gift of twisted genius allowed him to operate at multiple social levels.

"He was good enough to assemble a team of predominantly female operatives, move information and funds with non-digital techniques, and deceive all parties into believing he was serving their best interests. He even deceived Mercedes into thinking he was Steven Christopher. Pretty good con actually. Then, after s etting up so much, he began to text clues using Mercedes phone alerting people where to intercept the Muslim extremists.

"This was after he had engineered the transport of weapons and uranium into their hands, almost as if he wanted them caught with illegal goods. Our team speculates that even though he was a money-grubbing parasite, he also acted like a vigilante with a grudge against radical Muslims."

Juan let those comments sink in before he continued, "As far as we can track, it seems he fleeced the Muslims for the oil he was to pay for, blew the whistle on the uranium transport after he helped get it loaded, and ran guns as a part of ePETRO to the North Koreans. While we can't quite prove it, we are fairly sure he got those same Muslims to whack Marge and Mike, then drained their offshore accounts.

"Quip, with the assistance of ICABOD, helped identify the real Steven Christopher which was when things began to come together. Stuart Chesterfield was always one step ahead. He would have wiped out the data center in Panama if Brayson hadn't intercepted him. Our team firmly believes he would have vanished into another new identity if he hadn't been stopped."

Petra, Julie's sister suggested, "What if all the ancillary activities were established to provide a cloaking mechanism for Stuart. Looking at it from a different angle, using nefarious business partners to traffic in unsanctioned goods, Stuart pits all the players against each other so he could orchestrate their collective demise by turning them over to the authorities. He would have been able to walk away with all the money while his opponents were either incarcerated or dead. Bad guys in jail, no one hunting for you and with a new identity, one could set up shop somewhere else. Pretty slick business model, don't you think?"

Julie added, "The other loose end is, we didn't find pirated funds. Your theory of a thief stealing from thieves does seem plausible, but only if you have funds for your new business. You would have thought that based on his maniacal preference for analog communications over digital, we should have found gobs of hard currency, but we didn't."

Everyone was solemn after the briefing summaries. The R-Group inner circle, Julie, Juan, Quip, EZ, Petra, Jacob, Otto, and Wolfgang reflected their teammate's expressions as they puzzled over the details. ICABOD was on the call, but no one could envision how the supercomputer processed the details being presented.

Wolfgang offered, "I admit this ending is a bit of a paradox for us. When we follow the money, we find the money. Simple, right? Only this time we followed the money, and it vanished. The pirated funds from ePETRO, Mike Patrick's cloaked accounts, and Marge's even more cloaked accounts all tracked into the hands of Stuart Chesterfield, aka Steven Christopher, but then abruptly vanished. I must confess, I'm not accustomed to being outwitted in the world of financial cat and mouse. It's disconcerting!"

Julie protested, "Wolfgang, money just doesn't disappear into thin air! It had to go…somewhere!"

Juan insisted, "It doesn't make any sense. We tracked the AIMs, we tracked the uranium theft, we tracked each and every one of the bad players, and we tracked all of their ill-gotten gains to one off-shore account owned by Stuart Chesterfield. Yet now all we have is a piece of mail marked *please return to sender.* How is that possible?"

Quip was uncomfortable with such an illogical presentation. "Surprisingly, I'm like Wolfgang here. All this mismatched information has chapped my ass too!"

Otto rolled his eyes and sternly stated, "Well, thanks, Quip, for your pithy vulgarities! Can't you remain in the business world vernacular while we reason through this?"

Quip seriously studied Otto a moment and then asked, "You're not going to put me in time out again, are you? Because if you

are, I want all my crayons and drawing papers while I sit there."
EZ discreetly nudged him, even though the video captured the
movement, and Quip nodded grudgingly.

Musing out loud, Jacob suggested, "What is that basic law
of physics? Nothing is created nor destroyed, but rather is in fact
converted? It occurs to me that trying to run with that much
money is quite impractical. We are talking millions here. Moving
it to another banking institution leaves fingerprints and begs for
trust from someone who is unlikely to ever be trusted. So given
those parameters, what's a master criminal to do?"

Quip, not missing an opportunity for levity, volunteered,
"Government relief? Food stamps? Accosting auto drivers at a
stop light with a hand drawn sign saying *my millions are gone!
Please help! God bless!*"

Petra and EZ both studied Quip, undoubtedly sizing him up
for the amount of duct tape they will need to shut him up.

Jacob, totally used to and unruffled by the irreverence continually sprinkled throughout conversations with Quip, continued,
"He converts it to digital currency. The funds vanish into the digital
world with the promise of self-contained, highly mobile digital
currency which sidesteps banking over-sight and government
reporting.

"If this group and our own ICABOD cannot find it, I would
submit that he converted it to something that doesn't conform
to our conventions. If that is the case and he had lived, he really
could have vanished."

Petra started to grasp the logic of Jacob's concept and
added, "If he used one of the new crypto currencies built on the
Blockchain financial algorithms, he could literally vanish with
all his wealth. He could have lived anywhere he wanted and
had everything."

Julie chuckled as she set the reality bar. "Of course, he didn't make it out with all his ill-gotten gains because he didn't make it out. However, it still begs the question, where are the funds? Can they be retrieved or moved or even located?" Wolfgang nodded as he started to jump on the bandwagon. "This line of conversation helps to steer us in a potential direction on *what* to look for, if not the where yet. Still useful brainstorming."

Otto remarked, "If this is the case, it would seem we have a new attack vector to consider when dealing with the financial players in the digital landscape. Quip, I think we need you, Petra, and Jacob to work this angle and report back to the team. If all of our adversaries can vanish so completely with their stolen funds, if crime lords can fall off the grid from investigators, if the world banking community can be made irrelevant, then we have a major new global threat, and we need to get ahead of it."

They all nodded in agreement.

Quip then asked, "Can I say something now?"

They all shook their heads in unison, and EZ in particular said, "No, honey. You have your work cut out for you in finding the source."

Specialized Terms and Informational References

http://en.wikipedia.org/wiki/Wikipedia

Wikipedia (wIki' pi: diə / *wik-i-pee-dee-ə*) is a collaboratively edited, multilingual, free Internet encyclopedia supported by the non-profit Wikimedia Foundation. Wikipedia's 30 million articles in 287 languages, including over 4.3 million in the English Wikipedia, are written collaboratively by volunteers around the world. This is a great quick reference source to better understand terms.

Analog a signal, in which information is encoded in a non-quantized variable, as opposed to a digital signal. Relating to or using signals or information represented by a continuously variable physical quantity such as spatial position.

Blockchain originally block chain – is a distributed database that maintains a continuously growing list of ordered records called blocks. Each block contains a timestamp and a link to a previous block. By design, blockchains are inherently resistant to modi-fication of the data — once recorded, the data in a block cannot be altered retroactively. Blockchains are "an open, distributed ledger that can record transactions between two parties efficiently and in a verifiable and permanent way. The ledger itself can also be programmed to trigger transactions automatically."
(*see* cryptocurrencies)

Cryptocurrencies A cryptocurrency (or crypto currency) is a digital asset designed to work as a medium of exchange using cryptography to secure the transactions and to control the creation of additional units of the currency. Cryptocurrencies are a subset of alternative currencies, or specifically of digital currencies. Bitcoin became the first decentralized cryptocurrency in 2009. Since then, numerous cryptocurrencies have been created. These are frequently called altcoins, as a blend of bitcoin alternative. Bitcoin and its derivatives use decentralized control as opposed to centralized electronic money/centralized banking systems. The decentralized control is related to the use of bitcoin's Blockchain transaction database in the role of a distributed ledger.

Digital in technology refers to something using digits, particularly binary digits.

Encryption In cryptography, encryption is the process of encoding messages (or information) in such a way that eavesdroppers or hackers cannot read it, but that authorized parties can. In an **encryption scheme**, the message or information (referred to as plaintext) is encrypted using an encryption algorithm, turning it into an unreadable cipher text (ibid.). This is usually done with the use of an encryption key, which specifies how the message is to be encoded. Any adversary that can see the cipher text should not be able to determine anything about the original message. An authorized party, however, is able to decode the cipher text using a **decryption** algorithm that usually requires a secret decryption key that adversaries do not have access to. For technical reasons, an encryption scheme usually needs a key-generation algorithm to randomly produce keys. Encryption can be done to any data, voice or video packet.

Enigma Machine An Enigma machine was any of a family of related electro-mechanical rotor cipher machines used in the twentieth century for enciphering and deciphering secret messages. Enigma was invented by the German engineer Arthur Scherbius at the end of World War I. Early models were used commercially from the early 1920s, and adopted by military and government services of several countries — most notably by Nazi Germany before and during World War II. Several different Enigma models were produced, but the German military models are the most commonly discussed.

German military texts enciphered on the Enigma machine were first broken by the Polish Cipher Bureau, beginning in December 1932. This success was a result of efforts by three Polish cryptologists, working for Polish military intelligence. Rejewski "reverse-engineered" the device, using theoretical mathematics and material supplied by French military intelligence. Subsequently the three mathematicians designed mechanical devices for breaking Enigma ciphers, including the cryptologic bomb. This work was an essential foundation to further work on decrypting ciphers from repeatedly modernized Enigma machines, first in Poland and after the outbreak of war in France and the UK.

Though Enigma had some cryptographic weaknesses, in practice it was German procedural flaws, operator mistakes, laziness, failure to systematically introduce changes in encypherment procedures, and Allied capture of key tables and hardware that, during the war, enabled Allied cryptologists to succeed.

Fusion In *nuclear* physics, *nuclear fusion* is a reaction in which two or more atomic nuclei come close enough to form one or more different atomic nuclei and subatomic particles (neutrons and/or protons). ... The opposite is true for the reverse process, *nuclear* fission.

Geo-locator is a utility for getting geo-location information, geocoding, address look-ups, distance & durations, time zone information and more. A lightweight electronic archival tracking device

IP address An IP address (abbreviation of Internet Protocol address) is an identifier assigned to each computer and other device (e.g., printer, router, mobile device, etc.) connected to a **TCP**/IP network that is used to locate and identify the node in communications with other nodes on the network.

RFID Tag is part of an ID system that uses small radio frequency identification devices for identification and tracking purposes. An RFID tagging system includes the tag itself, a read/write device, and a host system application for data collection, processing, and transmission.

Supercomputer a computer with a high-level computational capacity. Performance of a supercomputer is measured in floating point operations per second (FLOPS). As of 2015, there are super-computers which can perform up to quadrillions of FLOPS.

TCP/IP computer address Transmission Control Protocol and Internet Protocol is collectively the common Internet protocol suite in the computer networking model and set of commu-nications protocol used on the Internet and similar computer networks. It is commonly known as TCP/IP, because these were the first networking protocols defined during the Internet's communication development.

Three factor authentication A tried and true method of identification in secure technology usage. Typically, something you know (such as a password), plus something you have (such as a smart card), and something you are (such as a fingerprint or other biometric method).

Yaqui Indians Native Americans who inhabit the valley of the Rio Yaqui in the Mexican state of Sonora, Mexico and the Southwestern United States. The Pascua Yaqui Tribe is based in Tucson, Arizona.

Discussion Questions for

The Enigma Dragon

Book Club Leaders … contact Charles and/or Rox to participate in a special meeting to discuss the book; the concepts; and the evolution of the series. We always encourage readers to post individual reviews on Amazon.com. And thank you.

In-person gatherings are possible if you are in the North Texas region. Otherwise, Zoom is always an option.

Discussion Questions

Did the idea of locations worldwide pique your interest?
- Were you delighted to learn about locations around the world?

- How did you like the interactions between team members on assignment?

- Did you take sides with the POV of any of the team members?

- Did you empathize with one or more of the characters and why?

What do you think of Julie and Juan with their business model?
- Do they complement one another's strengths?

- Was the foreshadowing effective?

- Do you think it's important for a woman to take risks if she feels she can win?

Did Julie missing set you on the edge of your seat?
- How were you affected by Juan's reaction to Julie missing?

- How would you react if your significant other went missing for any reason?

- How did you feel when she was found?

Did you have any empathy for the leaders of ePetro?
- Do you think Mike Patrick received his just deserts?

- Was Marge's betrayal a surprise, or would you have liked a different ending for her?

- What was your reaction to anyone supporting a government on the terrorist list for the United States?

How did you relate to Steven Christopher?
- Have you known anyone like this character?

- Is he a character to be pitied or despised?

- What would you like to do to him?

What themes surfaced in the story?
- Have you ever been in a situation where you needed someone to save you?

- Have you ever been in a situation where you did not want someone to save you?

- Have you ever had to step in and help someone out of a dire situation?

Breakfield and Burkey are happy to work with your club on your answers and impressions.

Read a snippet from **Book 10: The Enigma Source**

the Enigma Source

Breakfield and Burkey

Greed, Power, and Corruption: What's New

Poland, 80 years ago

Military troops all had their favorite places to blow off steam. This one was large, with areas for local musicians, reasonable food, a range of alcoholic beverages and a few private rooms available for a price to indulge in other refreshment fare. Only those from money or with high rank could afford them. In this case, the man waiting for someone had both.

Kondrat Mickelowski was of the older, more honorable, wealthy families that struggled with the constant regional conflicts that had been brewing for almost 20 years. His commanding presence was complimented by his height, speech, and impeccable grooming, all of which spoke to his status. His jacket was of the finest wool, cut in line with the fashionably rich of the times. Though his family indeed had position, money, and property, the values of education, human kindness, and a logical view of cause and effect had been instilled from birth. These are the values he imparted to his only son.

Life in this place in any position, he believed, was short lived while the maniac in Germany gained ground. That lunatic, in the opinion of many across Europe, surrounded himself with cruel and greedy men without conscience. Reflecting on the various recent conflicts, negotiations, treaties, and shifts in political power, he realized things were coming to a head. Hence the request for this meeting with his son, the Wolfgang.

Lively noise and revelry from the soldiers coming in for a start to the weekend spilled into the private dining area. Dark beers were flowing, in line with the weekly pay vouchers delivered earlier in the day. Military units from all sides were doing exactly as the strategy planners intended. Here's the target, the reasons are above your pay grade, and when these invaders evacuate this place, all will be well. Warsaw political leaders felt the annexation of the railway junction at the City of Bohumin was the only stop gap to German invasion.

Noise levels increased in the private room as the door opened and his son entered. He cut a fine figure in his uniform and had earned the rank of lieutenant, even at his very young age. With his education and training, he had entered service at 16. Tall and commanding like his father, he strode to the table, and as his father rose they embraced. They sat in adjacent chairs and the barmaid brought in steaming plates of food and two brimming steins.

Kondrat looked up graciously after she had set the provisions down and said, "Madam, thank you. That's all for now."

The barmaid was taken aback, as she'd expected his customary scowl, rather than a kind word.

The Wolfgang, who added a small smile and a twinkle in his blue eyes, also voiced, "Yes, thank you, madam."

Uncertain but pleased, she grinned, curtseyed and left without a word.

"My son, how was your travel? Any issues?"

"No, Father, though the rumors swirling about the New Order and what they plan are everywhere. It seems to be inevitable, regardless of the negotiations by our leaders."

"Agreed. It seems that the mandate is for a total Germanisation of Europe, one territory at a time. Without the intervention of the west, it is only a matter of time. The various delay tactics are just that. Our families, languages, traditions, religions, and associations will be wiped out if the lunatic is not stopped."

"How can I help, Father? What can I do? I am rising in the ranks and gaining ground from those currently in power, though I sense some reluctance to share information. Officers are having sidebar correspondence with those outside of Poland. With the latest border change negotiation, it seems we are being painted as a German annexation. Is that how you view it?"

"Exactly, and it will only get worse. I have a unit I would like you to request transfer into, though it will appear to be a demotion. Meanwhile, I am going to try to liquidate some of our assets and place them outside of our country. I will let you know where and the details for access. It won't be as much as I would like, because I want to make certain that our staff and the surrounding community have a share to help overcome what I feel certain is going to be devastating to everything you know and how you were raised.

"Men who get addicted to power, especially over other people and land, stop at nothing to gain what they want. This is one of mankind's biggest failings. There always seems to be some narcissistic psychopath who quietly rises up with the right message to gain his or her agenda. With education or the right influential circle, they often further their power addiction by military means. But you should know that our threat from the Nationalists in Germany is not the only consideration. The Soviets to the East are uncommonly quiet in this theater of aggression, and that is just as troubling."

The young lieutenant nodded and stated, "Father, how do you stop someone like Hitler, or is it even possible? The old wounds from the Great War have left many feeling guilty and ready to acquiesce to calls for repatriating lost territories, regardless of new national identities. Poland finally pulled away from the Kingdom of Prussia after the Treaty of Versailles set the stage for our independence. Now here we are again, being looked at as another territory to be annexed by Germany."

"Honestly, my son, I sadly think that a bullet to the head would be the most effective. However, it is morally wrong, period! The best way to stay ahead of the interlopers is to stay ahead of them and not let them get a foothold. Vigilance, coupled with better information and methods to apply the information, is the right solution, though it is the most elusive. As an example, if you can watch all the pieces on the chessboard during the entire game, you can know the traps in advance to know what to avoid. It is a skill that few possess."

The lieutenant was lost in thought about the commentary as he finished his food. This logic flow was not a new concept to him. However the current world situation was much closer to home. "I will make arrangements for the transfer, Father, when I return to Command. Do you think it will be enough to make a difference?"

Kondrat emphatically stated, "It always makes a difference to do the right thing, especially against tyrannical maniacs. Thank you, my son. You are the hope of the future. Stay safe. God speed."

CHAPTER 1

Did You Really Need a Different Introduction?

Present Day

In his cheeriest voice, Otto greeted, "Bruno! How are you, friend? It's been ages since we've spoken! I was beginning to think that our last round of business was the end of our interactions, but I am delighted to see I was mistaken. How can I help you and your associate? It is not often that I am approached by one of Interpol's finest cyber detectives and one of the directors of the Global Bank. May I assume that this has something to do with the latest developments in the cryptocurrency markets and the ensuing theft that occurred?"

Bruno sat dumbfounded for a moment, unable to respond. In his Instant Message window on his PC, he was alerted to a new message.

> How does this man know that I'm on the call?

Bruno, somewhat dazed, responded:

> You said you wanted the best...
> no one sneaks up on these people...

Otto puzzled a moment, then asked, "Bruno, are you still there? Are you okay? Can you hear me?"

Finally Bruno cleared his throat and responded, "Otto, this is my anonymous calling line that goes through a bank of anonymizing servers just so I can have a completely cloaked conversation with people demanding extreme security. How did you know it was me? And, furthermore, how could you possibly have guessed who was on the call with me? Finally, why do you suspect we are calling about cryptocurrency matters?"

Otto suppressed a smile and innocently replied, "Oh, pardon me, Bruno. Have I made some misstatements to your distinguished guest?"

Bruno clucked his tongue in annoyance and continued, "On second thought, I don't really want to know all the tricks of the magician. Allow me to introduce Tonya Van Den Berghe from the Global Bank.

"Otto, I was asked to make introductions, but as you can see, Tonya, these are the people we call on when we need that which cannot be done. I'll leave you two to talk in private. I assume that the voice tunnel is encrypted, Otto, after my initial but naïve outreach to you. Good day to you both."

Otto didn't have time to reply to Bruno's hasty departure, so he offered, "Tonya, apologies if your call didn't catch me unawares. We work very hard at being informed. That way when we are called upon to help we can take up the assignment quickly. How may I be of service to you and your organization?"

Tonya, relatively young but well-educated and informed about the world stage, quickly moved past her initial surprise, almost smiled, and acknowledged, "Otto, I believe your demonstration clearly proved your point about your organization's effectiveness. You are correct, I am calling with regards to cryptocurrency matters and some very high-profile thefts that lead us to believe the Global Bank has been compromised.

"To that end, I would like to meet and discuss the contents of a package I need to provide you. It will give you all the details we have so far, but there are some things that I cannot discuss over the phone, even though I rather believe that the line is certainly encrypted. Would that be possible?"

Otto nodded and answered, "Understood. In a chat window that I'm opening up on your computer, I will place the location of a cyber-Drop Vault. We use this with special customers for secure document and data sharing. It will help us to begin work immediately with current information. When and where would you like to meet? I presume that time is of the essence."

Tonya smirked as she replied, "You know it, Mr. Magician!

"I will upload the information within the hour. I would like to meet with you or possibly your right hand designate the day after tomorrow in Paris. I would prefer that we keep discussions on this topic out of our headquarters in New York City, though I assure you I have the support of our Managing Director in this matter. I can, of course, provide credentials."

Otto reviewed the background information on Tonya, including several photos provided by ICABOD, the team's Artificial Intelligence Supercomputer. The young woman had graduated in the top of her class from Harvard Business with a focus in International Finance, with no extraordinarily high financial portfolio and her remaining two years of education debt being paid monthly. The photographs provided included professional headshots of her even smile, her heart-shaped face framed by shiny chestnut colored waves that just reached her shoulders. The photo date was three months ago and included her physical attributes of height at almost 1.8 meters and a lean 59 kilograms. It struck Otto that her facial lines were very sophisticated, yet she seemed approachable.

He commented, "Based on the nature of the discussion, credentials will be necessary. I will have you meet with Wolfgang

Mickelowski, our Financial Director in Paris, at noon on Wednesday. Unless you have an objection, we will arrange for the meeting to take place in a secure conference room at Regal Financial in La Défense, just west of the Paris city limits. I have an associate on the Board of Directors of the main branch of the institution's headquarters in Zürich."

Tonya replied, "That is very agreeable. Thank you, Otto, I look forward to meeting with Mr. Mickelowski."

The call was disconnected and Otto called Wolfgang. They chatted for a few moments and decided the best course of action was to assemble the team. They agreed to a time, and Otto waited for the package upload from Tonya to read en route.

Tonya Van Den Berghe studied the desk phone, then reached for her personal cell phone that was still capable of making an encrypted call, and dialed a familiar number from her contact list identified by only an icon. Once the encrypted call was launched, she steeled herself for the pending conversation.

It seemed like an eternity before the call connected, and a pleasant voice answered, "How did the call go with Bruno's recommendation? Do we have the services of this unbiased group in Switzerland?"

Tonya replied, "Yes, Madam Director, we have their services, but, boy, what a creepy call! I mean, the man Bruno connected us to, Otto, knew right away who we were and almost to the letter of what we wanted. It was almost like he knew the work to be done and we would only need to verify the terms and conditions. Bruno seemed uncomfortable and bailed from the call. I finished the negotiations.

"Madam Director, I'm not completely comfortable with this type of contact, no matter how highly your Interpol contact, Bruno, recommended them."

The smirking voice on the other end of the call asked, "Do you feel we are on the right trajectory?"

Tonya had some trouble reeling in her irked state of mind but offered all the professionalism she could muster.

"Yes, Madam Director, we are on the right trajectory with these people. Not only did they know exactly who was calling over a supposedly anonymized voice channel, but they picked up on my presence, while correctly surmising the nature of the call. I've not witnessed this kind of digital sleight-of-hand before, and, well, it made me feel like I was right out of the University again.

"Since I took this job with your organization, I've only been embarrassed and humiliated twice during my tenure. The time you first pulled me aside and suggested that I not dress like a low class/no class call girl, and now this time with Otto the Magician."

The Director chuckled and gently reminded, "Oh, so not the time I stumbled into your office after hours and almost interrupted you with, what's his name? Though we were peers at our previous job, you do work for me know. Well, never mind. What are our next steps with the Magician? I assume they took the project, but what fee did you settle on?"

Tonya swallowed hard and admitted, "I…we didn't discuss a fee, only a meeting place and where to ship the advance materials so his team could begin work."

The Director sighed like someone ready to chastise an underling and then commented, "I'm glad your taste in men has improved over the years, but remember that even a low class/ no class call girl discusses price before putting the goods on the table. This is most unlike you. You need to take charge and not get rattled when you are in charge of an assignment."

Now mortified, Tonya stammered, "I didn't get rattled. Okay, I got a bit rattled, but when we meet in Paris I can…"

Thoroughly enjoying the teasing she was delivering to her associate, the Director soothed, "Tonya, it is a part of working in this field.

"I can tell you that because he did the same thing to me many years ago. I was an up-and-coming professional who thought she could hold her own in a male dominated world of high finance. My ego had to be ambulanced off the premises the first time I encountered him. I thought he might help you adapt more readily."

Tonya was stunned at the admission. But before she could say anything the Director responded, "That encounter helped me to get to this position. I'm hoping that someday it will help you get here too."

Tonya, somewhat chastened, quietly offered, "Thank you, Ingrid. I will try and be that person you believe I am."

Ingrid stepped back into her hard-edged Director role as she sharply reminded, "Understand, we need all the resources we can muster to intercept these disruptive cryptocurrency Johnnies and their cottage industry before one of these products catches on. We need time to get ours to market before we lose control of global finance. We don't want to be caught making buggy whips while the internal combustion automobile is being rolled off mass-production lines. Time is not on our side in this matter, so whatever Mr. Magician wants to charge is fine. If he and his organization can help us hold our position until we are ready, then his price is chump change compared to what our next position will be. If he doesn't, then he will be paid with useless currency, and none of it will matter anyway."

Tonya swallowed hard and stated, "Yes, Madam Director. I understand."

CHAPTER 2

It Looked Good on Paper
...The Enigma Chronicles

The panic and tension thickened throughout the building as each person entered, then frantically pushed and shoved those ahead of them to gain the front spot to demand their funds. The directors watched the increased madness through the glass walls of the meeting room, yet were powerless to stop the ever-growing chaos. It was a classic run-on-the-bank scenario like the old films and photos portrayed from the 1920s in the U.S. There was no shortage of desperate people having an anxiety attack concerning their funds. No one wanted to wait patiently in line for their money. The pushing and shoving continued to escalate within the line but did not quite reach the head of the line. Police were there to try and keep order, but most of them ended up joining the human tidal wave of desperation. This was just one frightened mob in one location in this small struggling country oppressed by debt. Some of the other banks in this impoverished country had wisely refused to open until communication avenues with the panic stricken improved.

In this formerly thriving city, the military, which was really only a volunteer militia, was called out to assist when martial law was declared. Its lack of success in controlling the crowds added to the chaos. Comprised primarily of weekend warriors, the militia had never been trained to be a true peacekeeping force.

Friends and family begged and cried to them for personal support efforts, and the militia members' subsequently weakened resolve was like accelerant on the crazed population. The police began to exit once they received their funds, leaving only the privately hired mercenaries, politely called internal security, to protect the banking institutions.

Here, inside the country's central bank, Mathias wondered how long he and his directors would be safe behind the internal security force and bulletproof glass. The images from the outside cameras convinced him that trying to go out to his favorite restaurant for lunch would be insanely unwise. It occurred to him that if this mob scene couldn't be brought under control, he and the other directors would be trapped here. He began to feel queasy at the thought of surviving on vending machine food until the mob was contained and under control, which might take days.

Mathias had a way of working with any group due to his ability to appear like those around him. He could be imposing if he rose to his nearly two meters and 90 kilograms, with his broad shoulders, squared facial structure and dark well-groomed hair. His suits were custom made in Hong Kong of the finest materials, and they suited the part he was playing in this scenario. As Mathias watched the chaos surrounding him, he had to admit this experiment had failed, not because the technology didn't work, but because people believed they were being swindled out of their money. What Mathias and the other directors had failed to realize was that in order for the regular population to make ends meet, they had to operate in or with the underground economy. To function in the underground economy, cynically called the EU, one needed hard currency for conducting business, which was highly mobile even if it was fiat money. Yes, several European governments had declared fiat money to be legal tender, but historically, money was backed by physical commodities such as gold and silver. They lacked understanding of the continual devaluation as those resources dwindled.

With his British accent, Mathias captured the ear of the authorities. His sales pitch suggested that by shifting everything to digital currency, the government could put an end to the EU. Then they would finally get the tax revenue they'd been missing. The powers-that-be had completely missed the fact that the loss of mobile hard currency would simply drive the entire population, heavily dependent upon the EU, into a subterranean-subsistence level of poverty. The governments involved in this joint experiment had made the classic mistake of pushing the population into a position where they now had nothing left to lose. Now, with the poorly trained but armed militia joining the frightened mob, and no police willing to defend the new world order, things could not have been blacker for the digital currency plan.

One of the larger, well-fed directors meekly asked, "Did the specialty donuts get delivered this morning? Can you ask the private security persons if they are on their way up?"

At that same moment, gunfire cracked several corners of vertical glass panes in the directors' meeting room. The eminent threat of the collapse of the fractured glass walls was immediately on the minds of the directors at the table.

Alois Dutch, who was always addressed as Dutch, entered through the lavatory door adjacent to the boardroom. He was imposing in his loose suit, which obviously concealed his holstered handgun. His gravelly voice barked, "The donuts are here, but the coffee is still brewing! Who wants to wait, and who wants to go? The chopper is on the roof, but there is only room for three!"

Mathias frowned and retrieved his own personal 9mm semi-automatic. He promptly made the selecting votes. All the frightened directors stared in shocked disbelief as Mathias shot them all in rapid succession. After one shot each to the head, Mathias turned to Dutch and calmly stated, "We now have room for the donuts, but let's pick up coffee along the way. I would like to have room for the cream and sugar to be added."

As a seasoned mercenary, Dutch wasn't surprised at the efficiency of the meeting's abrupt ending, so he responded, "Good by me. I've always thought the coffee here isn't strong enough for my tastes." Dutch was about the same size as Mathias, but his blue eyes and blond hair echoed his German heritage. The lines of his face, permanently turned down mouth, and haphazard scars spoke to his uncompromised lifestyle filled with brutality.

They both got low as they exited out the back door, away from the disastrous scene, and quickly moved toward the stairwell that would take them to the helipad on the roof. Mathias had snatched his ever-close metal briefcase, containing his standard escape materials, after eliminating the competition for seats in the helicopter. The special purpose briefcase was also bullet-proof. With its side sling, it made for a perfect shield should any more stray rounds head his way. As they climbed higher in the stairwell, the noise from the lower floors receded, and it was almost quiet as they got to the last door leading directly to the roof.

Dutch did a quick spot check from out in front and then motioned to Mathias to follow. They both swung quickly into the helicopter. Once the door closed, Dutch pounded on the glass behind the pilot and with a thumbs up indicated it was time to go. The pilot pulled the helicopter up to clear the building edge then smartly pushed the craft forward, gaining speed as quickly as he could.

Dutch smirked as he commented, "Maybe we need a new line of work. I mean, there must be something wrong with getting your whole agenda adopted by the Finance Minister, rubber stamped by the governing body of this backwater country, only to have to escape with our donuts, yet leave the coffee behind as we run for our lives."

Mathias ground his teeth in anger and remarked, "You know, I can ask the pilot to take you back and drop you off if you prefer."

Dutch knew he was on thin ice. "Alright, I'm fine here." Then he shifted the discussion as he added, "I have to admit, we almost pulled this one off by the numbers. But just like my CO used to say after a failed operation, *it sure looked good on paper!*"

Mathias stewed a moment as he mentally reviewed the carefully laid plan. "I know this model will work, Dutch! I just need a larger target audience! This one was just too small and too prone to backward superstitions. If they accepted my financial model…"

Dutch cut him off as he questioned, "We're going to try it again, huh? Now, you can always count on me for another turn at the roulette wheel, but I maintain we don't try this again without our trusty contingency plan in place! By the way, what is our plan B?"

Mathias offered a chilling smile and responded, "We will do a larger country where they have more to lose and more for me to gain! We hunt where there is lots of financial turmoil already present, because it will hide our footprints."

Dutch, now in something of a humoring mood, asked, "You don't think someone will notice that you're pitching a distributed digital currency to displace a centralized paper currency? It seems a lot like being out on a first date, where you're staring down the front of your lady's low cut evening dress and humbly proclaiming you admire her for her mind! She ain't buying it, and they won't buy it!"

A wry smile crossed Mathias's face as he admonished, "Dutch, your problem is that all the time you spent in the Deutsches Heer made you too cynical. You know what they say in marketing financial concepts: packaging, packaging, and packaging!"

"Yeah, but they also say that in taxidermy work!" Dutch couldn't contain his sour look.

CHAPTER 3

Redefining What a Long Day Means

It was late in the day, and Su Lin had just finished tending her animals, in particular her favorite pig, Franklin. At 160 kilograms, Franklin could have been a formidable adversary to her slight Asian build, being less than half his weight. Over the years of their friendship and her training, he'd become more of a barnyard pet and confidant. As she tidied her long silky black hair into her typical braid halfway down her back, she mused about how thankful she was that Franklin had outgrown his tendency to want to sit in her lap, as he had done when he was just an armful.

Franklin was a very bright hog who took everything in stride, and he showed a genuine affection for Su Lin. However, today Su Lin was distracted. Every unusual noise seemed to pull her attention in a different direction. Ever in tune with his human companion, Franklin stopped to test the air with his extremely sensitive nose. Su Lin halted her activities to study the surroundings of the familiar Georgia farm, but nothing looked wrong. Except that something seemed wrong. A most unsettling feeling came over her as she walked back from the pens to the house.

Andy's hound dog, Wrinkles, was fast asleep and didn't bother to raise his head up to watch Su Lin trudge back from the pens as he usually did at this time of day. Wrinkles' afternoon siesta was always secondary to the kitchen snacks that he got when Su Lin began to cook supper.

Su Lin studied the large hound as she approached and remarked, "I must agree with Andy's assessment of you, Wrinkles. If you were any more laid back, you would be constantly slipping into a coma. You must have played pretty hard today, to not even get up to begin pestering for snacks."

Su Lin stopped just outside the door and looked around the property one more time, hoping to alleviate her unsettled feelings, but the well-kept Georgia farm with its large welcoming home was perfectly in place. They had recently repainted the home in brick red with white trim, giving the house a certain quaint elegance without pretension. She shrugged her shoulders to loosen the cloud of doubt she felt and went inside. Su Lin paused at the mirror in the mud room, verifying that her hair was in place, and no dirt was apparent on her ivory skin. Even though she'd had servants for much of her adult life, she enjoyed her work with the animals.

As she closed the screen door, it flashed through her mind that locking the door would be a good idea, even though they never did. Andy always wanted folks to be able to drop in. He'd insisted you couldn't be neighborly if the door was locked. However, she decidedly wasn't in the mood to discuss how southern folks in the country always left the doors unlocked, and she went on in to check on Andy and see if he was ready for dinner.

Andy's office was a cross between a high tech server room, operations area, office area, and something of an electrical power drain on the grid. If he wasn't wearing his headset while talking to one of his many customers, or signed into a high tech webinar, he was building something for testing or trialing in his operational headquarters known as the Rock-n-Roll Domain. It wasn't uncommon for Su Lin to check on him, only to find him totally absorbed in some new technical project with some rock music playing at varying decibels in the background.

As she wandered closer to Andy, she noted that his white hair was a bit long, but nice with waves, offsetting his broad shoulders which suited his big hands. When he hugged her close it was like being wrapped in a cocoon of gentle protection. He was by all standards a big man, just shy of two meters and nearly 90 kilos. She smiled with fondness, until she drew closer and noted with dismay all the high-caloric junk food packages strewn around, mostly empty.

She immediately fussed, "Andrew! We've talked about this! Your heart attack was supposed to be a wakeup call for your poor eating habits! The doctor said if we cut back on all the junk food, you could lead a normal life. Honey, you promised!"

Andy sheepishly offered, "Aw, sweetheart, I have turned over a new leaf. You notice that I no longer have that big salt block used for cattle on the table at suppertime. Now, doesn't that count for something? Besides, all the healthy cooking you have been doing should make up for some of the small splurges I have now and again."

Su Lin retorted, "That's because I feed all the fat trimmings to Wrinkles, who by all accounts likes your new diet. And say, what's wrong with him today? Usually he is all over me when I come back in the afternoon from the pens. Have you been feeding him your favorite concoction of cheese puffs dipped in melted fudge ice cream again?"

Andy rather soberly remarked, "Nope! Not since that last time when we had to clean up after his bazooka-barfing-from-both-ends episode. Not me, ma'am."

Before she could admonish him further, she heard something in the front room area and cast a quizzical look to Andy before she went to investigate. When she walked into the front room, she saw a Chinese man, with the bearing of a military type, complete with his short cropped black hair and sinewy arms, sitting way too comfortably in one of the over-sized leather chairs, casually waiting.

Su Lin didn't recognize the man, only the type, and she immediately disliked him. Trying to keep the alarm out of her voice, she called to Andy without taking her eyes off of the stranger. He was neither menacing nor friendly in his presentation to her, but he said nothing.

Andy barged into the room and stopped short upon seeing the stranger. He sized up the situation quickly and demanded, "Who the hell are you, and what the hell are you doing here?"

Andy, being ex-military police, always carried his 1911 Colt 45 in a holster at the small of his back and quickly reached for it. At almost the same time, he felt two cold weapons on either side of his neck. Then some very cautious, practiced hands carefully confiscated his weapon. Andy froze but still rotated his eyes from one side to the other to take in the two Chinese enforcer types holding guns at his neck.

Once the disarming process was completed, the seated man looked toward Su Lin, "Ah, Colonel Ling Po, how nice to see you again. It's been a long time. Apologies for the surveillance you apparently noticed and the intrusion, but you have been extremely difficult to find.

"Please, don't worry about the enormous dog out front; he is merely sedated. I didn't want to risk an unpleasant encounter with him while we …um…talked."

Andy, trying to reconcile why this man called Su Lin by the name from her former life attempted a bluff as he bellowed,

"No one barges into my farm house and pulls a gun on us. It's even worse when that uninvited stranger speaks to my wife, Su Lin, using an incorrect name and sedates my animal without any idea of who we are! You boneheads have come to the wrong place, so git out!"

Completely oblivious to Andy's rant, the intruder continued, "I don't expect you to remember me, but certainly I remember you, Colonel Po. When you were put in charge of the Cyber Warfare College in China, all of your adversaries thought you had been neutralized. It is obvious that they were wrong. You managed to build an excellent power base, then crush your opposition quite completely. I believe the Khan incident that you engineered was probably the best example of assassinating someone using cyber means."

Su Lin swallowed hard and sternly replied, "Now I remember you. Major Guano, the henchman for Chairman Lo Chang. I hardly recognized you without your smock and hypodermic needle."

The intruder almost smirked as he confirmed, "How nice of you to remember. However, I must point out that I am now a full Colonel, and Lo Chang is no longer Chairman in this world."

As usual, Su Lin's intelligence launched her response, dripping in sarcasm. "I understand. One criminal out and another one in his place. Some things never change, do they?"

Colonel Guano tightened up somewhat and continued, "It seems you had some highly motivated help in leaving our, uh… facilities in China. It has taken some time to find you again."

Andy was trying to mentally find a way out of the situation. He did not like being in this position especially with Su Lin the target. He was not happy with the ongoing conversation and the familiarity that Colonel Guano was showing toward Su Lin. But Su Lin motioned to him to stand down during the ongoing banter, like she had a better understanding of their capabilities. Cutting her eyes between the two henchmen and back to Andy helped remind him not to attempt anything foolish.

Guano, still seated yet certain he dominated the conversation, continued, "Your vanishing act from China was most impressive and, I must say, a little vexing for us. As usual though, you couldn't stay hidden for long. Your brilliant research that coupled nanotechnology and genetic engineering helped cast a bright light on your trail. Of course, the shabby incident with that crazed Doctor Pekoni helped us to zero in on your current location.

"Oh, and congratulations on your marriage to Mr. Greenwood. We know you tried to keep the ceremony small and quiet, but the blood tests did help to confirm that you are indeed Lt. Colonel Ling Po, aka Master Po of the Chinese Cyber Warfare College. My hunt is now complete."

Su Lin, afraid of what Andy would think, cast a quick glance at him before she responded, "Let's pretend, for arguments sake, that you are not an insane delusional errand monkey and that I am this Colonel Po. What possessed you to travel halfway around the world, looking for someone who obviously doesn't want to be found?"

Guano steeled himself and answered, "You built an early prototype of, um…a financial program that was demonstrated to several influential party members and left quite an impression. It had, as I recall, a remarkable security routine called the Grasshopper Loop, which made it unbreakable to even the most persistent hackers. My leadership has sent me to retrieve that code and its author, in the most discreet but expeditious manner."

Andy was nearly undone with this threat. Su Lin smirked in a mocking manner and informed him, "I don't have that program, but it is not true that it was unbreakable. The code was broken by, shall we say, a highly motivated hacker. Your quest to locate the author of the code is simply a fool's errand. The code Master Po allegedly wrote that was purported to be unbreakable is as vulnerable as any freeware, downloadable from your favorite cell phone website.

"Take you and your abhorrent henchmen out of our house and leave us alone."

Guano rose out of the chair and bluntly stated, "I was sent to retrieve it and you. And I will do exactly that, with or without your cooperation."

Before any further instructions could be issued by Guano, Andy used his huge hands to grab both henchmen's gun-wielding hands, pushed the assailants' weapons to point at the other, and using his thumbs, pulled the triggers simultaneously causing them to shoot each other. Unfortunately, the hot muzzle blast of both weapons seared Andy's eyes, instantly blinding him.

Su Lin's military training kicked in, and she dove for one of the weapons just as Guano drew his. Andy, though blinded, instinctively knew to go to ground around the dead Chinese henchman and look for his missing Colt 45. He wasn't sure what he could do once he was armed, sightless as he now was, but he wasn't going to give up as long as Su Lin was being threatened by Guano.

Just as Andy located his Colt 45, two shots rang out, and the room fell silent.

About the Authors

Breakfield – Works for a high-tech manufacturer as a solution architect, functioning in hybrid data/telecom environments. He considers himself a long-time technology geek, who also enjoys writing, studying World War II history, travel, and cultural exchanges. Charles' love of wine tastings, cooking, and Harley riding has found ways into the stories. As a child, he moved often because of his father's military career, which even helps him with the various character perspectives he helps bring to life in the series. He continues to try to teach Burkey humor.

Burkey – Works as a business architect who builds solutions for customers on a good technology foundation. She has written many technology papers, white papers, but finds the freedom of writing fiction a lot more fun. As a child, she helped to lead the kids with exciting new adventures built on make believe characters, was a Girl Scout until high school, and contributed to the community as a young member of a Head Start program. Rox enjoys family, learning, listening to people, travel, outdoor activities, sewing, cooking, and thinking about how to diversify the series.

Breakfield and Burkey – started writing non-fictional papers and books, but it wasn't nearly as fun as writing fictional stories. They found it interesting to use the aspects of technology that people are incorporating into their daily lives more and more as a perfect way to create a good guy/bad guy story with elements of travel to the various places they have visited either professionally and personally, humor, romance, intrigue, suspense, and a spirited way to remember people who have crossed paths with them. They love to talk about their stories with private and public book readings. Burkey also conducts regular interviews for Texas authors, which she finds very interesting. Her first interview was, wait for it, Breakfield. You can often find them at local book fairs or other family-oriented events.

The primary series is based on a family organization called R-Group. Recently they have spawned a subgroup that contains some of the original characters as the Cyber Assassins Technology Services (CATS) team. The authors have ideas for continuing the series in both of these tracks. They track the more than 150 characters on a spreadsheet, with a hidden avenue for the future coined The Enigma Chronicles tagged in some portions of the stories. Fan reviews seem to frequently suggest that these would make good television or movie stories, so the possibilities appear endless, just like their ideas for new stories.

They have book video trailers for each of the stories, which can be viewed on YouTube, Amazon's Authors page, or on their website, *www.EnigmaBookSeries.com*. Their website is routinely updated with new interviews, answers to readers' questions, book trailers, and contests. You may also find it fascinating to check out the fun acronyms they create for the stories summarized on their website. Reach out to them at *Authors@EnigmaSeries.com, Twitter@EnigmaSeries,* or *Facebook@TheEnigmaSeries.*

Please provide a fair and honest review on amazon and any other places you post reviews. We appreciate the feedback.

Other stories by Breakfield and Burkey in
The Enigma Series are at **www.EnigmaBookSeries.com**

We would greatly appreciate
if you would take a few minutes
and provide a review of this work
on Amazon, Goodreads
and any of your other favorite places.

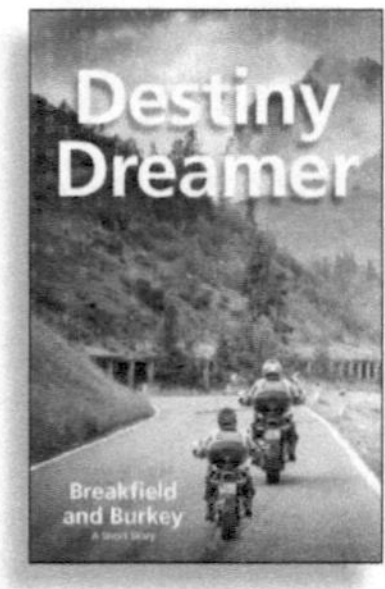

Other stories by Breakfield and Burkey in
the Heirs Series are at **www.EnigmaBookSeries.com**

MAGNOLIA BLUFF CRIME CHRONICLES

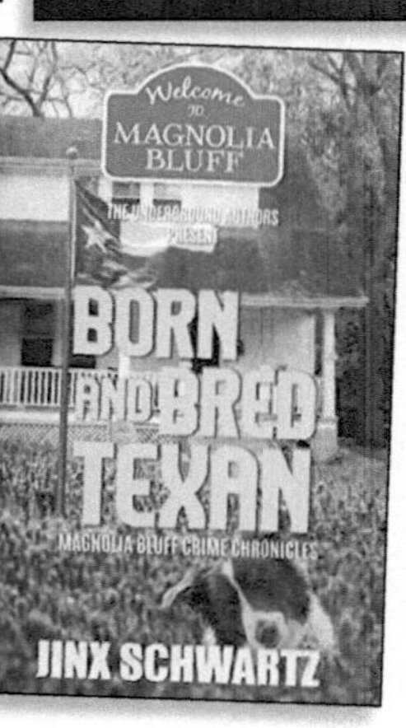

MAGNOLIA BLUFF CRIME CHRONICLES

The Enigma Wraith The fourth entry in Breakfield and Burkey's techno-thriller series pits the R-Group against a seemingly untraceable computer virus and what could be a full-scale digital assault.

The Enigma Stolen Breakfield and Burkey once again deliver the goods, as returning readers will expect—intelligent technology-laden dialogue; a kidnapping or two; and a bit of action, as Jacob and Petra dodge an assassin (not the cyber kind) in Argentina.

The Enigma Always As always, loaded with smart technological prose and an open ending that suggests more to come.

The Enigma Gamers (A CATS Tale) A cyberattack tale that's superb as both a continuation of a series and a promising start in an entirely new direction.

The Enigma Broker …the authors handle their players as skillfully as casino dealers handle cards, and the various subplots are consistently engaging. The main storyline is energized by its formidable villains…

The Enigma Dragon (A CATS Tale) This second CATS-centric installment (after 2016's *The Enigma Gamers*) will leave readers yearning for more. Astute prose and an unwavering pace energized by first-rate characters and subplots.

The Enigma Source Another top-tier installment that showcases exemplary recurring characters and tech subplots.

The Enigma Beyond the latest installment of this long-running technothriller series finds a next generation cyber security team facing off against unprincipled artificial intelligences. Dense but enthralling entry, with a bevy of new, potential narrative directions.

The Enigma Threat Another clever, energetic addition to an appealing series.

Novels by Breakfield and Burkey in The Enigma Series
www.EnigmaBookSeries.com

The Enigma Factor

The Enigma Rising

The Enigma Ignite

The Enigma Wraith

The Enigma Stolen

The Enigma Always

The Enigma Gamers
A CATS Tale

The Enigma Broker

The Enigma Dragon
A CATS Tale

The Enigma Source

The Enigma Beyond

The Enigma Threat

SHORT STORIES

Out of Poland

Destiny Dreamer

Hidden Target

Hot Chocolate

Love's Enigma

Nowhere But Up

Remember the Future

Riddle Codes

The Jewel

Kirkus Reviews

The Enigma Factor In this debut techno-thriller, the first in a planned series, a hacker finds his life turned upside down as a mysterious company tries to recruit him...

The Enigma Rising In Breakfield and Burkey's latest techno-thriller, a group combats evil in the digital world, with multiple assignments merging in Acapulco and the Cayman Islands.

The Enigma Ignite The authors continue their run of stellar villains with the returning Chairman Lo Chang, but they also add wonderfully unpredictable characters with unclear motivations. A solid espionage thriller that adds more tension and lightheartedness to the series.